I0691970

She had been searching for so long, the task now seemed impossible. How could she go on?

Something woolly pressed against her arm. "Marble." Rose desperately wanted to get something right, though part of her knew better. Then a substance, both stringy and wet, a hunk of grass in a wad of wool and spittle, along with two sincere-looking eyes fixed on her face.

"No! No! That's not what I expected. Get away! Get away"

The sad-faced little sheep eased off.

She wasn't crazy. She knew the creature was a sheep. But just when you had a cuddly sheep in your arms, it turned into something hideous. No sense in it, but there it was.

The mental dam that held her back from desperation leaked, little by little, until she couldn't hold back. Oceans of tears crashed against her hold on reality. She had always counted on winning Michael back, but now she knew better. There was no order left in her life. She tore at her hair. She ripped her nails against the stone wall. The love of her life had come face to face with her and had stalked away.

She had to do something, but what? It was dark now. No moon. She worked her way along the wall until she returned to the beginning. She sucked at the blood on the tips of her fingers. What if she could suck it out and stop living?

She whimpered.

She cast out the once-beloved name, like a bat in her hair. "Michael! Michael," she shouted across the castle's demesne. She bellowed the name. She sobbed the name. A shrill scream like that of a wounded horse rent the clouds.

She covered her face with her hands and cried. "Puppy. Oh, Puppy…" She lifted her face to the sky, collecting scattered raindrops in her mouth and on her cheeks to join her tears

At last she stumbled across the courtyard where she had eaten the sandwiches. "Four walls. Warmer." She was unable to concentrate any more. Weariness got the better of her, and she hunkered down inside a ruined passageway. She made a small package out of her body as best she could and...just...disappeared into her only comfort—unconsciousness.

HALF AND HALF ROSE is an edgy story about a quirky heroine and a sweet, hunky hero, married to each other and insatiably in lust, only to be torn apart by a tragedy neither one seems able to overcome.

After binge drinking, Michael rolls the car on a forest road, killing their unborn child. Neither he nor Rose can get past the tragedy. Unable to cope with Michael's alcoholism and the guilt both feel, Rose flees to Ireland in order to save herself. Michael keeps his mysterious issues close to the vest and shadows the love of his life from across the ocean. When they change their minds, and Michael disappears, the stakes increase, and it's up to Rose to reclaim him. If she can only find him…

Another Citrus County novel, set partially in Ireland.

KUDOS for *Half and Half Rose*

In *Half and Half Rose* by Judith Kammeraad, Rose Flanagan is about to have a baby when Michael O'Leary, her husband and the love of her life, wrecks the car while driving drunk. Rose loses the baby, and the grief and guilt that both she and Michael feel cause them to separate. Rose flees to Ireland and tells Michael she doesn't want to see him ever again. But when Michael disappears, Rose realizes that she still loves him. But how can she tell him when she can't find him? The story is engaging and intriguing, heartwarming and heartbreaking, and will have you laughing, crying, and sighing all the way through. And the sex scenes are hot! A wonderful read. ~ *Taylor Jones, The Review Team of Taylor Jones & Regan Murphy*

Half and Half Rose by Judith Kammeraad is the story of a man and woman in love, in lust, and married to each other. But when tragedy strikes, they suddenly discover that the bond they have isn't strong enough to overcome the guilt and grief. Michael O'Leary, the husband, has a drinking problem. He crashes the car while drunk and causes his wife, Rose Flanagan, to lose the child she's carrying. Michael blames himself, and so does Rose, but she also blames herself for letting Michael drive in the condition he was in. Neither can forgive him/herself, and they can't seem to talk about it so they can't work through the grief together. Eventually, they separate, and Rose goes to Ireland, tracing her roots and looking for her grandfather, who seems to have disappeared. As Rose travels the country, Michael tries to win her back by sending flowers and notes to the locations where she is staying in Ireland. But Rose isn't ready to forgive and she tells Michael to stop stalking her. Michael responds with a firm "goodbye forever" message and then promptly disappears. Only after Rose discovers that he has vanished does she realize that she was wrong and that she still needs and loves Michael. But he is gone, and she doesn't know where to find him. Unless she can pull off a miracle, Michael may be lost to her forever. *Half and Half Rose* is a touching, poignant, and compassionate story of grief, courage, and the struggle to forgive. Filled with enchanting characters, intriguing mysteries, spicy sex scenes, and vivid descriptions, it is a book that will warm your heart and break it at the same time. All in all, a very compelling tale. *~ Regan Murphy, The Review Team of Taylor Jones & Regan Murphy*

ACKNOWLEDGMENTS

Sincere gratitude to my keen-eyed critique partner Carol Megge and to beta reader Jennifer Taylor.

Thank you, Clifden, Ireland, for your encouragement and for giving me Rosemary.

Other Books by Judith Kammeraad:

Teach me Too
Ani's Lover
Little Peanut's Wild Ride: Little Peanut Makes a Baby
Little Peanut's Wild Ride: When Puffy Died

Half
and Half
Rose

Judith Kammeraad

A Black Opal Books Publication

Black Opal Books

BECAUSE SOME STORIES JUST HAVE TO BE TOLD

HALF AND HALF ROSE
Copyright © 2017 by Judith Kammeraad
Cover Design by Jackson Cover Designs
All cover art copyright © 2017
All Rights Reserved
Print ISBN: 978-1-626947-03-0

First Publication: JULY 2017

Published by Black Opal Books **http://www.blackopalbooks.com**

DEDICATION

To Peter S. Kammeraad, my beloved husband,
who takes me around the world.
Love is a journey, you my safe harbor.

Part 1
Flight from Paradise

Citrus County, Florida

Chapter 1

June:

Rose Flanagan's world hung upside down. Blood rushed to her head, and as far as she could tell she was blind. And tied up.

"Michael—" She squirmed against her bonds and groped with her left hand—the only one that would function. She caught hold of his bare wrist. It hung limp, his pulse undercover. Her heart pounded into her throat. "Oh, God, oh no! What—what's wrong?

She shook his inert arm. "Michael, what's that horrible smell?"

Acrid. Something like smoke but more powdery. It forced her to hood her eyes. Fire? Her lungs reached for oxygen, but a piercing pain tore through her belly, ripping out a tortured shriek.

"Michael! Help me, Michael!"

The substance in the air made her retch. Why was she so woozy? Awareness and dread rolled through her guts, hunching her over as far as she could reach. She curled a protective arm over her abdomen—an instinctive gesture ever since the child took shape inside her.

A viscous wetness soaked her from crotch to navel, and she knew its name. She knew, but would not acknowledge.

Her lungs grabbed for air, and let it all out in a piercing shriek, which spiraled down to a sob.

"Baby girl. Ohohoh, Rosebud. Oh, God. No!"

She rode just under the crest of panic. Struggling against her restraints, she gasped for a full breath before another wave claimed her.

"Michael!" In agony, she screamed his name.

Finally he groaned.

"Michael, thank God! What happened?"

He grasped her arm. "Rosie—I'm so sorry. Are you all right, baby?"

Before she could respond, a stronger pain rumbled through her, squeezing her low in her belly and confusingly jumbled. She heard herself scream, buffeted with horror and unwilling realization. She couldn't bring the primal out-break under control.

She didn't see her husband in the darkness that wrapped around the oaks in the Withlacoochee Forest, but she heard his fear. God, she smelled it in his sweat.

"Rose, is it the baby? Try to loosen the seatbelt, honey."

The fingers on her right hand refused to function. More liquid gushed out of her vagina. The intense muscular tens-ing and relaxing confirmed that this was all wrong. She touched the gooey liquid with her good left hand and brought it to her face. Her nose wrinkled as she recoiled. It smelled like a kettle of copper pennies.

The truth turned its death's head on her.

The lump in her voice brought her down to a low moan. "Michael, there's blood." She sobbed and gritted her teeth against another spasm. "No, God, don't let it be true." She struggled to catch her breath and ride the next squeezing pain.

This was too bizarre, her common sense told her. Part of her Irish imagination? You couldn't give birth upside down, could you? She laughed and shivered until the next pain, all the while struggling to turn herself upright.

Michael uttered an inarticulate murmur.

"Michael, help me—please—It's too early. She can't come now—here. You've got to stop it, Michael. Get help, please!"

He groaned when his restraints snapped free. Metal creaked as he kicked his door open.

"Oh, damn! My arm is broken. Coming around to your side, Rosie."

At last her door swung free, and he fumbled with her seatbelt, cushioning her with his body as she slid down to the sedan's headliner.

"Get out, Rosie, come on. Lean on me."

But the waves had taken control. She fought to keep from going under with her precious cargo. She panted and puffed and rubbed her belly in circles with her good hand.

"No, Rosie, no. She's shy of seven months. It's not happening. Not so far from the hospital. Not on a dirt road, for Christ's sake!"

"Get your cell phone, Michael. Please, get help."

"I can't, Rosie. I can't. Can't find the phone. Please hang on."

She could only stare at the florescent sticker affixed to the dash, a photograph of an orange and pink shrub rose he'd planted to celebrate their pregnancy. "Look at that rose, Rosie. That's you. And its little rosebud is just like our baby attached to you. Our little rosebud." His voice had resonated with joy.

Now his voice quavered. "Focus, Rosie. Look at the rose. Look at the rosebud."

She wasn't listening anymore, not to him. He rested a palm on her belly. She shoved it away.

Instead, she spoke to the child inside her. "I'm sorry, baby. I know I can't save you. Oh, God!" Her gut wrenched until she managed to grab control of her breathing again.

Rose recognized what had to happen.

She couldn't stop the expulsion from her womb. Using the little self-control she possessed, she had to do something else for her daughter. She must let Rosebud experience a good death. The baby's sense of the world came through her, the mother, didn't it? Her heartbeat, her breathing, her emotions, her fear. Her grief. Her child would never live a single minute in the world outside. Rose knew that. So if this time together, right now, was to make up Rosebud's total experience, part of that was up to Rose.

"Don't let her die afraid, please, God. Don't let her feel what I feel now." Tears snaked down her cheeks. She struggled to stifle her wild gulps for air. "Let me give her one great, wonderful deception. God, forgive me for my lie."

Then Rose let tranquility in. She breathed in and out, riding the waves, cresting the peaks and bobbing in the calm intervals. "Baby girl, listen to Mommy now. You don't need to feel afraid. You will never know about loss, and you will never cry." She swallowed the sound of her sobs and continued the effleurage on her belly. "Just know I love you, and stay peaceful, my love. Mommy will help you get to the end, and then you will be with God."

She sang all the lullabies that came to mind. She thought of the quilt with colorful ponies on it. "Maybe you will see it from Heaven. I wanted to wrap you in it and walk you up and down to show you our pretty home and grandpa's horses. Your little toes would peek out, and Puppy Joe would lick them, and your laugh would tinkle like his dog tags and make your daddy laugh too." She chortled as if enjoying herself. It didn't sound right, but she had to make do.

In the moments before dawn, distant sirens screamed toward them. Within minutes, headlights focused on them. Voices shouted. At first, Rose instinctively closed her eyes against the brightness, but soon she saw everything—the old Maverick upside down, the blood on Michael's face, his arm hanging limp. She wished she were back in the dark with her child. Just the two of them in unwitting bliss.

Two emergency technicians approached the car and addressed Michael. One of them knelt next to her. "We're going to put you on a stretcher, Ma'am."

She kept rubbing and murmuring. "Mommy's not afraid,

baby. Stay calm. Think of Puppy Joe and the pony quilt."

Michael's voice was low and urgent, and then the EMT leaned in over her. "Ma'am, we're going to remove your slacks."

"Hush, little baby, don't be afraid..." she crooned, part singing, part crying, part laughing.

"Get behind her, Sam, and let her lean against you."

She moaned. "Don't touch me, don't move me."

The EMT mumbled close to her personals. "I can see the head. Can you push the baby out, ma'am?"

She knew her baby's first struggle for breath would mean its death.

"No—no—Michael, don't let them take her. Tell them I want to keep her here with me." She shuddered. "Oh, baby, I love you so much."

"Push, ma'am!"

No, she would not push her child out. Not when birth led to death.

"I've got her. It's a girl, a tiny little girl with all her fingers and toes, ma'am."

Her throat was swollen with agony. "Is she—is she—"

The tech turned to Michael. "Are you believers, sir? Hand me that bottle, Sam." Then he swiped water over the little bald head in the name of the Father, the Son, and the Holy Spirit. He handed the tiny form swaddled in Michael's shirt over to Rose's good arm, and Michael leaned in over the body, close to Rose's face.

She smelled the sour odors of Irish whiskey and sweat.

ℰᘓℰᘓ

Later, Rose recalled signing forms, though the details eluded her. What had happened to Rosebud's little body? In her imagination a burly, masked man shoveled the baby girl into an incinerator. "No, no. I didn't want that."

She sobbed until the nurse hung a different bag on the IV

pole above her and relieved her of the ability to think.

Dilatation and Curettage surgery removed the placenta and miscellaneous products of conception, as the nurses called them. "But that belonged to my baby," she protested. An anesthesia haze kept her ribs and fingers from hurting.

A resident hovered above the gurney. "Wake up, Rose. Can you tell me what happened to you?"

She curled her arms around her abdomen as well as she could with one useless arm and tubes in the other. "My baby." Her voice had shrunk to a hoarse whimper.

"That's right, Rose. I'm sorry for your loss."

"I was always afraid of this. I'm barren, you know." Did this make sense?

"No, Rose, you did fine. It was the trauma that forced your body to expel the fetus. She was a perfect baby girl, and you would have carried her to term if not for the crash."

Rose was surprised she had any tears left to give.

The resident patted her shoulder. "You came through the D and C great. Now you rest. You've got hand surgery ahead."

Rose floated. "My baby?"

Rosebud danced into the room wearing a yellow hair ribbon and panties with lace across her bottom. "Bye, Mommy."

Rose reached out. "Wait, sweetie. Let me give you a kiss."

Rosebud's skin was the softest thing ever. Rose kissed each cheek and the fat little belly. The tot giggled and gave Rose a sweet, sloppy kiss from her rosebud mouth.

A nurse jolted Rose out of her dream, bringing on a spate of new tears.

"Don't cry, honey. It's just morphine and antibiotics. You've got quite a rampant infection. Your fever is high as the town drunk. Can't you tell?"

"What happened? Why do I have a fever? What about my hand?"

"Infection happens sometimes." The nurse shrugged.

"You have to get that under control before the surgery. The doctor is concerned about protecting your future fertility more than your hand right now. You can give birth without a hand, but not without your female giblets." She gave Rose a pat on the shoulder and turned up the drip.

"Where's Michael? I want Michael."

She remembered she was mad at him, but she wasn't sure why. She just wanted him to hold her. She wanted to press her face against his heartbeat and take in his smell of rose petals and pure soap and testosterone.

"You're in isolation, honey. Nobody can come in here but medical staff. Your parents were asking for you."

"Please, can you find out about Michael? Is he all right?"

"Oh, yes, I have a note here on that."

Surgeons had placed a titanium rod into Michael's left arm to realign the disarticulated parts of his humerus. The note was in a stranger's handwriting. A curving symbol at the bottom started her weeping again.

"He's left-handed. He signed that with his right hand. It's—it's his—his Irish triple heart. He always signs his notes that way, ever since we decided to have a child. He never gave up on me when I couldn't conceive." His triple heart showed her he still hadn't given up, even now.

"I should—be with him—take—care—take care of him."

She'd always done her best to look out for Michael, though she let him think he was the dominant partner. Her white knight.

Halfway to oblivion, Rose rambled about the first time they'd played knight and damsel. That night Michael had thrown off whatever had numbed him in recent years. "Claiming me, ravishing me. It freed him somehow. It made it all right to roar in victory."

She recounted how, later, the game-playing had become more real, more elaborate. "I sewed him a knight costume and he bought a metal helmet and sword." Her lips curved up in a grin. "He used it on some of the trees out back. Then he besieged me." She licked her lips. "He set me on fire."

The unyielding infection kept her in the isolation room for a week after Michael went home. Before he left, he looked in through the glass panel in her door. He raised his right hand to the window, and she placed the fingers of her left hand against it. He bore a stoic expression, but the lines around his eyes were new.

⌘⌘⌘

Rose's bruises and broken hand and ribs started to heal, but, with her forced isolation, she and Michael had no chance to mourn their loss together. When they skyped, she noticed Michael's expression was flat, his eyes guarded, though, otherwise, his face had always appeared so animated, so full of adoration.

"Got to go. See you soon." He raised his good hand to the screen, and it went dark.

Rose spoke to the mindless laptop. "Maybe you don't want me to see how you feel. Please don't treat me that way."

⌘⌘⌘

At last Rose returned home, and she and Michael faced each other across the table, bereaved rather than hopeful, as they had been once.

He studied the table. "Rosie, you look pale—and thin."

What had happened to the wonderful blue eyes that had held her spellbound? "You look…different." Distant. She didn't touch the steaming cup of tea he placed in front of her. Instead, she broke down in sobs each time she looked at the face she loved—and hated—for killing their child, though she would never admit the negative tinge of her feelings.

Michael's jaw hardened. Had they lost their once effortless connection?

"Please, Michael, I need to talk about this with you."

He waved the idea away, his voice rough. "Rose, I've been mourning for a week."

She gulped down a sob. "But not with me. Please, we need to talk."

He lifted dead eyes. "What can I say? It's over. I can't think about it anymore. I have to get past it, and so do you."

Rose lay on their bed sobbing, while Puppy Joe cuddled against her empty belly. He wore his ears folded backward and poked her with his nose, showing how much he wanted to comfort her.

"Why isn't Michael here, Joe? I can't do this without him."

From the bed, her glance caromed off the vanity mirror to a scene in the dim hallway where Michael brooded, his right arm hugging the cast on his left. So close to the bedroom, he made no attempt to approach her, as if this were the limit of his trust. His downcast eyes, slack posture, and lowered head told her all the shame and sorrow he could not put into words. But she needed him to say those things to her.

His hands covered his face, and he sank ever deeper against the wall. In the dark, she reached out to him with her misery. "Come to me, Michael." Just a few steps closer. Just a few words of shared comfort.

He did not reach out. Instead, he left her with tattered hope—hope that the threads of feeling between them were still strong enough to bind them together.

Michael uttered an animal moan and wrenched himself away from the hallway. The door of the old refrigerator creaked open and shut with a rubbery slam. Bottles clanked in Michael's hand. He stomped out of the house, slamming the screened door behind him. Once in a while she heard the bottles clank together or smash against a tree. Four Budweisers—all a one-handed man could clutch against his chest. His boots pounded down the steps and scrunched on the gravel path. The door to the shed creaked open.

Presently he stumbled back to the front yard. "Yabba Dabba Doo!" Blows smashed onto splintering wood. Puppy Joe cowered into her side with a whimper, joining her ragged sighs. Grunts of clumsy exertion joined the groans and cries floating through the night into her shriveled heart, wrung dry.

 espace

For weeks, Rose's mother had looked in on her every day, and Puppy Joe had become like another appendage.

"Oh, Mommy, he actually chopped Rosebud's bush into slivers. What can I do with a man like that—all suppressed passion and booze? I feel like I'm in a private hell."

Maria smoothed her daughter's hair. "Losing the baby was terrible, and you feel you can't get past it, don't you? I don't know how to advise you, honey, but I do know you have to go on."

Rose was glad her mother was a sensible mutt, with none of the Irish stubborn streak her father's father claimed with pride. This made Rose a half breed, Grand-dad Sean had judged, and she had yet to decide which half was dominant.

Rose's father Aidan came down from the main house every day too and forced her out for walks on his south Inverness spread. Getting you out of the house is like maneuvering a breached foal out of the mare.

She hugged him. "Oh, Daddy, you always make me smile." The corners of her mouth turned down, and she buried her face in his chest.

She reached a hand into the corral to rub the equine faces extending quizzically back at her, while Aidan's deep voice spoke soothing words to them. To her too. He handed her a wrapped peppermint, which always meant he didn't know how else to make things better. Always before, her work on the ranch had lifted her mood. So had Aidan's homespun advice. Even his voice.

But this time her whole spirit had suffered a compound break. Her brimming eyes sought his face. "Dad."

Aiden took her hand. "Appreciate every moment when you feel a little bit okay, honey."

She grinned, knowing what was coming.

"You know what I mean? Sometimes okay is good enough. There's plenty of time to reclaim your joy. I'm telling you what I know from experience."

It was more than okay to stroll under the live oaks in the company of the man who had made the most of his own sad situation.

Rose snuggled against his arm. "Daddy. I know you still love your mother." Seeing the encouragement in his face, she posed the question that hurt. "Do you ever hate her as well for what she did to you—for the way she left you?"

He stopped amid a stand of longleaf pines, pulling her into a side hug, and his quasi-firm voice presaged his answer. "Have you—have you started to hate Michael, girl? Because hatred is always a step away when love is strong."

She rested her head on his chest.

He made her look at him with a finger under her chin. "Could be Michael hates you too for what he did, and for what he cannot give you. You had so much together all these years, and now you've lost so much. You might say you both lost paradise."

Chapⲧⲉʀ 2

July:

Rose suspected what Maria was up to, coaxing her to spend daylight hours at the White House, as Michael had dubbed the family home. Mother and daughter savored the calm in the north-facing studio.

"You always were a natural landscape painter, Rose. I'm so glad you ended up getting your degree in fine arts." Maria hugged her daughter. "I love how you've adapted traditional art into your own style."

Rose emitted a desolate sigh, though a rush of warmth followed her mother's efforts to cheer her.

Maria moved mismatched squares and triangles of printed cotton around. "I've always liked bits and pieces, collage and quilts. Maybe it's because my heritage is such a mixture, while at least you're half Irish. Your dad used to call me his patchwork girl, though I know your grandfather wished his son had married full Irish." She snorted.

Rose put down her pencil and met her mother's eye. "I'm glad you made me an artist, Mommy. It's keeping me sane. If it weren't for you and Dad and Puppy Joe, I don't know…"

There were no more words. Maria's face told her there didn't need to be.

ᥫᨳᥫ

Lately, Rose dragged her wretchedness with her like a

sack of manure. Now and then, some escaped, and everyone knew how it stank.

Maria set down her teacup and peered over her working glasses. "My poor child, you're not getting over it, are you? Will you at least talk to someone?"

Rose's smile sagged. Even her paintbrush drooped.

"Did you have someone in mind, Mama?"

"Mmm…remember that nice woman we met at your last pre-natal visit?" Maria stopped short, reddening, before hurrying further. "Lyla something, I think. From the winery. She got on the topic of her psychologist, a life-saver, she told me. Her father-in-law goes to him too. She gave me a coupon for a tour of their farm. An alpaca on it. Cute. I'm sure I could find it."

ℰↃℰↃ

August:

Two weeks later, Dr. Meadows sat back in his leather chair and inspected Rose through his thick glasses. He sported a walrus moustache and thick eyebrows without a single hair on his perfectly shaved head. Her voice always dropped a half tone when she saw him.

His index finger groomed his moustache. "So…let me get this straight. You think it's your fault you lost the baby. That's over my head. Explain how you came to that far-fetched conclusion."

Rose couldn't stop twisting a strand of her hair, yet she felt foolish for doing it. She blinked at the intense Florida light that slitted through the plantation blinds. She hated it when people pressed her, but she soldiered on without protest, setting her lips in a line.

"Yes, it is my fault, because I should have been mindful of Michael's alcohol consumption at the party, and I shouldn't have let him drive."

He steepled his fingers. "Oh, you're saying you should've watched him all the time?"

"Yes. No." She brushed her answer away like a fly. "During recent years Michael always drank at parties. He always drank at home for that matter. I knew it, but I guess I was sick of the fact that alcohol dominated our lives. I wasn't exactly in denial…I just wanted our life to be normal once in a while. Like it used to be. Awareness got away from me that night." She crossed and uncrossed her legs.

Dr. Meadows laced his fingers behind his head and leaned farther back. "And what was it like when your life used to be normal?"

Her arms rested by her sides, while she let her mind wander back to the good times. "It was delicious. Michael came home from work, dumped his tie and jacket on the sofa, and undid the top buttons of his shirt. I loved the way he looked at me—as if to say, *later*. Then he took a sweating glass of iced tea in one hand and a small pruner in the other and walked with me through the rose garden he'd planted through the years. Some of the bushes were five feet tall, all gorgeous and Florida friendly.

"He always used the same words. 'Rose, I'm in Paradise right now. The work of my own hands in front of me and the love of my life by my side.' He always kissed me after that. For a long time. It was a tasting more than a guzzling."

Jotting down notes as she spoke, Dr. Meadows looked up when she paused. "Go on," he prodded, with a little half grin. Shoot! She must have that sappy, love-soaked look on her face.

"Then we had dinner together and talked about our day. I told him about the people who had come for their riding lessons. Maybe about my drawing. He related anecdotes about his day in the law office in Inverness. Even if his day had been the same old same old, he made it sound interesting, and he always made me laugh. After that, he cleaned away the dishes while I tidied the kitchen and living room.

Then he—" She pulled up short, feeling the redness suffuse her face.

"Don't worry, Rose. I think I'm familiar with what comes next. Go right ahead."

She felt a bashful grin curving her lips. "Then he stretched out his hand to take me to the shower—the first touch was electric." A smile played on her mouth. She was almost to the good part and done twisting her hair, so she hugged herself.

"And?"

"We soaped each other up." Her eyes slid away. "Lather, thick and slippery. Mmm…Drawing with our fingers on each other's sudsy bodies. We soaped and resoaped, just for the pleasure of it." She snapped back to the moment. "We went through a lot of soap."

"Mmmm?"

"Michael led me through to our bedroom. A lot of times we oiled each other up with rose-scented lotion. We traded backrubs. He liked to massage my feet—" She shuddered. "Sometimes we talked." She fell quiet. "We did a lot of role play, especially since his emotions started locking up a few years ago—you know, not letting me see how he felt, not crying any more. Gosh, he used to cry a lot in the old days."

"Go on."

"Well, he liked role playing—knight and damsel most of all. He was pretty good at pretending to rescue me. Or he was an ogre who carried me off and turned into a prince at one taste of my lips. Sometimes I was an unwitting virgin, and he was my teacher."

A hot flush captured her up to her ears, as a swampy feeling took over everything south of her Mason Dixon line.

Dr. Meadows gave her a sharp look. "So Michael was your savior. He always took care of you, inept as you were. Was that it?"

She shifted in her seat as the idea squirmed in her head. "Mmmm…I guess that's true."

"Don't you think you set yourself up?"

"Maybe I should have assumed the role of the knight?"

"What do you think?"

"Now that I recall, I think Michael needed me to save him sometimes. Maybe he needed me to ravish him and carry him to a safe place away from his demons." She bowed her head with regret. "Over time I realized he did have demons, though he wouldn't let me know what they were. Now it's too late."

"Is it?"

She recalled Michael's recent entreaty after a bout of guzzling beer. "Come on, Rozhie. Just. Stop. Nagging me, damn it! I can stop drinking any time I try. It's never too late."

She tossed her head from side to side. Her voice sounded strident, even to herself. "What about me, though? I need to save myself. His Guinness and his Jamieson are going to drown both of us if he keeps on this way. He hasn't stopped drinking, and his emotions are still blocked, though he has no trouble shouting at me. Meanwhile, I can't stop crying."

∽∾∽

September:

The cottage bedroom fell silent with a thick sense of loss. Rose and her mother packed up the baby clothes that had remained in the hope chest Michael had given her years ago when hope had been a pulsating, living thing. She lingered over the quilt with the vibrant appliquéd horses.

Maria laid an arm around her shoulder. "Don't you want to keep that for a while? You'll still use it, you know."

Her eyes were wet. Rose hated the fact that her pathetic self-pity saddened her mother.

Rose blew her nose on a well-used tissue and stuffed it back in her pocket. "I spent so much of my life trying to conceive. We used to tell each other we were on a quest for our holy grail." Rose made air quotation marks around the word *quest*. Should she even reveal such things to her mother? No choice. She was an emotional pimple straining toward rupture.

She groaned. "That was why we…we were so…diligent in the bedroom. 'Here I am,' he would say. 'Ready to reconnoiter, troops. Where is my staff sergeant? Ready my pistol, adjutant.' We used to laugh ourselves silly."

Maria smiled. "Good, honey. It's a treat to hear you laugh."

Rose shook her head. "You know, when I lost the baby I lost my past and maybe a lot of my future too. I'm afraid I'll never have a child, Mother. I'm afraid without Michael I won't want to make one again. Not with some other man. And maybe not with him either, if he—Michael was one of a kind—once."

"It hurts more when you give in to that kind of thinking, Rose." Maria sniffled and turned away. She lowered her voice. "I lost my grandchild, you know. I can't accept that this is the end of my dreams." She fumbled for a fresh tissue.

It was Rose's turn to comfort Maria now. "I know you loved her, Mommy. I appreciate that. You would have been the best grandmother ever. I think about that. I do. I play them over and over in my mind—scenes of you playing with her, teaching her to sew, showing her your world."

Maria nodded.

"You do understand, though, don't you, Mama? It kills me to be with the man I adored—without having sole possession of him, that is. He and I aren't alone together anymore. He has another lover now, and her name is Booze."

"Oh, Rose, I have always loved that boy. It feels like I'm losing a son in a war he can't return from."

"I know, Mama. That's just how I feel. I'll never stop wanting him…but I'm turning to dust in his hands. That's why I have to move out. It's killing me to see him all the time, when he's not really mine anymore." She stumbled over the stone in her throat. "You do understand that, don't you?"

Maria placed a hand on each of Rose's cheeks. "I know why you need to spend time apart. Just don't kill something that could still live."

Rose blew her nose and dried her eyes. "It's kind of like weeding, isn't it? Sometimes you pull out the wrong plant."

Maria walked over to a chest of drawers and emptied out the newborn-sized onesies and receiving blankets. She cleared her throat. "In the meantime you need your work on the ranch. You're a gifted riding teacher, even if you don't ride, and you're good with the horses. I don't know if it's enough for you, though. Maybe you need something else to occupy you the way your drawing used to." She fingered a white lace baby dress. "I wonder if you could feel that way about quilting. Maybe it could get you back to your repre-sentational art. You know, creating a scene from applique and patchwork?"

The stone on Rose's heart lightened, and she smiled.

"Let's see what we can do, shall we, sweetie?" They embraced for a long time before they lugged the boxes out of the cottage.

e∕ɔe∕ɔ

Rose returned to the comfortable leather chair opposite the desk.

"So, you moved out. Left the house you shared together piece by piece. Is that it? Why did you draw the process out so long?"

"It was easier to get used to that way." She opened and closed her fingers. "Although, not easy enough. I have to pass my house—my former house—to get to the main road. I must admit, that hurts."

"It's all right to hurt, Rose. Emotions are sometimes the only thing a person owns, so it's good to know which ones you've got in the bank."

Rose raised her eyebrows.

"In other words, you need to own your hurt no matter what you decide to do about the marriage." Dr. Meadows studied her face as if assessing it for later. "It's not the house that hurts you, Rose. Passing it by does that, just like failing to deal with your husband. You don't have to stop looking at it, remembering it, even visiting it. The same goes for Michael. He can still be in your life somehow if you want him there. You don't have to cut off an arm to treat a hangnail."

Recalling Michael's role in her life made her squirm more than ever. She forced herself to stop twisting her hair. Michael in or Michael out, the pain would stay with her. Could she salvage anything good from her marriage?

"How are you really doing, Rose? What have you been up to since you left him?"

"I took a lesson from Michael's plant husbandry—I'm working with my hands. I'm growing a quilt. It keeps me absorbed."

He gave her a quizzical look and steepled his hands.

"I started quilting before I met Michael, but somehow I never had time after that. He kept me so busy." She thought about some of Michael's ideas of *busy*. She hoped Dr. Meadows didn't notice the blush she felt flooding her features.

"Tell me about how you two met, Rose. Tell me about the early days. Those may be the emotions you want to take from the marriage."

She pondered what she should leave out. Those days were so full of carnality that she feared she might give the wrong impression. Or maybe she feared the right impression. "We…er…met during our last year of college—at an outdoor concert. We sat on blankets on adjoining squares of grass. I saw him staring at me. He was not subtle, but not rude either. Just engrossed. 'Not interested in the concert?' I asked."

"'I'm distracted,' he admitted. 'I prefer this view, but I

could see better closer.' That line made me laugh. I felt feisty."

"You look feisty right now. What did you do then?"

Rose fondled her armrest. "I patted my blanket, and he moved over. I don't know why I did that. It wasn't my way, but I didn't even think about it. Before long my hand was in his. He traced messages into my palm, and we laughed like gagging seals."

"You were uninhibited, and you had fun."

"We sure did. I think about that evening a lot these days."

"What happened after the gagging?"

"When the concert ended, everybody went home. Everybody but us. Michael dragged his blanket over us..." In her mind, Rose was back in the day, rolled up with this stranger who felt so familiar and so dead-on right for her. They had narrowly avoided the lawnmower in the morning.

"That was it. After that, we were together every day and every night. My parents embraced Michael right away, and we married on our graduation day. Grandfather approved, because Michael was full Irish like him and Dad. This meant Michael must have the *Irish values* in his blood." Her mouth sagged with reservation.

"What exactly does that mean?"

"He never could explain. Maybe he made those values up. I'd like to find out some day."

"So you two connected right away. Did you ever think it was too soon?"

"Well, it didn't hit me that way, because I'd heard so much about my grandparents' torrid romance back in the sixties. She was from Ireland. They saw each other at meetings of the Irish-American club in college, but if it weren't for JFK, who knows how things would've played out?"

Doctor Meadows stopped fondling his moustache and sat up straighter. "Oh?"

"You see, when they heard about the assassination, they ran out into the quad with other students, all crying. The two of them ran straight into each other's arms. Quick as a snake can wiggle, Grandmother was pregnant with Dad. That's how Grandfather put it."

"Now that's a romantic story. I can see why you would think your love affair might be the same."

"Well, I guess theirs wasn't romantic enough. In a few years, Grandmother left him. I don't know why. She was on a visit to her family, and she never came back. Thank goodness she left her son here with his dad. That was my father, and here I am—without her, without Granddad, and without Michael." She looked at her lap. "You knew Granddad retired to Ireland, right?"

Dr. Meadows offered a subtle bob of head and shoulders. "How do you feel about your grandmother abandoning her husband and son, Rose?"

She picked at her skirt. "I'm confused. I've missed her all my life. Yet she can't have loved them...us very much. In my book she has a lot to answer for."

He chewed on the earpiece of his glasses. "And yet you've left Michael."

Hands moving in agitated jerks, she avoided his eyes. "That's different. If I keep living with Michael, his drinking will kill me."

"So you've left him to save yourself." He studied her. "How do you know what your grandmother had to live with in her marriage?"

Rose had no answer to that. She tugged at the top of her blouse. "I know...um...I know that a child would be better off without an alcoholic, pent up father."

Or would Rosebud have made Michael better somehow? Could love put Humpty Dumpty together again?

෧෨෧

November:

"I love quilting with you, Mom."

Maria cocked her head. "But?"

Rose lifted her palms and weighed them left and right. "I'm partly like you in my life, Mommy, willing to stick to my plan, determined. On the other hand, my artistic temperament is more free-flowing. I get antsy but can't act on my impulse. I don't know how to integrate both sides of me into a quilt, much less into my life. You're so balanced."

Maria lowered her eyes. "It's true. You don't seem to take after me that way—at least not right now."

Rose gave her mother a hug. "Anyway, I'm so glad your family name is part of mine."

"Clever, wasn't it?" Maria lifted an eyebrow. "*Rose,* shortened from *Belrose*, with all my mixed up non-Irish heritage."

They laughed like co-conspirators.

"I always thought your grandfather made you conflicted, though, Rose, always spouting off about being full Irish."

"Yes, he did force the Irish pride on me. Poor Granddad. I love him, but he pressed me into emotional bondage. I wonder if he set me up to be the wuss I am today."

Her mother wrinkled her brow. "How do you mean, Rose?"

She waved her hands with impatience. "I put up with Michael's alcoholism far too long. His charisma eddied down into anger and outrage. I accepted that, though it gave a sour taste to my beautiful memories."

They remained quiet for a few minutes, pursuing their own thoughts.

Rose shrugged off the weight pressing on her. "I do miss Grandfather. I hope he's all right by himself, so far away in Ireland. I'm sort of sorry he inherited the family cottage." She shrugged. "I feel mean saying that, though. He was so happy."

"Well, right now let's take care of your artistic quandary." Maria reached for Rose's hand. "Come look at the album I made of my youthful experiments. I think you'll be surprised.

❧❦❧

January:

"Cheer. Cheer. Cheer. Trrrr!" A cardinal chirped through the open window while Rose related her memories to Doctor Meadows—a process by now as smooth as rotary cutting calico, in spite of his alarming eyebrows.

"I like to imagine myself back in those lovely days of our early marriage. I don't have to give up all the good memories if I can't keep the marriage, do I?"

"Is that what you want?"

"Are you kidding? I even lick the last ice cream out of my dish. I always hold out hope that something's left." They shared a laugh.

She gave him a contented smile. "Our work together is better-oiled lately, isn't it? You know how to turn on the switch, and the insights just pour out of me. It reminds me of when Daddy backwashes the pool. Dirty water just spurts out of that thick blue hose."

He smiled at the turn of speech. "You're doing very well, Rose."

"By the way—I'm happier with my quilt design. Very free form and thought-provoking. That's what I've been doing day and night since last week. Scenes from life, with rivers and mountains and children and dogs. Primitive Americana. A lot of movement, arrested in the moment if you know what I mean."

"I do. And you changed the subject."

Taut puzzlement lifted Rose's eyebrows.

Dr. Meadows leaned forward. "I don't think your troubles started with Michael's drinking. That's his attempt to avoid dealing with unpleasant thoughts and feelings. Focusing on his symptoms is your way of avoiding your own emotions."

She shifted in her chair. "But—"

"Think about it. When did things first go wrong with your great passion? That's your homework for next week. Now tell me about the quilt."

❧❧❧

On her way back to her parents' home, she passed the house where she and Michael had created a marriage and a child. Michael approached the car, a hopeful smile on his handsome face. The sight made her heart leap into her throat.

"Hello, Rosie." When did his eyes grow so sad?

"Hello." She couldn't think of anything else to say. Or rather, she thought of too much.

He drew a line in the dirt with his boot. "This is awkward. What's up?"

"I, uh, I miss the roses."

"I miss the Rose. When are you coming home?"

She could barely breathe in his presence. She looked away and shook her head.

He handed her a late season pink rose. "Here. Take this one with you." He leaned close to her open window. "I can still give you roses, can't I?"

Maybe they could still be friends. Maybe, when she stopped wanting him so much. It should become easier any time now.

She reached the main house in time to snag a cup of tea with Maria.

"I'm so glad you invited me to live here with you, Mommy. It lets us spend time like this together."

"I like it too," Maria replied. "As long as you're sure it's what you want. It's hard to work on your marriage if you don't live with your husband."

A torrent of sadness spilled over her. "I know you disapprove of the separation, Mommy. It hurts me, too. But I can't be with Michael now that he drinks so heavily. It's too

crazy-making for me. I didn't marry a man who spews nonsense and stumbles around cursing at night. I need to get
away to save my sanity, though God knows it tortures me to
the point of madness."

On her mother's massive project table, Rose unrolled her
king-sized plan for a quilted panorama and laid the finished
part atop it. "I've made a lot of progress. What do you
think?"

Maria clapped her hands together and slung an arm
around her daughter. "Oh, Rose, this is quite wonderful, and
you do have a lot done. I like how you've combined quilting
with appliqué and embroidery."

Rose pointed. "Yes, see here—down at the bottom—the
big pieces form the pond and the grass of the park, as well
as the big tree. Those I fastened in place on the backing
first, except for parts like the top half of the tree that will
cover scenery in the distance. Then I added the batting and
basted the layers together as I went along. To be machine
quilted. Of course I crafted the smaller pieces first and attached them separately with appliqué and a lot of embroidery. Look, leaves and all the bushes, ducks in the pond and
dogs playing with children."

"Yes, and I didn't miss the couple with their legs sticking out from behind the tree."

"Oh, you caught that. Yes, and, of course the most work
is the grandparents on the park bench with their grand-
babies."

"I suppose that's your father and me, front and center."

Rose nodded. "I always hoped so."

"And so it will be, some day."

芝芝芝

February:

Every week Rose told Dr. Meadows more about her

landscape quilt and the significance of all the scenes she'd depicted.

"This has been quite an undertaking, Rose. Does it represent your life?"

"Maybe the life that could have been, but I don't know where my future goes yet, so the quilt gets more fanciful as I go higher. See? There are Dorothy and Toto with their friends in that field."

"True, you're acknowledging the unknown. Wait and see, eh? Don't forget, though, who's designing your life." He supported his chin in his left hand, as if ready for a long story. "Have you thought further about the place where things went wrong in your marriage?"

"Well..." She chewed on her lower lip, thinking how to start. "I suppose the trouble began with a series of disappointments. For one thing, after being honeymooners for years we started trying for a baby. After a while, our bedroom turned into a factory with a work stoppage. I'm not saying sex wasn't still first-rate."

She wound her legs around each other. "But sex wasn't just for pleasure anymore. Whether the act took or not was the main issue. We were in denial for years, but finally we realized we weren't digging in fertile soil. I felt ashamed of myself, and I know Michael felt less of a man. We seldom approached each other for the joy of it, though passion was still a factor. The fact is, now that our project was a dud, we found reasons not to...indulge. Not to fail."

"So you had intercourse after that?"

"Oh, yes, we still wanted each other. And sometimes desperation took over. As a lover, Michael delivers quite a jolt."

"Anything else go wrong?"

More homework.

On the way home, Rose passed the garden where Michael bent over his roses. Knowing he didn't see her gave her license to feel imprudent sensations.

The sight of his backside drove electricity up inside her,

but she forced herself to drive on. Life-giving. That's what the sight of him was. Still. Six months and six days after Rosebud's death. She still burned with desire for him.

At least her feelings weren't dead, even if she couldn't have him. She pounded the steering wheel and drove on. Tears fell on her words. "Oh, Michael, Michael. Why did you have to ruin things for us?"

The next day, Michael waited in the road, in order to waylay the car. His face twisted in a grin. I knew you would come by. I think I spend more time watching for you than I do at work." He shuffled his feet. "Writing out contracts doesn't do much for me anymore."

"We could switch. I could spend a day straightening up your office, and you could come and muck out the stables."

"Ha! Not much difference, now that you put it like that."

By God, he still had fire. She couldn't help buying into his smile—and his beautiful, searching blue eyes. They were like catnip to a tabby. She reveled in them, and they never failed to shoot a pain of lust into her.

"Rosie, it kills me to see you pass by. You should be living here. Joe is worn out running from house to house."

He was holding her hand through the open window, rubbing the sensitive place on her palm, which he knew so well. Their eyes locked, and she was lost in the passion she knew would never let her go. Not as long as he could look at her this way.

His voice was husky when he released her hand. "Come look at my new rosebush. It's already got a blossom."

She hesitated, but when he opened her door, she followed him into the garden. Dozens, maybe more than a hundred bushes dotted the well-tended beds he had designed during their marriage. Each one stood as witness to his love for her, as he'd often maintained.

He led her to the new bush, with a porcelain white blossom.

"A hybrid tea?"

"Yes, but almost no thorns. It reminded me of us and the

way we can be." He showed her the name on the tag. *Home and Family.*

In the next moment she was in his arms. He brushed her lips with his in that tentative way that made her loins beg for him. Their searching mouths became one organ, probing ever deeper, rejoicing in the taste and fragrance and velvet touch that was *them*. His incorrigible hardness pressed against her, and he gripped her buttocks tighter to his groin. The aching and throbbing inside her drove her to desperation.

She broke away and hurried to the car, past the beer bottles that poked out of the trash.

⁂

Rose sat in the chair across from the doctor's desk, crossing and uncrossing her legs. The sun filtered through the slats into her face. She was going to have to say something about that one of these days. She moved the chair a little. God, she felt testy.

She caught Dr. Meadows hiding a smirk. What was that about?

His moustache spilled over his hand as he rubbed his mouth. "Well, Rose, what about the quilt?"

She leaned toward him and spread out her arms. "I found out my mother also quilted landscapes when she was young. Mine is going to be huge with many hills and valleys, like a real life. The landscape extends into the far distance. Near the top all the rivers empty into a large one along with waterfalls off the mountains. Above it all, you'll see a hot air balloon rising into the atmosphere. Symbolic, don't you think?"

"Very. Uplifting."

They indulged in a joint laugh.

She thought of her last visit to the cottage. "Michael loves symbolism."

"Is that where you get it from?"

"I'm more images. He's a word man."

"Don't sell yourself short. You have quite a way with words yourself."

She told him about the new rose and how its name had fanned them into a burst of romantic feelings.

He raised his eyebrows. "So? A new start?"

She shook her head. "Doctor Meadows, I feel angry at Michael, not just hurt."

"Do you now?" He raised his eyebrows and looked at her over his glasses. "Hmmm. We'll have to talk about that." He changed the subject. "Tell me about your homework."

She understood he wouldn't forget the topic she had broached. She was proud he trusted her not to take the easy way out of their conversation. She was ready to peel back all the layers of her life to him, even the distasteful ones.

"You asked what else went wrong in our marriage. Your instinct was right—there were other things that happened to sink our happiness. The worst was when Michael's father died. He worshiped his father, a good man, though sometimes a hard father in his last years. My grandfather called him staunch Irish, and they became close pals. My dad was not such a fan of Michael O'Leary, Senior, though. A hotshot Ocala lawyer he called him. Maybe Daddy was envious of his education."

Dr. Meadows's eyebrows rose closer to his hairline. "Oh?"

"Yes, you know my grandfather moved to Citrus County to establish his horse ranch? My father worked hard in the business all his life, while Granddad made it a going concern by hob-nobbing with important people in the horse culture." She crossed her arms across her chest. "Cinderella, my dad called himself. He's funny but serious, my dad."

"Dad loves Michael, but he wasn't so sure about Senior, especially the intense drinking. Then, of course he was sorry to see how ripped up Michael was when his dad…died."

Doctor Meadows gave her time to empty her thoughts out under his lens.

He steepled his fingers. "Tell me."

"It wasn't so much that he died. He killed himself."

"But the papers reported he fell."

Rose's ears moved back in surprise. "You knew?"

"Some things I do know. You think I'm wrong?"

"Yes." She looked into her lap, her shoulders rising to her ears. "He killed himself. He walked right off a cliff. That's when Michael started to fill in the cracks in his heart with drink like his dad did."

Doctor Meadows nodded. "Hmmm…How do you know he did it on purpose?"

"Michael was there."

ღჯღჯ

March:

Rose labored on the landscape quilt in the big, sunlit studio. "Get down, Puppy! Look what he's done, Mommy. He bit off part of the pattern. What's gotten into him these days?" Joe spun around and around chasing his tail.

"Maybe he's not getting the attention he needs?"

Rose opened the door. "Michael should be home from work. Find Michael, Puppy."

He sped down the road toward the cottage.

"The poor thing." Maria strained after the dog. "A product of a broken home. It kills me. He's losing weight rushing back and forth."

"I know, Mommy, but neither of us wants to give him up. I do know I'm going to put him into every landscape quilt I ever make."

Maria nodded. "You're taking to this genre."

"Look, I've put in the road where it goes past the park and the little town across the road. It's going to be tricky to wind the road around the hills all the way to the mountains in the background."

"I see, and you've got to make the details of diminishing size to maintain perspective."

"I'm learning so much. Not just about art. About the really important parts of life. See the wedding party at the church across from the park?" She hugged herself. "I can't wait to show it to Michael."

Maria looked at her out of the sides of her eyes.

Rose felt sizzly all over. "Oh, God, I can't believe I said that."

ల౩ల౩

The next day, Rose stood at the office window. "I see you've got some new plants in here. They need more light, but not just now and in my face." She adjusted the blinds.

"Very good." Doctor Meadows nodded. "I wondered when you would stick up for yourself. I hoped I wouldn't have to take up smoking to push you along."

Rose turned away from the window. "It took a while, didn't it? Well, enough is enough. I guess that's part of what happened to Michael and me. Too many drunken snits, too much silence, too much unhappiness—and I accepted it. It didn't mean we stopped loving each other. We just stopped being good for each other, and that's why I left."

"The drive for survival."

She plopped into the chair. "I'm still in danger of falling for him every time I see him, and then we'll be right back where we were."

"I see."

They were silent for a while.

"Doctor? Do you think it's all right to show Michael the quilt?"

"Does it feel all right?"

"Well for some reason I just want him to see it, but I'm afraid too. I'm afraid I won't have any willpower once I'm in the house with him."

"Willpower is useless if you don't want it."

"But…" She wriggled in her seat.

Strands of gray had grown into Doctor Meadows's moustache in recent months, too many with her name on them, she figured. They sighed at the same time.

"I think you're getting sick of me rambling on about Michael. You probably think I focus on him too much and not enough on moving on." She pinned him with her stare.

"Do you think that?"

She pounded a fist into her palm. "Yes, yes. I'm sick of myself. I'm totally stuck on him, and I can't progress when I'm always around him."

Dr. Meadows cleared his throat. "Let's change the subject. Does Michael know that his drinking is the deal breaker between you?"

His abrupt gambit took her aback. She helped herself to a few deep breaths. "Yes, we went to AA together once but he scoffed that he could handle it himself if he only had a chance…meaning if I gave him a chance. Umm. That sounds like I'm responsible for him drinking or not drinking, doesn't it? That is not fair."

"You're very perceptive, Rose. Just a little late."

Chapter 3

April:

Rose's hands shook when she climbed the porch steps of the house where she used to live and rang the bell with her elbow. She was glad the rolled up pattern and the nearly finished quilt filled her arms. She was glad she had something to talk about besides the same old problems.

Michael appeared in the door in a sleeveless t-shirt and bare feet. She'd forgotten how the sight of his feet made her all sweaty. She felt that way now. Oh, dear!

She concentrated so well on gobbling him up with her eyes that she barely heard him speak.

"Hello, Rose." He dried his hands on a dishtowel. She always hated it when he did that. Linen was for glass.

He hid the towel behind his back. The act made his chest jut out, drawing her attention to his pectorals and making her remember what it felt like to rub her hands over them.

"It's nice to see you here. It's been a long time." His voice sounded a little throaty, and, head down, he looked at her over his eyebrows "I was just finishing my meal. There's a lot of custard left. Want some?" He opened the screen door wide.

Oh, man, first bare feet and now his homemade custard.

She looked at the floor. "I...uh...I just wanted to show you something."

She remembered the door always squeaked when opened too wide. Now the sound brought back memories of times when Michael was the one with his arms full—an arm full of field daisies, bags of fruit, and a pretty twelve week old sheltie displaced in a divorce settlement he'd handled. The pup, already named Joe, had licked them both as Michael had pressed him into her arms.

"Come on, then." He and his grin helped her crowd in through the screened door. Now a handsome teenager, Puppy Joe followed her in from the porch.

"We really should find a way to keep track of his whereabouts, Rose. I'm afraid we'll lose him on his sorties."

"Well, when he's not with you he's on the White House porch with his ears up and his nose in the air."

"Yes, he knows when it's time for somebody to come home."

Come home. The words resonated with her, tingling in her chest. She licked her lips. "I was afraid to come here."

"Afraid of me? Rose, you don't need to be afraid of me."

"I'm afraid of myself and how I'll react to being with you."

"It doesn't have to be like that."

He was telling her everything she wanted to hear, but she couldn't say what she wanted him to know. Her voice felt dry as oil-poor corn bread. She thrust her bundle at him. "I...uh...I just came to show you this. Where can I put it?"

Papers he'd brought from the office overflowed the dining table. His eyes twinkled. "It looks intriguing so far." He examined her with a look that always made her heart turn over. "Come in here. Let's lay it out on the bed."

The part of her that was hurt beyond healing wanted to pull back, but she followed him, anyway, into the room they used to call *Paradise*. She uttered a small sob. He opened his arms to her but stepped back and turned his gaze to her bundle.

"It's a quilt, isn't it? A huge one, I see." He gestured with his arms wide. "And intricate, if I know you."

If he knew her? The memory of his intimate knowledge of all her curves and crannies itched at her.

"Let me get us some iced tea, and you can guide me through it." Without waiting for an answer, he quitted the room.

She heard him rummaging in the kitchen while she fidgeted beside his bed. His pillow showed the dent where his head had lain. She knelt beside it and touched it with her fingertips. With a groan, she let her face sink into it. She took in the familiar scent of his shampoo and soap, wishing she had time to take in the scents lower in the bed, where the most personal parts of his body had reposed.

"Iced tea for my lady," sang the artificially jovial voice. "Unsweet, just the way you like it."

She jerked her head up off the pillow, presenting him, she knew, a very red face.

Showing him her project was comfortable, though, and suggestive of old times. She pointed out minutiae of the scenes, and he professed interest in every detail. Michael was always like that, drawing out time together as if it were precious. Finally he helped her roll up the quilt and pattern in a tidy bundle. Slowly, suggesting he didn't want to finish the task.

Side by side, they made their way to the door, where he handed her the bundle. "I miss doing this with you, Rose. You should be living here with me."

"But you know why we have to be apart, don't you?"

He shrugged. "I know what you think, but I'm going to get on top of things. Someday you'll be back in this house with me, Rose. I know it."

She extended a flexed hand as if to say *stop*. "I do still have feelings for you, Michael, but I need to try to get over them. I can't let your drinking kill me. That's why I have to go away."

He staggered forward, as if he'd lost his balance.

"Michael, Daddy is sending me to Ireland for a while."
Now he would get mad at her, or at Aidan.

His voice was thick as bean soup. "The quilt is amazing,
Rose." He turned away. "At least I didn't kill your creativi-
ty. You deserve to salvage that much from our marriage."

◈◈◈

Afterward, Rose gave Doctor Meadows a rueful smile.
"At least I didn't say 'I can't let your drinking kill me *like it
killed our baby*.' I wouldn't have been able to look at him
after saying something so cruel."

Doctor Meadows wiped his glasses and let the silence
pile up. "But that is part of what you're angry about. That
and his failure to be forthcoming with his feelings. And the
drinking, of course."

Rose balled her fists. "To tell you the truth, I wanted to
tell him to step up and lob his big ball of anger and sadness
into my court, so I could deal with it. But he just watched
me get into the car and drive away."

She stood up and twisted the slats open. "And that was
the last I saw of him. And this is the last I'll see of you until
I get back. A month at most. I hope I can handle it." She
gave him her hand.

"You can handle it, Rose. Good luck .I hope you find
what you want over there…and here."

◈◈◈

Packing prodded the next few days to race by. At last it
was time to go. She told her inner sceptic she was off to do
the homework that would bring her back in better shape.
Rose made herself sound crisp and decisive when she bade
farewell to Maria. She couldn't handle any wavering.

"Watch over Puppy Joe, will you, Mom? Hopefully he'll
accept staying with Michael all the time, but he may come
around looking for me."

"Maybe he'll come around looking for me. Aiden and I know how to take care of him too, you know." Her expression softened. "Your absence will be hard on that dear doggie."

"You do understand why I have to go, don't you Mommy?"

Maria made a *mmm* sound down in her throat and then turned away. "Just keep telling yourself what your motives are. When none of them is left, come home. Just come home.

Rose took in one more look around the ranch from the porch of the White House. The big oaks, the pines, the double fences where the thoroughbreds and saddle horses exercised, and—most of all—the little house that backed up to the woods. Michael's house. It could be a long time before his tempting proximity presented no danger to her peace of mind.

She squared her chin, murmuring a farewell down the road. "I'm moving on now, Michael. I won't come back the same."

"That's so true." Maria held Rose's face between her palms. "Remember, darling. You may forget the places you visit in the next month, but the people you meet and the lessons you learn can change you forever.

"I hope so, Mommy. I hope some things will change. I know I'll miss you most of all."

"No you won't, child."

☾☽

May:

Rose hoisted her twenty-six incher up to the scale. "Shannon, Ireland. I'll keep my backpack."

"Are you one way, then?"

Rose shrugged and gave the attendant her passport. "I'll stay until I find what I'm looking for."

She turned away from the counter and perused the crowd for a face she didn't want to see there, yet longed to gaze upon. A few men possessed the tall, slim physique and tumbling dark hair she scanned for, two or three of them with the right kind of eyes. No, Michael wasn't here, just the thought of him. That was everywhere. The knot in her belly relaxed, as it usually did when she knew they wouldn't come face to face.

Her father was here, though, the very last of the pure Irish in her family, thanks to Maria, who'd brought the line to an end. Grandfather disliked Maria's wantonly mixed blood, and did his best to restore Rose to a Celtic sensibility. But not her dad. Aidan always insisted his daughter was perfect as God made her. His little half and half counted as cream, after all.

Aidan motioned her over to the spot in front of the window where he minded her backpack. One of the dark-haired Irish, just like his father, Aidan stood out from a distance. Handsome men and passionate they were, and she had kept their surname when she'd married Michael O'Leary.

"Well, then, Rose, all set?" Aidan's voice caught a little. "I can't believe my girl is going on a grand adventure in the homeland at last." He waved her protest away. "Sure, I know you're nearly thirty years old, but you'll always be my little girl, and your mother's too."

"Yes, I know that, Dad." She hugged him to keep away the tears that burned her eyes. "Thanks for arranging the guided tour. I don't know when I'd get another chance to see the land our family once called home."

Her father held her at arm's length, searching her face. "Well, you deserve it, darling. You need it after all you've been through. Maybe it'll do you good, and you'll find out who you really are in the process. And who you want to be."

"I hope so, Dad. I think I've known myself merely as Michael's half-breed wife for too long, thanks to Grandfather going on about the Irish thing. Thanks for helping me get away."

He patted her on the back. "Thank you too, for promising to look up your grandfather after the tour. Stay as long as you like with him. It's great he retired at the ancestral cottage, but he needs to stay in touch. Give him a verbal thrashing for me, will you? Make him promise we'll hear from him."

Her mouth quirked in commiseration. "I'm sure he's all right, Dad."

Aidan shrugged. "Maybe he's carousing around, spending all his money, and that's all right." He sniffed and wiped his eyes. "I worry about the old fellow. After all, he is my da and the only parent I've got."

"I know how you feel, Daddy. You're my da."

He gave her a squeeze. "Wait 'til they see you over there, Rose dear. Next time I see you, you'll be bringing a big hulk of an Irishman home." He pinched her cheek. "Don't be afraid to look around."

Rose turned and waved to him as she proceeded into the security hall. She dashed away a tear and adjusted her backpack. It had ground her down to say goodbye to her father, so much her ideal that she'd married a man with his dark hair and blue eyes, his honeyed voice and gentle manner. She sighed. And now she had to leave them both behind. She squeezed her eyes shut. "God, take care of Michael."

She thought she felt eyes on her backpack, so she turned around, and there he was. Her heart contracted forcefully. All she could do was stare, as her legs turned to noodles. Yes, it was Michael all right—puppy dog eyes, curly hair, and that look that shook her up inside. Even now he made her feel the way he always did, all mush and jelly. But she was still angry enough at him to blow an artery.

He closed the remaining feet between them. "Rosie, I'm so glad you didn't go through security yet. I'd have to buy a ticket to see you then." He wrapped his arms around her, backpack and all. "Darling, I couldn't let you go without saying goodbye."

She felt squashed in more ways than one. "We talked about this, Michael. We're not together anymore." A pinch in her groin belied her words, but she refused to heed such sensations any more. "Why did you come? You know how I feel."

Michael's eyes were wet, forcing her to look away. She was always a sucker for those eyes. He'd been a man who used to cry freely before he got dammed up. She'd loved him for that then, and—damn it—she loved him for his more infrequent tears now.

"Please, Rosie. I know I'm to blame for everything. The baby, the drinking... But I can turn things around. I promise I will." He tipped her face to make her look at him. "I know you still love me the way I love you."

Her heart turned in her chest, but she wouldn't give in. "I just can't go through it anymore, Michael, the drinking and how you act when you aren't yourself. Your refusal to share your feelings with me. I know you belong to your demons now, not to me, and I deserve better. You're not the man who used to be joined with me at the hip."

"Please, Rosie, you're everything to me. I stopped drinking, and I'm getting help. I can't lose you, sweetheart."

Rose moved past the security agent, and the queue sucked her in. He'd already lost her. That's what she told herself.

⁄⁄⁄

Rose blinked when she saw the interior of the Air Lingus jet. Thank goodness, some seat room. She could still feel the buttery flesh of her seatmate on the Atlanta leg of her journey. Thank goodness, that wouldn't happen again.

On that first flight, a jiggly warm arm covering part of her body, with the hot sun from the window, had put her into a fitful dream about Michael. He'd smiled into her eyes, again the soul mate she'd married eight years ago. Gloriously naked, he half reclined on a sheet of velvety rose petals, and she melted into his muscled, yet yielding flesh. When she'd awakened, she'd found her generously fleshy neighbor patting her knee.

There was plenty of room on this second flight, to Shannon. Rose stood on her seat to bustle her carry-on into the overhead bin. Her weight-lifter grunts mortified her. She strewed furtive glances around, hoping she had attracted no attention.

A light voice spoke at her shoulder. "Don't hurt yourself. Let me help," Bright turquoise eyes looked at her. "Really."

"Thank you. It must be the boulders I packed."

"You'll need those where you're going. Wait until you see the Irish rocks. You're not Irish, I take it, except for your hair. It's the color of rosewood."

"I'm partly Irish. Just call me Half and Half."

"How do you do, Mizz Half and Half. My name is William. And this here is Claris." He pointed to the woman beside the window.

He was easy to talk to. Nice. But surely he wouldn't have commented on the rosewood if he knew how she hated her dark red hair. Grandfather loved it, because it was the part of her that looked most Irish, he'd thought. It reminded him of his wife.

Rose apologized for not speaking to Claris until now. "How do you do. I'm Rose." Claris listed toward the wall, looking miserable. She stared straight ahead, her eyebrows forced together. At short intervals she sniffed. "I'b sick. I thig I bight throw up. Eben better, baybee I'b dyig."

Will raised an eyebrow and cocked his head at Claris. "Allergies."

Claris gave him a pained look. "Dabbit, Will, why dote you help be?"

Will fished some antihistamine tablets out of his pocket.

Claris popped two into her mouth and gave him the evil

eye. "God forbid they'd give us water od this tid cad."

Rose gave her a bottle she'd filled near the gate. Claris turned her face to the rivets holding the wing together. Will and Rose chattered until dinner time. Hmm! This guy was good at getting information from her.

She indicated the Gators emblem on her baseball cap. "I'm from central Florida. My family runs a horse farm in Citrus County. You've probably heard of the big corporate farms in Ocala, near us. Well, ours is a small concern. Saddle horses. My great-grandfather always wanted to run one of the horse farms in Ireland, but he couldn't afford it. That's how the Flanagans came to the States. My grandfather built his father's dream, and now my dad runs the ranch." Rose took a deep breath. She couldn't believe she'd talked so much. "We've been in Florida since the late sixties."

"Ogay. Dow I'b dyig." Claris whined

Will ignored her.

"You do look Irish with that glorious hair."

"That's one of the things my grandfather always used to say. He told me to remember I'm Irish above all and hang on to my Irish qualities, er, values. I don't know just what that means. Maybe I'll ask him when I find him."

"Is he lost then?"

"Sort of. See, he inherited his family's home in Ireland and hasn't contacted us for a while. We're not too worried, but who knows what he's up to? I'm playing family detective. After my three week tour, that is."

"Ogay, id's workig now. I'm goig to sleeb, you two, and the berson who wakes me ub is going to be sorry."

Will patted Claris's hand but otherwise ignored her.

The man was charming, but shouldn't he pay more attention to his wife? He was an interesting companion, but Rose could see something was not as it should be between them.

"Why are the two of you going to Ireland? I can tell you're not Irish."

Will chuckled. "Is it the gray-blond hair and Boston intonation?"

She nodded. "And your laid-back manner. I can't imagine you hoisting a Guinness with one hand while bashing a fellow's head in with the other."

"Well, I am more of a talker than a fighter. I work at a prep school. I'm on sabbatical. So, I'll do some lecturing and some research, but first I'm going to travel."

Talk of the places he planned to investigate got them through their rubber chicken and soft-cooked peas.

"Do you know this is an actual Irish dish—mushy peas?"

Will shuddered. "God, who would kill perfectly good vegetables for this? I like to eat them raw, right out of the pod."

"So do I, and my puppy likes to eat them out of my hand."

After dinner the captain warned of turbulence ahead. The plane pitched forward.

"No kidding," Will exclaimed, his fingers gripping the arm rests.

Rose felt the blood leave her face. "I'm not partial to this. I don't even like the nerve shredders at amusement parks. I don't enjoy pitching and rolling and ups and downs. I prefer to be on an even keel."

Will gave her his arm. "Well, if we go down, I'll let you fall on me. It will be my pleasure."

What a funny man. So nice. What about his wife? Rose wouldn't have liked her husband making over a female companion like this. But who knew what Michael would get up to now? She compressed her lips.

Presently, Will braced both arms over his chest and joined Claris in a nap.

ℰↄℰↄ

Rose rummaged in her backpack for a sweater, since the

cabin walls gave off a chill. Loneliness made her cold too, especially now that her conversation partner was dead to the world. She'd rarely traveled alone since Michael and she had married. Except for his drinking, she had loved being married, and she missed it now. When would she ever get over this? A marriage lost was a life-long sentence of bereavement.

Her heart pitched forward when she found an envelope jammed inside her backpack's outer pocket. Michael and she had done this when one of them had been away from home, even for a single night. She'd assumed the custom would stop now, but her name wiggled across the envelope in the scrawl she would recognize anywhere. "To Rose, my heart's desire."

She moaned softly. "Oh, no...oh, Michael." He would never let her go. A band formed around her heart, scary but comforting too. Truth be told, she had missed finding his sweet little notes in the house. Despite her resolve to make a clean break, it felt delicious to settle in to read this one.

My *darling Rose,*
You can't forgive me for the past, and I understand that. You have good reason. I know I have ruined everything, so things can never be the same between us. I just hope we can preserve our feelings for each other in some form, like a wasp in amber. I just hope you understand I have to maintain hope to stay alive. At least for a while. Let me have that, Rose. Please.

I'm going to try everything I can to win you again. I won't say "win you back," because I know the best I can hope for is to possess you in some new way. If it's a different connection, a different relationship, I can accept that. Just, please, don't sever our bond beyond mending.

I'll never stop thinking of the closeness and passion we had. I know, though, that you deserve the life you want, with the man you want, and that might not be me.

Enjoy your trip in the homeland, Rose. I truly hope it gives you what you need.

All my love, Michael

P.S. No, I'm not going to stalk you forever, darling. I just want you to know you will always be my Rose. You'll hear from me once in a while, until I am able to stay away.

On the card's back side she found a drawing of three shamrocks with their long stems forming the shape of a heart.

How could she have fooled herself? She would always love Michael and want him in that old way, but she deserved better than what their life had become—grief and regret, with a soupçon of recrimination and a lot of anger. She had to move on.

She tried to swallow past the lump in her throat, pressed the missive to her lips, and closed her eyes. Now and then a tear or two squeezed through her lashes.

In her dream, a giant bottle of the dark, liquid temptation that was his new love whirled around in Michael's embrace. Next to them, a tiny girl jetéd and twirled by herself. Her organza skirt ballooned and bore her through the windows into the garden, beseeching Michael with outstretched arms. "Daddy, please. I'm too light."

He did not seem to notice her absence. Rose reached out to him, crying. "You killed what we had together."

Why must he love his Guinness more than he loved her? More than he loved Rosebud? Why had she loved him too much?

Part II
Trying to Forget

Ireland

Chapter 4

Rose intended to say goodbye to her companions, but by the time she grappled with her hand luggage and endured two Swedish wrestlers bearing in on her person, she felt deflated. William struggled to make Claris stand up—husbandly attentions that won Rose's approval. Meanwhile, the throng stampeded her forward and out to the concourse.

Fresh off the bus to the Strand hotel in Limerick, she milled about the lobby waiting for a room assignment, and, even more important, decisive news of the group's missing luggage, now on its way to Dublin on the eastern side of the island. Apparently she and her clothing were slated for separate vacations.

Many were in the same boat. Everyone wanted a shower and a change of clothes after a long day and night of travel. She wandered from group to group exchanging personal information that no one would remember. She wouldn't, anyway, given the fried state of her brain. She felt like an Easter egg with the insides sucked out, and she said so, making the others laugh. Maybe they would remember her for her egg brain later on. Goofy was better than pathetic.

People started going off in pairs and groups of four as they scored room keys. The process reminded her that she had always been half of a couple. She couldn't see herself as a solo act. Yet there she stood, alone on the sculptured carpet. Loneliness flooded her despite the throng.

She remembered other hotels and riding upstairs hand in hand. Unfamiliar rooms became home as soon as Michael swiped the key card. He always carried her across the threshold laughing. Always, he uttered the same phrase. "Now this is our marriage bed, should you choose to accept it," and he hummed the theme song to *Mission Impossible* until they collapsed with hilarity.

Rose grabbed a turn at the guest computer in the lobby. Her parents responded to her email at once, though dawn barely filtered through the pin oaks on the farm. They must have been up all night waiting to hear from her.

She typed fast. *Is there anything new on the ranch?*

Aidan replied. *Not much, though we heard an awful howling on the property last night. I went out with my rifle, checking for coyotes. It was Puppy Joe. I've never heard him like that.*

Maria added a postscript. *Yes, the poor little guy. But Aiden didn't tell you the worst part. Michael was there on the porch, crying his heart out too. The two of them togeth-er. I'm going to have him drop Joe off at our house when he goes to work and pick him up on the way back. That way I'll get to check on both of them. Don't worry now, honey. Have the time of your life.*

How could she, when she couldn't get Michael out of her mind? She returned to the lobby and gazed from the window at the city Limerick, but she imagined Michael standing on his porch instead, his thick, dark hair disheveled, his forelock tumbling over his forehead. His blue eyes grew larger than ever, their rims red. He wailed her name over and over before he fell to his knees. "You've torn my heart out, Rosie. Look." Just as he opened his bloody white shirt, she gasped and forced her gaze onto the street scene before her instead. She knew the desperate turns her fantasies often took. There was no way she wanted to be in on this one's dénouement.

"Are you alone, then?" conjectured a cracked voice at the level of her chest. "I know this is grim, but you look like it's too late. We'll get our rooms all right. It's never too late to sleep or to fall in love. That's my slogan."

Rose turned her head from side to side and rubbed her face. "Just so tired."

A cackle issued from the diminutive woman. She wore spectacles that made her eyes enormous. "Didn't you ask for a roommate?"

"Hah, uh…" That would be a mean trick, to pair someone up with a sad sack who was liable to cry all night. "No, I—"

"Well I didn't either. I snore, and I can't put anyone through that, unless he can't hear." She snickered. "Besides, my kids are paying for this trip." Her laugh tinkled like a bell on a cat. "In case you're wondering, it's a present for my eighty-fifth birthday, and my name is Mildred."

At that point, two porters bearing keys appeared to whisk them to the glass elevators. In a moment they found themselves looking down at the foyer from six floors above.

Mildred plastered her face to the glass. "Whoo-ee! What a thrill. I wonder if anyone can see up my skirt." Mildred's magnified eyes twinkled at Rose. "There's always hope."

∽◦∽

Limerick:

By walking straight on the Ennis Road, Rose could cross the Shannon River on the Sarsfield Bridge into the heart of Limerick. "Wow," she mumbled into her guidebook. "Michael would want to climb underneath this old swinging bridge." An MBA and attorney, he always wanted to see how things functioned. It was beyond her, why he'd never studied engineering.

"That's right, darling," he whispered in her head. "It's

vital to investigate the guts of things—or people. That's how you come to understand them." His earnest eyes pierced her soul as he spoke. Rose wrapped herself in her sweater, shivering despite the sun.

Lorries and automobiles whizzed by on the left side of the street. She leaned on the stone balustrade to catch her breath and enjoy her first view of the river. Across the bridge, the Georgian city center showed off its abundant smear of red brick. To the right, the river chugged along downstream. She consulted the map showing its estuary and the Atlantic Ocean, where emigrants sailed for New York, clinging to hopes for a better life. She imagined the moment the vessel broke free of land, passengers waving and shouting and embracing each other.

Today, people and prams bustled along the concrete embankment of a park near the hotel. There was plenty of white water here, and it looked like a cold place to swim any time of the year.

Rose bounded across the road for a view from the upstream side. To the north, the thirteenth century Thomand Bridge led to Saint John's Castle. She and Maria had read reams of information in preparation for the tour—her parents' gift to her.

"Come with me, Mommy."

Her mother had chuckled. "No, Rose, you'd have too much fun with me there. You need to be alone in your head and in the homeland just now."

"Is that what Ireland is? I've never felt that way, though maybe I should."

Maria had clasped her daughter in a snug embrace. "I'm a product of random breeding. If you ask me, home is where you want to be." Rose could use a good hug like that now.

She couldn't believe she stood on a spot where Aidan's ancestors had come to imagine a new life."

She crossed over the Shannon to the four story brick buildings and their storefronts. Autos, parked or in transit, crammed the first cross street in several unmarked lanes.

Mounded red and yellow bouquets took up the center of the roadway, and fluttering blue and white pennants hung across the street at intervals, far into the curving distance.

She decided to seek a closer view of the castle, somewhere to her left, so she wound along whichever streets she judged nearest the water. At last, the warren of buildings opened out into a park with shade trees and a view of the river.

Her Canon captured the castle and, in the foreground, a squirrel on the park railing. She deposited her weary backside onto a bench and sketched her version of the scene.

A tiny girl in a full-skirted dress stared in her direction before following a group downstream. Would-be artists occupied benches all around, many with pads and coffee containers. Mmm… What she wouldn't give for a good old-fashioned coffee.

"I'll share if you let me have part of your bench." She looked up at a smiling young man with unruly red curls and a short Irish nose.

"It's as much your bench as mine, but no thanks on the drink."

He tipped his billed cap and possessed himself of the end of her seat. "Well, thank you for that, and I can see how you might think I would try to slip an aphrodisiac into the coffee, you being so lovely. You're wise to decline." His eyes mocked her, and he lifted the lid on his steaming coffee, close enough so she could take in the aroma.

Mmmm…That smelled heavenly. It was just what she wanted. Instinct leaned her toward his cup. "Oooh…"

"Well, don't fall over. Change your mind? I'll let you drink first if you show me what you've done there."

Fresh life flowed into her with the caffeine and unaccustomed boldness.

"Well, are you going to stop?"

Wincing, she handed over the cup. "Sorry, I didn't mean to do that." She watched him help himself to a deep draught.

His shoulders relaxed. "Ahhh…I needed that. All right, then, hand it over." He pointed to the sketch pad on her left. "You show me yours and I'll show you mine." He beamed at her facsimiles of the river and the castle ahead of them. "This is lovely. I imagine it's what everyone's after at this spot, but you've got something unique. Something to do with the light. And the squirrel's a nice touch." He nodded. "I'm bad with buildings myself. Are you a professional, then?"

Pleasure sent a warm flush over her face. "No, I wanted to be, but it didn't work out." Unpainted, her planned portrait of Rosebud with Puppy Joe stuck in her mind forever. She didn't tell him that. He stared at her enough as it was.

"What's the matter?"

He leaned forward. "I don't like to tell people, but I have a feeling you'll never hold it against me."

An uncanny feeling licked at her. "What is it?"

He handed her the coffee cup. "Now there, nothing bad. My grandmother was a seer, and unfortunately the curse came down to me. I see things in people's eyes, that's all." He shook his head. "Unfortunately, women don't find that attractive in a man. Sometimes, I see something they don't like. My curse…compulsion…is the reason I drew this." He tore out a page from his pad and handed it to her.

A sweet sadness washed over her when she recognized her image. In her eyes shone the reflection of a toddler's face, a reminder of her unfinished past. Or things to come? Rose stared at the drawing for a long time.

By the time she finished, the young man and his second sight were gone.

℘℘℘

Rose kept winding her way toward the castle. Near noon she stopped in a side street. At Locke Pub's patio, an iron railing, hung with overflowing pots of geraniums, enclosed wrought iron tables. She backed herself into a round-backed chair at a small table near the bar, where unreadable script identified all the specials. She opted for local fish and salad with strong Irish tea. With her face to the door, she could keep an eye on anyone coming in for a plate or a pint or a quiet hour with the newspaper. As she ate, Rose indulged her love of drawing people.

An elderly couple sat down on the window seat, took out their novel and magazine and proceeded to ignore each other, except for the woman's occasional touch on his arm.

A small girl settled into a corner table with her mother. "Now, Libby, eat yer chips, luv. Dawn't gawp at the lady."

"But, Mummy, I want red curls like that, please."

Rose smiled expansively at the pair while the mother blushed. "They think of the daftest things, dawn't they? Still, there's nothing like a wee babby."

Half a dozen seventy-something men claimed a table near her. Their laughter and half-heard jokes occupied her attention while she finished her meal.

She approached their table. "Pardon me. I'm American, and I'm not in the know about Irish pubs. May I ask you...Is that your regular table? Do you come here every day?"

The skinny one with the quirky eye answered. "Oh, grrreat. She thinks we're pub rats." They chortled and elbowed one another, and Rose warmed with embarrassment.

"Sorry—I—I just wondered about the customs."

The man with enough white hair to cover two heads soothed her. "Don't worry, dear. He's just teasin' because he doesn't see many pretty ladies these days."

The one-handed fellow stuttered. "No, I mean, we come here once a w-week, and we always sit here, but the table doesn't exactly be-belong to us, ya know." A few of them got red in the face.

"Well, it just looks like you have a lot of fun together. I was wondering what got you together in the first place."

"Look, it's like this." That was a man with a low, sexy

voice, who peered deeply at her V-neck. "We're all retired."

Rose felt a flush rising up her neck as she returned Sexy Voice's glance.

Two of them, from their looks twins, spoke at once. "Yes, and guess where we used to work."

The one-handed fellow wiggled his fingers. "We used to be expert bead stringers."

Rose startled, looking where his other hand was meant to be while all of them laughed.

"Pay them no mind," said Sexy Voice, giving her a deep grin. "We all worked for the post office. Can you believe it?"

"Yes." Quirky Eye looked—she figured—at One Hand. "When he was on his route, a poodle bit off his hand." To them, this was hilarious.

"Well, my grandfather used to tell me the Irish like to have fun. He was of pure Irish descent, Celtic through and through, and he warned me to remember I'm full of the Irish myself."

They murmured to each other. Sexy Voice chuckled. "No Irishman is pure."

She shrugged. "I'm here to find out how his judgment applies to me and what he meant by it."

They embarked on an argument about what it meant to be Irish.

"It's the small nose," offered the twins together. "Uptilt-ed."

"Nauw, it's the full hair," added the bald one. "Curly."

"We love talking. Some of us talk all the time." The skinny one elbowed the one with the hand, who colored up ominously.

"How dare you say that?"

"It's true, you argumentative sot."

"Are you implying I imbibe?"

One of them turned to Rose with a shrug. "We're a wee bit impulsive, now and then."

"Hard to comb, it is."

"Get off it. We already talked about the hair."

"Did not."

"You stubborn arse."

"Well," Rose decided, "I'd say you six are a friendly, personable sample."

"And we love having fun. And arguing."

"Not me."

Where would her mail go, Rose inquired, now that she was on the road—assuming someone would want to write her a letter? She pictured the man who might want to find her. She'd loved to watch Michael walk the letters to the mailbox—how his buttocks and hips swung his long legs. How it made her want to take hold of his backside right now and press him against her.

"...that depends," One Hand was saying. "The writer would have to know the itinerary, the hotels, the coach company. Like that."

Sexy voice stood up and leaned in to her. "If someone wants to find you, there's always a way. You never give up. That's Irish."

Rose smiled to herself. So much testosterone in the air, but all her life she'd only had pheromone receptors for one man. The man who knew enough to find her.

ぐうぐう

Five yards from the pub, a small boy rode his scooter from one corner to the next and back again. He reminded her of herself as a child, unable to detour from her inner map. Even now. Couldn't she be impulsive like Michael? If so, she'd be in bed with him right now, her plane ticket crumpled in her pocket.

She'd veered away from the river, so she corrected her course left into a small street, where a betting office surprised her. "Well, a bookie." She'd like to go into Saint Margaret's Cathedral and the betting office too, but she kept on walking anyway. The castle of King John, brother of Richard the Lionheart had pride of place on today's program. First things first. Once she had seen the castle videos, animations, and spectral holograms about thirteenth century life, she retraced her steps. What if her priority had taken up so much time that she never got to number two on her bucket list?

As Rose neared the corner, the bookie closed in her face. The church door had locked as well, but the iron gate of the cemetery stood open. Under the oak trees lay row after row of gravel-covered graves outlined with bricks. Granite monuments identified those once beloved and unloved alike—all were as touching to Rose as a good novel. Around the corner, in a shaded spot, she spied a tiny stone with a statue of a lamb. "Our baby," it read. Rose knelt on the gravel and laid her hand on the stone.

Where was her baby…their baby now? Just as she thought it had curled up and moved on, her grief awakened. She balled her fists and cried out. "Our baby should have a grave…and a real name. Oh, Michael, where were you when I needed you? When she needed you?" She wiped her face on her already sweat-drenched shirt.

Back at the hotel, she idled under a hot shower and rubbed the complimentary shampoo into her hair. She swirled her gamey t-shirt and underwear around on her sudsy head and finished up with the miniature bar of soap. Then she set her alarm clock and tumbled onto the bed naked. She dreamed of the baby girl who, in the drawing, lived inside her—and of the man who'd put her there.

After her rest and a joyful meeting with the spare shirt and undies from her backpack, she revisited the guest computer. "Dear Michael," she typed. "Arrived safe and sound. Don't worry. Having a raucous good time. Hope you will too. Take care of Puppy Joe." She blew her nose on a sheet of scrap paper. "Don't think about me."

そそそ

"How-ya!" The next morning, Gary the driver helped Rose haul her stiff body up the steep bus steps. "It's a little close today, isn't it, but there'll be grand craic—fun, as you say, and the sunshine is a gift. Mind yer head on the coach." Rose nodded to Mildred in the seat behind the driver and flopped down on the left behind the tour guide's station, where she could best see the countryside looming up at her. She lumped her raincoat and her backpack on the seat beside her and turned away from the aisle toward the window.

"Well, I see you took the best seat on the bus." This came from Sue, who, in the airport, had recounted her life's story. At least Rose hoped she had already heard that entire load of misery.

"I saw you put your suitcase in the luggage compartment. It must have come during the night, like mine did."

Rose forced her face into the imitation of an interested smile. "Oh, good." She hoped that wouldn't egg Sue on too much.

"Think so, huh? My new luggage got torn apart, I'll have you know. Things couldn't get much worse, but they will." Sue grabbed her sour-looking husband by the jacket. "Come on, Lou. Don't stand there talking, or we'll get a terrible seat." Rose was relieved when they moved on.

A very large, hairy man came next, "I hope you checked that your valuables are secure." He questioned each traveler, "Your jewelry all right?"

"Keep your mind off our jewels, pervert," Lou snarked from his newly claimed seat.

"Sue and Lou. I can't believe their names rhyme. And their surname is Pugh, as in stinky," stated a crinkly voice behind her. It accompanied a shock of white hair, bushy white eyebrows and bright blue eyes.

Rose turned around on her knees to get a good look at the man. "Yes. And they look exactly alike. They both work in a sewage processing plant." She wrinkled her nose.

The gentleman behind her dampened his voice to a confidential register. "They look like their noses are turned up permanently…like the whole world smells bad. Pee-you."

Both of them laughed harder than Rose thought discreet. She offered her hand. "Alistair, isn't it? I heard the guide call your name at breakfast. I'm Rose. I'm from the U.S.A. You're Australian, right? So's Mildred here."

The tour guide, Ally, called for attention. "Did you all enjoy the welcome dinner on the grounds of Bunratty castle last night? It dates from 1425, with a Viking and Norman structure before that."

Mildred reached over the aisle. "Isn't Ally cute? She's got the wild, floaty hair and the Irish nose."

"Oh, I've got that too. My father used to tap me on the tip of my nose a lot. He liked to say he could always depend on me to *turn up*. It was a joke."

"You're pale like her too."

"Michael claimed he could find me in the dark."

"Brilliant." Ally started her wind-up "Well, I hope you enjoyed your walk in Limerick yesterday. How many visited St. John's Castle? St. Mary's Cathedral? How about all that Norman and Georgian architecture?"

After the enthusiastic mumbles, Ally explained the counter clockwise rotation system on the bus. "If you don't want to move, you may sit in the rear seat. That's the way of it, and I'm dead stubborn."

Rose nodded. "Mmm, Granddad used to use that expression."

Mildred whispered behind her hand. "That's strange. Last night Ally seemed so friendly and kind."

"Damn. This means tomorrow I'll be behind myself. Tomorrow you'll be in front of me, and I'll be able to keep an eye on you for days until we cross into the other side of the bus. We'll never get back to the seats we have now."

Mildred smiled at her. "Well, at least we won't get into a rut."

Rose admitted ruts were one of her weaknesses. She moved closer to the aisle, so they could talk head to head about the welcome festivities and the pretty streets and cottages at Bunratty Castle last night.

"What did you like best, dear?"

"The welcome dinner, Irish music and dancing. And spending the evening in a thatched barn!"

Since he was eavesdropping anyway, Mildred included Alistair, who was eyeing her while she scooched over the aisle. "Didn't you think the pretty streets around the castle were wonderful?"

Rose clasped her hands in elation. "Yes, the thatched cottages are charming. Isn't it strange having the pavement come right up to the house? What's up with that?"

"Wouldn't that have something to do with keeping the rain water from making the ground too soggy around the house?" For this suggestion, Mildred judged Alistair a genius. She joined him in his seat, and Rose could hear him rumble on in an explanation of engineering, punctuated with her high-pitched giggles.

Mildred spoke to her through the crack between seats. "I really liked that t-shirt you had on last night. You must have gotten your luggage before the rest of us."

Rose explained that she'd brought the fancy t-shirt rolled up in her backpack in case she needed it. "That was a picture of my puppy Joe on the shirt."

"Oh, what a sweet puppy. Do you still have him? Don't you miss him? Who took the picture? It looks like a professional did it."

"Yes, I miss him very much."

Mildred tittered. "The dog or the man with the camera?"

Rose laughed. "My ex took the photo and gave me the shirt before I came on the trip."

"What a considerate man. Too bad he's ex." Mildred's forefinger made a slashing motion across her throat.

Her remarks brought to mind the events of last night, when they'd all gathered before dinner. William had stood next to the bus. At first, she'd failed to recognize him without Claris. And standing up. As soon as their eyes had met, he'd hurried over to her. "Hey, pretty lady. Remember me? You look as though you don't."

"I—I—William—I must have been out of it earlier. I didn't even realize you were coming on this tour. I thought you had to head off to a university assignment."

"And I missed the same bits about you. I only remembered your plans to find your grandfather. It seemed we told each other our life's story on the plane, except for the *what next* part."

She noticed the faint laugh crinkles around his eyes.

Later in the evening, Rose had seen him on stage dancing with the folk performers. Long limbed and limber, he possessed the loose, unselfconscious mannerisms of the Scarecrow in *The Wizard of Oz*, her favorite movie once. Claris had been wrapped in a black cape and a scowl and hunched over a table in a corner. What was wrong with that couple? Maybe Claris didn't approve of William's unabashed shenanigans? Rose admired his ability to give in to impulse.

This morning William and Claris sat two rows behind to her right. William twinkled his eyes at her from time to time when she looked in his direction. Had he toured Limerick earlier, as she had? Or had he and Claris remained in the hotel room? They were a couple, after all.

Everything about this bus culture reminded Rose of what she had lost with Michael. She sank back in her seat and thought back to many an amorous afternoon when she and Michael had ignited the sheets in hotel rooms. They'd always traveled with a cooler of food in case they didn't get out to dinner. "Everything I want I have right here," his lust-husky voice stated, while he unbuttoned her blouse, "and I'm a starving man."

She would always remember how heat smoldered in her when his voice turned low and dark. And his eyes. Those eyes that pierced into hers, all the way down to her melting south pole.

Chapτer 5

Cliffs of Moher:

Ally's microphone squealed. "First view of the ocean!" Grandfather had always wanted to ride at the Cliffs of Moher. She wondered if he'd been here lately, fulfilling that dream. All those years breeding saddle horses in Citrus County made him a capable horseman, but still… She winced.

Grandfather and Michael had scrutinized photographs of the cliffs, with their drop-offs to the sea. Posted signs were intended to keep tourists from the fragile edge. However, judging from photos of daredevils walking on since-eroded surfaces, the cliffs offered a short countdown to tragedy. The two men had laughed at her squeamishness.

In every way, Grandfather had taken pleasure in Michael. It had been his idea for the newlyweds to build a house on the ranch, so they could all live near each other. Yet he'd been the one to retire to the land of his forebears. Rose shook her head at the irony.

With Mildred in tow, Rose made their way to a viewing plateau. "You would never catch me so close to that edge. See those kids clowning around? One wrong step, and…I know I couldn't save them." What a nightmare.

The precipice recalled her father-in-law's death. Michael

hadn't wanted to talk about that afterwards, though he'd once been open and expansive about his emotions. She recalled him slumped on the couch hour after hour, eyes cast down, hands covering his head. He'd started drinking soon after his father's demise, and nothing had ever been the same again.

"Yes, I can see some of the rock broke off." Mildred bent closer to the danger zone. "What's the matter, dear?"

Her kind eyes prompted Rose to confide. "I don't know if you've heard of the Pictured Rocks on the Lake Superior shore? My father-in-law fell off those cliffs when we were there on vacation."

"Oh, you poor dear!" Mildred made a clucking noise as she slipped an arm through Rose's.

"We were tortured about the secrets he may have taken to his death. My mother-in-law kept thinking of him going to hell for the sin of self-murder."

"Suicide. But why would she think that way?"

"Isn't that the church's idea—that he couldn't live to ask forgiveness?"

"It's a big assumption, my dear." Mildred clucked again. "My Bernie was a minister for over forty years. He always said you never know what's in a person's mind at the end."

After ascending a further incline, they stopped to catch their breath.

Mildred pointed "Look, there's a peregrine falcon." As they watched, it took off at top speed, and snatched a little crow with orange feet out of the air.

Rose grasped her hair. "Awk!"

Mildred patted her arm. "You're a sensitive soul, dear."

On their left, they took in the view of the shoreline to the south. The surf charged in and out of large sea caves at the foot of the cliffs. Maybe it had been like this on the cliff where Michael's father had taken his plunge. Rose pictured him as he'd stood on the headland, bereft and in need of deliverance from whatever hell he was in at that moment. Maybe his mind called out to his higher power as he fell to his doom? Mildred's voice startled her away from his imagined scream.

"My Bernie and I once made love in a cave like that. We were in a small boat, and it kept rocking back and forth." Her eyes turned up in their sockets. "We did things that day that were illegal in several states."

Rose tittered. "Mildred, you are some woman."

After Mildred turned back toward the touring coach, Rose reviewed her own passion in a rowboat. It had been uncomfortable, but unforgettable. Michael's hands rough and urgent on her body. The sweaty taste of his skin. His slippery ownership of her mouth and nipples and personal places. His roar of laughter when they'd capsized the boat. All the sensations jangled her synapses, even in memory.

That was all over now. The boat, the glorious sex, the man. She wasn't disappointed that she'd failed to forget such moments. After all, she was unlikely to experience anything like them in her lonely future. Why not indulge herself with a steamy memory now and then? They were better than dwelling on her loss.

She pushed on to O'Brien's Tower, a small eighteenth century monolith, where she looked straight out to the Aran Islands.

A thick voice behind her startled her. "A descendant of old King Boru built this to promote tourism. Turns out it worked." The voice belonged to the hairy passenger from Rose's bus. Justus, wasn't it? The guy set her teeth ajar. Justus peered at her through his cola bottle lenses. "Here, darlin,' let me put my arm around you and squeeze under this arch with me, so Harry there can take our picture." She took a helping of tolerance from her mental toolkit. After all, they were destined to form a tight community for a few weeks.

On the other hand, Justus's greasy lack of personal hygiene turned her stomach. She was amazed at the kind of man she attracted, now that she didn't have a husband. Justus lifted her hand. "Are you married, young lady? I see

you're wearing a nice wedding set—yellow gold, nice soli-
taire, a few small rubies and diamond chips." He inclined
his lips to her hand. "You should've left that home in your
jewelry box."

Once rid of her admirer, Rose scuttled along to the end
of the path, from where she looked north to a different section of cliffs with their grassy plateaus. Alone with that
horizon, her mind took in the sounds and the briny odors of
the sea, the cliffs, and the grassy terrace. Puffins with their
comical orange beaks preened on the ledges below and
groaned and growled to their peeping pufflings in their bur-
rows. Once under the sod with their young, the adult birds
sounded like lowing cows.

A kestrel emitted its chittering call over the cliff tops.
Rose wrapped her sweater tight around herself.

A woman's voice screeched. "Colin! Colin! You get
back here."

Rose forced her attention to a reedy voice. "Go see puffins. Fly, Mummy."

Arms and legs pumping, a toddler headed for the precipice near Rose. She opened her arms and took a step forward, just as he veered toward the cliff's edge, wings poised
for flight. "I fly, Mummy. Watch me!"

The woman's cracked voice barely managed a scream.
"No, Colin, no!"

Rose felt her hands and feet go numb. All her senses focused on the frantic pounding in her chest. She tackled the
tot in midair. One foot closer to the precipice and they
might have tumbled onto the rocks together. She focused on
the fragrance of baby powder mingled with the smell of her
own fear.

The child flailed in her arms, but she did not loosen her
grasp on him, though he pounded her shoulders. "Let me
fly! Let me fly!" Wailing, the child buried his face in Rose's
bosom. His mother fell on him and on Rose.

"Oh, God," bawled the mother. "You saved my baby."

ℰↃℰↃ

Rose was the last person back on the bus. She trembled slightly, and Ally raised her eyebrows at her. While the bus continued northbound, Rose clutched a scrap of paper and a photograph. She thought about little Colin's baby-powdered body. And about Rosebud, who'd smelled of blood and amniotic fluid. She blinked rapidly and then stared at the coastline as they headed north.

Mildred stretched over to see what Rose held.

"It's someone I met after you left. This is her little boy." She zipped the paper and the photo into her backpack and turned back to the window. "She wants me to write her." Rose lost herself in the vista of sea and sky.

ℰↃℰↃ

Tall hedgerows planted atop and around them, stone walls bordered the two-lane road. "Whoa." Rose addressed Mildred. "It's disastrous to veer into the bushes here."

"Yes, especially on a bicycle. The bushes would tenderize your body like a fork and the wall beneath them would finish the job."

Rose chuckled at Mildred's imagery. She remembered her own tendency as a child to ditch her bike on the side of the path, usually onto the sparse Bahia grass and magenta phlox that formed the verge in Citrus County. Roads were different here. Tight curves. Were it not for their seats high up in the motor coach, the passengers would have little view of the countryside. The driver's tunnel vision would leave him no plan B if and when he came head to head with another vehicle.

She chalked up a score in the air. One for the land of her birth, zero for Grandfather's Irish paradise.

Sights and sounds of the road set Rose reflecting on her responsibility to keep her eye on the straight and narrow whenever Michael drove too fast. Now she could relax and trust the driver.

Today the rotation placed her three seats back in the bus. She couldn't see much to the front at this distance, but the screeching of brakes and a surge of adrenaline resulted from a near crash with a minivan on an ess-curve. Behind Gary, their driver, Sue let out a head-splitting screech. Others, especially the tall-bodied ones who could see past the seat backs, contributed equally to the din.

In the second seat, Mildred unclenched her fingers from her arm rest to peer at Rose through the seat crack. She spoke loud enough for Sue to hear. "Thank you for not screaming in my hearing aid, Rose."

Rose smirked.

The van had no choice but to back slowly around the curves behind it, while the bus inched forward. What if the van collided with traffic to its rear? Relief swept over Rose when it sped up and backed into a lay-by to let them pass. Her nails had dug into her sweating palms.

"Don't worry, Rosie," Michael crooned in her head. "I got it under control." The image of his cocky eyes made her sweat more.

The opened-up view of rocky hills to their right and the sea coast rising to headlands on their left announced the approach to the Burren, a sparse landscape where boulders and slabs of limestone capped the ground. Ally was into her spiel. "They say there is not enough water here to drown someone, not enough wood to hang someone, not enough soil to bury someone."

Mildred looked coy. "Hee-hee. I'd better not die here then."

Alistair took the bait. "Don't worry. With your trim little figure, you'd fit in a crack. Besides, I'm sure Ally is exaggerating."

Ally eyed them. "No, it's true. They also used to steal soil from each other back in the day."

"The sheep look fat enough, despite the scarce grass."

Rose narrowed her eyes. "I'd hate to graze my horses here, though."

Ally agreed. "Yes, but this grass is especially nourishing. The lambs get rich milk.

All Rose could think about was a little lamb running toward her across the grass, where she'd snatched him up from the edge of the cliff. Little Colin. Maybe she wasn't the weakling she'd assumed she was. She eased back on the seat and pulled in a deep breath, a knowing, satisfied smile on her lips.

 барб

The Burren:

It was too bad Rose had given up riding as a child. She'd always missed it, and she loved petting the animals and brushing them. She frowned, thinking of the childhood incident which had quashed her equestrian pursuits and set her up for some of the apprehension she'd felt, even today.

It had been her first solo ride on the big chestnut stallion Thunder. Her sheltie Charlie had trotted along behind them, nipping at Thunder's heels and then pulling even with Rose to bark his excitement. Charlie's silver fur flashed in the sunlight. Every time she glanced at him, his well-brushed coat caused her to smile. His eyes flirted with her, his lips spread in a big doggie smile, and his tongue lolled. She was crazy about him.

"Go, Charlie! Show this horse how you can run."

The dog had hesitated as if checking the intention in her eyes. He'd glanced ahead, then stared at her again. She'd pointed to the open meadow ahead. "Go!"

He'd taken the ground in great leaps of his forepaws, flicking the ground with his hindquarters. He owned the meadow.

"Go, Thunder. Run after Charlie!" The horse had broken

into a gallop, fence posts and live oaks passing them by. Thunder had closed on the speeding dog.

She'd pulled the reins. "Charlie, watch out!" What had happened next still composed her nightmares. After the horse had limped home alone, her father had found her, curled around the broken silver body.

She'd never sat astride horseflesh again.

Ally announced a stop at the karst formation beside them. "The terrain consists of deep fissures and cracks. Please keep well away from the cliffs, and take care not to break a leg in a crack, right? Brilliant." Claris bulleted out of the bus, apparently eager for the fresh air. William rolled his eyes at Rose as he passed her seat. Claris rushed to a nearby boulder with her romance novel. Rose couldn't understand those who spent their outdoor time with their faces attached to a book or electronic device.

Scraping the ground with his shoe, Will lingered outside the bus. When Rose started her descent down the steep steps, his eyes lit up, and he held out a hand. What a nice man. Like Michael had been when he'd loved her more than drink. Will warned Rose about the wicked footing at the Burren.

She nodded. "This reminds me of the beach. When I was a child, I'd carry around a pail full of watered down sand. Then I would dribble it onto the beach and watch it harden into a terrain much like this, only smaller. I'd maneuver a little action figure—Super Woman—around the knobs and holes."

"Whoa!" Will grabbed her around the waist. "Look what you almost did." Rose lifted her foot out of a crevice "Your leg could've ended up dangling between earth and sea, and you might've broken it. Come on. You can put it down on firm ground now."

She shivered. "Thank you William. I guess I had a close call."

"Come on." He held out a hand. They found their way stone by stone over the cracks and holes until they stood near the rim peering down to the waves that broke on the rocks below. "Hold on to my belt, Rose. I promise I'm very sure-footed."

Rose had her eye on a teenager who stood a few inches from the edge. All at once he screamed and wheeled his arms. "Aaaah, save me!"

A teenaged girl approached the boy. "Stop it. You're scaring me."

The boy took her in his arms, laughing. The girl's fists pounded what she could reach on his arms and back.

"Oh, Will, that's mean. Look. She's crying. You wouldn't do that, would you—scare someone on purpose for a joke?"

"Well, I doubt it's a mere laugh the boy's after. And, yes, I may have done some play scaring in my day. I wasn't always perfect."

Rose fisted him on the arm two or three times. He chuckled. She sneaked a glance at Claris. Still not of this world. "Oops! I shouldn't have done that. Claris wouldn't like it."

"Ahh...don't worry about her. She's hit me plenty of times herself."

What a strange relationship those two had. If the wife didn't mind her husband play fighting with another woman, what else could he get away with?

e/ɔe/ɔ

Rathbaun Farm:

Ally strolled down the aisle with her microphone. "For you Floridians—" She looked at Rose. "—this dissolution of the limestone bedrock is the same thing that forms sink-holes."

Rose shivered inside her wool-lined raincoat.

Ally looked them over. "You look a little the worse for wear. Well, how about a cup of hot tea? We'll be at the farm in two shakes of a lamb's tail. Pun intended."

Meanwhile, Lou and Sue informed the group of some grim facts about Irish sewage treatment. "Did you know it's possible for septic tanks to leak into karst rock like the ones at the Burren?"

"Sue's right. You know, under the latest laws, the Irish government requires inspection of wastewater plants and tanks."

Will engaged Lou. "Maybe because the EU sued Ireland over the lack of mandatory inspections."

Gary got into the game. "Yes, we aim for disposal without endangering human health or the environment. The liquid goes into the water, but we hold on to our sludge."

Will's eyebrows met each other in an expression of distaste. "And pathogens and toxins."

Perhaps because others looked as queasy as Rose felt, Ally won out against Lou's rhetoric. "Well then. Everyone on this bus has some personal tie to Ireland, but no passenger possesses Irish citizenship."

It tickled Rose to hear she was not the only half and half.

"My groups usually have a lot of folks who always wanted to visit Ireland for its beauty, or because they read about it."

Rose raised her hand. "Or family—umbilical ties."

Ally giggled. "Brilliant. I'll call you the Belly Buttons."

"That would be great for George here." Alistair, pointed to the thin, red-haired fellow in the seat across from him. "He's a cop. He could be a Belly Button Fuzz."

Everybody groaned.

"How about the International Shamrocks?" William suggested in a quiet tone.

"Yay for the Shamrocks!"

Ally tapped her microphone. "And here we are at Rathbaun Farm for the best cup of Irish tea you'll find."

Moments later, teasing, bubbly Frances Connelly welcomed her guests at the door to her plastered and painted stone cottage, which, like most, stood in a paved yard with potted flowers set out on the pavement. A few foundation plantings in the front grew up the wall to the overhanging thatched roof, which made the building resemble a furry mushroom.

Their hostess waved them into the salon, where a turf fire burned high, and to her lunch room beyond. Along with her scones and tea, she treated them to a brief recounting of the farm's two hundred year history.

"It's about time we stopped." Sue stretched. "I was going to stiffen up permanently, wasn't I, Lou? He's not listening to me. He lost his new camera somewhere."

Rose wrapped her hands around her steaming teacup. "I agree, it's not a moment too soon. Mmm. These scones are delicious with the fresh butter. And the strawberry jam."

"I can't eat those. I'm carb free. That's how I stay so thin. You might watch it yourself." Sue wandered to another table and chided Lou for helping himself to the scones.

"Oo!" Maryann sat near Rose with her sister Jocelyn. "Sounds like somebody's jealous of your boobage, dear. And your other ass—ets." Jocelyn cackled.

Heat flashed up Rose's neck. Did anybody hear that? At the next table, Will rolled his eyes and grinned.

Alliances formed when people heard she'd almost fallen through the limestone at the Burren. She didn't know whether to call attention to William's role as her savior. At a table in the corner, Claris was busy with her book again. Was Will in trouble? He seemed to enjoy the conversation at his table anyway.

"You shouldn't go off by yourself." Sister Ann eyed her. "Next time, join our group."

Frances's husband Fintan popped into the tea room to invite them to tour his sheep barns. Rose hugged the middle of the group as they trudged herd-like down the drive between the farm buildings. In the barn, Fintan demonstrated his shearing techniques with yearling lambs.

Sue hissed. "Look how he's got the poor thing on its back. Oh, now he's flopped it on its side.

The young border collie Buff sniffed at the lamb and vied for attention from Fintan. He petted Buff, and the dog stood down. "These sheepdogs, they're constantly tagging in with their masters. Totally devoted they are. They never give up."

"Our eighty acres are largely in pasture now," he told them, "so it's mostly the lambs that keep us going."

Alistair raised a tentative hand. "So there's good money in Irish wool?"

"Not at all. That goes off to third world countries. It's the meat that makes our living. Lamb."

Sue let out a strangled squeak. Others fell silent. Fintan released the lamb, which stumbled off into a corner, naked.

Buff made a dramatic pass, herding several lambs past the barn and into an outside pen. After a round of photos in front of the pen, some of the humans returned to the warm house. Rose sat down near the fire to work on a sketch of Buff.

Will spoke from the companion chair. "Very good, you could make a living doing that."

She gave him a full smile, pleased that he'd noticed. "I don't know. I kind of like giving my drawings away— which reminds me—excuse me, will you?" He looked so alone when she left him sitting there, despite his apparent ability to fit in anywhere.

Outside the sheep barn, she met Fintan with Buff. "I always wondered how someone holds on to a sheep while shearing it. That was so interesting how it just let you lay it on its back and turn it every which way like a bale of hay."

"That's right. They're pretty meek when you get the upper hand, and, though you're gentle with them, you can't think of them as personalities, you know." Buff laid his forepaws on his master's thigh and drummed for attention.

"I especially enjoyed the demonstration of Buff's herding abilities. He was brilliant."

"Oh, yes. You noticed that then?"

"Yes, my family has always kept a border collie on our

horse farm. The one my dad has now reminds me of this little guy." She scratched behind Buff's ears. "My own dog is a sheltie, and he's talented with squirrels."

"What's his name then?"

"Puppy Joe. I mostly call him Puppy."

The farmer laughed. "What? That's not a name for a dog. A real dog would be Joe."

Rose laughed too. She handed him the page from her sketch book. "I drew Buff's picture. You can have it if you want. It's important to have pictures around of the ones who love you, as your dog obviously does."

He scratched his head. "Well, I don't know, but these dogs have a strong urge to please, like some people. You may say they're always courting their special person, and they don't let anything put them off you either. You can call that love if you want. Some might appreciate that attitude in humans, as a matter of fact."

"And some of us try to discourage such devotion."

He wrinkled his forehead. He walked away rubbing the back of his neck.

Their hostess ran up to Rose as the group piled onto the bus. "You're Rose?"

Rose nodded, a question forming in her mind.

"This must be for you then."

"Wh—what?" Confusion and suspicion flooded her, as Frances pressed a perfect pink rose into her hand.

"Don't ask, and I won't tell, and I'm not supposed to tell." She nodded with a conspiratorial glance at a folded piece of paper in her hand. "You probably know who sent it to you, anyway and what he's trying to tell you."

Rose opened her mouth to speak, but nothing came out. Her mind had turned to gelatin.

Frances spoke with emphasis. "I guess I don't need this paper anymore." She placed it on the tarmac, in front of Rose's shoe. "Have a lovely trip, and try not to make any daft decisions, love."

Back on the bus, Mildred gestured with her head at the paper in Rose's hand. "Well?"

Rose held the paper for a long time, while she pressed the rose to her lips. She recalled the first time Michael had given her a rose.

He'd drawn her close. "When we get married, I'm going to plant a rose garden, just so I can hand you a blossom every day. When we need to be apart, I want you always to have one nearby and hold it against your succulent lips to remind you of my kisses." Then he'd brushed her lips with his and segued into a deep and lingering kiss that made her feel warm inside, even now. "I want to give you a rose every day of our lives. Remember, no matter what, you'll always be my Rose."

She smiled as she recalled how he'd kept his promise. When they'd completed their cottage, he'd proclaimed the event worthy of a rose bush or two. Then he'd planted the front yard full—tea roses and grandifloras and old garden roses in all the colors of an overjoyed rainbow. Everything known to thrive in the south. True pink *Belinda's Dream* and *Apricot Candy* and blood red *Chrysler Imperial* basked in full sun, White *Blanc Double de Coubert* and pink *Butterfly* sheltered in the shade of a grand old oak. Michael had made the sandy soil fertile and babied his roses leaf by leaf.

After several years of practicing, they'd conceived, and Michael had celebrated with a single young rose bush near the front door. It announced their fecundity with bursts of yellow and deep pink. Michael presented Rose the tag from the bush.

"This name will always remind me how I feel today, my love." The tag read *Yabba-Dabba-Doo*.

Rose forced herself back to the present moment, though her eyes swam with tears. She unfolded the paper she wasn't supposed to see.

Dear Mrs. Connelly of Rathbaun Farm,
My wife Rose Flanagan will arrive at your farm on a

scheduled stop with Ireland Tours. Will you please do me a favor and present her a rose from your garden? Please don't explain where it came from. I believe she will know what it means.

You see, by the time you meet my Rose, she may have made a decision I can't bear to hear but must accept. The rose is just a tacit reminder of what she means and will always mean to me.

Rose couldn't read any more. She pressed her lips to the signature at the bottom of the page. She closed her eyes and turned her head to the window as tears rolled down her cheeks. What was it Fintan had said about faithful sheepdogs? "They keep courting the ones they love? They never stop."

Chapter 6

Galway:

That night, Rose rutted in her bed until she could articulate what she wanted to say. Alone in the hotel computer room, she typed her message "Dear Michael, got the rose. You knew I would like it. Thank you, but it's not necessary. Hope you find new things to keep you busy."

She rubbed at the ache in her chest. She had to admit there were some new things she didn't want him to get into, though that was no longer her business. So far there had been no e-mails from him.

There was one message in her inbox. "Rose, honey, as you know, I've kept tabs on Michael. So far, he always goes out after supper. Not to a bar I hope. Time for bed. Dad."

"Immediately, a message from Maria popped up.

Hi, Rose, sweetie. Aidan's message was a little negative. Still, I take the news as encouraging, and you will too when you hear what happened the other day. I was on my way to Inverness when I passed Michael on his porch. He wore a dirty T-shirt and hadn't shaved in days. I asked him why he wasn't dressed for work.

He gave me a look out of hell. "I can't work, Mom. I

can't sleep. I can't eat. I can't think. But don't worry, I'm going to the doctor this morning."

I saw he had your pony quilt in his arms, dear. He nearly broke my heart.

Rose stared at her empty hands. She drew her arms up, over the ache in her throat and bosom. She barely had the energy to stand up. She spoke to the image permanently entrenched in her mind. "I'm so sorry, Michael. I didn't mean it to hurt so much."

With a heavy tread, she retraced her steps to her room, where she stood under the shower for a thousand years.

That morning, while the Shamrocks toured the Connemarra marble exhibit outside of Galway, Rose wandered away into the grounds, where Mildred found her crying.

"I can't concentrate on a collection of rocks, and I suppose my face is too swollen for decency. I'd probably ruin the trade in there."

Mildred held her without making her explain.

Slated to stop in Galway center for a late lunch, most of her companions were excited about a bap with ham and a cup of tea. Rose, though, felt growly through her glued on smile.

"Forget lunch. My stomach is like a rock. I want to see the city. After all, I'm looking for my heritage in this county. That means on the ground, not in a bus. I've got under an hour."

"I applaud the change of mood, but heritage is not defined so easily." Mildred had won her attention. "I suspected my Bernie had Aborigine blood in him. I traced him, but his tendency to make a walkabout whenever I gave him a chore list was nothing but laziness." Rose laughed at the odd story, and Mildred patted her arm. "Watch your step while you're searching, dear. I read the paving stones aren't the best."

"Try St. Nicholas's Church," suggested Meredith, a nurse. "Do you know Christopher Columbus prayed there?

Look, you can see the steeple from here. Ahead and to the left. Early fourteenth century I think."

Rose set off down a twisting thoroughfare teeming with activity. Carved wooden business signs hung over the street. No sidewalk. Every second storefront contained a cafe, with tables and chairs and potted plants claiming space on the roadway. She had to pick her way along the paving stones, with potholes competing for her attention now and then.

The next thing she knew, one eye peered directly into one of those holes. The other examined the pavers. Several voices shouted at her. "Get up! Get up!" Their tone was strangely compelling. Why would she want to get up? Everything was fine down here. She couldn't fall any lower. For the moment nothing hurt—as long as she didn't move.

"You must get up!"

"Come on, you can do it."

"Can you move? See if you can."

Goodness, people were upset. She felt like a sheep, dozing under a tree, with dozens of sheepdogs nattering at it. This was a great view of stones, holes where stones should be, and feet. Sandals and hiking boots, mostly. Funny-looking toes. Now a pair of knees. Strong thighs. A crotch. A man's crotch. Right in her face.

Somehow familiar, a deep voice spoke her name. "Rose, I'm going to stay with you. Only I doubt I can get down any lower. What do you think about sitting up? No rush. Just a suggestion."

The voice made her want to comply, so she pushed up with her palms. Her right arm rebelled. "Ow, that hurts!" she appealed to turquoise eyes.

"Good job. The arm hurts, does it?" He palpated it.

She pulled away. "That's what I said." She had to tug on her mental reins to keep from snapping. "Why are you following me, Will? Why are you repeating what I say?"

"See if you can move it, will you?"

"Where's Claris? Ow! That hurts like crazy."

"Mmm, grouchy. Good. Now brace yourself on my arm.

Use your other arm. There you go. Up…up…good."

She was on her feet. Nothing hurt down there, though one shoe bore evidence of a brief scuffle with another pothole. Ugh! Lousy construction workers. No better than in the USA. Worse.

Will made her raise her injured arm straight ahead, up, and to the side. Then he compared it to her good arm.

"What are you doing, Will? Why are you ogling my chest?"

He blushed. "I'm not, woman, just your collar bone. Nothing's broken, and your arm moves fine, but it's going to hurt worse before this is over."

She felt grumpy. "Well, I can't do anything about it. Too late. I'm a cripple, ogled by a stalker, even in my condition."

He chuckled. "Still have your personality, I see. Now look across the street. There's the provider of all necessities to American tourists. Aim for that."

She felt wobbly, as well as wounded in body and in self-confidence. They tacked their way through the sea of college students and tourists to the fast food store front, a shy and narrow afterthought among the businesses, remarkable only for its red and blue paint. She took the one remaining seat in the establishment, while William fetched her a bag of ice.

"Ice cubes. I haven't seen that since we got here."

"Yeah, this was their entire stash."

She opened the bag and took out a cube, which she popped into her mouth. "Mmm, good."

"Uh, wrong move. Get your jacket off and place this on the hurt muscle. We want to keep the inflammation and stiffness down."

William was right about the ice. By the time he finished answering her questions, her arm had stiffened but did not bruise. Not yet.

He insisted he hadn't followed her—not much. He'd been on this street to look for the university, where he planned to spend part of his sabbatical. In fact, he explained, he meant to travel here and there about Ireland, and he would have a chance to look up his daughter Bridget, who'd married an Irishman.

"And what about Claris? Why isn't she with you?"

"No way." He shuddered. "She's begun her search for the finest Irish wool, as she's a textile artist. She's convinced she'll find the Holy Grail of textiles here. I just hope she ships it all home. I'm getting too old to carry her stash."

The image of Will as a camel swayed across her imagination.

のかか

Connemara:

If Claris had found what she sought, her expression didn't show it later in the day when she and Will stuffed themselves into a corner bench at O'Donnell's bar in Clifden. The permanent crease between her eyes had deepened.

Some of the others draped themselves on the bar or in barrel-backed chairs at tables. Rose was not into bars. She snorted. This looked like one of those boondoggles foisted on tourists in lieu of more eco-cultural spots, but she had to be a good sport. Wouldn't it be odd if a watering hole gave her a sense of Grandfather-like Irish belonging? This was the hometown of his ancestors, she realized with a jolt, and she'd return here after the tour. She studied the bar patrons. What were the odds of him showing up right now?

"Rose, Rose, come sit with us." Six or eight Shamrocks crowded into a semicircular embrasure. "Tell us about your adventure. How's your arm?"

Mildred was there, next to Alistair, patting a bit of cushion on her near side. Paddy, who believed himself the reincarnation of Oscar Wilde, sported a flowing orange scarf purchased in the city. Several other Shamrocks bent over their glasses of Guinness. It seemed Rose's fall had endowed her with notoriety. Probably she could score a half dozen painkillers right there.

"It's stiff, and it hurts, and I can only get it to half staff now, but I'm relieved my right hand works." She flashed back to the night she'd broken that limb,

Meredith handed her a bottle of ibuprofen, still warm from her fanny pack. "Keep icing the arm."

Her companions around the table demanded she show them her sketch pad, which had made her an instant celebrity earlier. Their handsome waiter plied her with Irish cream whiskey, the house-recommended pain reliever. Alistair nudged her. "Drink up. Two rounds are included with the outing."

Everyone sat shoulder to shoulder listening to a local musician play six different guitars, Irish pipes, a flute, and a small drum. Rose grew ever warmer.

William flashed her a helpless glance across the room as Claris became more animated, maintaining an iron grip on his arm. Why didn't he pay attention to his wife? Rose didn't like this about him. Otherwise, he was so nice. Thoughtful, like Michael. Her thoughts went to his roses. All the roses. All the time.

William took the microphone. Rose clutched her throat as his tenor voice soared with the familiar strains of "An Irish Lullaby." The crowd sang the chorus with him.

"Too-ra-loo-ra-loo-ral, Too-ra-loo-ra-li,
Too-ra-loo-ra-loo-ral, hush now, don't you cry!
Too-ra-loo-ra-loo-ral, Too-ra-loo-ra-li,
Too-ra-loo-ra-loo-ral, that's an Irish lullaby."

Tears flowed at the memory of Michael singing this song to the child once inside her. "And now, for my little Rosebud," he used to say. "This is to show you Daddy will always protect you."

Instead, he'd killed her.

CASCO

Knock, Sligo, and the Donegal Coast:

It had been a troubling morning. Sue had found her missing purse in the trash minus a wad of cash and a list of her passwords, and Meredith's jeweled rosary had vanished into thin air.

Justus acted as if these incidents were personal. "God damn it! "Didn't I warn you people?"

His wife Marge's sparse white neck whiskers trembled. "Oh, dear, now you've all set him off." What secrets lay in that marriage?

After a night fraught with nightmares, everything reminded Rose of her marriage and her past.

She strolled through the massive gardens and furnished rooms of Kylemore Abbey, a castle before Benedictine nuns took it over. She imagined herself such a building, and at first it was more fun than pretending as a living creature. She cast a fond eye at opulent furnishings and a rose garden the owner had planted for her, his beloved. She stuck out her front porch, feeling grand with her thirty-three bedrooms. Later, laughter bounced off her walls as little girls came for the nuns to instruct them. In the present, people spoke in hushed voices within her walls. So much for Rose's imagination, which always returned her to reality, thank goodness.

Rose stood on the shore of the lake, celibate and barren, like the nuns.

She lowered herself onto a bench and rummaged in her bag for a leftover scone from breakfast. She came across Michael's two roses, pressed into her paperback novel. Should she throw them away to help her forget? She raised the faded blooms to her lips. Their fragrance lingered, one she would forever associate with him and the garden he'd cultivated for her.

She could no more throw the roses away than discard the recalled scent or the handsome face always present in her mind's eye. "I can't shake you off, Michael, though I'm doing my best to move on."

At the village of Knock, the Shamrocks scrambled over the grounds of the shrine. Meredith tagged along with Rose. "What a terrible time to lose my rosary. I planned to go in for some heavy praying. Not that I can't do it without the beads...but you get in the habit."

Rose's lips perked up in appreciation of the pun. "Here, take mine. I'm half Protestant anyway."

They ended up at the wall of the parish church, where fifteen people had claimed to see Mary, Joseph, and Saint John with angels and a lamb. Rose imagined an apparition of her own—Michael with open arms. "Please, Rosie. Please love me again." His fierce eyes sent her stumbling into the church.

There, too, Michael's voice pleaded in her head. "I can't forget you, darling. Please forgive me."

Her throat constricted with tears. "I can't." She covered her face. "I can't." People stared.

She exited the church with Mildred. "You told me your husband was a pastor. What did he say about forgiveness?"

Mildred frowned and scratched her head. "He used to say 'Get used to it, because we all need it every day.' And he said to get used to asking for it and extending it. Sometimes I used to nurse a snit about something he had done. 'I forgive you for pouting, Millie,' he would say, 'and I feel so much better.'"

Rose mulled this over.

"You know what else? Sometimes Bernie used to make up things to be sorry for, like spilling the salt, so I could have the pleasure of forgiving him. Oh...I did enjoy making up with him. The more I forgave, the more...uh...apprecia—tion I got." Her eyes went to a bygone place.

Rose was relieved to curl up on the bus and escape all the chatter and her troubling thoughts.

e/se/s

Later, Mildred peered between the seats. "Do you like Yeats's poetry? We're coming up on the famous church-yard. Grab your camera. This is Drumcliff, and that's Sligo Bay. There's a table mountain that reminds Gary of a pile of cow pats."

Rose yawned and stretched. "Did I miss a lot—besides that?"

"Ally reading aloud from a book of poems."

"How was it?"

Mildred mimicked Ally's exaggerated smile. "Brilliant."

They both giggled.

"Unfortunately, I was the one who lent her the book. Some of the poems I liked until now. I'll show you some later, but—don't worry—I'll spare you the declamation."

Rose smirked. Bless Mildred. What an irreverent, re-freshing person.

She followed the crowd to the poet's grave, where a guide read more poetry and told anecdotes She enjoyed that, especially the spicy bits. She elbowed Mildred. "What do you think Yeats meant by that—'the tragedy of sexual in-tercourse is the perpetual virginity of the soul.'" Mildred raised a finger to her lips.

Wandering among the monuments by herself, Rose came upon an undersized stone near a tree. She knelt to read the inscription, which stung her eyes at once. "Our little Posey. Born too soon for our arms. Borne up to God's."

She knelt there, her mind blank as polished granite.

"God, what am I going to do? Give me a sign." A shad-ow covered the grave.

"Excuse me ma'am. I knew you were coming. I know you by your hair. It really does look like a burgundy rose. He told me I'd find you among the graves, especially those for the children."

Rose turned around to see a frail gentleman. "Who are you?"

"I'm the man who gets the letters. People write to me from all over the world. Or they write to the church. Sometimes they write to Jesus." He shrugged. "They want to place flowers or tuck notes under the pebbles near a stone, so I do that. You'd be surprised."

"What? Who?" She trembled, anticipating the answer she already knew.

"I don't have the man's name, but he went to a lot of trouble and expense. He sent this rose along with the bit of poetry. It's by the local bard. 'Consolation' if you want to look it up."

She clutched the rose to her lips. Tears made it hard to read the words.

...Where the crime's committed
The crime can be forgot.

‹›‹›

The lines echoed in Rose's mind. *The crime can be forgot. The crime can be forgot.*

A river of tears flowed through the landscape of her soul. "Oh, Michael, I'm trying to forgive you, but I can't forget. Can't you get out of my head?"

At first she failed to see Mildred nearby. "If it hurts so much, maybe it's up to you to do something about it."

Rose handed her the poem.

"Oh, yes. I know this one. I agree it's a heart-breaker. Do you know what it means for you?"

Rose nodded. "It's practically written for me." They leaned against a tree, while she shared her unsuccessful attempts to deal with her loss and with Michael's ongoing tryst with alcohol.

Mildred tapped her front teeth. "That's a tough one to forgive."

Rose nodded, shuddering out a last sob.

Mildred handed the poem back. "Rose, are you happy the way things are now?"

Rose shook her head.

"Do you want him to leave you alone?"

"No!" Rose's spirit leaped. What? Was that true? Eddying confusion soured her belly.

Mildred urged her to the path. "The bus is leaving. Life goes on, you know, with us or without us."

ᕙᕗᕙ

After a day viewing the deeply serrated Donegal coastline, the tension skittering through the bus gave Rose a headache. Behind her, Alistair carried on a long-winded dialogue about the Second World War with William. Darn it! The men's boring discourse set her teeth on edge. And so did the fact that Will had left Claris staring out of the window and blowing her nose.

It was a relief to clamber out of the cramped bus at last. Ally herded them into the Belleek pottery company like carsick cows. Rose's antipathy to over-decorated trinkets had increased with the throbbing of her temples. Was this tour doing her any good at all?

To her surprise, the demonstrations piqued her interest in the production of the fine Parian china. A greenware specialist told them about trimming excess clay with a fine knife. "One slip, and the whole piece goes into the waste bin. And don't think I can get away with anything. Somebody in the next department evaluates my work."

Wide-eyed, Rose turned to Mildred. "This man must've performed the same picayune motions for thirty years. My goodness, I couldn't work like that for ten minutes."

"I hope his private life is more exciting than this."

The painters' brushes produced exquisite miniatures. One wrong hairline stroke, and their project was done for.

Rose supposed the smashing specialist, who worked over the rejects, left for home without a tense muscle in his body—or else with an overwhelming sense of waste.

Sue screeched. "What? No seconds? I was counting on that."

Rose pressed close to the bin where thousands of Euros worth of fine pottery met their doom every day. "For once I agree with you, Sue. I don't require anything to be perfect. As an artist, I like quirky things and people."

Mildred whispered close behind her. "Now you're getting it."

"Anybody want to smash something?" The tour guide placed an exquisite cream-colored ewer into the receptacle. A hush moved over the Shamrocks. Everybody stepped back except Rose, who peered hypnotically inside. "Here, madam. Have at it." The worker handed her the hoe-like smashing tool.

"What?"

A couple of the Shamrocks snickered behind her.

"Me?" For a moment she thought she saw the smashed skull of her beloved dog Charlie under Thunder's hooves. She shuddered. "Not me. I could never smash anything."

Hands on hips, the craftsman in the work smock stared into her eyes. "Don't want your chums to know the truth about you?" He looked her up and down. "I'll bet you could really go to it." His sarcasm struck at her anger bone.

"Hm-hm," she croaked. "I'd feel way too guilty to ruin something so nice." She looked around at the Shamrocks, who leaned forward, eager to see her id at work.

Some of them wetted their lips. "Do it, do it, do it. Go, Rose, hit it, smash it!" The smasher found its way into her hands.

Justus pounded his fists on the bin. "Smash his head to pieces. Grind him to bits. Get even!"

Rose administered a tentative tap. She tapped a little harder. God, what a wuss she was. She felt the ewer crack without a sound.

"Okay, we'll leave it at that. Anybody else want a try?"

Rose glared at the people crowding in on her. They shrank back, while she planted her feet far apart. "Grrr—Hah-yak!" The ewer split in two. She hauled off on the enemy. "Yak! Yak! Ah!" She bore down with all her weight. Over and over, her pulse pounding in her throat.

William pulled her away. An embarrassed silence shrouded the Shamrocks. Then they all started to cheer. "Brava, Rose! Way to go, Rose."

Justus fluttered his moustache at her. "Got him right in the balls! It was better than seeing you naked." His wife Marge looked ready to smack him.

"Holy Red Sox. I'd like to rent your services sometime." Claris seemed breathless.

Rose's legs shook. Craving a glass of water, she headed from the department while her admirers hung two by two on her arms.

Sue giggled. "You actually snarled."

"Did I? I'm sorry."

Mildred took her hand. "Oh, you did. It was wonderful."

"Any souvenirs? Gifts? An elegant-looking woman with porcelain roses at her ears approached. Some of her companions slipped into the gift shop.

Rose fondled her earlobe. "No thanks. I got what I came for."

The official consulted a photograph in her notebook. "All right, Madam…Rose. This is for you. You're a lucky woman." She placed a small box in Rose's hands.

One by one the women slid into the coach seat next to Rose. Ally first. "You know you'll have to show everyone what you've got. Those are brilliant."

Sue was next. "Very, very pretty. If I were you I'd scrub them down good with a toothbrush every time you wear them. You'd be surprised what kind of filth, skin, mites get stuck in jewelry."

Rose made a gagging sound.

Jocelyn donned her spectacles. "Be careful you don't

damage a sweater with any sharp bits."

"May I look at those closely?" Marge brought the ear-rings close to her tiny eyes. "I like to check for flaws. Most people can't see them. I, of course, am very aware of things others can't see and don't want to see."

Rose wondered how, with whiskers under her own chin, Marge could detect flaws elsewhere.

Mildred slipped to Rose's seat. "May I see? Is this from…him?"

Rose nodded. She could sense the tears building in her sinuses, much the way seawater did when she swam in the Gulf. "I feel as though I'm in over my head, Mildred. What should I do?"

"Don't cry over it, dear." Why not just accept it the way it's meant…a tribute to a pretty lady." Mildred examined the ear baubles, squinting her eyes into focus. "Heavens, this is the best kind of gift. Something you can keep close whenever you want."

Rose peered at Mildred. No earrings, no necklace, no bracelet. Probably no body jewelry. She snickered. Mildred gave her a puzzled look.

"I'm sorry, Mildred. I was picturing you with nipple rings."

"Not for me, nor for you, I imagine. You don't make im-pulsive decisions, do you, dear?"

Rose pursed her lips, "No, but I wish some new pierc-ings could fix my life." She touched Mildred's left hand. "That's a lovely ring."

"Yes, it's the only jewelry I wear…the only jewelry I care about. As long as I can look at it all the time, my Ber-nie is always with me. I'll never take it off. It's getting a little loose, though."

Marge gushed. "Oo! Look at that ring, Justus."

Justus heaved himself into the aisle, looking more unsa-vory than ever, with an unrecognizable substance dribbled on his flyaway beard. "That's a beautiful ring, and it's an antique. Don't drop it down the drain, little lady."

Lou threw up his hands. "God knows, it's amazing what goes down the sewer."

Rose was positive he was about to tell them. As he nattered on, she composed a message to thank Michael for the gift and rebuff him at the same time. It might work in cyberspace, but in her head it didn't ring true.

⅏⅏⅏

Derry:

As the bus neared Derry, Ally asked for a volunteer who knew the melody *Londonderry Air*. Several of them recognized the tune.

"That's the same as 'Danny Boy.'"

"A hymn..."

Mildred raised her hand. "'Apples and Roses.' We had to memorize it at school. Something about kissing and blushing and sighing and breasts. We considered it naughty back in the day."

"London Derriere. It's a British bum."

Ally gave Paddy a dirty look. "Rrright. The tune is everywhere, even in movies and in a computer game."

When William got up and sang *Danny Boy*, there wasn't a dry eye in the bus.

Alistair trumpeted into his handkerchief. "Damn. I always hated war."

A few minutes later, they pulled up in Derry's Guildhall Square. A natty bald-headed guide mounted the bus steps and addressed them in posh English.

Lou poked his wife. "A Chinese guy, and he talks better than any of us."

The guide bowed slightly. "Yes, and I'm married to a French woman. We adopted two kids—an African and an Indian. At least no one is American." Then his rich bass rolled out the story of *The Troubles* in Ireland.

Sue looked flummoxed. "Shoot! I thought it was all about religion."

Paddy coiled his scarf around his neck with a grand gesture. "That's an American for you."

Their guide prodded them down the street toward the neo-gothic Guildhall, his umbrella leading the way, while some of the females prattled.

"My, it's imposing."

"And red."

"No, silly. It's black. The British all have that."

Mildred smirked. "Are you talking about the building or about his bumbershoot?"

"What did you call it? Is that a dirty word?"

The guide touted the stained glass and the large pipe organ inside the main hall. He broke up their tittering to remind them they had an hour to view the building, eat lunch, and meet the bus. He used his umbrella to point.

Paddy looked ready to pass out. "I'll always remember that umbrella."

Laughter rippled, with Sister Ann the loudest. Even Rose did her part.

The Shamrocks had little time to peruse the interpretive panels about the Irish plantation system and *The Troubles*. Mildred let Rose grumble for a while about fixed programs on tours.

Then she pressed her lips together and crossed her arms. "Well, dear, were you in a mood to organize your own solo trip? You've got that guide book in your pocket, but I don't see you rushing about Ireland on your own. How often have you sailed your own ship?"

"That's one thing I hate about myself. No initiative."

A little later, Ally announced time to walk on the only complete city wall in Ireland, four hundred years old and never breached despite several sieges.

A deep laugh rolled out of Justus. "That's why it was called The Maiden City."

Rose thought back to Michael's fondness for laying

siege on her. She let her mind go back to that game, hot blood settling in her loins. He emerged from the shower, his warrior shoulders wide and powerful, his hips trim and primed for engagement. He hadn't taken the time to shave his face, and a dark forelock forewarned of tortures ahead.

"Well, maiden, I've scaled the wall and taken the fortress. Now you're mine. What say you? Shall I rub your holy grail into insanity, or do you give in to my mounting your hill at once?"

She'd sat on the edge of the bed, pretending to tremble. Well, really trembling at the sight of his weapon.

"Grrrr!" He'd seized her by the laces on her medieval underwear and tugged her chemise and breast binder over her head. "Now give me those braies." She kicked off her panties. His dagger swung in front of her face, swelling as it advanced.

"Oh, Lord Michael. Mount me then, if you're man enough."

She was far away from the scenes of Derry passing by.

The bus maneuvered in front of one of the four original city gates. Ally was adamant on the timetable. "One hour. If you don't make it to the third gate in half an hour, you won't make it around, so come back the way you went."

Mildred peered at Rose hard. "You're sweating. Are you all right? What were you thinking just then?"

"Coming, little lady?" Justus hurried Mildred along with a hand under her elbow and an impressive belch. "Remember, don't give up that ring if the British attack."

Mildred brightened and held up her hand for him to examine. "Bernie gave me this."

Justus became more attentive. "It's an old European cut, solid platinum and diamond, over half a carat in the center stone, I'd say. Hmmm…The ribbed design is unique. It could be a retro engagement ring, or it's original, and you've taken care with it."

"Hey, what about me?" Marge called to him.

"Exactly." Rose muttered. "There's way too much familial neglect going on." She had to admit, Michael had always been super attentive. Except when he drank.

Will disappeared into the post office, laden down with bags of yarn. He dropped some of them, and Claris lit into him.

Rose turned to Mildred. "The poor guy's trying his best. Somebody ought to say something to that woman." Michael's parents came to mind, a couple who'd alternately ignored and picked at each other in their final years. Until he'd killed himself.

Rose marched up to where Claris leaned against the wall. "Claris, I'm going to say something to you, and I hope it helps your relationship."

Claris looked blank.

"You don't treat Will with respect, as far as I can see, and, though he's not very attentive to you, he doesn't deserve that."

Claris squinted and made a *get away* gesture with her palms. "Okay, thank you, but I'm guessing you're no better. She'd hit a nerve. Rose opened her mouth, but Claris wasn't finished. "What's the matter with you today? You're awfully cross."

"You're right. In fact I'm irked...about a lot of things, including how you treat Will. You always act like you're mad at him and he can't do anything right. I would never act that way."

Claris took a deep breath. "Sure you would. Don't forget, I've seen your temper when you smashed the pottery. Didn't you have a sibling or friend to take things out on?"

"Yes, but I never treated my husband that way. Though he yelled a lot when he was drinking."

"Well, Rose, everyone has someone he loves enough to yell at. Let me know when you want to talk about what's going on with you. And if you think you can do better with William, you can take him on." Claris took refuge in the post office, leaving Rose with her mouth open.

Rose mounted the stone steps and strode along atop the

fortification. Maybe Claris had the right idea. What made Rose think she knew how to treat a husband better than others? She looked back to the Michael of her past, the bereaved son, who'd sat at the table for hours, his head in his hands.

She'd yanked his hand. "Come on, Michael. Let's go for a walk."

"No, Rose. I don't feel good.'

"Well, you won't feel any better just sitting there. Come on. You need to get out."

"I can't Rose. I need to think. I've got to figure out how to get over this."

"Why? All you do is think. I want to get some exercise. It will be good for you too. Please."

"If you want to do what's good for me, why don't you leave me alone?"

Leave him alone? Hurt and angry, she'd slipped out of the house and taken the car to Inverness without saying goodbye. An hour later, laden with a bag of sketch paper and pencils, she'd found him bereft, pacing on the front porch. When he'd caught sight of her, he'd sprinted down the walk and caught her by both elbows.

His voice had trembled. "Where have you been? I was so worried. I can't stand it if I lose you too."

"Is that your business? You didn't want to do anything with me. You just sit there sulking, and I'm supposed to watch? Well, I can entertain myself. Don't worry about it."

She'd stamped into the house, slamming the door behind her. She'd been in bed before he got inside. That night, he'd slept on the couch.

From then on, he no longer sat at the table feeling sorry for himself. The next day—and most days thereafter—he'd brought a six pack home after work.

Chapter 7

The Causeway Coast:

The next day Rose hiked on the rocks at The Giants' Causeway. What a weird place this was, with blocks, columns, boulders, and pools, all formed from cooling eruptions. All slippery wet. What if she fell while she was alone? She was much too accustomed to having Michael with her to hold her hand or keep her within reach, especially since his father had died in that horrible way. She noticed William a good distance behind her. When he caught up to her, she would ask about Claris. She passed through an arch and around a corner and alit on a column just the right size for a seat. After mulling over her intended spiel, she realized William should have caught up to her. She picked her way back over the rocks and crevices, only to find him lying in a tidal pool, battered by the surf.

She sprinted toward him. "William! William!" She huffed and gulped. "Can you hear me? Did you slip? Are you all right?"

His eyes were closed.

She darted back and forth at the pool's edge. "William, wake up! Are you breathing? Did you hit your head?"

His eyes opened, and he appeared to search his memory. "What?"

"What do you mean *what*? What happened to you?"

Rose dipped her hand in the pool. It was a windy day, but the water in the pool was rather warm. Will's footwear and outer clothing draped nearby columns. Wearing only a t-shirt and plaid boxer shorts, he relaxed in sun-warmed contentment.

"Mmmm?"

"Will, you idiot! Get out of there. The tide is coming in."

In no hurry, he stretched his arms out wide and swished them in the water. She helped him get to his feet on the slippery rocks. As he transitioned into the sea wind, his teeth chattered.

She tried to manage a soft tone. "Come on, Will. I'll help you take off your wet shirt." Scowling, she removed the clingy, wet material from his arms and over his head with jerky movements, while he hung on to her. It had been a long time since she'd seen this much of a man. He looked pretty good. She ratcheted down her irritation and helped him don his sweatshirt over his bare chest.

"Turn around. But first hand me my pants. My fingers are waterlogged."

She pictured him fighting his way out of his sodden boxers. Thank heaven he didn't ask her to help with that, but she zipped up his jacket and tied his shoes. Dry shoes, dry jacket, dry slacks. Good. William was shivering now and slapping his body with his arms.

"How did this happen to you, William? Did you slip?"

"I always wanted to bathe in a tidal basin. B—boy, that was a wrong decision. Everything was all right, except for the wet clothes against my body in the wind. I should've taken all my clothes off."

Rose chuckled. "Why didn't you then? You were all alone in your private bathtub. For the moment."

"It was you. I knew exactly what you were going to do, and I didn't want to gross you out."

Confusion hobbled her tongue. "How? What—"

"Er—you always do what makes sense. I knew you would turn back when the others got too far ahead.

The ends of her lips turned down in chagrin. "But how did you know?"

William looked down at the wet boxers in his hand. "I'm a psychologist as well as a historian." He reacted to the look on her face. "I've been studying you, you see."

By now William's teeth were like castanets. They headed into the wind on their way uphill. Rose walked in front of him to cut the breeze.

He laughed. "N—no, Rose. You're not big enough."

She snorted. A buxom five foot four, surely she came to his shoulders, though, come to think of it, since he always lowered his face close to hers while he listened, she had no notion of his height. Perhaps he was actually quite tall, even as tall as Michael. Wait a minute—what was that under his layered hair?

"Will, are you hard of hearing?"

He pulled his hair back from both ears to expose the devices. "I guess this blows my cover as the Shamrocks' sex symbol. Anyway, you can see I'm no longer young."

She noticed the streaks of gray and grasped for an appropriate remark. "Why, Will, how old are you?"

It turned out he was thirteen years older than she was. She noticed the fine wrinkles around his eyes and the laugh lines at his vulnerable-looking mouth. If only Michael would look this way at William's age he would electrify women still.

He told her his deafness came from a love of rock concerts. "It's ironic, because I love music more than ever now. I especially have trouble with female voices, so don't take it personally if I seem not to hear. Either that or I'm ignoring you."

She was careful to speak with her mouth close to his face. Talk turned to the legend of the giants Ally had told them about.

"It was interesting, but I didn't hear all of it. If you remember, Ally doesn't always have her mic up to her face, and I need that."

Rose repeated what she could remember of the legend of Finn McCool, a giant who constructed the causeway and had his wife wrap him up like a giant infant, so his enemy would fear the baby's parent, Finn himself.

"So Cuhullin put his finger in the baby's mouth to feel the strength of his teeth. Did you hear this part? What do you think happened? Finn, posing as a baby you know…he bit the bad guy's finger off, so he ran away screaming."

"Rose, you are so animated when you tell stories. You will make a great mother someday." Will blushed.

Rose pretended not to notice. "What I like about this story is the idea of people taking back control of their lives. Sometimes it's the giants and ogres, you see, but maybe it's someone you love who casts you as an underdog in the end."

"How is it you know this, Rose? Did you have someone like this in your life?"

She nodded. "My grandfather came pretty close to playing that role. I told you he retired and moved to the family home in Ireland, right?"

"Yes, you mentioned you're going to look him up after the tour."

"Well, he lived with us since my grandmother left him— all my life and most of my father's. I always accepted what he told me and let him call the shots, because I loved him so much."

She shuddered, remembering she had repeated history with Michael.

"Well, Grandfather taught me the importance of being Irish, even though I'm only half and half. 'Always remember that when you're in trouble.' His exact words."

William opened his mouth to speak, but let her soldier on.

She fumbled with the strings of her hoodie. "Well, I'm more or less in trouble now, and I'm trying to find out what he meant—find what's in me—once and for all." Her racing mind searched for answers, even while she talked.

The wind whipped them. William gave her a squinting grin. "I'd like to know what you yourself think"

She gnawed on the end of her thumb, disconcerted by the question. "Well, I hope my Irish will help me overcome weakness. Michael was sometimes a stinker when he drank. My acquiescence was as much to blame for the end of our marriage as his behavior was." Her chest tightened. "I shouldn't have put up with that."

"But, Rose, that can't be your fault. A catastrophe like that would confuse anyone. You couldn't know what to do." He put his arm around her.

His protectiveness brought a lump to her throat. She decided to trust him with her self-doubt. "The truth is, I need to decide who I am as a single person and what I will do with my life. Paint? Teach? Use my art history degree? I feel like a child. I don't want to be aimless and unfocused all my life."

William turned her to look at him. "Rose, weighing options does not make you aimless."

"You're so understanding, but you never felt lost the way I do, did you, William?"

She bit off her words, for a sad expression claimed his kind-looking eyes.

"Ever since my wife died."

A gaggle of Shamrocks rushed up to Rose and William.

"Where were you?"

"You missed the lecture. What happened?"

Last of all, Claris appeared. "You're all wet. Go get your extra clothes from your backpack."

Rose stood with her mouth open like a baby bird, waiting for the other half of the worm. The welcoming party bore William away, grist for the gossip mill for now.

She eyed the stones beneath her sodden shoes. "What happened?" Had she heard right? Had Will been a widower? Was Claris a replacement for a much more beloved wife? There was no chance to ask him now. Claris practically had him by the ear, and it was time for the Shamrocks' drive into Belfast.

She hoisted herself aboard the bus. "I know. I'm wet, I'm late, and I'm cross."

The eyes Mildred turned on her suggested contact with an extraterrestrial. "What happened to you?"

"Don't ask. I don't even know."

ɛ∕ɔɛ∕ɔ

Belfast:

Mildred patted her head over the top of the seat. "Better take some deep breaths, dear. We're due for the Titanic exhibit, and I know how you feel about that."

"Yes, another tourist trap we're forced to visit."

Some hours later, the bus maneuvered around a bend, revealing a giant monument ahead. Several sections formed peaks at least ten stories high she judged. Rose took a step back, taking a few seconds to get her words out. "Oh, it's the bow of an enormous ship."

Ally wrapped up her pitch. "As you approach the building, you'll get the feeling the passengers had when they walked up to the ship. It's exactly the height of the Titanic's hull without the decks above. Brilliant, eh?"

Rose sucked in a small breath, pressing her hands to her cheeks. She and Mildred worked their way up inside the monstrosity via a series of elevators. They pored over maps, room plans, and photographs. Reconstructions and holograms let them imagine they were really aboard ship.

Rose's fingers itched to handle the linens and china on display. "Wow, Mildred, look at the embroidery. Can you imagine the ironing?"

Alistair eyed the sets of china. "It looks to me like they made plates smaller in those days. He patted his belly.

Mildred made a tutting sound. "Did you see the tiny sleeping quarters in third class?" She pointed. "Only one toilet for the whole floor."

Alistair groaned. "Just imagine the stampede in the mornings. I hope they all made it on time. Do you see how the hoi polloi locked the poor buggers downstairs when the ship started to sink?"

Rose cringed. She remembered how it had felt to be trapped in the overturned car, with Rosebud's desperate hurry to get out and her own need to remain calm.

Her companions went on ahead, arm in arm, while she lingered over the tales of people who had died, and those who'd survived. Rose was there with them in her imagination—a pajama clad lad leaping into the sea, corpses next to half-empty lifeboats, an attendant shooting men as they claimed lifeboats. She heard women screaming in the darkness and explosions that attended the ship's final plunge into the sea. Tears rolled down her face.

A kind voice and a pair of arms gentled her. "It's all right, Rose." There was a question in Will's eyes. "You really do feel things deeply, don't you?"

She sniffed. "It's too sad. Families got ripped apart, and it didn't have to be that way."

He steered her over to a bench and produced a tissue. "What set you off, Rose? I guess there's more to your distress than you're telling."

"I hate boats. I used to be afraid every time we went out in our canoe. We have alligators, for God's sake. It's easy enough to lose someone on land."

Rose stopped to blow her nose. Red puffiness had settled under Will's eyes. Maybe she'd better tread gently. "What about you? Don't these things get you, or can you distance yourself pretty well?"

William guided her over to a bench. He cleared his throat, and when he spoke, his voice was thick and coarse.

"We used to have a small runabout with a high performance outboard. A beautiful mahogany Hacker it was. We actually lived near the factory on Lake George at the time. I asked my wife never to take it out alone, but..." He shrugged and cleared his throat again. "Sorry, I haven't talked about this for a long time."

"It's okay, Will. You don't have to."

He brushed her concerns off with a wave of his hand. "It's just hard to tell about...and hard to hear. Well, one day my wife ended up near a park where I was meeting with a student. We'd taken a break under a willow tree overlooking the water. I saw her looking back and waving." He stopped and swallowed several times. My wife loved gunning it in that boat." He rocked himself back and forth. "Well, the accelerator got stuck. She hit a dock."

Rose's hands flew to her mouth. "Oh, oh no, Will. Was she...how did she..."

"It was horrible. The boat kept on running full force, crashing through several piers and a boat house."

Rose forced herself, for Will's sake, to regain control of her nausea. This time it was her arm that crept around his shoulders.

"Ahh, Will, I'm sorry, so sorry." She already knew the answer to her next question, but she had to ask. "Did you—could you—save her?"

He covered his face with his palms. "There wasn't much left."

It was hard to see the repugnance on his face.

"Later someone found her wedding ring. Still on her hand." He shook his head "Part of her hand."

Rose trembled. "Oh, no—Oh, Will."

He wiped his eyes with his fingertips. "I was a mess. My wife left me with two small children and memories of a scene nobody should have to witness. And I was no good for anything for a long while. I couldn't even care for my children properly. Not long afterward, Claris became part of our household. She was good with the children. We needed her."

Rose's frontal cortex flashed into *full on.* So that was

how William had found Claris. It had been nothing like the way she had married Michael—her heart bursting with tenderness and longing and the need to spend every day together.

ↄ⊙ↄ

It was late when the Shamrocks checked into their next hotel. The desk attendant handed over a brown envelope with Michael's handwriting. Rose drew out a folded sheet of paper.

Sorry for this, Rose. I guess the sight of my handwriting makes you cringe, but looking at this photo every day hurts too much. I thought of throwing it out to save my sanity. But then I realized you might want to remember how you looked on our wedding day. You can cut me out of the picture if you want. Michael.

She strode over to the trash receptacle and tossed the note and the photo inside as if they had burned her fingers. Then she snatched them out again. She slumped and burst into tears.

ↄ⊙ↄ

Newgrange:

The next morning, she couldn't miss the dark aura arising from Mildred. She didn't eat breakfast, and she turned away when the Shamrocks forced the issue.

Gary tried teasing. "Come on, Missus, I saw ya making the best of the rashers and eggs other days. There's nothing wrong with yer gut today, is there?"

Ally uttered her encouragement. "Mildred, dear, ya stayed under yer covers a long time this morning. Got to rabbit on, don't we?"

Rose took her by one arm, and they soldiered on to the bus park. Gary gave her a hand into the bus, and Rose took the seat beside her. She leaned in to Mildred and whispered. "What's wrong with you, Mildred?" Only when Rose discovered her naked finger did Mildred admit she'd lost her wedding ring.

"It was all I had left from my Bernie. It's like losing him a second time." Mildred broke down in Rose's arms. The Shamrocks whispered and rumbled behind their hands.

Justus growled. "I told you, people, there's good reason to watch your valuables. Now look what happens when you don't." Rose wanted to administer a good kick in a place that would make him more sensitive. Marge wagged her chin whiskers.

Up front, Gary spoke loud enough for them to hear without the mic. "Jaysus, That ball-bag's brains are as useless as tits on a bull."

Ally attempted to get them interested in their route through the Mountains of Mourne. "This is Ulster, with the highest mountains in Northern Ireland—all granite."

Gary cleared his throat. "Most of them back there are having a kip, Ally. Can't you hear them snoring? It's useless to blather on."

Heads bobbed while Ally talked about an old whiskey smuggling trail from Newcastle. It was a pity to miss all that, but Rose's focus had dimmed its lights.

Gary's voice on the microphone startled her. "All right ya lot. Time to go up the yard. Toilets are over there. Ya can have a fag, but don't miss seeing this monument, or I'll be cheesed off."

"Ooh," Rose moaned. Her voice was but one in a sour chorus.

Nevertheless, Gary kept ragging on them. "Newgrange is five hundred years older than the pyramids and as big a mystery as Stonehenge. The passage tomb inside is only nineteen meters into the mound. So what's the purpose of the rest of the structure?"

Ally made a histrionic grimace. "I would tell you about it, but in your present shattered states, I would just make a hash of it."

Rose cringed. She knew how Ally felt, having made the acquaintance of low self-esteem long ago. She straightened up in her seat and opened her mouth to say "Sorry."

Ally met her eye. "Just kidding. I'm not allowed to guide here in the National Trust. The official guide will tell you the story of Newgrange. After that, if you come with me, you might hear me talking very quietly about it."

Lou pushed to the front of the pack to argue with the guide. "Three thousand BC. The world is not that old."

William rolled his eyes at Rose and tapped his head. She smothered her laughter.

The guide nodded at Lou. "See the small window above the entrance? On a couple of days in December, the sun shines through there, lighting the entire passage for a quarter of an hour. Did the megolithic people build all this for a few minutes of light? She encouraged the Shamrocks to venture into the passage.

Alistair folded his hands. "An astronomical device for sure."

Jocelyn hung next to the guide. "Imagine…they knew so much about astronomy …and they didn't even have metal tools."

Rose's eyes widened. "Yes, and just think—we know they existed. Did they possess only the here and now, or did they imagine us?" Rose found it ironic—people could dig up history, but she could not revive the happiness in her own past.

Claris wandered apart from the group, surveying the field around the site.

No time but the present to force a showdown. Claris shrank back from Rose's touch.

"Sorry, uh…you must have been deep in thought. I didn't intend to scare you."

Claris looked like a teddy bear without its stuffing. "All

this—all the people so long ago, dead all these years. I've been thinking of those my family lost."

Rose didn't expect this sentimentality. She felt the sting of tears in her own eyes. "I...uh...guess it's hard to go on..."

Claris gazed into the distance. "Yes..."

They headed back toward the bus. "Claris, William told me how his wife died. I know you had to fill big shoes. I just want to ask you something that's been bothering me."

"Hmmm?"

"Maybe it's none of my business, but why don't you act more affectionate toward him?"

Claris shot her a pained look. "What about you, Rose?"

As Rose recoiled from the ambiguous question, a gaggle of Shamrocks swarmed them.

"Mildred isn't doing well, Rose."

Alistair's arm around her, Mildred occupied a bench near the toilets.

Jocelyn paced up and down. "Where the hell is my umbrella? I swear I'm losing so much on this trip. First my locket and camera, then my gold bridge, and now this. I know I'm absent-minded, but this is too much."

Rose rubbed her hands over her face. "Gosh, everybody's nerves are really jangled. You don't know if bad luck is lurking behind you or if it's just a bad person."

Jocelyn paced faster. "Well, if this is a prank, I hope it's over soon. And may the monster who's responsible tumble down the steps into Gary's toilet."

Resplendent in another new outfit, today Paddy looked more like his hero than ever. 'Some cause happiness wherever they go, others whenever they go. True friends stab you in the front.' That's what Oscar wrote."

Alistair pounded him on the arm. "Good one, my boy."

Rose grinned at him. "Yes, Paddy, you get more like your idol the closer we get to Dublin. I swear you hear him calling you."

Paddy raised his chin and turned up the corners of his

smug mouth. "Yellow is a good color for such a morbid place, don't you think? I sent a selfie to my sons and my ex-wife. They thought I went too far, but my live-in thought I looked delicious."

Gary eyed Paddy. "A little bit molly, what?"

Rose put her finger to her lips. "Don't listen to anybody. You're perfect, Paddy. We need a ray of sunshine like you. I just wish we could put a stop to this sabotage."

Her reserved nature notwithstanding, she'd always fancied herself a potential sleuth. Maybe this was the time to see what she could do.

ↄ∕ↄↄↄ

Dublin:

Rose heaved a heavy sigh. "Another captive tour and forced time in the gift shop. I can't believe this is a top attraction in Dublin."

"But the Guinness Store House gives us a free drink in the Gravity Bar overlooking the city."

"Is that right, Ally?"

"Yes, and dinner is included. Can you see that glass tower? It's the shape of a pint glass."

"I don't want any dinner." Mildred clutched her purse for dear life.

Gary gave her a slight push. "Away with you! The dinner's grand. And the Guinness is just what ya need. And don't worry about that git that stole yer ring. He thinks he's got us flummoxed, but we'll get him, that ball of shite."

Rose walked Mildred into the elevator.

"Hold the lift! Hold the lift!" shouted a young female with three inch spiked hair, a two inch skirt, and five inch heels. The door wheezed shut in front of her young man. "Bollocks! That eejit's going to end up snogging with some scab in the alley. What a lot of cheek when he came here with me!" She tottered out on the top floor and stormed off to join some of her clones.

Mildred's levity had a stretched edge to it, but this was an improvement from a day obviously spent in the basement of her soul

They squeezed into a space at a tall bar table, where two of the Shamrocks heaved Mildred onto a stool. A waiter sloshed glasses of dark brown ale down on the table.

Rose touched her arm. "Look at this, Mildred, and do what I do. The best slug of beer is the first one. That's what Michael used to say." She swallowed two thirds of her Guinness down at once. "Good old Michael...he was right, because the rest of it tastes revolting."

Everyone at the table laughed at that. Why was she just now discovering the fun of traveling with a posse?

In the dining room, William played with his pasta salad. "Our itinerary says this is Ireland's most visited attraction. I can see why from watching you. You were pretty funny after you swilled that Guinness."

On the other side of William, Claris turned away.

Rose's hot cheeks got hotter. "I can't hold my liquor. I didn't drink for so many years, because I didn't want to encourage... My husband is a drunk. What do you think of that?"

"I figured that from some things you hinted at before. It's a terrible affliction."

"Yes, I know it. His father was the same, an unhappy person." Rose's eyes stung. "My husband was happy...we were both happy until...well, until he started drinking. I don't understand for sure why he started and why he wouldn't stop...for me."

William handed her a spare napkin.

"You know, drinking can be a coping mechanism for demons inside a person."

"That sounds scientific. How do you know so much?"

William blanched. "I have an alcoholic son."

"How's that?"

"My son is a drunk—was a drunk since he was fifteen. He can't drink anymore these days."

"Why not?"

"He almost died of alcohol poisoning when he was seventeen." William looked away. "He has brain damage."

Rose cursed herself for bringing up a topic of such obvious distress to Will. "I—I'm sorry."

Will's voice turned throaty. "He can't care for himself. I can't do it all, and I certainly couldn't ask Claris. My boy lives in a nursing home now. I visit him, but I can't make a life for him. He still has to do that himself. The worst thing is—he still suffers from the depression that started him off."

She nodded her understanding. "Michael's dad killed himself."

William pinched the bridge of his nose and sniffed. "One way or another, self-punishment is not unusual. I do it. My daughter Bridget did it. I think that's one reason why she's an expatriate. There are so many things I can't undo for my kids." He told Rose how, for the past several years, he'd visited schools and youth groups after work to share his son's story, hoping some teenager would realize he could get help before it was too late. "Here. Here's a picture of my boy. His senior picture."

"He's handsome, just like you." She bit her lip. "I mean, he looks so bright and aware."

"National Honor Society. Mensa. Chess Club. He was going to be valedictorian most likely, and he had a scholarship to the University of Michigan. Now he can't change his own diapers."

At last Rose escaped thinking of her own problems. She shed tears for Mildred and for Will. Her heart felt pounds heavier from sharing their loads. Still, it was good to know hers wasn't the only heart where loss had moved in. If it decided to stay with her, she would learn to get along with it.

∽∾∾

The Shamrocks spent the rest of the afternoon in a woolen shop. Rose had to admit it was fun selecting gifts for those she loved, including Puppy Joe. She fingered a multicolored scarf in a cashmere blend. "We do have cold weather in northern Florida."

Mildred gushed over it. "Ooo. That should substitute for petting your puppy until you get home. What a luxury." She stroked the scarf. "I was planning to purchase gifts for all my grandchildren and nieces and nephews, but...uh...I don't see anything suitable."

Rose sensed her financial straits. "Look, Mildred. Why don't you buy some of this fine wool and make Irish Rose hair ornaments for the girls and coin purses for the boys. They'll always remember you made them."

Rose already had Mildred's address in Sidney. She slipped it to the sales person with her credit card and the scarf while Mildred admired Will's new cap. She wrote on the back of one of her artist cards, "Enjoy in memory of our time together! Rose O'Leary." She passed it over to be included in the package.

The sales agent bit her lip. "This doesn't match the name on the credit card, madam."

"Oh. Oh, dear." What a Freudian slip. "I must have written my husband's name." She added "Flanagan" in parentheses. She suspected this absent-minded slip was not the first such blunder. "What is my subconscious telling me?"

The agent tut-tutted. "That's nothing. I regularly call my old man by my first lover's name."

Rose hustled out of the store. She slid into three smiling rows of Shamrocks posed on the front porch.

"All right." Justus handed over his Nikon. "I guess mine is one of the few cameras we've got left, isn't that so?" The last words sounded like "Told you so."

Chapter 8

Standing queue are you, darling?" Ally asked Rose. "I'm surprised you Americans aren't all toting tablets and laptops everywhere you go."

"I should have thought of that," Rose replied, "but the mystery man would have stolen it by now. Look how many smart phones we've lost."

Finally, a wi-fi station came free, and Rose connected with her mother, who recounted an incident from the previous afternoon.

When Michael came to pick up Puppy Joe, he accepted some unsweet iced tea. He drank it with me on the front porch. As always, he was pleasant. Charming. A sweet, touching man. I wished I could hear his laugh. He was happy that Joe's so well-adjusted with us. I assured him the dog's no trouble. Michael asked what I thought about letting Joe move in for a while. I told him we love that little guy. I told him you do too, and we'll do what it takes to make sure he's here when you get back. We don't know what Michael's planning, Rose, but don't worry. We'll take care of this.

Rose read the passage several times before she focused on its meaning. She shook off her confusion and moved on to Aidan's missive.

Michael's always monkeying around with those rose bushes and with the dog. By God, I never saw a pup so besotted with a man. It's touching in a way. The minute he hears that car pull up to the cottage we can't hold him back. Off he goes, and we can see him from here, jumping all over his master.

Anyway, Michael installed underground sprinklers. I guess he wants to make sure he doesn't forget to water the roses now that warmer weather is on the way. Joe jumps around in the sprinklers. Gets Michael to chase him. Seems to be good for both of them.

Back to the dog—Joe has had a hard time lately when he stays with us. He keeps looking in the room you stayed in and cuddles on your bed a lot of the time. He has to have your nightshirt with him. I guess it has you on it. During a storm, your mom puts his thunder shirt on him for his anxiety, kind of like a straitjacket. I wonder if they come in my size.

℘℘℘

She tapped on the keys. *I wonder if they come in my size too. Can you find out what Michael's up to?*

Rose looked away from the screen, her eyes not focused on the here and now. In her imagination, she stood unseen behind a garden rife with spurting sprinklers. She watched Michael and Puppy Joe cavort. A ragged towel around his neck, he wore only his old gym shorts, a size too small and an enticing showcase for his backside.

"Go, Joe! Go!"

Puppy Joe ran faster around the curving paths in the cascading water.

Michael pumped his fists, his handsome face the picture of excitement. "Go! Go! Where's Mommy? Get Mommy! Get Rose."

The sheltie performed figure eights around the beds. He

bit at the sprinkler heads and, gargling, attempted to drink from them. He sneezed and yapped and practically shook himself inside out.

Michael hooted his delight, collapsing on the steps.

Puppy shook himself, sending water flying at Michael, who leaped off the steps and pounced at him. He carried him to the porch like an infant, wrapped in the towel. "Who's my boy? What's the matter, Joe? No Mommy?" He held the wriggling terry cloth package tight on his lap. His blue eyes sparkled, but sadness tinged his voice.

Rose wanted to move closer, beyond the curtain of water. Instead, Michael deposited Joe onto the floor boards to shake himself, and he removed his sodden shorts and tennis shoes, revealing parts of him that perked up Rose's body with desire.

Michael stood up and rubbed himself with the towel. Everywhere. Rough. At last, he stood his spade against the porch post and bundled the wet objects under one arm. "Come on, boy. Let's go in. There's a lot to do before Mommy gets home." He looked back through the gushing water, directly at her.

Rose shook off her fantasy and returned to her floor for a pre-bedtime party with Mildred. They moved camp into Rose's room, so she could share the biscuits she'd acquired that day. Besides, she couldn't wait to show her friend a purchase she'd kept secret.

"This is for you, Mildred. I know you'll think it's a consolation prize, but, well, I want this to remind you that love can't be lost, not love like you had with your husband. Put it on before I make the tea. This is a party."

Inside the box lay a silver ring with the Irish three-pointed love knot wound around the band. "Oh, Rose. It's beautiful."

They wept in each other's arms, their tears intermingled with laughter. Rose imagined the grandmother who'd abandoned her years before she'd been born. Mildred sniffled into a tissue and handed one to Rose.

Rose plugged in the electric tea pot and picked up Mildred's room key to fetch her fine wool and crochet hook. And her favorite tea bags. She left Mildred turning the ring this way and that in the lamplight.

She thought of Michael, who had gained—after she'd left him—an enhanced relationship with her dog. She hadn't even brought a photo of Puppy Joe, except for the one on her t-shirt. Would she recognize him by the time she left Ireland? Would he know her? Would he still be hers?

The door to Mildred's room was slightly ajar. Rose's hackles came alive.

Not knowing if an intruder had already entered or if his arrival might be imminent, she slipped into the shower, hoping the plastic curtain would muffle the galloping sound of her heartbeat. After a few minutes, the sweat from her scalp dripped into her eyes. She imagined it hitting the tile floor with a surreal *ping!*

A shadow on the bank of closets opposite the open door outlined a bulky figure rifling through the bags on the bed. Now and then the intruder cleared his throat or emitted a labored sigh. Finally, the light went out, heavy footsteps shook the floor, and the door clicked shut.

She opened the adjoining door. "Mildred, you'll have to come here and see if your suitcase is packed the way you left it."

∽✐✐∽

Rose hadn't slept, and it was an early start in Dublin. Fuzzy as she felt, she noticed there was something different about Sister Ann.

"Where's your cross?" Mildred demanded with a mouthful of oatmeal and raisins.

"Good Jesus, my crucifix! It's gone, chain and all. I thought the clasp was getting a little loose."

Rose wrung her hands. "Oh, no! Not another loss." She put an arm around the nun.

"Oh, Lord, my mother gave it to me when I took my vows. It's gold, with a big piece of glass in the middle." She glanced around the circle that gathered. "You remember it, don't you?" She leaned in to the group. "Only it's not glass."

Everyone moved closer. "It's my grandmother's diamond. Mama considered it my insurance policy if I ever wanted to leave the convent."

Marge leaned closer. "Was it insured?"

"No, and I don't think I can tell anybody at the convent what happened. Reverend Mother wouldn't like that I held on to something so valuable."

Marge's chin wagged more than ever. "Well, Justus will be upset. He's always telling you folks to be careful. What can you expect with a loose clasp or an open purse, or an unlocked door?"

Rose was so glad she hadn't brought the gold locket from Michael with her. Unthinking, she felt for it against her chest, the way she often reached for a phantom puppy nose against her leg. Some things were always part of her, especially where Michael was concerned—what he had done and said, what he would do and say. The way he'd presented the locket.

Grandfather Sean's favorite border collie had died in his arms. It was hard to hear his heart-breaking sobs. Eventually, he'd emerged from his bedroom with the little body in his arms and carried it into the yard.

"My good little gal. I'll bury her down by the pond, so I can see her grave from my window."

The family had followed him. Michael had dug the grave. After Sean had laid his pet in the ground, he'd wiped his eyes. "If you love somebody, you'd better get used to this. Eventually, you'll lose her." He'd marched to the house, the family trailing. Rose had cried herself numb.

Michael had folded her arm in his and they'd proceeded to their little house. On the porch, she'd turned to study his face.

"What, darling?"

Her dry lips trembled. She grabbed on to him. "I…It scares me sometimes how…how much I love you." She blinked rapidly. "Oh, Michael, I couldn't stand to…lose you. It would kill me." She'd whimpered.

Michael had held her arms and peered into her eyes. "Are you afraid you'd lose my love, sweetheart?" He'd placed her hand on his chest, so she'd be aware of his heartbeat. "You know my heart belongs to you, Rose. When I die you can have it stuffed and wear it around your neck."

She'd shouted. "What? That's a terrible idea." Then she'd laughed until she'd hiccoughed. "Oh, Michael You are so bizarre."

His eyes had been wet with laughter too. "I know it, Rose. Maudlin. But it made you laugh."

"You always make me laugh, Michael. I'm still scared of…you know…the end."

"Well, my love, then how about this…for second best." From his pocket he produced a small box with a large heart-shaped gold locket. Inside a closeup of him and a lock of his hair.

✺✺✺

Rose's face emerged from her guide book. "Where are the London Plane Trees? It's O'Connell Street, and I don't see them."

"Yes, hmmm!" Ally giggled. "Noticed that, did you? They were all cut down in the first years of the new century and replaced with art projects, monuments, and other kinds of trees." She soothed the torrent of protests by pointing out the Irish granite, limestone, and red brick used in the imposing neoclassical buildings.

Saint Patrick's Cathedral received a quick drive by. In the library at Trinity College, the Shamrocks filed past two glass-cased volumes of the ornately illuminated *Book of*

Kells. William bent over the glass. "Imagine, the monk who produced this has been dead more than a millennium."

Claris motioned him on. "I bet he went blind first."

Ally organized them on a street corner. "Now we're going to see Merrion Square, one of the five Georgian squares left in the city. That house there is the family home of Dublin's favorite son, Oscar Wilde." Everyone looked at Paddy, who blushed.

"We'll take fifteen minutes for an inspection of the statue in the park. See? You can see him from the corner here, posed on a slab of quartz. His shimmering garments are granite, feldspar, and green jade, and other stone, and they look just like cloth. Some think it fitting, considering how he was thrown into jail for homosexuality, that his face is turned away from the Parliament building."

Most of them ran fingers over the monument to make sure there was no fabric involved.

Lou challenged Ally. "How do we know the statue looks like him?"

"His grandson posed for the likeness. Is that good enough for you?"

Dressed in an outfit similar to the one in quartz, Paddy assumed an identical pose beside the slab.

Rose read a quotation from Wilde's obituary. "His abilities were sufficient to win him an honored place as a man of letters, but they struggled in vain against his lack of character." The words choked her.

Paddy's mournful visage was less than comical now. "Am I just like Oscar, Rose?"

She placed a hand against his smoking jacket. "You have the same fashion sense, but I'd like to get to know the real you, Patrick. You're one of a kind."

With an hour to spare before a slated departure from the city center, Rose treated herself to a cup of tea at a crowded second story cafeteria. In the company of her romance novel, Claris sipped her tea at a table with a view of the park. Rose knew how engrossed Claris could get when fiction was involved, so she slid into a chair opposite her and waited for attention.

At last her companion appeared to float into a vague awareness. "Mmm?"

"I take it you don't mind if I sit with you, since you're not paying attention anyway."

Claris's conscious mind gave the impression of impending emergence. "Wh—what? Oh?"

"I notice you often lose yourself in your book."

"Oh—hi. Oh, yes. I'm notorious for that." Claris chuckled. "It's not just books. My own fantasy too." She slipped her tea napkin into her book and closed the page.

"How about a scone and another tea? It'll be my compensation for intruding on your privacy."

When Rose returned with a plate of cinnamon scones and a large pot of tea, Claris's face lit up. She helped herself to a big bite. "Mmmm! Just what I need, and I didn't know it. You are right. I do go deep under when I'm absorbed. The same when I'm weaving or spinning." She shook her head self-consciously. "It's bad of me socially, I guess."

Rose couldn't disagree. She nodded.

"See, I don't change, because I figure my habits don't do any damage. Yet here you've gotten the impression you're unwelcome to sit with me, when really I'm happy you turned up to keep me company. Tell me about yourself, and you'll be surprised how well I can listen."

So, Rose's heart came unlocked to Claris. She prattled on and on about Michael and Rosebud and Puppy Joe, and even about Michael's drinking and how their dreams had been dashed and their marriage ruined.

It was almost time to meet the bus when Rose realized she had done all the talking. There was so much she wanted to know about Claris.

They exchanged a few words more as they hurried for the bus.

"How long have you and William known each other, Claris?"

"All our lives, of course, but I didn't pay much attention to him early on. I was so much older, you know." Claris chuckled. "He thought I was much too bossy anyway. Of course, when we were older, we had more in common. I was friends with the children's mother, and the children...well, who wouldn't love children? Naturally I was eager to take them on when their mother passed."

So that was how it had happened. Had Claris been in love with William even before his wife's death?

∞∞∞

Back at the hotel, another envelope awaited Rose. Her lips pressed together. "Oh, Michael. You can't let go, can you?" She inhaled a long breath and shook her head, irritated yet intrigued too.

She forced her eyes out of focus while a half sheet of paper emerged. The words evoked Michael's voice.

Hi, Rose,

Your mother mentioned you miss Joe. Here's our best picture of him. Maybe you notice I cut you out of the picture. I guess you don't need that part, but I want it. I planned to cut me out too, but then Joe would lose an ear and a paw.

Don't worry. He and I will be here waiting for you.

Rose's eyes filled with tears. She spoke to the man in the picture—to his sensuous eyes and wayward, skillful lips.

"You're killing me, Michael."

∞∞∞

After dinner the friends sipped tea in Mildred's room.

"That's a beautiful picture sticking out of your purse. He looks rather...gorgeous. The dog is cute too."

That night, they put their plan into operation. Mildred clutched her arms to her chest. "Be careful, my dear. I know sleuthing appeals to you, but don't take chances. If there's trouble, make sure I can hear you in there. You have nothing to gain, really, you know."

Nothing besides proving herself capable. Rose pursed her lips.

Rose left Mildred hunkered near the phone in her room, turning out crocheted roses and ready to call for help. She cracked the door to her own room and hid in the slippery bathtub barefoot and armed with a shillelagh she'd purchased for Aidan. Why must Detective Rose always operate in the bathroom? After a while, she heard Mildred snoring through the wall. Great. She was on her own.

At some point, she heard a metallic sound at the door, like someone depressing the plunger of a ballpoint pen. Then again, a click. A change in air pressure. A slight breeze, but why? She hung tight to the plastic tub liner, her heart thrumming in her chest. The hall door creaked. A tiny sound, but so ominous.

She heard the scrunching pile of her carpet as someone stole around. A heavy foot struck the table leg hard, triggering a deep growl. What if he came to the bathroom for a towel to staunch his blood? Mildred was right. This could turn dangerous.

Her sweaty toes lost their grip on the ceramic surface. Behind the shower curtain, she slipped to her knees, cowered on the tub bottom, and wrapped her arms around her head and chest. Where was the shillelagh now that she wanted it?

She could hear heavy breathing—his raspy, hers labored. She realized he'd want to avoid dealing with a witness. Pretend not to know someone was there.

Big feet clomped to the door. The door slammed shut.

Rose inched her sore muscles over the side of the tub and flopped onto the bathmat, where she lay until her heart stopped playing doo-dah. With her face so close to the hall carpet, she noticed the impression a shoe had made on the smooth, thick pile. A big shoe. She rummaged in the drawer for paper and traced the outline of the wide, long shoe print on two sheets of paper. Next, she whitened the print with bath powder and snapped a photo. All she needed now was to find that shoe.

℄ℨℰℨ

The Wicklow Mountains and Ballyknocken House:

In the morning, the Shamrocks chugged through the Wicklow Mountains, once the most anticipated part of Rose's trip. However, she missed some of the scenery, because she and Mildred crocheted dozens of Irish roses for her ladies' society.

"I can't believe I'm letting detail trump the mountain vista. Mildred, I could crochet these roses in my sleep. Do you think we could make something else?"

"What? Like a snare for the intruder?"

"I can see the headline—'Irish Wool Ties up Thief.'"

Mildred fingered her new ring and sighed with contentment. "Rose, I know this ring is supposed to stand in for my wedding ring, but it reminds me of more than Bernie. It reminds me that you can find all kinds of love anywhere. And you're one of the most loving people I've met."

Rose snorted. "So why am I so stubborn, and why can't I forgive and forget?"

Other questions crowded around in a feeding frenzy. What was Michael up to? Would her new sleuthing chops impress him? Had he found someone new? Was he going to forget her after all? How would she feel about that at the end of the day?

Aidan had encouraged her to notice new men. She looked down the aisle at William. Such a nice man, and he made her feel safe, whereas Michael brought an element of contention and danger to the table. His motor was always on, while William was the calm of a fair day. So far, she enjoyed his friendship, but how did she really feel about him as a man? The image of him naked eluded her.

Gary knocked on the microphone. "Attention! Here we are at Ballyknocken House, where ye'll meet a famous television chef, and I hope I get something to eat. I've a mouth on me, and the scones here are grand. I could use a cup of cha too."

Rose pretended to fumble on the ground for her crochet hook. Five whopping pairs of feet passed her on the way out.

Gary was right. Chef Catherine's scones and tea were just the thing to give Rose some get-up-and-go. She rummaged around roses and herbs and forget-me nots in the garden, photographing the display with the Wicklow Mountains in the background.

At the front of the cottage, she came across Will. He stood under an evergreen arch, handsome with his silvered temples and eyes like the Irish Sea. He radiated stability and kindness.

"Hello, Rose. Come stand here with me. Let Claris take our picture."

Rose handed over her camera too.

Ally rounded the house at that moment. "You know what this means. Forever friends. Get in there too, Claris. Mildred. Let me take one of all of you."

The aproned chef, strolled over from the rose garden. "So this is the man then." She turned to Will. "You could really present the rose yourself, mister."

William blushed and stammered, denying credit for the bloom in Rose's hand "Not that I wouldn't like to be the one."

Rose looked at him startled. Her mouth felt dry, her chest hard.

"Oh, so you've got more than one suitor. Good luck to you then."

Claris eyed her closely. "What's the matter, Rose? Your face is the color of your hair. There's nothing to be embarrassed about. You're divorcing your husband, and you deserve the attentions of another man."

Rose's startled eyes ricocheted off Claris's face to William. He took a step closer, and confusion laid its claim on her. She swallowed several times. "Claris, I...I don't understand. Wh-What about you?"

Claris crossed her arms, setting her mouth in a grim line. "Haven't I nagged him enough about being too shy? Why shouldn't he throw his hat in the ring?"

Rose wasn't in Kansas anymore. She stammered. "What? Why? I...I don't." Someone jerked the bones right out of her legs. The world turned black.

William moved forward to keep her on her feet. "Come on, Rose. This is too much of a circus. Let's talk over there."

In the garden of the next door guest house, they claimed a wrought iron bench.

"So you thought Claris tried to pimp out her own husband." A deep laugh flew out of William's throat. "That's what she deserves for being so bossy. She's been trying to fix us up since the plane. Didn't you get it?"

"But, William—No. That's not right."

He returned her stare. "Claris is my sister, Rose."

ℰᴕℰᴕ

Kilkenny and Waterford:

The bus breezed through Kilkenny with no time to tour the castle, so Rose vowed to return there after she'd visited Grandfather Sean. More and more she anticipated that future part of her adventure. Images of times spent around the corral with the big, handsome man lingered in her memory. Though he'd never set foot in the homeland, he spoke with a lilt—a legacy from his immigrant parents, she supposed, or from his short years with Grandmother Rose.

She recalled his blessing on her wedding day. An arm around each of the newlyweds, he'd turned to Michael. "Never let her go, boy. Hold her close."

Perhaps he had wished he'd received similar advice when he had encouraged his wife to visit her Irish family. When the worst had happened.

Rose was close to tears when she entered a lunchroom. She ordered a bowl of soup and a bap with ham. She picked at the meat that hung over the roll, willing herself to stop replaying her inner slide show. "I'm always hanging back, waiting for something to happen in my life," she told her inner judge and jury. "It's not my fault I've got two men interested."

So Michael had arranged for another rose. She'd judged he would have stopped by now, but part of her was relieved. Would he ever give up on her?

After all, she'd traveled nearly halfway around the globe to get away from him. Wasn't it time for him to stop wanting her to return?

"May I sit with you?"

Rose looked at the hand on the back of her chair.

"Claris. Yes, please do."

The women exchanged raised eyebrows and sighed at the same time.

"I owe you an apology, Claris. I created quite a scene. I created several scenes recently. I'm sorry. There's no excuse for being dense and rude. You must have considered me awfully uncivil all this time. And slow."

Claris chuckled. "Just a little."

Rose tossed down her bap. "So much time wasted."

"Not your fault. Will's right. I am too bossy, and I'm always trying to push women on him."

Rose covered her eyes. "I don't know what to say."

Claris handed her a card. "We've got very little time left on this trip. Here's my email in case you want to talk later, maybe while you're with your grandfather. William will be on the lecture circuit, and we plan to visit my niece, but one can always find a way onto the internet. I have to say, I'm a better friend than a sister, and maybe you need one."

∽∾∽

After the long journey to the southern coast, the Shamrocks checked into their hotel next door to the Waterford crystal center. There was just time for Rose and Mildred to stroll around the fine glass exhibits arm in arm. They agreed on the unique beauty of the specimens, and they joked about glass blowers inhaling.

Rose gave Mildred a fond squeeze. "You were right about finding someone new."

"I can't believe you never noticed William sniffing around you."

"What?" Rose tilted her head. "William?" She snorted. "No, I meant you, Mildred."

Afterwards, Rose hurried to the office center at the hotel and snagged a computer. There was a message from her mother in her inbox.

Michael still goes out every night. He looks so clean cut—all dressed up in a suit or open collared shirt with a tie. He's had a fresh haircut, almost the way he wore it at your wedding.

Yesterday a woman drove up to our house, looking for him. Later, I saw them ride away in her Mercedes. Don't know what it means, but he seems to be doing better. More focused. Cling to that thought.

∽∾∽

Rose delayed her reply for later, but she typed out a note to Michael. *Thank you for the rose at Ballyknocken. It is lovely.* She wanted to add, *Does this mean you haven't moved on with someone else? Has there been anyone else?*

Are you still drinking? I wish I knew what was in your mind.
But she didn't.

☙☞☙

Tonight was pub night in a small fishing village. At first, Rose questioned her decision to accompany the group, but why not have some fun? Did she have anything better to do than moon over her past? Wasn't Michael going out with some woman every night? She shoved her hair out of her eyes and clenched her jaw so hard it cracked.

Some of the Shamrocks stayed in for the evening, leaving plenty of empty coach seats. William and Alistair hunkered down next to each other in historical discourse. Rose plopped down in today's assigned seat and slid over to the window. Marge sat down next to Sue, while Justus lingered outside. He hauled himself up the steps—quite a chore for such a massive man. He kept coming down the aisle. There was plenty of room for him to sit alone.

Rose sent a concerned look at Will cater-corner behind her. He caught it and waved. Rose's eyes bored into him. She hoped they conveyed "Save me." She squeezed against the window and averted her eyes.

Justus marshmallowed into two thirds of her double seat. Leaning close to her face, he expostulated about the day's events. His wiry whiskers nearly touched her skin. Her stomach lurched at his reek of sausage and onions and beer. Especially beer. Her eyes were lasers directed just past Justus's right ear at Will. They locked eyes, but he remained in place. Ten long miles to the village of Dunmore East on the southern coast, and all the while Justus never closed his mouth.

After a precipitous ride on a narrow road, the bus descended to the pier, from where they could photograph the harbor, the cliffs, and the village. Justus did not leave her side. Was he stuck? Was it possible the warmth of their bodies had made him wider? His thigh now rested on her lap, and the placement of his arm along the back of her seat gained him even more torso room. Her entire left side now swam in sweat which she couldn't be sure belonged to her.

William looked slightly amused. She stared pointedly at him. Why didn't he leap to her rescue? Michael would have done so.

At last they entered the pub with its thatched roof, where a classical tenor played the guitar and sang. Rose couldn't get into the music, because she kept glaring at William across the bar. Irritation roiled in her head. After she lurched outside to get some air, she approached Gary, who lounged against the bus.

"Guarding the belongings?"

"That's right. Just doddering and having a fag. Why the puss on ya? Don't ya like the music?"

"My mood has been bad since the ride here."

He laughed. "That I could see. Don't mind the eejit. He was just messing with ya, starin' at yer diddies and all, but I thought ya'd eat the head off him." He chuckled deep in his throat. "Anyhow, here comes the chap you wanted to see."

William slouched near the doorway, hands in pockets. He stepped over to her. "Hello, Rose. What brings you out here? I was concerned something was the matter."

She glowered. "You didn't have to worry about me, Will. It's too late now."

His eyes twinkled. "What are you talking about? You had such a good time with your companion on the ride."

She wanted to tie his ears in a knot. "You know I was looking at you for help. You didn't save me."

He looked serious now. "You're right, Rose. I didn't."

"Why not?"

"You didn't need me to rescue you. You know how to save yourself. You just think you don't."

She crossed her arms. "What?"

He moved closer and then stepped back. "Rose, you don't know the power you have."

Later that evening, Rose read Maria's e-mail account of a delivery addressed to Rose at the big house.

"I couldn't believe what I saw when I opened it. Honey, you should look at the website for a picture."

Rose keyed in the URL for a photograph of a multiple-petaled rose, every leaf ridge and fold realistic down into its dewy-looking throat. Waterford crystal.

She laid her head on her arm and cried. "Oh, Michael, will you never give up? You think you have to make me love you again. You don't need to. If only…"

She typed furiously, thanking him for the gift. She assured him she needed a man she could depend on, not one to stuff worry down her throat. *Maybe I can find a man like that again someday, though maybe that ideal died with your drinking. I know I can't go back to the constant upheaval.* She clicked *send* and gave the waste basket under the desk a good kick. She stared at her inbox, shoving her hands into the pocket of her jeans to resist the urge to pull her hair. Then she burst into tears.

She escaped into the elevator. "Dammit, Michael! I shouldn't have said those things. I'm such an ass." Her voice became a soft, fluttery sob. "I'm sorry. I probably hurt you a lot."

That night she dreamed of him with a new woman. She pummeled her pillow, "Who's the slut you're seeing, Michael? We're not divorced. You still belong to me."

ღჯღ

Blarney, Cork, and Garnish Island:

Rose walked through the castle grounds and up to the tower that led to the Blarney Stone.

"Mildred, you shouldn't go up there."

"I can make it."

"I know you can climb the steps, but if you want to kiss

the stone you have to lie with your head in a hole, and people hold your ankles and dangle you down so you can reach it with your lips. Is that what you want?"

Sue made the face of a prune. "Yuck. I heard it reeks of Chapstick. I'll do it, but I feel like wiping my lips with disinfectant afterward."

"I'd want to scrape the skin off my mouth." Mildred retched.

Rose birthed an absent-minded smile as they walked arm in arm to the bus lot. "I don't need to kiss a piece of infectious stone after the kissing I've been through the last eight years."

"You bet. One time Bernie and I—"

"Shh!" Rose held Mildred still. "Look at that. Look into the bus."

"Who is it, Rose? What's he doing?"

"He's going through backpacks, and they can't all be his."

"I wish I could see better. He looks like a big guy. Don't let him see you."

While the bus loaded, Rose held Ally back.

"I saw something on the bus, Ally. I'm pretty sure who the thief is, so—I'd like to talk privately with you at the hotel."

Gary boosted Mildred up the steps. "There ya are, me old flower." Her smile covered her face up to her ears.

The Shamrocks were shocked to hear that Lou had become deathly ill at the gift shop. Gary furnished some of the details. "He had a bad dose. I saw him, weak as a kitten."

Ally pursed her lips. "His wife scolded him while he was puking up a dozen bars of Butler's chocolate. Maybe it was hard on his heart. We can't say anymore just now. All you need to know is that he went to the hospital. He's in no shape to continue the tour."

Whispers went through the coach on the way to Cork.

Rose admired the vista of this sixth century city from across the River Lee—imposing towers and five and six story buildings in every hue. In the town center, they had time to explore the shopping district or find their own lunch. Rose suspected this was a ploy to protect the virginity of Gary's bus toilet in a cubby beneath the rear steps. "I keep her pristine," he'd announced. "Nobody crapped in her yet."

Rose watched her companions disappear in every direction—Saint Finbarre's Cathedral, Shandon Church, Red Abbey. William took off after a taxi, muttering "Saint Anne's Psychiatric."

"That sounded odd." Rose wrinkled her brow.

Ally agreed. "Bang on, it did, but that one's no eejit. Trust it, he knows what he's about."

Gary pocketed his keys. "Well, I'm off to do me messages. The coach is locked."

Rose, Mildred, and a few others set off to find a coffee. Cozy in a couple of adjoining snugs, they sipped coffee with Irish cream in it.

Mildred hugged herself. "These tiny booths are perfect on a chilly day."

Marge acted unusually sociable. "They're perfect for a low-keyed canoodle."

Some speculated that Lou had been the thief, trying for an excuse to get away from the group.

Mildred spoke in an oversized voice. "If he's the one, he's a wanker."

Other patrons looked at her with their mouths agape.

Rose whispered into her ear. "Mildred, do you know what that word means?"

"No, but the young folks say it a lot, just the way I did. A wanker."

The way folks laughed, Rose was sure anyone could tell they were already hammered.

The bar-keep approached. "What's all the ructions, girls? Do I need to call the guards?"

Rose hoped he wasn't serious. All they needed was time in gaol. "Mildred here is eighty-five years old, and she thinks it's time she learned some foul language."

The bartender howled. "In that case, crack on. Here, have a biteen more of the Irish. Better have some crisps, too."

"Does this mean we're on the tear? Even though we're a little mature for it?" Sister Ann's voice was blurry.

"It certainly does, Sister. There's no mistaking it, even if you were as old as the mist. Are ye from the coach around the corner?"

"What coach?" Mildred cooed, fluttering her lashes at him.

"Never mind. You can't walk. It's bucketing down. I'll bring them down the back way. Meanwhile, keep filling yer tanks."

The ladies kept on laughing and pouring Irish cream from a bottle on the table.

The bar-keep's voice sounded near the back door. "Here they are. They've just been acting the maggot. The old one was especially bold. She got quare motherless. Ladies, pull your socks up now." He murmured confidentially, "I guessed they were on holliers from somewhere far from home. America maybe?"

"Something like that." William brought out his wallet.

"No, no, man. It's on me. They brought in people off the street to see them. It's been jammers in here since they started in. Class craic."

The women raised their glasses. "Class craic!"

Chapter 9

Rose figured this was a sort of time out for drunks, the four of them strung out on the back seat of the bus. Giggles fizzled out of them, like gas out of a balloon.

Mildred danced her shoulders to inaudible music. "Hee-heehee! I think the barkeep fancied me. What do you think, Sister?"

"He was pretty well built. Almost as hot as my high school boyfriend."

Rose rubbed her face. "Whoo! Michael never saw me like this."

Mildred gave her a look. "Maybe he should have."

"Maybe. Look at the others, ignoring us. It's amazing how much you can find out about a person from the backs of his ears. Any one of us could be a ruthless criminal."

"I can't believe it." Sister Ann fingered the place where her crucifix used to rest. "Something so wicked lurking amid so many beautiful flowers."

Mildred nodded, a sage expression on her face. "Yes, where you find flowers there are always weeds."

Meredith shed some giggly tears. "Except by now our gardens at home have flowers among the weeds."

Caffeine and booze sloshing in Rose's skull preserved her gray matter in perpetual agitation. She thought about her rose garden at home and the high point of every day when she and Michael used to walk through the waist-high bushes "Oh, Michael, you are the man who made me bloom."

These thoughts brought to mind an afternoon when they had gathered an armload of fifty long-stemmed roses, all of them different. His eyes followed her movements while she arranged them in an oversized pottery vase.

"Rosie, some day you and I will travel to Ireland and purchase a big crystal vase. Then I can look through it while you arrange the roses. Let's pretend."

He stripped her down to her cotton bra and panties and positioned her behind the clumsy vase. "Mmm, I can see you behind there, darling."

Giggles bubbled up through her nose. "You cannot see through pottery, you rogue."

He gave her a promising kiss and removed her brassiere. "Try it now."

She stood behind the vase. "You're so silly. You still can't see me."

He kissed her on both breasts and fingered her nipples. "You're right, the view is much better close up." His voice sounded hoarse now. "Try it again." He skimmed her panties over her feet and dropped them onto the tile. Behind her vase, she quivered, yearning for his next move.

"No good, baby. You're right. I can't see, but what I see in my mind's eye is etched there forever. I will never forget what you look like, even if you go far away."

He covered her body with kisses that burned not only where he placed them, but inside her. "Ah, my Rose!"

She loosened his jeans and took hold of his manhood like a lifeline to still her trembling.

He lifted her, set her on the counter, and coaxed her thighs apart. He explored her with slow fingers.

"Oh, Rosie. I feel you ready for me." He slid her toward him until her personal wetland made contact with his—

"Hey, Rose. Rose!" William called. Time to get off the bus. Come on, girl. "What were you thinking of? We're at the harbor for the boat to Garnish Island. Seals, remember?"

She tottered to the ferries at the Bantry Bay dock.

The prerecorded guide on the ferry skipped every third or fourth word, so that Rose riveted all her attention on deciphering the message. "The Island…Garnish…renowned…gardens…with beautiful…and rare specimens…which survive here, in…mild and rare…"

"My goodness! It's amazing how much one figures out from incomplete clues." Mildred pointed. "Oh, look! Look at the rocks."

A colony of seals basked in the middle of the bay. Some of them barked and skittered about. They made her think of Puppy Joe, good for one last play session at bed time and then stretched out at the foot of their bed while Michael drew her into his arms.

Rose hugged herself, dragged back to the here and now out of remembered heat.

Mildred continued on her philosophic bent. "Strange things come up when you're not expecting them." She pointed at the croupy animals. "Smell their fishy breath?"

"Harbor seals." Justus hovered behind Rose's ear.

She shuddered. "Mildred, you make such astute remarks."

❧❧❧

An hour later, Rose and William strolled along gravel paths on Garnish Island.

"Will, I never saw anything so lush as this walled garden. Look at these enormous hydrangeas." The garden's competing colors thrilled her artist's heart and overwhelmed her senses. There were too many flowers to take in properly. At least the wall lent boundaries to this lushness. Four…no, five layers of textures and colors organized themselves into tiers, from climbers to the shortest of borders.

Yet the scene was like a canvas painted with finger paint, its wrongness nagging at her heart.

These trails brought to mind paths she'd hiked at Rainbow Springs Park or Shalom Gardens, with Michael beside her. His tight t-shirt set off his biceps. His jeans fit his lanky legs and narrow hips so that her thighs wanted to rub against his with each stride. Her hands yearned to brush against denim. He'd thrown an arm around her shoulders, his slender wrist and long fingers dangling in her sight, teasing her with what they might do against her skin. His lips brushed her ear when he whispered, and his laugh rang out, sending joy singing into her heart. He looked into her eyes, blue on blue, in a way that smoldered down to her toes.

Michael was the man who should inhabit this panorama with her, but he wasn't here. Damn him for ruining it for her.

William stopped. She was sure he saw her distress. "Will—I—"

He held out a hand to stop her lips. "Rose, I can see this garden doesn't mean the same thing to you as it does to me." He searched her face, as if looking for something to contradict him. "Come on, let's find a place where we can sit down."

A short stroll brought them to the Italian Garden, where a stone folly overlooked the mountains. They sat on steps that flanked the reflecting pool.

"Rose, I told you about my wife. Now it's your turn. I know why you left Michael. Tell me why you wanted to stay, why you did stay a long time despite the trouble." He paused. "Tell me why you loved him...love him...because I know you still do."

Pain shone in his eyes. His voice on the brink of tears brought a lump to her throat, but none of that could hold her back once she breathed in his invitation to indulge herself.

With a cleansing sigh, she blurted out everything she'd wanted to repress. "From the moment we met I adored Michael. I loved the way he looked at me and reached out for me. I couldn't stop looking at him, and I wanted to touch him all the time." She snagged a quick breath before racing on. "I loved his funny antics and the way he laughed. I adored the way he listened, the way he understood. He filled me up with new animation. I lived for the way he drank me in and never got enough. I loved our arguments...and making up. I was in heaven when we made Rosebud, and even the grief of losing her made me love him more." Rose's voice broke, and she shook her head. "It would take forever to tell you everything."

She covered her face with her palms. "It kills me to give him up. I'm beginning to think I'll always love Michael. I just can't have him."

She saw the tears in William's eyes and warmed to him. "You made me realize my life isn't over, William. But there's a big chunk of it missing."

He rubbed his eyes. "Rose, let me tell you something." His voice was thick. "I lost my wife abruptly. I never had a chance to say goodbye. It was worse than if she'd left me and allowed me to hate her. I missed finding closure somehow." He gritted his teeth. "It's essential to say goodbye and know you mean it. Did you do that with Michael?" He peered into her face. "Did you?"

"I told him I couldn't be with him now that his drinking was his primary love. It was like a piranha nibbling at us every day. I got out before it killed everything, even our memories."

"Did you mean what you told him? A hundred percent?"

"Yes, I did—I thought I meant it." She felt her certainty drain away.

"My dad says I've got to live my life, and he's right. He says I can move on and love someone new. Do you think that's true, William? Do you think it's that way for you?"

He gnawed on a callus on his thumb, stoppering his mouth. "Yes, a person can travel forward, but only...but only if the other train on his track has really left the station."

They perused their reflections in the pool. "Look, Rose. Can you really see yourself with anyone else? Do you really know what you want?"

"I know I like you, William. You get me, and I enjoy being with you."

"Yes. But don't I deserve more? Don't you?"

တာတ

All the way back to the hotel, Rose reviewed what she
was going to say to Michael. She raced to the occupied
computer room, where pacing back and forth felt like wearing a track straight to Hell in the carpet. She had to get away
from the brink.

She took the elevator to her floor and peered at herself in
the long mirror at the end of the hall. She stepped closer,
staring into her own eyes until she imagined they were Michael's, the same blue as hers.

She sobbed softly. "Oh, Michael. Rosebud would have
had the same eyes. I know what I dream about, Michael,
and it's not this life."

She let tears fall, trying her best to keep them quiet. "Often enough I've listed the things I won't put up with…the
drinking, the closed off anger, you not telling me what's
wrong." She shrugged, cutting off her list. "What's killing
me is the desire to tell you…what I do want."

She failed to connect by phone. She raced downstairs.
The now available computer pulled her in like a confession-
al. She felt ready—compelled—to tell Michael what she
really wanted to say, including how hard it was to live without him. She had it all in her mind, as if she'd been writing
the script for months.

"How could you ruin what we had? How could you not
love me enough to throw away the viper that sucked us dry?
I'm so mad at you, but I need to be mad with you. With
you—you hear? Not away from you. I need to tell you about
Rosebud, and you'd better damn well listen." Oh yes, she
was ready.

She wiped her sweaty palms on her jeans. Even so, her

trembling fingers slipped on the keys when she tried to type. She started over, entering her message box first, before tackling her mission.

An email from Michael awaited her. She read it fast, panting and without comprehension. She ached so horribly with longing she couldn't think. Then she took a deep breath and read it again.

Dear Rose,

Thank you for being so patient with me. You gave me time to indulge my fantasy of winning you back. Remember our game of storming the castle? Well, you're not the kind of stone and mortar I can conquer anymore, but a flesh and blood woman with a mind of your own. My heart is bleeding with love, but I can't force you to put up with the unforgivable things I've done and the foolishness I might subject you to again.

Maybe you thought you didn't make your intentions clear to me. Be assured, I understood you. I just didn't want to listen. I do owe it to you to take you seriously. I just didn't want to believe you would walk away for good.

None of this was your fault, Rosie. It wasn't you who prolonged our agony. You did what you had to do. And I did what I had to do. I'm sorry if I put you through too much. I had to try.

You remember we always wanted to travel? Well, I'm going away. I notified the firm, and I'm going to see some of the world while I wean myself from our old happy surroundings. I'll take a break from social media for a while, too, so I'm not tempted to contact you.

This is the only way I'll get over you, Rose. For the first time, I see I have to get past our marriage, our house, our garden…everything I loved.

I hope knowing what I intend to do will make it easier for you to move on and give you a chance to live the life you want. Be happy.

Love, Michael

Rose pounded the desk, struggling to regain her breath. "No! Nooo," she wailed. A lead curtain closed on her life. She clutched her fists to her raging chest.

This is what I asked for—but it's not what I want.

When Rose opened her eyes the next morning, they felt swollen, and her whole being hurt. When the truth hit, it was corrosive acid. She muffled her weeping with her pillow, turning herself inside out with sobs. She took her time with self-pity, for her actions had destroyed the meaning of future tense. No need to act as though she were part of the living, breathing world. Besides, this was a free morning in Killarney, with no one to see her falling to pieces.

Then she remembered the meeting.

છ∂છ∂

When Rose showed up at Ally's room, Justus was already there. That sight made her knees buckle. What had made her get in over her head like this? She grasped the end of the table, drawing herself up straight.

Her mind cleared. Of course she could handle him. Never again would she kow-tow to an overbearing presence. She stepped forward, making her voice firm. "Justus."

"Hello, Rose." He double locked the door behind her.

"What are you doing? Unlock that door."

He brought out a tolerant smile. "Pipe down, Rose. You've caused me enough trouble. Here, take this. Put it where it belongs later today."

It was an antique wedding ring.

Ally's voice sounded from the bathroom. "Do take a seat, Rose. Justus will fill you in. Listen carefully."

છ∂છ∂

The Ring of Kerry:

After lunch, the Shamrocks piled into the bus, what was

left of them. Ally announced that, in addition to their previous losses, another Shamrock had ended up in the hospital during the night. The two sisters had also come down with a virus. It was a shame Jocelyn must go home without her recently lost gold earrings.

Today's new seat assignment brought Rose close to the front once more. Alistair was now in front of her beside Mildred, whose jacket hung over the back of her seat.

Rose had her eye on it.

By the end of the afternoon, the Shamrocks had experienced the mountain scenery on the Ring of Kerry.

Mildred gripped Alistair's arm. "My, that was inspiring, but I would have liked to go all the way through the Gap in the mountains. Preferably in a jaunting car. Don't you think so, Alistair?" The way she looked at him from under her lashes made her young in Rose's eyes.

"Yes, a funny name for a horse cart, though. And today's excursion should definitely take longer than one afternoon. We didn't need the shopping morning."

"Speak for yourself." Paddy sported a new conservative tweed jacket with jeans.

Claris turned up her nose. "Well, I'm in mourning. We didn't stop at the lace-making center, and that was going to be a high point for me."

Finally, Ally broke up the melee. "And now we're approaching Muckross House, sixty-five rooms of gorgeous Elizabethan Revival, where we'll have our tea. We need it."

In the car park at Muckross House, Mildred took Rose's arm. "I've never seen such a grand house."

Rose offered her arm. "And now we have to walk down that long drive between those trees. Do you think we can make it, Mildred?"

"Don't worry, Rose. I'll hold you up."

"What were you two talking about today, with your heads so close?"

"Oh, not much. Alistair told me about his farm and how he's sold off most of the cattle now that he's getting older.

Did you know he's only eight years younger than I am?" Mildred looked up with a twinkle in her eye.

"You like him, don't you?"

"Well, maybe he thinks I have money."

They had a good laugh at this idea.

"Anything else? I'm sure your conversation wasn't merely about cattle."

"His son can take his dog anytime he wants to travel." Mildred bowed her head. "He wants to visit me in Sidney."

Rose hugged her. "Way to go, Mildred."

They wound their way through the gardens to the back of the house, where a glass facade enclosed a tea room. They wiggled into overstuffed chairs around a low tea table.

Mildred fixed Rose with a firm eye. "Your turn. What happened?"

Rose told her about Michael's departure and how she had realized the truth about herself too late.

"I've ruined everything, Mildred, even worse than Michael did with his drinking. At least that was an affliction we could have dealt with together. I was just plain stupid running away."

"But, Rose, you said he wouldn't admit he needed help."

"I know, but that was then. I hear he's been going to Alcoholics Anonymous meetings every day." She reached out her hands in helplessness.

Gary emerged behind her. "So, your man's having a recalibration, and now he's legged it."

"Does everyone know my business?"

"Well, we're not dense. Everyone knows you're keen on him, and your resolve to stay off him is as small as a mouse's diddy. You should just find the lad and go at it."

Ally poked him. "Lay off, Gary. Can't ya see she's mortified with your talk?"

"Jaysus, I'll lump off then."

"No, Gary." Rose reached for his arm. "You're right. Can you sit down here and tell me what else I should do?"

"We're not allowed to eat with ye, no, but if ya see me in

the garden that's a different situation. I've got stories for ya all right."

At that moment, Alistair strode up to Mildred and offered his arm. "Care for a stroll before the rain starts? Look, you can see the lake from here." He wiggled his eyebrows at her, and she laughed. "The grounds are lovely."

Gary looked personally responsible. "That's right. It's because the muck around here is so good."

Mildred swallowed the rest of her tea, stood up, and shoved her leftover scone into her deep jacket pocket. She blanched and staggered. "My—my—"

Gary stepped forward. "What is it, missus?"

"My—It's—"

Her hand drew out a bit of platinum and fire.

"It's my ring."

That night at dinner the Shamrocks celebrated Mildred's discovery with wine all around.

❧❧❧

The coach drove them to Tralee to attend the National Folk Theater's presentation about an Irish girl who seeks a better life in New York. Rose wondered what her grandfather had found to keep him in Ireland. Something more precious than his family?

It was late when the Shamrocks returned to their hotel. They murmured hurried goodnights and scattered to their rooms. As she flew to the business office, Rose's mind was on the possible contents of her e-mail account. She felt a little breathless as she tapped the keys that might connect her with Michael. Nothing.

She checked her sent messages to review how she had answered Michael's goodbye missive of the previous night. She typed an urgent follow-up.

Michael, stop! Don't go away. I want you to be there

when I get home. I am not having the easy time of it you im-
agine. I need your help.

I should have known it all along—I can't get over you
without you. I know that sounds crazy, but please write
back. I don't know how to do this anymore.

I still love you.
Rose

Next she entered the addresses of both her parents, turning for comfort to those she had always been able to count
on.

Mom and Dad,
I have news for you, and it doesn't make me happy. Mi-
chael wrote that he's going on a long trip. What do you
know about this?

I hope you get this message soon, because I am beside
myself.

Love, Rose

Almost at once, a message from her father popped up.

Dear Rose,
Michael doesn't seem to be around any longer, honey.
He came to us last night and gave us the same news you got.
When I checked his house at daybreak, it was locked up,
and his car was gone.

He can't have gone far. He took the dog.
Love, Dad

That night Rose set her alarm earlier than needed for the
morning's departure, so she could get an early crack at the
computer. A message from her mother awaited her.

Dear Rose,
Still no Michael. Last night the woman who picks him up
stopped at the house wondering where he was. I'm afraid I

gave her a hard time. I demanded to know who she was and why it was her business.

"Why? Didn't he tell you?" she said. "My husband's his sponsor. He goes to meetings right from work. We live down the road from you, so Michael and I drive together."

Sorry, darling. Try not to worry.

෧෨෧

Dingle Peninsula:

The next morning, Justus was last into the bus. He was clean shaven, well-dressed, and fifty pounds thinner, with elegant manners and a well-modulated voice. Rose watched the Shamrocks' reactions, smirking to see all the mouths hanging open.

Justus took the microphone. "Good morning. I want to reintroduce myself. I am your bus line's detective, and this is my associate Max."

Max wore a suit and tie with thick glasses. He was shaven, except for his white neck whiskers. When the Shamrocks recognized him, a collective gasp sounded. "Yes, it's me, out from undercover. I can tell you it was hell getting my ears pierced for the role, but we really got into it." He gestured toward Justus with his thumb. "Thank God, I didn't have to wear a fat suit like the boss there."

A smattering of laughter went through the coach.

"The company has watched your thief for a long time now, especially after he or she pilfered a duchess's million dollar ring. We've caught the culprit, who is off to gaol."

Justus gave a bow. "I want to apologize for playing my part so disgustingly well and also for entering some of your rooms in my search, though I had a warrant. It wasn't personal, but I did find some interesting…uh…souvenirs in your luggage. I hope they work on the current in your home country."

Mildred tittered. "Hee-hee! Nice of you to mention it."

Alistair put his arm around her when she blushed. "That's my girl. Always resourceful."

Justus cleared his throat. "Now then, we have retrieved stolen valuables found in the thief's luggage. Photographs of the items are circulating around the bus. If you recognize your property, please write your name on the back. No duplicate signatures, I hope." He scowled like a lord.

Mildred glowered. "You. It was you who put my ring in my pocket. Trying to make me think I was nuts."

He kissed her hand and winked at Rose. "It was a pleasure."

"Who was the thief?" Several Shamrocks clamored at once.

"I'm not supposed to tell you, but you can guess. You can take your pick from all the people no longer with you."

A cheer went up through the bus. "Yay, Justus."

"If you don't mind, I'm going to see you through to the airport at Shannon. Oh, and I am not married to Max."

There was plenty of laughter that day, and much speculation as they wound their way through the Dingle Peninsula. It let Rose shift her mind away from her tortured heart.

℘ℵ℘

Rose scampered to the computer room. "Got it," she mouthed, as she slid into the chair and logged on. "Come on, Michael. Stop getting even with me."

She let out a shriek. There was no message from Michael, except notice of the suspension of his e-mail and Facebook accounts.

Her father's message asked if she could leave the tour early to start her journey to Grandfather's home. "You know he hasn't contacted the family for a while, and now he hasn't answered queries from his bank. He's going through his money fast. Can you help extricate him from this mess when you see him? Very worried about the old boy."

Michael was an attorney and an MBA too. He would know what to do, but she had driven him off the face of the earth, hadn't she? What kind of dimwit would do that? She clenched her fists and moaned. "Michael! Damn it, Michael!"

Rose caught up with Ally and Gary in the bar, and told them what she needed to do. Ally called for a limousine to take her to the car rental booth at Shannon airport early in the morning.

Rose let herself down on a stool. "There's one thing I don't understand about you two. You always have such strong accents when you're with the group, but you don't speak that way without us."

"Well, madam," Gary explained in his Oxford best. "The tourists expect it, you know."

On the way back from dinner that night, the Shamrocks sang all the folk songs they'd learned on the bus. Then people scattered to their rooms. Rose lingered on the hotel forecourt while several of her companions dispensed a hug or a handshake.

Mildred embraced her, whispering. "I'll say goodbye now, Rose. Sorry, I won't be in my room later tonight."

Rose giggled and then sobbed. "Oh, Mildred, you taught me so much. Thank you—and be happy."

When she turned back to the lobby, William stood in her path. He spoke with a quavering voice. "Goodbye, Rose."

The tenderness in his turquoise eyes melted her heart. She stood on tiptoe to wrap her arms around his neck, while he adjusted his height to her embrace. His day-end whiskers pressed against her cheek, stiff but soft.

"Goodbye, William." She kissed his cheek. When she opened her eyes, he was gone. Just like that. "Goodbye, Scarecrow," she whispered. "I'll miss you most of all."

Part III
The Search

Clifden, Ireland

Chapter 10

June:

The rented Fiat lacked pep, but it carried Rose uneventfully to Galway on the N18. She was determined to sort Grandfather out and high tail it home to the ranch.

By the time she got there, Michael would have returned, and they could talk things out face to face, as never before. She played over the moment when she would step up to their little house and catch him unawares on the porch, an errant forelock intruding on his forehead and his sparkling eyes arresting as ever. She imagined the shock and joy on his handsome face, lined with suffering on her account.

William had been right. She had never faced Michael down the way she should have done if she meant their separation to be final. So many issues remained in shadows, while she foundered in a murky quagmire of *poor me*. Why his need to be the alpha hero in their role play? Why the compulsion to mourn alone?

For God's sake, was he afraid of real life?

She wielded a mental axe against his bottles of beer and whiskey. The liquid morphed into his oozing tears, which he concealed by turning away. She shouted at a sheep on the verge. "Take that, Michael! Take that!"

She pounded the steering wheel. Now that she was set on tearing all obstacles out of her way, nothing could best her desire. Not an ocean. Not a whiskey bottle. Not a role-playing macho man wanna-be.

A wrong turn at Salthill took her onto the ocean road, an alternate route toward Connemara. Her guidebook promised cliff top views over the sea ahead. Narrow byways called her to tiny towns with Gaelic names. She patted the dashboard in memory of Rosebud's sticker in a poor, totaled car consigned to a junkyard somewhere. She spoke to the child who had died in that car. "Everything I do from now on is for our family, Rosebud, though your daddy doesn't know it." Was she the only one who still thought of them as the triple shamrocks? Did Michael still doodle the three-lobed heart? She cast off a tear with her hand, pressed her lips together, and depressed the accelerator.

On the cliffs near Spiddel she got out to stretch her legs and let her gaze wander over the seascape, with its view of the Aran Islands. The "Awk-awk-awk" of sea birds faded before they dived into the sea, whose sinuous voice overlaid everything, like the sound of a mother's heartbeat in utero. Had her pulse, in fact, comforted Rosebud?

The Cliffs of Moher, great, peaceful titans, lay in the distance, She thought again of little Colin running into her arms at the cliff edge. She'd taken that incident as a sign of her mission to find her true north, and her time with the Shamrocks had pointed her in a surprising direction. She lifted her chin to the wind. Her sigh blew away on a puff of sea air.

"You still belong to me, Rosebud, and I'm going to get your daddy back too." Elevating her face to the breeze, she spread her arms as if to lift off from the cliff and soar above the surf, making love to the rocks below. "Don't worry, honey. I know I can't fly, but I can walk. I can plod. I can even crawl if I have to. I'll get us where we need to be."

It was all so simple here. The crash and susurrations of the sea. The whisper of air both cold and soft. The salty smell of...what? Blood? Life-giving fluid within the sea's womb? She wanted to tell Rosebud how women crouch and clutch their thighs, gritting their teeth to bring forth new life. "Thank you, Rosebud, for giving me that know-how." She would be talking to her baby girl the rest of her life.

She blew a kiss into the air and drove off toward Clifden, home of Grandfather's ancestors. They had lived and died working in the Irish horse breeding industry, without owning any of it. She felt them in the wind. How glorious the Connemara cliffs would be for riding. She had tended horses all her life, most of it without riding. She had to get past her emotional baggage to reclaim the Flanagan spirit.

Though it was only late morning, the sea air had made her peckish. Her boxed lunch aboard, she turned onto a small road that led to a dirt parking lot When she'd finished her boiled egg and roll, she searched out an appropriate bit of cover. A short way into the weeds and nettles stood two trees entwined. Stepping closer, she saw what gave the trees their shimmer.

Little pieces of ribbon and paper covered the leaves and twigs. Each carried a prayer or wish. Baby shoes hung there too, along with lockets, photographs, and locks of hair in ribbons.

"A fairy tree. How perfect." She tugged a length of toilet paper out of her pocket and tied it around a small branch. "See that, Rosebud? I promise I'll come back again with the words to my own fairy wish. And you know what that will be."

e/∂e/∂

Rose reached Clifden in the early afternoon and made her way straight to a bakery for raisin scones, her grandfather's favorite. The town made a different impression from the last time she'd been here, on the tour.

The baker rubbed his gnarled hand over his mouth.

"Flanagan. I know the house. The heir from America took it over. Plenty from here went over the water in the bad times, and plenty from there came back, even those that were born on the other side." He tapped the side of his nose. "Always thinking they have the true Irish in them." He coughed out a dry laugh and scribbled directions to Grandfather's address. "Just over two hundred souls in that neighborhood. Hope you get along with all of them."

The true Irish. Something Grandfather would say.

Her drive through Clifden complete for now, she took the 341 south and then a small offshoot to Ardbear Cottage. "What an odd name for a village or hamlet, whatever it is." At last she reached the address she'd been looking for. The driveway reached up to the house. No grass. No bushes. *Pretty secluded*, she texted Aidan.

She heel-toed up to the front door and knocked repeatedly. It didn't feel as if Grandfather expected her, though both she and Aidan had left voice mail messages. It was so like him to be out gallivanting. She stepped to the windows to look for signs of life, but, like sunglasses, curtains kept a person from seeing the eyes that looked back. Her heart thumped an irregular beat. What if Grandfather were lying in there dead or helpless?

He had always left an extra house key in the farthest bush from the front door, the fifth on the left at home. What about here, with no foundation plantings? Several feet away lay a dead hydrangea in a capsized flower pot. Pure Grandfather Sean to purchase items that struck his fancy but fail to care for them.

She poked inside the leaves of the plant. She fingered the dirt in the pot. A bit of metal poked out of the hole in the bottom. Knocking the plant from the pot, she darted with her prize to the door. Within a minute she was inside, a white cat behind her.

She hurried through the sitting room, kitchen, and bedroom on the ground floor and then mounted the steep staircase to check out bedrooms above. Back downstairs, she threw open the door to the bedroom closet. Not much in the way of clothes.

She took a shaky breath. "Grandfather, where are you?" She knew not a soul heard her.

A cupboard door slammed. Someone was in the house after all. She followed a draft from the kitchen. To her relief, the window giving onto the vegetable garden stood wide open, and the back door swung in the breeze. She raised both fists to her head. "Grandfather! Where did you go? What were you thinking?"

A circuit around the garden revealed nothing except the white feline rolling in a patch of catnip. Garden tools stuffed the shed. No fertilizer, though the vegetables bespoke faithful care. At least she would not starve here.

A barn at the rear of Grandfather's plot showed recent signs of horses. A dung heap occupied the far corner of the fence near an open gate. "Aha! Manure!"

What if an assailant had murdered Grandfather for his clothes and wallet and hid his body somewhere near the house? That would explain the slightly *off* stench. What if he'd escaped with the horses through the back gate to the woods?

She drew several deep breaths to quiet herself before picking her way through the garden patch.

At the living room desk, she failed to find Grandfather's personal effects. She tried to order her memories of the things he always carried whenever he left the house. His phone. His wallet. Yes. She recalled how he used to tease her, urging her to unload his pockets until she found a peppermint. His small notebook! Waking or sleeping, he always kept it near him. "I'm so forgetful. This is the only memory I've got," he used to say, usually tweaking her nose in jest.

She wiped a hand over her eyes. She dropped down on the coverlet on Grandfather's bed. In that position, her eyes met the bedside table.

"Mmm...the notebook. There it is." She curled her lips.

"Evidence of speedy departure, Grandfather? You'll be back."

Her weary bones took grateful possession of the bed.

ოაოა

The scraping of metal on moist glass grated on Rose. Skritch-skreeech! Rude. She fought her way out of her slumber. Grandfather's notebook reminded her where her train of thought had left off. She wrapped her hands around an oversized flashlight from the dresser the way he had taught her to grip a bat. She scuffed her socks on the floor like dust rags as she slid toward the door. That cat better not be sharpening its claws on her suitcase.

Nothing in sight in the living room. Cautious now. Step...step. Wow, what a stench coming from the kitchen. She scratched her sweating palms. She rounded the desk toward the kitchen arch and raised her torch as two booted feet and kneeling jeans came into view.

Rose waved the flashlight, though the torso and head that belonged to the kneeling limbs were wedged into the refrigerator. "What's going on here?"

The bonk of scalp on metal came from inside the appliance, followed by a high-pitched voice. "Holy shit!"

"Come out of there, unless you're trying to kill yourself in the wrong appliance." Her imagination hesitated. Could you do that in a gas fridge?

"You'd better get out of here," ordered a disembodied voice.

A rotund belly in a flannel shirt backed out, along with a comely face, its strands of blonde hair escaping from a rubber band in all directions. The eyebrows lowered over turquoise eyes underlined the scratchy words. "I'm pissed."

"Why? I can see you're up to no good. Something stinks in there. Maybe you stuffed the dog inside?"

The figure on the floor lifted out a decomposing trout by

the tail and plopped it on the floor. "Is this yours? Have you been squatting here? You'd better run away before I call the police. And take this carcass with you. After you help me up off the floor. Ooof! Shit!"

Rose's eyes stared, and her jaw sagged, but her feet didn't move.

"Come on. Drop that ridiculous torch and give me a hand. I wouldn't have had to get down here if you hadn't stunk up the house."

"Oh-my-God-oh-my-God-oh-my-God!" The flashlight clattered to the floor. "Stay, stay there. Oh, my God." She inhaled deeply. "Are you okay?" She saw the answer by the murderous cast in the visitor's eye. "Take it easy. Give me the fish."

Rose grabbed the rotting hunk of protoplasm by the tail. It fixed her with a viscous eye. The cat right behind her, she tossed the offending object out into the vegetable garden. She grabbed a shovel that leaned against the house and spaded it under.

Her guest sprawled against the refrigerator, a *why-don't-you-kill-me-now* look in her eye. "I emptied out everything else. You could have taken the garbage bag out to the can while you were making heroic with the fish."

Rose moved the bag to the back door. "Come on. Let's get you off the floor."

"Shit, no, I may as well finish this bottom shelf. Once I'm up, I'm up." After a histrionic groan, she turned her sudsy steel wool pad to the glass shelf. Meanwhile Rose found a way to prop the door open.

All in all, to Rose's way of thinking, the refrigerator woman proved amazingly limber in her condition, and Rose provided minimal help to a chair at the kitchen table. Rose took the adjacent seat. "You'd better explain what you're up to here."

The blonde woman made a moue of irritation. "You're the intruder. You explain."

Rose sighed. She filled the kettle and put it on the gas.

The blonde's expression softened. She struggled out of her plaid shirt and revealed a svelte figure in a t-shirt, except for her baby bump. "Oh, well, I'm the do-for woman of the gentleman who lives here. I'm Bridey."

"I'm Rose. I'm his grand-daughter."

Bridey's eyes flickered to a framed picture on the desk. "Shit!"

"Why do you always say that? I thought the Irish youth always said *fock or feck*."

"The coarse buggers. Half of them don't even know or care what that actually means." She loosened her hair band, letting her straight, fine hair fall around her shoulders. "Shit! I'm not Irish." She dropped her accent. "I just married a big, dumb, Irish sex maniac." She scratched her head. "And he's the reason I'm so irritable."

The tea water boiled and Rose grabbed the bag from the bakery and shoved it toward Bridey. "Do you like raisin scones?"

Thank Heaven Grandfather kept tea. Good strong black Irish tea, high test. They drank cup after cup until they achieved the proper wide-awake buzz. They filled up on scones and licked their fingers. The cat stole his share.

໕ເ໕ເ໕

"What's the cat's name?"

"Pickles, he likes to lick out pickle jars."

"So." Rose positioned an impish quirk onto her lips. "You know Grandfather. Prove it."

They traded epic tales about him until the bag was empty and even Rose's belly felt bloated. "I feel like a raisin with all the wrinkles soaked out. Raisin bloat."

"Huh…you should try the blueberry scones next time. Blueberry bloat."

"Blueberry bloat." Rose mimicked intoxication.

They giggled until Bridey declared her belly stuck under the table.

"Well, then, as we've talked ourselves into the evening, you'd better stay the night and talk some more. I already know your husband isn't living at home."

Bridey gave her a skeptical look.

"Well, you're alone at this hour, right? We have lots of room upstairs."

Bridey opened her mouth to object, but Rose struck the coup de gras. "Guess what I found in the cupboard—cans of American baked beans. Grandfather loves them."

"They should do well with the bloat we already have."

Bridey talked about her Irish husband, whom she had met at an American university. He'd graduated, and she'd dropped out to follow him back to his hometown. They'd traded the news of her pregnancy and of his enlistment on the same day, and he'd deployed overseas two weeks later. She rubbed her arms.

"Turns out, since his dad was American, he's got dual citizenship, like my baby will have. He'd joined the American marines. Before long he told me he'd gotten a posting to the Middle East. Somewhere. Top secret." She waved her hand vaguely. The dumb shit should have known that had to be dangerous. You just know he's in a war zone doing something heroic, damn it!"

To Rose, Bridey's cross demeanor looked like fancy dress covering her worry. Rose spoke a little of her own marriage, but directed attention mostly to the mystery of Grandfather's whereabouts.

"Shit! I certainly don't know where he went, but he's been gone a long time, I know that for sure. Maybe a week or more, given the state of that fish. Too bad he couldn't have given it to the cat."

"Speaking of which, through the window I can see the little bugger digging up the garden."

"Oh, shit! He'll be sick."

They raced outside and pounced on the purloining pussy. They positioned several garden pots on top of the fishy burial site and carried the offending feline into the house, where they closed the windows and treated their scratched arms with rubbing alcohol.

Pickles slept all night on Rose's bed. "Silly cat!" Rose scolded. You smell like rotten fish." He burped and cuddled close. Under the covers, she grinned.

ೋೋೋ

After its morning bath, the cat sat on the living room window seat grooming itself.

"Well, Pickles, you don't stink now. That's important if you can't stay out of my bed. I'd still rather have Grandfather's border collie, seeing as he had to leave one pet home." A feline was useful for talking to, but not as good as a dog. She missed Puppy Joe like an absent toe.

"I can't get over Michael taking Puppy. Maybe he's going to snap his picture all over the world and send the photos in order to twist the knife into my belly." Senior citizens came to mind—the ones she'd witnessed snapping photos of their grandchild's stuffed toy at famous sites, in order to e-mail the pictures as a *wish you were here*. Michael got his mind around fanciful ideas all right. Just now she wouldn't mind the snapshots.

The cat hissed at a fly.

"Don't talk like that, Pickles. I'm right. Men take the most surprising things with them and leave even more important things behind. I never thought Michael would leave his garden untended."

Pickles kneaded the spot where the fly carcass lay.

Grandfather had prized one possession most. Rose's mind fastened on that now. He'd told her he always stashed it in a hidden compartment in his desk. "Grandmother consigned it to his keeping when she came to Ireland, and he took it with him when he moved over here," she informed the cat. "I know, because I looked for it at home." She scratched the cat's ears. He rubbed his cheeks against her hand.

She examined the drawers and underside of the desk and did find a secret niche. An empty niche. She was sure he would never risk losing that precious link to Grandmother, though she'd left him over fifty years ago. Would he carry it around in his pocket?

Rose paced. "Oh, Granddad, now I know you met with foul play. God help me. How can I brood about my own problems when you may be in danger?"

She dialed nine-nine-nine.

An hour later, Rose snapped the dust rag at Pickles, while Bridey ran the dry mop over the wood floor. "I know about your grandmother's wedding ring, Rose." He showed it to me often, and—you're right—he would never jeopardize his one treasure. It meant everything to him."

"So I was right to call the police?"

"You bet. That old fool's life may not be at risk, but he's up to no good."

Rose couldn't help scowling. "What a thing to say! A little respect for an old man, please."

"You don't believe me? Shit!" Bridey brandished the mop at the cat, to stop him clawing at a corner of the rug. "Come see what I found in his bedroom closet."

Side by side they peered inside. Bridey shoved Grandfather's left-behind clothes aside. A white muslin and lace nightgown and robe hung on a rack to the rear.

❧☙

Rose felt shut in without the rental car. Besides, the canned beans were gone, and, what with the quantity of vegetables she had consumed, she felt in need of a shopping trip in town. So she hauled Grandfather's bike out of the shed and pumped up the tires.

The police officer on duty had taken the news of Grandfather's disappearance lightly. "See, he's taken his clothes, but not all of them. He's not walking around in the nip. That means a journey but not a move. He forgot his notebook and his fish. That speaks to the old gentleman's cognitive state. Still, dense as he may be, he's obviously got an oul doll someplace, so you can't say he's not the full shilling."

Rose took her suspicions to all her near neighbors. Some shared a dismal view of Grandfather's survival chances. Others warmed to the possibility of a kidnapping. A few assumed he'd gone off with a local spinster, while others made thin lips and gave neither information nor opinion. Meanwhile, Rose drank tea from porcelain teacups in parlors kept for visitors. If nothing else, it was good to know her neighbors.

"So it's nice you met some people your own age. Any eccentrics in the neighborhood? I think I know the answer." Bridey pursed her lips in a smirk.

"Well, one lady says Grandfather promised to marry her."

"Who was that? Lydia about quarter of a mile down on the other side?"

Rose nodded. "It was. She was so sad. I really don't want to gossip about her."

"No, me neither. Lydia has been crazy for every man since her husband died in the Falkland war."

"It would be terrible to lose one's spouse in battle." When Bridey teared up, Rose clasped her friend's hands. "Oh, Bridey, I'm sorry I said that. Truly. I'm an idiot."

"It's something I have to face. We all have something to bear, don't we? " She looked closely into Rose's eyes. "I can see it's good for you to have a friend to talk to. I suspect you didn't do that much before."

"No, and it probably wasn't good for me to be tucked away on the ranch without girlfriends." She concealed her mouth behind her hands before lowering her shoulders with a sharp sigh.

"I just married Michael so young—too young, I guess— but what could I do when our grand passion took over? He took up most of my time, even when he wasn't there. You know, playing housewife, exercising the figure, sketching babies. I had my work on the ranch, but my concentration was elsewhere. I should have had a sister or an aunt. You know—more females around. Feminine teasing."

"I'm lucky to have a wonderful aunt. I wish I could share her with you. You'll love her when you meet her."

Rose had already met more delightful Clifden people than she'd imagined, like the lady who worked in the art shop. "You should meet her, Bridey. Gwen's a fifty year resident of Cliffden. Crinkly blue eyes and gray hair streaked with red. A natural woman with clay up to her wrists."

"Gwen stopped what she was doing when I told her about Puppy Joe. She took this as a sign, for she'd just finished sculpting such an animal. 'I saw a little dog like that recently, in town with his master,' she told me. 'I knew I was meant to capture him in clay—the dog, not the man.' You should have heard her laugh at her own wit, Bridey, the way my dad does." Rose paused in her story, gazing off to a place far away, where she imagined Aidan leaning against the paddock gate, his face split by a belly-buster.

She cleared her throat. "Anyway, Gwen gave the little figure to me. I'm to go back to the shop when I want to paint it." Rose's smile opened like a flower. "I'm going to do that. I'll enjoy making the statue look just like Puppy. That was nice of Gwen—to give it, and to understand what it would mean to me. I appreciate her."

Later she met with a gaggle of new girlfriends. "I'm sorry to dominate the conversation today. I just miss Puppy Joe so much lately. My poor boy was so wonderful to me when I needed him. We never enjoyed enough good times together, when he was still a pup, before I had to leave." She sighed deeply. "I suppose you all think I'm being silly."

Someone remembered observing a similar dog lately. "I wonder if that's the one your friend noticed. He was with a bearded, scruffy-haired guy. A stranger."

Rose's breath caught, and then she blurted out the name always close to her heart. "Was it Michael?"

Elaine made a chopping gesture. "Around here we wouldn't even notice a man named Michael."

Bridey scrunched up her brow. "Certainly not such an unkempt person. A guy like that would have to have his arms full of money to get a second look from me."

Chapter 11

A potted rose plant appeared on the tarmac in front of Grandfather's house. Rose found it atop a note from the ladies' society inviting Grandfather to a program.

"Shit." Bridey wrinkled her nose. "Man-crazy women resorting to gifts in their seduction attempts."

"It works," Rose told her as she placed the pot near the front door. "Michael used to woo me with roses all the time. They were absolute aphrodisiacs."

For a moment she was back in Michael's garden. He gave her such a hot glance. She wanted to melt with him into one filthy puddle of lust.

"You look tired, sweetheart." He wiped her hair behind her ears and held her face in his hands. Were your students difficult?" He placed a forefinger to her lips. "Shh, baby, breathe. I know your work is even more demanding than mine. You tell first."

She regaled him with a tale of the visiting toddler who'd fallen into the dung pile.

"My God, Rosie. To think I only had to deal with a divorce client who brought a gun to the meeting." Soon he had her bent over laughing and longing to kiss his provocative lips into submission.

"Seriously, sweetheart. Let me cook tonight, while you put your feet up."

She met his dancing eyes. "Better idea. Walk me through the roses while you select a few blooms for the table. Dinner's almost...well, dinner. After that, we can both, uh, put our feet up together."

"I like the way you think, sweetie, and you make me remember why I planted these roses for you."

Bridey gave her a peculiar glance and a sideways hug. "Why don't you just pretend this bush is for you, then, Rose? It'll remind you of better days. Come with the friends for supper at Mitchells. Great Irish fare and fish so fresh it winks at you."

Rose mounted Grandfather's bike and drove away with her into the village, the two of them abreast and laughing. What a lot of fun she had missed as a youngster, living and working on the horse ranch. These days, she'd discovered the knack of making friends, and she rode a bike without hands.

Hours later, giggles and shouts floated off them like shedding wool, as they left the restaurant in the company of several new companions.

Someone shared a bawdy joke. They all stamped their feet, hooting.

Rose bent over, trying to catch her breath. "There's nothing like a good plate of fish and chips to bring out the best in you."

"Or the waistline," whooped Bridey as she turned sideways and patted her pregnancy pouch.

"You sure it wasn't the wine that brought out the best?" someone asked.

They all shouted as they headed for their bikes. "No, no!"

"Bridey didn't even drink. Just mineral all night."

"Or Rose. And she's the silliest and worst of us all."

"Fok 'em all, Rose." Bridey held up a finger.

A ruined visage peered out of a shadowed doorway. The crone slurred her speech.

"That's right, girlies, fok' 'em all. Have your fun. No consequences these days. My own ma wouldn't let me get the pill. I begged her, but *no*. 'That's sinful. I'll have to tell your da. He'll take off his belt to ya and then you'll have ta inform the priest.'" She cleared her throat and spat. "Well, I did confess, and he had his way with me, the bloody wanker.

Elaine's pallor made her iridescent under the streetlamp. "No, Ma."

Bridey placed a hand on Elaine's shoulder. "Come on, she's out of it."

The group surged back. "Aye, Lydia's not the full shilling tonight."

Lydia raised a fist. "Out of it, am I? Eff off!"

Her focus zigzagged from one to the other, finally lighting on Elaine and Bridey. "You think I did something disgusting? So I did. It was right manky. At least I kept ya and raised ya, though ever after I couldn't stop thinking of what the miserable prick slipped me from under his cassock." She stumbled.

Bridey stepped forward to steady her. "Come on, oul dear!"

Lydia brushed at the air. "Feck off, ya floozie!"

She seized Bridey's arm. "Where's your own ma, heh? I see she couldn't keep you from being a slag."

Elaine put her arm around her mother's waist, but Lydia thrust her away.

"Ah, yer all dense. I know my daughter goes with the men. She thinks she's safe if she just eats the heads off 'em. But one of these days there'll be one more mouth to feed." She cackled at her ribald imagery.

Rose shuddered. She could land in Elaine's position. Her own grandmother could be anywhere, alone and living with delusions.

For that matter, where was Grandfather? She couldn't

stay in the cottage waiting for him forever. It appeared few knew him, and she'd finally given up asking about his whereabouts. The police had dropped their apparently haphazard search. The clerk had looked at her pityingly. "Leave the poor bugger alone. Maybe he got lucky."

Maybe so, but that didn't quash her worry. Both he and Michael could be in trouble somewhere. It would be so much better to know the truth, any truth, than to stick pins of doubt in herself day by day.

At Grandfather's house, Pickles imitated a limp fleece on the doorstep, and a second potted rose sat opposite the first. No note. These could be for Grandfather, but she didn't want to think that way. She turned to look at the full moon. "Where are you, Michael? I understand you're giving me time before you come rushing in to play the knight. I guess I can't blame you."

She studied the lunar orb. She could almost feel it pulling the tide, much as Michael pulled her heart from wherever he was now. Despite her failure to reach him, all was well. The ache still lodged inside her, but she felt his presence under the same sky.

She imagined him behaving as she had acted to him. He lounged against a wall somewhere at the ends of the earth, his arms across his chest, his long legs crossed at the knees. She read the nonchalance on his face as he looked away.

"I said terrible things to you, Michael, but I can't change what's done. You have to come claim me anyway. Either that or give me a chance to find you. Just don't take too long."

She picked up the cat. "Come on, Pickles."

The moon winked at her. "Another rosebush will land on my doorstep tomorrow or the next day. Whenever."

Someday it would have her man in tow.

∽჻∽

Rose paid several visits to Gwen's craft shop to paint.

"You're so detail-oriented, Rose. I admire how you show the way the light plays on the dog's coat. Try to bring out what he's thinking."

Rose furrowed her brow before breaking out in a smile. "He thinks about playing. He wants to play all the time. Work is his play, even if it's just herding a gecko around my parents' pool."

"Then show that élan in his eyes. Suggest the saliva on his tongue, with an extra drip dangling from his lip. Use extra thick paint to make it three dimensional."

Rose drew the work out, so she could return often. Her heart smiled during time at ease with Gwen. Her arms and shoulders felt loose at the work table. She indulged in more talking than painting. Seamlessly, she moved from the pottery to portraits and landscapes. Her heart was a ewer that emptied itself freely. Gwen positioned Rose's portrait of Puppy Joe in the shop window.

By now Rose had talked to enough people about her fruitless search for Grandfather. To Gwen, she confided "I came here to look up my family, but it hasn't worked out."

"No, I can see that in your eyes. Still, your mind is on something else."

So Rose told her all about her heart's desires. Michael and Rosebud were just part of her thwarted longing, now rekindled as she related how much she had once wanted to paint, to ride, to teach. No paint stained Rose's brush that day, and she wasn't close to the ending of her story—if there was an ending.

"Gwen's a true confidante," she told Bridey, "along with you. I don't know much about her, but sometimes, when she looks at me, I see myself."

Gwen did share stories about her life during the hours they spent with paint and clay. She had reacclimated herself as an Irish woman, after her American husband and child had died in an accident. "Sometimes I wonder if I did the right thing."

"Self-doubt is familiar to me, too, these days."

Gwen's hands fell to her sides. "Try regret. You'll like it even less."

⁂

Every evening, Rose returned to Grandfather Sean's cottage and fed Pickles half a chopped up pickle in a little brine with his cat food. He thanked her with extra caresses against the legs of her jeans. She was never surprised these days to find an occasional new rose bush on the pavement. Pickles kept his counsel on whatever he may have observed from the window seat. She picked him up and murmured into the thick pile of his fur. "I wish I could see what you've witnessed from that perch, kitty."

She peered out at the blooming collection on the tarmac.

"This is costing you a lot, Michael. Send me a picture of Puppy in front of the Little Mermaid instead. Or is it the Eiffel Tower this week? Better yet, send me one of you. Naked." She smirked at the image. Most of her hopelessness had slithered away when the roses had moved in, because she sensed his touch on them.

⁂

Gwen covered up her full sized sheltie statue to carry it to the show window. "Well, if the mystery man is yours, it looks as if he's going for a slow courtship. Is that the way he went after you before?"

Hot blood pounded in Rose's ears. She tried to slough off her embarrassment, but her feelings poured out to this surrogate auntie.

"No, it was all intense hormones and—frantic sex."

"So why the difference now?"

Rose looked Gwen in the eye. "I think you've got the right idea. Either it's not Michael sending the roses, or—he wants to take the intensity off the table. He wants to go for something else, like…"

"A slow burn?"

"Maybe, yes. Or he's doing to me what I did to him. I can't get that image out of my mind."

Gwen rubbed Rose's arm. "Yes, my dear. Tell me."

Rose's eyes focused on a place inside her spirit where all her mistakes and hopes ran on a continuous loop.

"Michael sits on a filthy mattress on the floor of a hovel somewhere. Everything about that place is run-down and grimy. He's rereading a copy of my email that commanded him to leave me alone. His mouth turns hard. He crumples the letter. Smoothes it out. Over and over. Each time, he has to read it again. Each time a tear falls on the paper. He clutches his chest.

"There's an ominous glint in his eye. 'You don't want to see me. You won't see me. You will wear yourself out listening for my words. Every day you will wonder where I am.'

"He turns to look directly into my eyes. I travel through his pupils to the center of his being. I feel his voice more than I hear it. 'Seeing me and hearing my voice will be your new longing. The desire to find me will become everything to you.'

"Then I cry. And I smile. Because he never utters the words I fear."

"What words, Rose?"

Rose squeezed Gwen's hand. "He never says, 'you can't.'"

❧❧

Gwen introduced Rose to her mahogany-haired daughter. "Guess what her name is, Rose."

Her mirror image offered a hand. "Hello, Rose. I'm Rose too."

"Rose too."

Their round, wide open eyes looked back and forth, and

their lips formed perfect Os. Forefingers pointed at each other. Rose fidgeted with her own tresses. "You're what I used to think all Irish women looked like. Er, I hope that wasn't rude."

Rose Too giggled. "Upturned nose, pale skin, curly red hair? Don't take offense, but you could stand in for my mirror."

"Well, I'm glad to see it. At school I was the only one. I'm glad to meet you." They shook hands.

A small girl rushed in and slammed the door. "Grandma, Grandma!" She took one look at Rose and came to a halt in Gwen's arms. "Oh—"

"If you like the Irish look, feast your eyes on my daughter. Come over here, Violet, and say hello to a new friend."

Violet stepped forward. "Hello. I'm five." Her intense blue eyes surveyed Rose from under thick lashes.

Rose's heart turned over.

Violet reached for her hand. "Want to take me to the play park?"

Gwen ruffled the moppet's hair. "Watch out, Rose. Once you start, you'll be going there every day."

Rose's hand closed over the little one in her grasp.

∽∾∽

It had been too many weeks to count since Violet had lured her to the park. Rosebud's dancing image seldom appeared nowadays, but she sometimes peered from Violet's eyes. Tranquility and delight flowed through Rose's veins whenever she watched the flesh and blood child on the swing. Her breathing came slow and easy as she leaned against the back of the bench. She laced her fingers behind her head, admiring the pair of pink crocheted Irish roses in the moppet's long hair.

Violet pumped herself up, and her feet flew into the air, while she trailed her hair almost to the ground. "Whee!"

Now and then, she sang. As always on such occasions, joy multiplied in Rose.

"Mmmm…" Rose yawned, lacing her arm through that of her companion. "Goodness. It's amazing you're old enough to have that sweet little girl."

Rose Too grinned. "I'm twenty-five. I was married at nineteen. My daughter's five. Got the math?" She called the little one away from the play structure. "Violet, darling, Auntie Rose wants to take you for ice cream today."

Violet bounced on her toes and spun in a circle. She tightened her little arms around Rose's neck. "Auntie Rose, you're a Rose like Mommy. I always wanted to be one, but Mommy says there aren't any more Rose names in Ireland."

Rose laughed and helped herself to a longer hug. "Well, you could be a hyphen. How about Violet-Rose? Just between us?"

Violet hesitated, eyeing her mother. "All right." She settled onto Rose's lap.

Rose buried her face into the smooth skin of the little shoulder. "You are delicious, Violet-Rose. You even smell like roses. I should know. My husband raises them at home."

"Well, I can be stinky too. Just ask Mommy. I need a bath every night. You smell like baby powder, Auntie Rose. Like Grandma."

"Yes, my daddy always gave me baby powder when I was little. He loved smelling it on me. I don't know why. So did my husband."

After a while, Violet struggled to get down. "Mommy, did you get the last Rose name?"

"Well, wise-nose, since you have to know everything, it was like this. Grandma's first husband died. They'd always agreed if she had a little girl she would be Rose."

"Was that Grandpa?"

"No, that was another Grandpa. He also died, you know."

Violet turned to Rose. Do you have a Grandpa?"

"Yes, I do."

"Can he be my grandpa too? It would make up for not being a real Rose."

Rose chuckled and ran her fingers through Violet's curly mane. "Why not?" The sincere little face always softened her grief-knobby heart. "When I see him, I'll tell him." Where was the old man? If he were dead, the police would have notified her. There had to be more places to search. She must have missed something.

Violet-Rose pouted, making Rose want to kiss her. "Oh, dear. It's too hard to keep track. So many Grandpas and Roses. No wonder we Irish run out of words."

Rose sniggered. "The Irish will never run out of words."

෴

Apparently her mystery suitor would never run out of roses. Rose picked up Pickles, who marked her with his scent glands wherever he could.

"Did you see who was here, boy? Next time get me a scrap of his jeans, will you? Something with his scent on it? You wouldn't know any bloodhounds, hmmm? And who's that fumbling with the gate?"

Elaine had come to apologize for her mother's behavior a while back. "I was so embarrassed. I couldn't lift my head up. She doesn't do this often, but once in a while Mother can really go off the rails."

Rose gave her a generous hug. "It's okay. I know it's not your fault, and she wasn't in control of herself. It's good you don't have to watch her all the time. You need to get out."

Elaine picked at the wounds on her arms, still scabbed from her most recent struggle with Lydia. "Yes, but where would I go that I mightn't get a frantic call? You can't just run off and hope your problems will disappear."

Rose gave Elaine another hug to hide her stricken feelings. "Why don't you come along on a hike tomorrow? It'll be fun."

Elaine sighed shakily. "I'm so glad you're not going to hold Mother's behavior against me. Thank you for that." She opened the front door to take her farewell. "You say you used to be a loner, but you're a good friend now, Rose." She glanced out at the tarmac. "By the way, did you notice your suitor lined an imaginary path to the door with all the rose bushes? He's dying for you to notice."

The next day, Rose insisted that Violet come along with the girlfriends, for the tyke was lodged in a tender corner of her heart.

Rose Too consented. "Just remember—she can't step along as fast as we can."

Bridey stuck out her belly. "We? There isn't any we. Does anybody think I can walk as fast as a five-year-old?" The two of them raced to the neighbor's house, and Violet won. They undertook a moderate hike along Sky Road, stopping often. Violet picked dandelions and spring gentian along the way.

Rose flopped down on the grass next to Bridey, while the others rambled farther. Rose pressed her ear to Bridey's belly. The lump inside moved out of the way.

"Ooo! I remember this part. Wonderful. It was the first time it struck me that Rosebud was a living, moving person."

Bridey's face paled. "Are you all right being around me, when—when—"

Rose's voice cracked. "You mean—when every minute from here out is—is more than I got to share with Rosebud?"

Bridey's eyes popped.

Rose wiped her eyes. "Don't be embarrassed, Bridey. It's okay to talk about her, to remember—she was—a real little girl." She scraped her throat. "My loss still overwhelms me sometimes. But I can be sad and happy at the same time. And I can rejoice for somebody else." She pointed. "Like you."

Bridey threw her arms around Rose's neck. Rose managed to jockey out of her friend's embrace to look her in the face. She made her voice as calm as possible. "What's wrong, honey? Come on, now. Give it up, or I'll imagine I've upset you too much."

Bridey's lip trembled. "I'm scared. I suppose Evan is scared, too. I suppose they give the troops plenty of whiskey to take the edge off."

It was Rose's turn to enfold her friend in comforting arms. "I'm sorry, Bridey, if my insensitive talk did that to you."

"It's not you, Rose. If anything, you're an inspiration, the way you've come through your trouble, the way you gave birth in frightening circumstances. I'm afraid for myself, pregnant without my husband. I told you my Evan has his vices, but I wouldn't mind how much he gambled or how much whiskey he sucked down if he were with me now."

Rose wrapped her arms around her belly, where Bridey's words had struck. At first her attention fell short of Bridey's next words.

"Why did he have to go overseas to fight, when I need him here with me?"

Rose held Bridey's hand while she wept. "Of course you're angry and afraid, babe. I feel exactly the same way." Yes, she needed Michael with her too—except she had sent him away, and she was the one who had gone overseas.

Their eyes met. "Look, Bridey. I'm going to help you while I'm here, and you have an aunt too, right?"

Bridey's face lit up. "Yes, and my dad too. I saw them both a while ago. We had a great evening, and they promised to stand by me."

ᴄᴎᴇᴎ

That night, Pickles's warm body cuddled up to Rose's back. Bridey's pronouncement ran through her mind, scratching a hole in her brain. "I wouldn't mind how much whiskey he sucked down if he were with me now."

Rose's legs moved in restless patterns, propelling the cat off the bed. "Maybe you would mind, Bridey. Maybe you would reject him for his vices." In her dream, Rose drifted, picking her way through a forest of words. Suddenly she stood on the cliffs near Spiddell, while disembodied voices sang in a monotone.

Rosebud was there, and a lean but well-muscled man with curly dark hair. Chain mail encumbered him. Nevertheless, he hoisted Rosebud, and they danced closer and closer to the precipice. Rose focused on the little girl giggles and the man's laughing baritone, which mesmerized her and lamed her will to act.

A gull flapped in front of the duo just as Rosebud grabbed for the dagger at the man's hip. He reached for her hand but lost his grip on her body. "No, I can't hold you." A piercing scream swirled around Rose like vapor. For a moment, it marinated her in fear.

When the gull passed on, only the man stood on the edge of the cliff, peering down at the sea. Childish giggles sounded below, intermingled with the steam drifting up from the rocks.

Covering his eyes, the man wailed. For the first time, he turned and looked at Rose, spreading his hands in appeal. "Where were you? I dropped my knife." His voice was a monotone. "I have to get it." He turned back to the sea and reached his hand down, down until he disappeared from the cliff.

Rose screamed—a raw, throat-ripping shriek. Her muscles broke free of their paralysis, but she failed to reach him in time. She covered her face. "No!"

Tinkling giggles reached her out of the foam churning on the boulders below. Michael's baritone echoed them. "Where were you, Rose? Where were you?"

Rose was poised to jump into the eddying waters. "No!"

Her arms stretched in front of her, reaching into the bedroom's darkness. The bodice of her nightdress was sodden with her tears and cold sweat. She wiped her face with her hem and padded barefooted to her grandfather's desk.

Pickles wrapped his body around her legs and fell asleep on her feet.

"Good old boy." She leaned down to tousle his fur. "You changed my opinion about cats." Her lips pursed. She began to write. "To the office of Overhulst and Knight, your employee Michael O'Leary recently took a leave of absence. If you know where my husband is, please tell him..." She crumpled the page and started a new one.

Four days later, Rose found an envelope in the mailbox. It held a bulletin from Christ Church downtown. Someone had marked the sermon title with rose-colored highlighter. It read "Seek and ye shall find."

"That's just creepy." Bridey shuddered.

Rose shook her head. "No, no, it's just like Michael to have someone in Clifden send it to him or directly to me, and so similar to the way he arranged all those roses along my journey. Maybe he collected the bulletins for months and mailed me one with the right text."

"Or delivered it himself."

"I would have seen him if he were here. God, his pheromones would have alerted me from miles away." She laughed, but her throat filled with knots. "What if he's in cahoots with Grandfather? He's got to get help from someone."

A look of awareness crossed Bridey's features. "Wait a minute. What church is that?"

Rose turned over the bulletin. "Christ Church."

"Oh, yes, the one up on Church Hill that overlooks the town. That's our Church of Ireland community. The rector's very nice. He would do anybody a favor, especially if the correspondent shared a little horse talk. He's always been a horseman, very keen on stallions. His wife's a sweetheart too." She elbowed Rose, a sparkle in her eye. "See if you can guess her name, Rose."

Rose Too groaned. "Ohhh! That's right!"

Rose looked from one to the other. "What?"

Bridey smirked. "You'll find out."

After lunch, Rose apprised Gwen of her suspicions.

Gwen tapped a clay-smeared fingertip against her lip. "Hmmm…You told me you wrote to your husband's employer. What exactly did you say?"

Rose rubbed at her temples as she tried to remember the precise words. "I asked him to at least tell Michael I'm looking for him."

Gwen reached for the bulletin. "My goodness! Then this was hand-delivered?"

"Yes, that way there's no stamp and no cancellation. It could have come from anywhere, delivered by anyone."

"Yes, that sounds like part of your man's slow courtship plan, if that's what he's up to."

"He's turned our relationship upside down. Do you think the words of the text are a direct response to my letter?"

Bridey grinned at her. "You're actually licking your lips."

❧❦❧

Now Michael's mystery was bigger than Rose alone, and plainly, her posse couldn't wait another day to play sleuth along with her. Bridey agreed to hide at the house after Rose went out the next day, in order to catch any delivery man in the act.

"Whether he's got roses or a letter, I don't care. Just nab him. Here's the camera. At least get a picture."

"Crap, Rose. I know what we're looking for. I can do this, though it's hard to stay in one place for long. The baby is kicking my belly to a pulp today."

Rose returned late in the afternoon, only to catch Bridey yawning.

"I hid on the window seat behind the curtain. All day." Her voice had developed a cross edge. "I didn't see anyone. No deliveries. Now I'm all stiff and sore, and my back is killing me." Bridey stomped off to the place down the road where she had concealed her bike—these days with training wheels.

"What do you think, Pickles? Did Bridey fall asleep while she was on duty?"

He yawned. Their relationship had progressed to a pinnacle of feline intimacy, she felt, for he had revealed his ticklish spot, and its satisfaction was uppermost on his agenda this time of day. He yielded his armpits to her fingertips.

"You old libertine. I bet you'd have a lot to tell me if only you could talk."

Sure enough, Rose awoke during the night to the sound of frantic yowling. Pickles paced from the bedroom to the front door and back again.

"Silly thing. You could have used the cat door if you really had to go." That idea brought her up short. She flung open the door and burst into tears. A new rose stood near the gate.

She dashed onto the forecourt and beyond to the street, bawling out the name in her heart. "Michael! Michael!" Her voice was one long sob. "Who's doing this, and where are you, Michael? How long are you going to make me suffer?"

Rose was more certain than ever of Michael's revised grand plan. He'd proved himself a romantic still, but he wasn't going to come charging out of the woods to bear her away.

Forgetting the hedgerows along the property covered a stone wall, she kicked them. "Oowww! Damn Irish rocks! Damn hedges." She hopped on one foot. "Grandfather, you're nuts with your Irish this and your Irish that."

She searched the clouds for some kind of moon, and jerked her fist at the heavens. "Give me my dog back, Michael!"

Chapter 12

I can't change the outcome of his little game, Bridey. I give up." Rose waved her hands around. "I know I made him suffer, and I guess he'll be done with this revenge when he's ready. Maybe I'm done too. I'm ready to stop playing and act like a grown up." She stood up and stretched her back. "I'd better concentrate on Grandfather." She wrung her dust rag. "All efforts to find him have failed."

"Shit! Your cell phone is a pain in the butt. Too bad I let Evan take our smart phone with him. It kind of defeats the purpose if I don't have my own to talk to him. I can sit home by the landline all the time as far as he's concerned." Bridey's sarcasm sounded a new low note.

Rose tossed the flip phone onto the couch cushions. "Well, I can't text with the people I'm trying to find, and I can't call them."

Later in the evening, she used Sean's desk top to open a message from Aidan. *Yr G-pa sent a ltr. Moved temporarily and not to worry. Ltr was on pink paper. LOL. Sorry for trouble. Dad.*

Bridey pounded on the table. "Sorry for trouble?"

"Crap." Rose made her mouth into a straight line. "I'll show him. I'm going about this all wrong. Instead of pining for Michael to come save me, I'm going to haul Grandfather out of hiding if it kills me."

ᥱᥴᥱ

Elaine staggered through the door into Brown's Restaurant, where some of the friends gobbled down the seafood chowder. She pulled on Rose's arm. "Listen. I found a wild man."

Rose chuckled, visions of a new suitor for her friend tickling her fancy.

Apparently Bridey thought the same thing, for her eyebrows wiggled à la Groucho Marx. "Just how wild was he, Elaine? Did he make your insides curl and your toenails fall out?"

"Hee hee." Rose Two rolled her eyes. "I could use some of that."

"No, no. I saw him, a wild man on a bike. Listen to me."

"Of course, honey." Rose laughed at her ribald friends. "Tell us. Why do you call the fellow wild?"

"Well, he was, you know, wild looking, maybe homeless. Long hair, unkempt, big bushy beard. All of it curly."

"Yeah." Bridey wagged her forefinger. "We've all seen guys like that in this day and age. No need to be afraid, though I've had it with facial hair mucking up handsome faces these days." She wiggled in her chair. "That's one good thing about military men."

"No, you don't get it. It wasn't just hair. It was h-a-i-r. Sprouting all over his lower face, sticking up all over, like he didn't care how he looked. Yeeech!"

Rose laid a hand on Elaine's, which picked at its partner. "Okay, we get it. You weren't attracted. What got you so riled up?"

"Jaysus, didn't you hear me? He was pedaling a bike for all he was worth, and on the back he toted a freaking wrapped bush."

Rose stared, waiting for her brain to catch up to her ears.

Elaine fluttered her hands. "Holy Christ, girls, what does a man like that want with a fokkin' garden plant?"

Suddenly deaf to their chatter, Rose stood up and moved away from the table.

She stepped outside and gulped the air. Michael had orchestrated so many novel deliveries of his courtship tokens before. They should find this hirsute fellow and ask him if he'd acted as Michael's agent, like a cat bringing home dead mice for a pal.

Bridey caught up with her, and, arm in arm, they continued down the street. She pointed to the floral shop. "Look. We can ask if they have a delivery agent who looks like that."

They continued in silence to the corner and waited for the light. "One thing I don't understand." Bridey stared at the parts of her feet she could still see.

They looked at each other.

"Well, you're always giving your husband credit for being resourceful. If he's really so capable, why can't you give him credit for maybe kicking his habit?"

Rose felt the blood drain from her complexion, followed by a small transfusion of shame. "You're right, Bridey. He attended a group, but I never thought he had enough resolve to stop drinking for good."

Bridey crossed her arms over her chest and sighed. "I think you never had faith in him at all. You were both too busy playing your freaking knight and damsel, fuck-me-in-another-new-way games. Well, good for you that it was all such fun. For some of us marriage is sunup to sundown serious."

Rose pretended to eye the treats in the bakery window. Why did she obsess about her marital hic-coughs when other people had real problems? At least Michael was alive and safe. Somewhere.

Bridey placed her hands on the sides of Rose's head and gave her the eye. "Maybe you're so mad at him because he stopped playing the way you wanted him to. Maybe he can't be your white knight anymore."

⚜

That afternoon, after Rose and Bridey pedaled up Ardbear Road from town, Rose waited while Bridey checked her mailbox. It contained a letter from Evan. "Don't go home just yet, will you, Rose." She massaged her belly. "Just until I read it. I have the shivers about this one."

Rose laid her bike there in the drive and waited in silence, all sharp edges inside. The letter sucked all the life out of Bridey's face. Rose hurried to her side just in time to catch her.

She walked her friend into the kitchen and propped her up on a chair. She tried to pry the letter from her icy fingers, but the best she could do was massage the stiff hands. It was almost a relief when she started to tremble.

Rose carried a cup from the stove. "Here, Bridey, try to take some hot tea." Rose touched a spoon with a small amount of liquid to her lips. Then another and another until Bridey's hands, with hers around them, were able to hold the cup.

"I'm so sorry, dear. So sorry this upset you. I can see it's bad news. Can you talk to me?"

Bridey moved her lips, but she'd turned mute.

"I hate to see you like this. I'd rather listen to you swear." Rose's fake smile strained at her lips.

Bridey stared at the letter on the table, her face expressionless. Her fingers scrabbled at it but failed to secure it.

"Come on, Bridey. Let's get you into bed." Her eyes cut to the envelope. Later you can tell me about the letter."

Rose half carried, half dragged her shivering friend to the bedroom, undressed her, and tucked her in with an extra wool blanket over the down comforter.

"I can call your mother-in-law, Bridey. Is that what you

want?" Damn it, she didn't even know the name of Bridey's dad. Liam something. "Do you want your dad?"

No reaction.

"I'm going to sleep on the couch. You rest, and I'll be right there." She pointed to the door.

Bridey trembled. Rose swaddled the covers around her, and she stilled, her eyes closed.

Rose waited in the kitchen until she heard weeping. She took her time warming a wet washcloth. Then she entered the bedroom in dim light, loosened the covers, and bathed Bridey's tear-swollen face. She slipped into the bed, so she could hold her

"Rose—I—he—next week they're going—a mission—casualties." Bridey gulped air and wailed herself dry.

"Shhh, now, Bridey. I get the gist. Don't worry. I'm not leaving you alone."

They cuddled together all night long, joined in scraps of misery and fear and hope. Rose tried to remember if she had ever lain in bed with another woman. Maybe her mother when she was very small?

No, it had only been Michael, since the night they met, and their co-sleeping had been of a different sort than this. There had been recurring awakenings to the other's body and a fitting together in splendid attunement.

This was nice, though. Lying together like halves of a perfectly matched bivalve, two of the same.

Rose had tea ready before dawn. Sniveling sounded from the bedroom, along with shrieks crossed with angry shouts.

Rose mumbled as she carried in the tea. They talked in short spurts while each drank two cups of Irish black. Finally Bridey asked Rose to read the letter out loud.

The recitation set Bridey to pounding the bed with her fists. "I'm so angry with you, Evan for going off into this horrible war. The stupid thing is—I think he did this for my American family, since I don't have a brother to represent us in the fight."

Rose thought of the question William had asked about

Michael. "Have you told him how mad you are?" If she could talk to him now, she'd tell him for sure.

Rose leaped up. "Are you hungry? Get dressed. I have eggs at my place, and I have an idea. Hurry up."

Not only did she have eggs, but a large loaf of Irish soda bread and some unsalted butter. What an apt repast for two women who'd cried and talked half the night and pedaled home before breakfast.

She suffered a show of feline indifference from Pickles, who'd apparently spent the night outside the front door. She picked him up and carried him around to the back, where he relieved himself in the garden. "Look, Bud, there's your cat door. It's good for going in as well as going out, you know." Pickles lifted his chin and turned his head. What had set him off?

⋘⋙

Scrambled eggs with chives, sliced tomatoes, and great hunks of brown Irish bread slathered with butter and honey more than filled the spaces where last night's missed supper should have lain.

"My dad used to pinch his belly and say 'I think I have a gap right here for another pancake.' Did your family ever talk like that, Bridey?" Rose asked.

Bridey laughed—a mere shadow of her former belly rumbling.

"That's the sound I want to hear from you, my friend. I'd even put up with your occasional crabbiness for one of your giggles."

"Yes, my mood is so uneven these days. I'm happy about the baby. I'm scared to death about the war."

Rose smiled while she buttered another hunk of bread. "Yes I noticed."

"It's that I can't see him, and I can't talk to him. And meanwhile I'm going through this with my little rolling, boxing lump. That's what I'm going to call him, I swear. Lump."

"Speaking of swearing…" Rose fished in her pocket. "You should direct that exasperation at the right person. Here. I'll borrow it back from time to time, but you carry it. Just don't melt it with all your phone sex."

૯౭౯౩

Letting Bridey have the cell phone lent new lightness to Rose's step. What did she want with the darned thing anyway? Now that Aidan had heard from Grandfather, the urgency in her life was cut in half. And she couldn't call Michael.

"See, Pickles." Her voice cajoled. He rushed over to his dish and lapped up the extra half teaspoon of pickle juice she'd added. "It feels good to do something for someone else instead of turning into a worry machine." She picked him up and tickled his armpits.

She did borrow the phone to send the occasional text to her parents. "No progress in my search for Gpa or M," she wrote. "Many ideas. Keeping B busy is good for me 2. Roaming about in town, etc."

૯౭౯౩

At a nursery outside of Cliffden, Rose showed her photo of Michael to everyone she met, customers and employees. A ruddy man in a company uniform mused over the photo she proffered while he sucked his teeth like sticky candy. "Well, we do employ delivery people. Many on bikes." He pulled his shoulders back. "A lot of the customers are local, one-at-a-time business. You know—the funeral wreath, the *thanks-for-the-good time* or *I'm-sorry* roses."

"Well, did you see anyone like this?" She pressed the photograph on him again.

"No, no. This is a gentleman. Can't see him delivering bushes." He shook his head. A knotty forefinger dabbed at the picture of Michael in better days. "Nice suit and tie."

Rose's shoulders slumped as she took back the photo.

He seemed eager to offer her a little something. "Of course, a person's looks do change, especially when he's got a rose bush in front of him."

Bridey fanned the embers of Rose's hope. "Don't be discouraged. Not a single soul recognized Michael, but that doesn't mean no one saw him. They just didn't see what we're showing them. I've got an idea."

Gwen had a copy machine in her shop. She cleaned the clay from her fingers. "Give me the picture."

In no time they sat around the table looking at two copies of Michael's photograph. On one of them, Gwen drew a ragged beard and mustache on the handsome visage, with long hair that curled in all directions. She laid it next to the untouched copy.

"There. That's the Michael people see now if he's the wild man with the roses. Not the picture you're carrying around."

Rose had never seen her spouse with facial hair, though she knew every bone and plane of his visage. A choking heaviness in her chest reminded her of the time, when Rosebud's death was still raw. Her forefinger touched the face in the photo. "My poor Michael. With all that hair, all I can see is your beautiful eyes."

Gwen copied the original portrait again and snipped away everything but the eyes, which she enlarged and ran through her copier. "Memorable eyes, Rose." She laid them in front of Rose. "That's the picture you need to show around. People will remember those eyes without all the distracting hair in the picture."

Gwen and Bridey looked at each other in silence while Rose held her hands over her heart. Her mind wandered into the past to eyes that had twinkled in mischief and broken her heart with their grief and passion. In her memory, tears threatened to spill through the long, dark lashes, and she heard the voice that went with them.

"You call the shots now, Rosie. When are you going to claim me?"

"I'm trying," she whispered, as Gwen wrapped an arm around her.

"Let her cry it out," Gwen told Bridey, who already had a pile of tissues out of her bag.

Rose used up the tissues. She squeaked in affirmation of Gwen's point. "Just can't—stop. Those eyes—they are Michael's—most prominent—feature. S—somebody will have—noticed. Somebody will—remember those eyes if they see this."

Gwen looked wise. "Yes, my dear, I do remember them."

Rose and Bridey stared at her. Rose stopped squeaking.

"I'm sorry I didn't put two and two together. I have seen those eyes. He's been in here."

Rose felt darkness closing in. "What? When?"

Bridey leaped to her feet and hunkered before her, pressing her head down. "It's okay, babe. Breathe."

Gwen urged a glass of water on her and placed a cool cloth against her forehead. Her smiling eyes intruded into Rose's darkness like the stable light at home, showing the way to safety.

Rose wrapped her arms around Gwen's neck. "What did you say?"

"Your husband has been in the shop, and I remember his eyes. In fact, that was the only detail I focused on at the time."

Bridey took hold of her arms. "Don't you see, Rose? That means it's real. He's here in Connemara."

Rose tore out of her chair and rushed toward the door. Gwen took her by the hand and, instead of restraining her flight, led her outside and stood her in front of the display window. "Can you see what's missing, Rose?"

Rose heard Gwen's words as if from a distance. She only pointed.

Gwen gave her a squeeze. "He bought it this morning." She set them both down at the table and plied them with strong tea. "Yes, I'm sure I never saw him before today. I always have a strong feeling about these things. For instance, I experienced a compelling, almost déjà vu sensation when I met you, Rose. Somehow I knew your eyes, though I'm sure we'd never met."

Rose chuckled. "I never told you, but I had the same feeling the first time I saw you. I knew your eyes and something about that little line next to your mouth. That's why I was so slow painting the little dog statue—so I could come back."

They both laughed.

"I still can't figure out where I've seen you before, and, yes, it's impossible. Unless you've been to Citrus County." She shrugged her shoulders.

Gwen applied lotion to her clay-dried hands. "When I saw Michael's eyes I detected the grief inside him."

Alarm spread itself through Rose's heart. "Wha—what was the matter with him?"

Gwen shook her head. "It was strange. My impression was of an old grief and a new one laid over that. He was perfectly calm, but there was something deep down. A number of times he said...what was it? 'Maybe she'll forgive me.' He spoke as if he didn't expect me to understand."

An unseen hand squeezed Rose's chest. They all fell silent.

Bridey spoke first. "I need to take Rose to the fairy tree."

"Yes, I agree." Gwen nodded. "The sooner the better. I'll go with you." She brought out some cotton rags, which they cut into strips. "Make them the length of a man's hand. If you remember the length of your lover's hand, that's best."

Rose caught Bridey testing the length of her strip by placing it along the curve of her breast. "No good, Bridey.

Your boobs have grown since Evan left. He'd get more than a handful now." They all tittered.

Rose guessed what hopes and griefs Bridey wrote on her strip. Come to think of it, the others were aware of hers, but a flush of embarrassment crept up her neck as she realized how little she knew about Gwen's private life.

"What are you writing, Gwen? If you don't mind telling."

Gwen smiled. "Well, you know my daughter Rose and little Violet. They'll be alone when I pass, so…"

They nodded.

"Then I'm adding a prayer for the past and future—my two husbands and little boy, and a wish for all the grandchildren that may yet be born."

An hour later, the three stood with their strips of cotton at the base of the two entwined trees. Rose recalled being here before.

"Scarcely a single empty space on the branches. Did either of you leave messages here before?"

Bridey looked at her belly. "Just when Evan left for the Middle East."

Gwen sighed. "When my son was little I left him with my husband and came here to visit my mother. My wish was for them to be well until I held them in my arms again. I prayed for my boy to grow into a good man and husband and father. I also added a clause about all his descendants getting their heart's desire." She fell silent.

Rose prodded her. "Well?"

"I guess I watered my message down too thin. As you know, my husband and son died while I was away."

Rose and Bridey left Gwen back at the shop before they pedaled toward Ardbear Cottage.

Rose worried her lip. "I know I promised to stay over tonight, but I'm half expecting a clay sheltie in front of my house. Do you mind?"

"Not at all. I want to see it too. Then I'll leave you alone with it."

They pedaled on to Grandfather's house, chattering about the statue and Michael's visit to Gwen's shop. Once they got to their destination, they spotted no statue at all. When they discovered who stood on the doorstep, Rose tottered back a step, covering her mouth.

"Holy shit, Rose!" No wonder Michael couldn't make his delivery."

Rose responded through gritted teeth. "After the last visit, I almost want to go hide in the bushes."

"Look how the cat's hackles are up."

Pickles ran hell bent for leather toward Rose and kneaded her jeans, mewling a frantic complaint. Rose picked him up. "It's okay, baby. It's a friend. No fear."

"Hello, there!" Lydia stepped out of the shadows under the eaves. "I bet you don't remember me. Maybe I hope you don't. Hee-hee."

"Of course I do. You're Elaine's mother. We've actually met a couple of times." Rose offered her hand. Pickles hissed. She buried her face in his neck. "Shhhh, baby!" She tried to tickle his armpit, but he was in full rigor.

"Well, I came to make amends and ask for another chance. May I come in?"

Rose eyed Bridey. "Uh, sure, I've got a little time yet. It's only around four o'clock."

Bridey waved from outside the gate. "Hi, there, Lydia. You're looking well. Rose, don't forget to, uh, call me before six for our...uh...you know."

Rose felt blank. "Uh...okay, Bridey, I'll be sure to call you before then." For goodness' sake. Of all people, Bridey knew Rose had no phone. Bridey turned her bike around and headed back down the road.

Pickles had his claws out. He grinned, showing his sharp little teeth.

Rose unlocked the door. "Come on in, Lydia. Don't mind my cat's manners."

"Pickles."

"Yes, how did you know?"

"Eh!" Lydia backhanded the question.

Rose pointed her visitor to a seat on the couch and turned on the standing lamp next to it. "What brings you out?"

Lydia's eyes sparkled in the lamp light. "I brought you a jar of my pickled vegetables. Sort of a peace offering."

"Well, I appreciate your thoughtfulness. I'm a canning amateur myself. Too bad. There's a big garden out back. I don't know if you realize this is my grandfather's ancestral home. But I forgot—you probably don't get over here much?"

There was that odd twinkle again. "Oh, you're wrong. I've been in this house a lot. Maybe you think you know your grandfather, but he's not what you think he is."

Rose's jaw slackened.

"Good old Sean is nothing but a womanizer. He played with my emotions, but he threw me over for that redhead he's shacked up with now, that slut!"

The hot blood threatened to spew out of Rose's ears. She had to remember this woman was not all there. She counted to ten while her inner tea kettle simmered down.

"You're quite wrong, Elaine. My grandfather has been a respectable gentleman all my life. He's a tender subject right now, because he is missing at the present time, possibly a victim of a crime."

Lydia looked ready to pounce. "That's what you think, Missy. I know exactly where he is."

The doorbell rang. Thank God for Bridey to the rescue. Rose flung the door open.

Elaine stood on the mat. "I'm sorry. I came for my mother. I could hear those remarks from here. I hope you disregard them. They're not true." She glanced quickly at the couch where Lydia's lips curled, her eyes vacant. Elaine steered Rose into the kitchen.

"My mother led a sorry life. She can't forget she lost her first husband and her son. I try to overlook a lot."

Rose brought her into the living room.

Lydia rocked herself. "A lovely visit, a lovely visit."

As Elaine ushered her mother out, Lydia chuckled "The cat eats pickles."

Rose found Pickles clinging to the drapes. "It's all right, baby." She disengaged his claws one by one. "Sometimes life makes people crazy, but not us, because you have me now, and I have you." She buried her face in his belly. "Zrbtt!" He scrambled onto her shoulder.

She shoved the pickled vegetables into the cupboard. "We're not having these tonight."

Chapter 13

Rose was still crabby the next morning when she pedaled to Church Hill, from where Christ Church dominated the countryside. "Well, Michael, there's a nice announcement board there. Did you post an ad on it?"

She left her bike near the path and trudged uphill on foot, past gravestones that, like the gray stone church, sparkled in the strong sunlight. She surveyed the hills and mountains in the distance while she listened to the peals of organ music from inside.

A middle-aged woman bustled from an entrance that proved unlocked. She turned at the sound of Rose clearing her throat. "Hello. Can I help you?" The crinkles beside her eyes made Rose's question come unstuck.

"I'm a visitor in town. I wondered if I could see the rector. Do you know if—"

"Lovely." She pointed at the door. He'll be happy to see you. I'm not kidding. He loves meeting folks from different places." She delivered an appraising glance. "I can tell you're not Irish."

"Tell that to my granddad."

"Is that right? Well, it's Adam you want to talk to. What's your name, dear?"

"Rose, Rose Flanagan."

"Well then, Irish after all. But American too, I'm guess-ing."

Rose nodded. "Half and half."

"Well, half and half Rose, my name is Rosemary, so you and I have the same name in a way, don't we?" Her laugh tinkled on the breeze that welcomed Rose to this spot. "Have Adam bring you along to the house when he comes for his mid-morning coffee, will you?"

Rose was still smiling when she shouldered open the door to the apse. In a moment, she found her way into the sanctuary, where the organ music swelled and eddied around her. Rose gaped at the decorative pipes of the in-strument on the left wall. Its booming voice vibrated in her chest.

When the organist noticed her, he ceased playing.

She held her hands folded before her chest, as if to hold in her heartbeat. "Go on playing, please. This music is so…big."

"Yes, it's mechanical of course. Way different from electronic sound." Caressing the keys, he spoke as if the music belonged to him.

"This isn't a really old church, is it?"

A pleasant voice spoke from the apse. "Good eye." It's only about a century and a half years old. The interior is pleasing enough, don't you think?" Backlit from a tall win-dow, full but fine white hair floated around the man's head as he strode toward her.

They strolled together toward the three tall windows and extensive white woodwork in the front. She spun around to take in the four double windows on each side. "It's so light inside, considering all the stone."

His eyes sparkled at her as he held out his hand. "I'm Adam, and you look hungry. Come next door."

In his study, Rose imbibed two cups of coffee with homemade cinnamon scones. She told him all about her mission to find her grandfather, and the rector promised to ask his Catholic counterparts about him.

Rose took a deep breath and looked around at the many books lining the walls of his study. She closed her eyes in the sunlight. This inspiring chamber reminded her of her mother's studio and all the times they had spent there together.

He inspected her narrowly from behind his sparkling spectacles, steepling his fingers. "But, my dear Rose, something else is on your heart. Don't you want to tell me why you really came?"

Rose looked at him for a few moments. She didn't want to radiate mistrust, but she could barely speak over the lump in her throat.

"Well?"

She inspected her fingers. "I never thought I could talk about this with a clergyman."

"Okay. That's all right, too."

The floodgates opened in her heart, spewing out the story of her marriage to Michael and their love and betrayal. Of their lost Rosebud and his inability to grieve in tandem with her. The clergyman retained an attitude of silent attention, so—finally—she recounted her decision to flee from the man who still drove her heartbeat. As she told him all this, she stumbled over the realization that, in a way, she felt dead without Michael.

"And is that the end of your story, Rose?"

"I tried. I ran away. I struggled to push him out of my world. Still, he fought for me like he always did...before."

He leaned forwards. "But?"

She couldn't stop now. She poured out the story of Michael's never-ending courtship of her in his quirky way—aware of her wishes to cut contact yet stoked by his need of her.

"You're smiling, Rose. It's all over your face that he won you over at last."

Tears fell. "Yes, though I'd been sure it would never work for us."

"So you feel Michael is the central fact of your world, but his addiction would inevitably destroy you?"

She nodded.

"That's a world without God, Rose, without hope."

There it was. She knew the preacher would fall back on the dogma she had learned in her childhood.

"It's sad, isn't it, Rose—life without a belief in order, without confidence that you can make things better?"

Rose snorted. "*I* can make things better?" Her eyes flashed.

He leaned forward in his chair, spreading his hands in an arc. "Did you never hear of forgiveness?"

Mildred's word.

Here she was, a deer in the headlights, and all he said next was "Let's eat." After all those scones.

Around the kitchen table, Irish brown bread with local cheese, washed down with strong black tea, impelled her to include Rosemary in a recap of her story.

"Then, after I realized I didn't want a life without Michael, he sent me a message I was unprepared to take in."

"What was it, dear?" Rosemary looked up as she poured the steaming Barry's Gold from the porcelain teapot. "Take a Hobnob, Dear. They're chocolate *and* salty."

Rose held the cookie while she answered. "He told me his plans for an extended trip with no connection to social media. He claimed he'd given up on me. It was a real good-bye." She pressed her hands to her temples. "The realization that I was too late broke my heart all over again."

Her hosts' silence transmitted their compassion.

Rose swallowed rapidly. "But—but—I find he hasn't given up. He just changed the game."

She glanced from one to the other. "He keeps courting me from afar, inserting himself into my life so that I know—or think I know—what he's doing. Subtle. He's no longer the white knight swooping down to take me."

The vicar frowned. "It's up to you now, isn't it? And how are you so sure what he's up to?"

She exhaled on a quivering sigh. "Because he's here." She had almost forgotten that part of the story. "That's why I came." She fumbled in her backpack and produced the church bulletin. "This was in my mailbox."

Rosemary passed the biscuits around again, while they looked at the folded paper. "Oh, yes, I remember that sermon, dear. 'Seek and Ye Shall Find.' A little subtle for some. All about second chances, but I suspected people turned their houses upside down looking for money."

The rector patted his wife's hand and turned to Rose. "What was your point, exactly?"

She gestured with her teacup while smoothing the bulletin on the table. "I deduced that whoever put that in my mailbox acted for Michael or attended that service and took home the bulletin."

They stared at her.

Rose drew out her words. "Maybe you saw that person and shook his hand. Maybe he talked with you. Maybe he is this close." She showed how close with her thumb and index finger.

Rose displayed the pictures of Michael before and after.

The clergyman cleared his throat. "Yes, he's been here quite a few times to the eleven-thirty service Sundays. A nice fellow, but down on his luck, I think. He doesn't look it, but he's quite a horseman. We had an instant connection. In fact, he already knew all about my background."

Rosemary touched his hand. "Everybody knows that, dear. It's on the internet."

Rose clapped her palms over her lower face. "Research. That's my Michael. I'm sure of it now, and I have to figure out how to find him."

ᏊᏋᏊ

Gwen's sheltie statue stood on the drive, a rose in a vial fastened to its neck. She clenched her fists. "Grrrrrrah!!"

she growled. Pleasure and vexation, half and half, "Michael, you make me so mad. If you want me, why is it I get to talk to everybody but you?" She picked up the cat, and marched into the house.

Pickles laid his ears back.

"What do you think he wants, Pickles? Maybe I'm supposed to go to church every Sunday in case he shows up there?" Her ears burned. She looked out at the gate. "Asshole! I'm not the weakling you thought. I'm going to get you."

The cat hid under the couch while Rose rummaged through the kitchen cabinets, trying to remember when she last went to the store. "Chocolate, chocolate, chocolate. Come to Momma!" At last she found a bag of crisps, half a jar of peanut butter, and Lydia's pickled vegetables. "Mmm! A balanced diet. Taters, protein, and veggies." She wolfed down what she could and offered Pickles the rest of the vegetables.

"I won't think about you-know-who anymore tonight. Let's have some Irish humor instead." She dragged Grandfather's easy chair closer to the television and flopped down. Her stomach rumbled. "Ruuulps!" That sent Pickles scuttling into the bedroom.

"Oh, God, the peanut butter is heavy on my stomach."

Two comedians traded lines. "What do a priest and a pint of Guinness have in common?" All she heard next was the roiling of her gut.

She pressed on her belly. Man, now acid. She rummaged in Grandfather's medicine cabinet and knocked back a double dose of antacid. The bottle shattered into the sink.

She belched and retched repeatedly, but nothing came out. Her heart hammered against her lungs. Something was very wrong. "Pickles! Are you okay?" Clutching her belly, she undertook a frantic search. Pickles lay convulsing on the far side of the bed. "Oh, my God. Oh my God! No, baby, No!" She picked him up under her arm, all the while trying to keep her dry heaving dry. She threw open the front door and struggled to the gate.

A car approached from the direction of Clifden. She propped herself against the hedge "Help! Help!" She launched herself in the direction of the vehicle and collapsed onto the roadway.

ᏈᎦᏋᎦ

Bridey wiped the sweat from Rose's forehead.

Half conscious, Rose turned her head from side to side. "Michael—Are you here?" Finally she fixed on Bridey's face and took hold of her blouse. "Tell Michael—I'm on to him. I need him."

"Okay, Rose. I'll do my best. Shit! Your complexion looks like something out of Tussaud's."

Rose tumbled back down into the maw of unconsciousness.

Rose smelled baby powder. "Gwen—Bridey?" She had the shakes.

Gwen held her, as Maria had done when she was little. "Shhh, dear. I'm taking over until Bridey gets back. Don't worry. You're going to be all right. You swallowed something very bad."

Rose looked around. "Where? What?"

The next time Rose opened her eyes Bridey was there. "Dad? Daddy?"

"It's me—Bridey."

"A dream—My dad was here. His eyes looked so sad. Then they turned into Gwen's eyes."

"Your parents are in America, remember? You're here in Clifden with me."

"What happened?"

"You were very sick. Then a car almost ran over you. You tried very hard to die, but I've got you now. Try to relax."

"The hospital—"

"Yes, It's interesting. I made some discoveries while I waited."

Rose struggled to stay in the moment. "Tell me—what happened."

She saw the effort in Bridey's grimace.

"All right, the doctor told me not to upset you, but I know you won't rest unless I tell you." She interlaced their fingers. "The thing to remember is you're all right now."

Rose made a helpless gesture with her free hand. She hoped Bridey could see her impatience. "Tell—me—everything."

"All right. Take it easy. You swallowed something. The doctor sent me to your house to find what it was. I found the medicine bottle in the sink and the remains of your so-called supper. Then I brought everything to the lab."

Rose pressed on her temples as if to force wayward memories back to life. "Yes, we ate a lot of comfort food. Did you find Pickles? I tried to—carry him."

Bridey fidgeted with her hair.

"What, Bridey? Where's Pickles?" Rose gripped Bridey's arm, choking on her vocal cords.

"He went to the hospital with you. Remember that, Rose. You brought him to the doctor." Bridey uttered a little croak.

Rose clutched Bridey's sleeve, her face crumpling. "Pickles? Oh, no!" She wailed as loud as she could, given her aching throat. She gagged. "What's wrong with my throat?"

"The doctor had to pump your stomach. Luckily you threw up earlier rather than later."

Rose wailed even more. "Everything I love I lose. Michael—Rosebud—Puppy Joe—now Pickles. For God's sake. My cat!"

Rose convalesced at Bridey's cottage for a few days. Bridey's family doctor made house calls. "You had a close call, miss. I hate to tell you what the chemist detected in the pickled vegetables."

They stared at him.

"Right, then. I'll tell you. It was—now take it easy—It was ricin."

They screeched at the same time. "Whaaat?"

"How could that be? I know Lydia's a little off, but she wouldn't try to kill me."

"And where would she find ricin?"

The doctor spread his hands. "Oh, a lot of people add it to food like a tonic. Maybe your parents forced a spoonful down you regularly when you were a kid. It's even in chocolate."

"Chocolate?" Rose whispered, eyeing the extra-large box of Butler's luxury Irish chocolates Rose Too had laid on the table that morning.

The doctor chuckled. "Think castor oil."

ᴇ/ᴈᴇ/ᴈ

Bridey came in singing. "Here's something to entertain you, babe. I found the Alcoholics Anonymous meeting room in the hospital."

"I thought there was a veil of secrecy over meetings in Ireland."

Bridey shrugged, patted her belly, and tittered. "Shit, give me credit for my power over men."

"Okay, well, that's very handy. I'll have to go hang out and see if Michael shows up, if I ever get out of the house again."

Bridey smirked. "I found something familiar when I looked in the waste paper. You doodle this figure sometimes. I never saw it anywhere else."

Rose's eyes practically exploded with her intense scrutiny. Then she burst into tears.

Bridey folded her arms. "That's what I thought."

That evening, Rose cuddled a mountain of pillows. The paper with Michael's signature—three part doodle—lay on her coverlet. She felt a little peaked still, but holding something he had touched set a butterfly of contentment fluttering inside her.

"I'm glad I could bring you Michael's lovey-dovey triple heart shamrock thing." Bridey looked smug. "But I've not shot my wad yet." She handed over a book with a castle on the cover. "From the treasure trove under your grandfather's bed. Note the passages he highlighted."

They cuddled up on the couch and read a few pages.

Bridey pointed out a picture. "There's been a castle over there since the twelfth century."

"The same family lived in it for over five hundred years."

Bridey stabbed at the page. "Look at that. The grounds are open to the public. There are inside tours during the summer. Hotel packages."

Rose looked up at Bridey. "I wonder…Do you think Grandfather went to this castle on vacation? Once he drove all the way to Ohio to visit some caverns mentioned in a novel."

"Gosh, yes, that sounds like him. Impulsive." Bridey studied the photograph on the cover. "You know, my dad is an expert on these castles. I wonder if he could give us some hints."

Rose read on while Bridey tapped out the number. When she returned, her face glowed. "Guess what? Liam—my dad—is writing a book on that castle. He usually spends Thursdays there, and he'll meet us. It's a couple of hours, I think, and it'll make a nice day. Want to go?"

It wasn't as if any living creature depended on her presence here these days.

⌀⌀⌀

A week later, they undertook the pilgrimage. Rose unfolded her stiff limbs. "That wasn't too bad on the bus."

Bridey rubbed out a cramp. "No, but it's good to get out and walk."

"I've been in Kilkenny before but had no chance to see the castle, so I'm hoping to look around a little before we hook up with your dad."

"I'm famished. You won't believe what I've got a craving for. Oxtail soup with soda bread."

They lunched at a wrought iron table right at water's edge, belly to belly with a picturesque bridge. Luscious planters of rose-colored geraniums hung from the railing within plucking distance from their table. Through the bridge's arch, colorful stone buildings lined the water on the opposite side.

Bridey inspected Rose's arm. "I see you forgot your wristwatch again. What's up with you?"

Rose shrugged. "I don't run my life according to a schedule anymore, I guess. You know—Michael wakes up. We have sex. He leaves. Housekeeping chores. Muck out the stables. That sort of thing." Rose sighed. "Time doesn't matter now. It's a temptation to sit here longer and drink in the scenery."

Bridey stood up. "Oh, no you don't. I'm within radar distance of my dad, and I want to see him."

Rose's book claimed the easy path skirted the Norc River to their left and the castle grounds high above their right shoulders. As they headed away from the city center, smaller houses appeared more tightly packed together on the far bank.

Presently they discovered a narrow entry into the castle fortifications. They climbed stone steps toward the grounds above.

"Give me a push, Rose."

The echoing giggles in the stair shaft increased their helpless merriment. Somehow they hauled each other past the last step and collapsed, panting, onto a manicured lawn.

"Huh, huh. I hope I never have to do that again."

Bridey panted. "This was nothing. Wait until we're in labor, coach."

"What?" Rose whimpered.

"Come on, Rose. It's already after three o'clock what with the ride and the lunch, and…well…enjoying ourselves. I'm afraid the building will close, and you won't get to see it. I'll go and find my dad. Liam's been excited, I know."

Immediately before them stood the castle, with its crenellated towers. They strolled around the massive complex to the courtyard nestled within three four-story wings.

"You enjoy yourself inside, Rose. There's the main entrance. We'll meet at those steps at five. Have fun." Bridey waved and disappeared through a small door.

"So many chimneys." Rose headed up the main staircase. She melted with artistic delight at the parquet floors and the rose-painted, sunlit galleries lined with portraits. She peeked into bedrooms, furnished with period furniture, and into a number of closets and bathrooms with surprisingly modern facilities. The furnishings so diverted her that she lost track of which floor she was on. And the time.

How remiss she had been in leaving her watch home. In any case, Bridey knew she was here, and surely there was still plenty of time before they had to meet in the courtyard. What would Liam be like? It was hard to imagine a male version of Bridey's pretty features.

Rose sneaked into a long storage room, where she discovered a collection of paintings and folios stored in slots or crowded on the walls. This counted as sneaky, nosy, and delicious at the same time. Reverent euphoria buzzed against her skin. Her tingling fingertip traced the air above the frame of a priceless painting, a James Latham—or maybe a Garret Morphy? She cast a furtive glance toward the door. She mustn't be discovered in here. It wouldn't do for Bridey's friend and a guest of her father, a respected historian, to end up in gaol. Quickly, she stepped to the door and closed it. Without another thought, she was back at her visual banquet.

"Check the doors in this wing, Maudie," croaked a disembodied voice in the hallway. We got to get out before the storm hits."

Rose heard the door handle rattle and the key jangle, but by the time she made her way to the door, she banged on it to no avail.

"Hello! I'm in here. Help!" No answer.

She settled down to wait with shelf after shelf of art to keep her company. Maria had been right. She really ought to continue her art history studies, so enjoyed in her college years.

Drop by drop the sound of rain gained Rose's attention, so she tugged open the sash of the small, fourth story window. Bridey's purple flowered umbrella hurried to the entrance below, along with a tall man with gray-streaked hair. "Bridey! Bridey! It's me. Look up!" It was useless. The gushing downpour must have covered her voice.

She returned to the painting of a tall-masted ship. It listed hard to starboard and headed for a rocky shoal in a roiling sea. The gale whipped the sails. The deck pitched beneath her feet. Barrels rolled in her direction. The rank sulfuric stench of rotting vegetation turned her stomach.

A ferocious crack of lightning put out the lights. Rose sat in the near darkness as rain sheeted down, spattering against the window. Thunder boomed and rolled around her. She was back at her cabin on the ranch in Citrus County. She lolled on the porch glider while she telephoned with Maria. Michael emerged through the screen door, the sleeves of his white shirt rolled up to show the faint hair on his wrists and forearms. He alit next to her, slung one arm over her shoulders, and pointed alternately to the sky and the phone with the other hand. His curving lips articulated the word *dangerous*. "Bye, Mom. Gotta hang up now. That last lightning strike was pretty close."

She took hold of Michael's free hand and rubbed her lips up and down his arm. "Mmm...Michael. Your fuzzy arms are some of the most sensuous parts of your body."

He gave her a slow wink. "Not the absolutely most sensuous part, I hope, my love."

He interrupted her giggle with his lips. How could a man have such cushiony lips? How could a soft kiss last so long? It started with a few feather-light sweeps across her bottom lip—exploratory, speculative, and finally confirming his claim on her mouth. Flesh asserted itself on flesh. The tip of his tongue demanded entrance. Her lips parted tentatively, and he licked inside them and over her teeth, contending for her compliance with his will. His deep, blue eyes peered deeply into hers. He did not need to spell out his intentions. They uttered a mutual sigh and settled against the glider. His hands explored her features. She was caught in his eyes.

His voice quivered. "Rosie—oh, Rosie. I like sitting out here with you." He rubbed her nose with his. The sheets of rain provided a curtain of privacy against the menacing world."

"Yes, Michael, I feel so safe sitting here with you. So safe—"

Lightning cracked nearby, splitting a century old oak to the ground. She shrieked. Her mind whirled back to another reality, where she shuddered in the dark.

She was on her feet, hammering at the door. "Help! Help! Get me out!" The tears swam over her face. She pounded and panted until her heart was on the point of exploding.

At last she heard Bridey's voice. "Rose! Rose, it's me. We're here to get you out."

A cacophony of voices. "Who has the keys?"

"Watch out, Liam!"

The racket deafened her. Her skin crawled with sensation. Cowering, she backed into a corner.

A familiar voice shouted. "Stand back, Rose! I'm going to smash down the door." Then a colossal crash and the sound of wood splintering before she collapsed into the tall man's arms.

"Wh—what are you doing here? I never expected to see you again."

Chapter 14

After a fifteen minute walk to the train station, William had settled Rose and Bridey into a first class coach, reached a bag of ham buns in through the window, and waved them off to Glasgow, where they would change trains.

By then Rose's strained throat felt relieved. She seized Bridey by the shoulders. "Look, Bridey, look what we discovered. Will…Liam is your father. For goodness' sake, you never referred to your dad as William. Didn't you ever deduce we were on that tour together?"

Bridey gave her a sharp look. "You're the one. Aunt Claris told me about you."

Rose let the barb go. Whatever Bridey had heard about her friendship with William could sit in the slow cooker until later. "And here we are, drinking tea, gobbling yummy ham baps, and waiting for the next surprise."

They sat in silence for a while.

A gleeful expression came over Bridey's face. "Chocolate."

"You know—you're right."

At the next stop, she disappeared into the station house and reboarded with more tea and a paper bag.

"It's even better when you dunk it in hot tea."

Bridey mumbled. "Mmm…Butler's. My favorite."

"I'm surprised you can eat so much, Bridey—Bridget—after what we went through."

Safe in her living room, Rose munched on the last of the ham buns. "It was nice of William—your dad—to get these for us—and to give you money for the train and taxi. It's good to be home."

"Okay if I stay here tonight? Our cycles are down at the bus station."

"Yes, of course. Tomorrow we'll get someone to fetch the bikes."

Bridey peered out from the window seat. "Well, the dog came back."

Rose scooched further down in the sofa cushions. "Yes, didn't I tell you Michael sent me Gwen's sculpture?"

"I figured, but that's not what I'm talking about."

Rose groaned. She didn't want to get hauled into something new in her state of bedragglement.

"No, look." Bridey pointed to a black and white border collie resting on the tarmac.

They tumbled over each other as they hurried outside. The visitor licked both of them soundly and whipped his fringed tail to and fro.

"Holy Cow! You act as if you're the welcome party and I'm the visitor, doggy."

"You're fast on the uptake, Rose. Meet Raven, a member of your family. This is your grandfather's dog."

എൗഞ

When William and Claris visited them a week later, a speeding ball of fur bulleted out of the house to greet them.

"Whoa, boy! Nice doggie. Whoa—Ha-ha! Wait. Stop. Ha-ha-ha!" The collie administered his Raven special and then trotted to his water dish in the kitchen, where he shared liberally with the tiled floor.

"That's my grandfather's dog," Rose clarified.

"You don't say." William toweled his face with the dish cloth. "Maybe you'd better get started. I sense a long story coming."

Rose told him all about her efforts to locate her Grandfather on his extended vacation.

William ticked off the facts on his fingers. "But the dog is here. His cat was here. Cats often stay at home if the owner's coming back. I take it Bridget fed and watered Pickles? Dogs go with their masters. Ergo, the master is close by."

"But why is Raven here now, and how did he get here?"

William pursed his lips. "Maybe he ran off and came back to his original home. Surely your grandfather will guess the truth and track him down."

Her stomach quivered. "Yes, or I can follow him through woods and brambles to find his second home." She drew a tentative breath and then released it. "Look at his condition."

Bridget tore at scores of burrs with the pin brush from the drawer.

William grinned at each of them. "Bridget tells me she asked you to be her baby's godmother as well as her labor coach." He moved a little closer. "Look, I know you'll never be my wife. We settled that. Yet you're going to be like a grandmother to my grandchild."

Rose lowered her shoulders, looking at him from beneath her lashes. Regret hung close. "I'm sorry for what I did to you, Will. You were so nice to me, and I'm afraid I used you to make myself feel better. I see that now."

He laid a hand on hers. "It was win-win. I enjoyed your company, and I still do."

While Bridey and Claris visited in the other room, William pumped Rose on her attempts to reunite with her husband. She fidgeted in her chair.

William's eyebrows drew together. "You look a little frail. You really aren't happy without him, are you?"

She didn't want to lay her troubles at his doorstep, but

there was no way to keep her frustration out of her tone. "I want to reconcile with Michael with all my heart, yes, but it may be too late, because he doesn't know how I feel, and I can't find him."

"That husband of yours just doesn't know when to take 'yes' for an answer."

She chuckled. "You've got that right."

"Well, I'm going to help you flush him out."

That afternoon William fetched a big piece of plywood and propped it up in front of the house with the potted roses as anchors. Then he handed a brush and black paint to Rose, who boiled her message down to a few words.

Michael, let me find you.

ℰↄℰↄ

August:

Rose and Raven lounged on Bridey's overstuffed couch after a spaghetti dinner. Bridey sank into the matching chair after turning on the television. "Oof! Evan wouldn't take no for an answer when he wanted this chair. Now I'm glad he got to enjoy it, but I live in fear that I'll not be able to get myself out of it."

"Don't worry, babe. You know I'll be along soon enough to haul you out. You can always sleep in it if you need to."

"True, but when I have to pee—oh, boy!" Bridey's pinched face looked as if that could happen at any moment.

Rose reflected on her allies, who cooperated in each other's ventures—from cleaning up vomit to making the sign. Never again would she limit herself to a life that revolved around one person. Rose ruffled Raven's ears. His eyes rolled back in his head with pleasure, and a light panting ensued.

"You're so easy, boy. Pickles was harder to read. I guess I am a dog person. Puppy Joe wore every emotion on his face…Well, I guess, after all this time, I really don't know what he's like. He must be grown up by now. I missed a lot, didn't I?"

Raven pawed her arm.

"I know, boy. You want more.' She scratched his head. Can you believe I left my dog behind, and now Michael took him away? "I didn't even realize I could take Puppy Joe into Ireland these days."

Raven's dark eyes penetrated hers. He uttered a soulful whimper.

"Yes, that's what I say. Ooo, that Michael. I don't know what I will say to him when I do see him. It may not be pretty. That statue, lovely though it is, is no substitute for the real Puppy."

He bobbed his head with each syllable. "Ruff-ruff-oo! Real pup-py!"

Bridey groaned. Familiar music played. "Shit. The news."

Rose pushed the dog off her. Funny how quickly he'd adjusted to viewing her as alpha cushion. "I'll change it, Bridey. I know why you'd rather not see it."

Bridey uttered a sigh of resignation. "Leave it. I know very well I may see something I don't like. It's been a while since Evan went missing. I don't even know if he's still in Afghanistan—or wherever."

"All right. I agree it's better to know, and no news is good news." She returned the love toy that was her body back to Raven, but her eyes didn't move from Bridey's face all the while the news was on.

It was the same news, as far as Rose was concerned, though the fighting extended farther through the landscape every day. It could have been the same footage, replayed daily. Terrorists murdering civilians, civilians hiding in doorways, marksmen stalking inch by inch through sun-strafed streets and roads, occasionally taking down a child or two in error, while the mothers ran after them screaming.

"Holy crap. I wish they could show something new. I

wish Evan never decided to claim dual citizenship. Just because his father was an American like me. What a hare-
brained scheme. He's determined we'll live permanently
near my dad in the USA. He's no mama's boy, you know."

The war correspondent's familiar face filled the screen.
"This is the masked man who has executed so many west-
erners, GIs, journalists, humanitarian workers. Videotape
shows the unnamed terrorist threatening to behead a man
shown in silhouette but believed to be an Irish or Scottish
national attached to US forces. The name of the prisoner is
as yet unknown."

"No!"

Shuddering took over Bridey's body as she wailed and
called Evan's name. Raven leaped from the couch, placed
his forepaws on the arm of the chair, and whined.

Rose switched off the television and bent over Bridey's
cowering form. "It's all right, Bridey. We don't know it's
him. Evan is just a run-of-the mill foot soldier, isn't he?
There's no reason to make an example of him," she lied.

After a struggle to get her to bed, Bridey lay with her
legs propped on pillows. She slept, devoid of motion, silent.
Rose saw her as a silkworm in a cocoon, waiting for her
world to unravel. She murmured to the inert form, "Crawled
in there to die, did you, Bridey? We'll see about that." She
consulted the doctor at the door. "I can call her family to
come. Shall I?" That was another way of asking if she
should expect the worst for Bridey and her child. Rose
knew what the worst was like. She would never forget.

The doctor eyed her face. "You're asking if she'll go into
labor." He patted her shoulder, as if he suspected her history. "There's no way to predict that, my dear. She's suffered
a shock, but there's no sign of labor yet—no cramping, no
bleeding."

Fidgeting, Rose sat on a straight chair next to Bridey as
long as she could. Finally her chain-yawning made her
wretchedly irritable. She scratched the dog's ears. "Come
on, Raven. Let's stretch out on the couch."

Raven lifted his snoot from the bed, laid back his ears, and gave a nervous yawn. He slunk out of the room behind Rose, peering behind him every few seconds.

"It's all right, boy. We'll leave the door open, so we'll know if anything changes." She stretched out, and the dog lay beside her.

Rose dreamed of the child she had carried inside her and of the unwanted pains that had forced the infant into oblivion. Tonight Rosebud stood beside her, holding her hand.

"Doing good, Mommy. Nice and calm. I'm not in pain, and I'm not afraid." Rosebud's face was reassuring and kind. "I know you can do it, Mommy. But where's Daddy?"

Rose saw Michael struggling to open the door with his dangling arm. He forced his way out of the ruined car, stumbling and falling around the wreck. Somehow Rosebud could see him too, and Rose knew it. They both cried together. Michael stood there with the saddest look on his face, but he didn't cry. "Daddy!" Rosebud wailed, on and on.

❧❧❧

Rose felt for Raven. She sat up, felt in vain for her shoes, and padded barefoot into Bridey's bedroom, where Raven whined at the bedside.

"Bridey?" Rose tried to keep her voice to a whisper, but a gasp returned her call. "What is it, honey? Can't you sleep?"

"My back hurts, and I feel sick."

"Oh, dear—anything else? Can I get you to the toilet?"

"I—I think I wet myself already."

Rose recalled the odor of blood and the sensation of oozing amniotic fluid. The waters of life. And death.

She turned on the light in the hall, though she knew what she would see. She was not mistaken.

"Hmmm! Huh! Hmmm! Huh! Hmmm!" Bridey's breathing was all light, humming exhalations between little inward gasps.

Rose tried to raise Bridey's shoulders up in the bed. "How long has this been going on?"

Bridey was starting to tremble.

"Okay, honey. You're right. You are wet. And you're— Good breathing."

"Mmmmmmmm! What are you trying to say?"

"I'm pretty sure you're having the baby tonight."

"Oh, shit! Dammit, Evan. It's too soon." Bridey explored her sex with her fingertips. "Oh, God! I'm bloody. I'm losing the baby."

Rose tried to hold on to her arms. "No, Bridey. You're almost eight months."

"Mmmmmmmmm! Huh! Huh! Huh!"

"See, honey? You're having contractions. Maybe they don't feel as you expected, but that's what's happening. And you're not losing the baby. Doctor told me the baby should live. He'll be little, but he'll be fine."

Bridey gasped. "Mmmmmm! Mmmmmm!"

"Listen now, Bridey. I'm going to call the doctor. He'll want to check if you can have the baby here at home, as you planned."

Rose fumbled in Bridey's bag for the cell phone and then waited for someone to pick up. "Oh, thank goodness, Doctor. Bridey is in labor. What should I do?"

The doctor gave her instructions and promised to arrive as soon as he could.

"Bridey, the midwife is out of town, but the doctor is sure you'll be fine until he gets here. Meanwhile, it's you and me. It's good we took the classes, huh?" Rose hoped her laugh didn't sound too nervous.

"Oh, man." Bridey, struggled to sit up. "I have to poop." Instead, she threw up. "Oh, shit! Now what?"

Rose struggled with the urge to laugh. "You're in transition." She rolled up the top sheet and shoved it off the bed.

Bridey gritted her teeth. "Mmmmmmmm! Mmm!"

"No, Bridey, try not to bear down yet."

"Aaaah! You fuckin' try."

Rose rummaged in the kitchen drawers to find towels. She grabbed plastic garbage bags too. On the bureau, she propped up a five by seven of Evan in his uniform. "There's your focus. Look at Evan. Light breaths now."

Bridey threw back her head. "Fuck you, Evan!"

"Not just now, babe." Rose had soaped her hands and arms in the kitchen. Now she slid the bags under Bridey's buttocks. "Oh—wow—something is happening. I'd better examine you, Bridey. Sorry. I'm a horse midwife on the farm. It couldn't be much different with people, could it?" She slid her fingers into Bridey's stretched out birth passage.

"What the hell! Oh!"

"Aha!" Rose's finger touched an object inside Bridey's vagina—solid with slippery hair. She grabbed a new towel, wiped her fingers, fluffed up more pillows, and propped Bridey into what she considered an appropriate position.

Just then, a car roared into the driveway. Rose sprinted to the front entrance with a towel, threw the door open, and raced back to the groans in the bedroom. She placed her hands on Bridey's abdomen, feeling for contractions.

"Okay, Bridey, trust me. I know how this goes. I can feel the baby, and you're acting like it's time to push, so do what I tell you. All right?"

Bridey groaned.

"Take a deep breath. Now push as hard as you can. Harder, harder, harder. Stop. That was good. Now on the next one, you push even harder. I want this one to count."

The doctor appeared on the threshold. He gestured for Rose to carry on.

"Uhhhhhhhhh! Uhhhhhhhh! I can't, Rose, I—"

"Yes, you can. Do it for Evan. Show him what kind of a woman you are."

"Mmmmmmmmmm."

"Go—go—go—go! Okay, relax."

They looked into each other's eyes. Bridey nodded. "Shit, Rose."

"I can see the head. One more time, girl. This is the one."

Bridey clenched her teeth. "Mmmmmwah!"

Rose saw the back of a tiny head and two elfin ears. She turned the head and shoulders and guided the little form onto a fresh towel along with a vast amount of what could have passed for intestines. She felt giddy. "Oh! My God—" She was looking at a blue-veined length of umbilical cord."

"Bridey, you did it! Here's your baby."

Bridey laughed and cried simultaneously. "Is he all right? Does he have everything?"

"Hah! Yes and no. Meet your baby girl."

ℰↄℰↄ

The next day Bridey couldn't stop chattering. Her Aunt Claris brought the newborn to her, fresh from her bath. The baby rooted for Bridey's nipple and latched on to nurse.

Rose felt a flush of pleasure. This was the way it was supposed to be. "She may be tiny, but she sure knows her business."

Bridey reached for her hand. "Rose, I was so scared—If I'd lost the baby, this was my last chance, in case Evan died too."

"Well, you didn't. And I don't believe in last chances."

Once Rose was satisfied that Claris could take over, she was in a hurry to notify Gwen about the birth in person. So much in a hurry that she only belatedly noticed Raven running behind her. "Go home, boy. You can't come with me. Go home." How many homes had he lost in recent months? "No, all I need is for you to fall back from the chase, roam around town, and get lost again."

Once they arrived in front of the shop, she retrieved her scarf from her pocket and tied one end to his collar, the other to her bike, which leaned against the storefront. She placed her hands on his muzzle and rubbed until he groaned. "Don't pull the bike down on yourself, will you, boy?"

He looked eager to please.

Another moment, and Rose was in the shop. "She's had the baby, Gwen. It's a girl."

Interrupted at her pottery wheel, Gwen looked up with a smile. "I surmise you mean Bridey? And everything went well? Take a seat, and tell me all the minutest details."

While Rose dumped her bag on a chair, Gwen covered her unfinished project and scrubbed her hands and tools. Her eyes never left Rose's face. "My goodness, sweetie. You have the glow of a new mother yourself."

Rose laughed. A comment like that had ceased to bring up fresh grief, though she still recalled examining her little Rosebud, with her large, closed eyes and rosebud lips.

"Yes, Bridey's baby does feel like mine in a way. I delivered her during the night. And you know what?" Her wide eyes searched Gwen's. "I feel contented to have got it right this time. My heart feels like a well-filled teacup." Their chuckles stumbled over each other. "I got that expression from my Grandmother, though I never met her."

"Yes, I remember we said that in my day."

Gwen leaped from her seat at the sight of Raven, his front paws on the shop window and a gnawed scarf in his mouth. "Oh, my!" She flung open the door. Raven smooched her all over, with little doggie expletives. A wriggling missile of joyfulness, he threw himself on Rose too and administered a thousand little play bites with as many overwhelmed yips.

Finally Gwen noticed the damage to the scarf. "You tied him to your bike? How do you know Raven?"

"You know him too? He certainly knows you."

"Yes, he stayed at my house for a while this year before he moved on. I guess he's what you would call the town dog."

"No, not really. Bridey says he belonged to my grandfather, who has eluded me for quite a while. I wish I could—"

Gwen staggered back, her eyes round as an owl's. Her hand went to her chest, and she uttered a little squeak. She fell onto a chair and grabbed for Raven, who clamored around her. She buried her face in the luxurious white fur on his chest.

The gesture kept Rose from seeing her expression. She dropped to her knees and pushed Raven aside. Gwen's face was whiter than paper, her trembling lips speechless.

"Why, Gwen, what's the matter? You're not having a heart attack or something, are you?"

Gwen squeaked out her words. "No, no, child. I think the...er...the good news of the...the birth has...uh...overcome me. I wasn't expecting...this. It...It's been quite a while since I've had a baby in my circle...not since Violet was born."

Rose furrowed her brow. "Come on, now, Gwen. Don't take it so hard. You're not alone. You have a wonderful daughter and granddaughter."

Gwen uttered a bitter laugh. "It's not that. I've just missed so much." She rubbed her cheeks. "I can't believe it." She clutched Rose's arm, her tone intense. "Oh, Rose, I can't believe I almost missed knowing you. You would have gone back to Florida, and I might never—" She broke off, shaking her head.

Gwen gulped back tears, and sobs tightened in Rose's chest, as though the tears were hers. "I'm sorry, Gwen. I didn't know this would affect you on such a deep level. Shouldn't we take you to the clinic down the street?" Rose held her tightly around the knees while entreating her to...somehow...let her in on the truth clearly clamoring for expression. "That's my fault, isn't it, Gwen? I've poured out my guts to you these past months as if you're family, though I know nothing about what makes you tick." She covered her face. "I'm so sorry. I never took the time." She grasped Gwen's hands. "Now I want to take care of you, and I'm going to learn what you need."

More tears rolled down Gwen's cheek. "I'm sorry, Rose. I haven't been easy to know."

Rose stood up and sat down next to Gwen, her arm around her shoulder. She fished in her bag for a tissue and blotted Gwen's face. "The truth is, you do feel like family to me. I love you, Gwen." She angled her body to peer straight into her eyes. "You do know I'll never forget you when I go home, don't you?"

"You said *home*, Rose. And that's not here."

"Yes, I did, but *home* can be wherever you love someone."

⁄⁄⁄

Gwen closed up the shop to leave early. She seemed more composed, more herself. Rose marveled, as often before, how, looking into her eyes, she knew she had seen them before.

Gwen's voice was bright and strong when she spoke. "Don't worry, Rose. You have a pretty good homing device in there." She tapped Rose's forehead. "You'll find the people you love."

Rose accepted Gwen's invitation to supper tonight. She turned to look at Raven and let her hair cover the side of her face to hide her embarrassment. She had dropped in on Gwen at the shop nearly every day while she'd resided in Clifden. Yet she'd never thought to visit her at her home. How often Gwen had invited her. "You'll have to come over," or "I'd love you to see my garden." Rose didn't even know if Gwen had a third husband in place, or a boyfriend. She looked awfully frail today, but she wasn't too old to live a full life.

Rose made her voice bright. "I'm eager to see your place."

"Good." Gwen's voice was pert and sunny. "When you're done with your shopping take the Galway Road east to the turning into the low road. Follow it south and around to the west and the Owenglin River. You'll see some du- plexes that back up to the woods. Here's the number." She ruffled Raven's ears. "Since this doggie's so good at follow- ing your bike, why don't you bring him with you? He'll like my cooking."

Raven yapped. Rose had planned to stop in at Christ Church that afternoon for the ladies' crafting meeting. She wanted to help with their quilting project, but now it was too late. At least she should explain her absence. She found Rosemary gathering herbs in her kitchen garden. Rose soaked up the overflowing contentment that attended this woman and this place. One look at the motherly figure in- stilled confidence that all would be well.

Rosemary gifted her with one of her big smiles. "Rose, dear. It's so wonderful to see you."

"I'm sorry I didn't come to the meeting. Something hap- pened."

Her friend kept her smile, but now it hung a little askew.

"What about this little gentleman?" She bent over, hands in her lap, herbs and all, affecting the tone many used on pets and toddlers. On her it sounded right. "Who are you then, laddie? What? Oh, a playful boy, are you?"

Raven bowed down on his forepaws as he wiggled his hindquarters.

"This is my grandfather's dog, Raven."

Rosemary's eyes widened. "Did you find him then?"

"No, but Raven came home. It seems he's visited other homes for a while. Right now he's contented to follow me everywhere."

"Can you come in then, the two of you?"

Rose was sorry to refuse but mindful of time slipping away as her appointment with Gwen neared. As she turned her bike around, she recognized the set of Rosemary's lips. "I know that face. What is it?"

Now Rosemary looked away, her eyes cast down. "I'm not supposed to say."

Rose's heart lurched. She caught her friend by both arms. "What's the matter? Please don't keep anything from me."

They locked eyes. "Adam saw him."

Rose opened her mouth to reply, but her tongue felt thick.

"He met with your young man." She nodded toward the house. "In his study. With the door closed."

"My Michael? Are you sure?"

"They were the eyes from your picture. He's been here before, remember. He had a dog with him too, a wee laddie, brownish with a lot of white. Very well-behaved."

"What did they say?"

Rosemary's eyes darted from side to side. "The vicar can't tell anyone, even me. Professional privilege."

"But?"

Rosemary paused a long time, twisting the chives into mush. At last she opened her mouth and then closed it again, without returning her gaze to her friend. "Well. I'm not the vicar."

Rose seized her hands as the herbs fell to the ground forgotten. "You—You heard something. You're going to tell me, aren't you?"

"Only a little, when I dusted the pictures near the door. That and the way he looked."

"Please, please, Rosemary. Tell me what you can."

"I didn't hear the whole context, you understand. His words were 'I've ruined my whole life. I've not been able to save...something, something." She scratched her palms. "One wrong move, and I'm lost forever.' Something like that. I heard some crying—the dog and the man both."

"Oh, God. Did Adam tell him that I'm looking for him?"

"Well, he wouldn't tell him that, would he? That's your business, and—come to think of it, this man didn't have the same surname as you. It could be somebody else."

"Nothing else?"

"Well, yes, I think there was some advice. I heard 'what

are you waiting for?' and 'why are you so afraid?' and the usual talk about God."

Rose covered her face with her hands, and Raven pawed at her leg. "Nothing else?"

"Just my overall impression. He's a man who's been lost. He needs someone to save him. And it's not going to happen in church."

Chapter 15

Rose wound through town and south to the river while her thoughts wove a tapestry with Michael and Grandfather and Bridey and Gwen. Why had the sight of Raven rattled Gwen so much? It was time for Rose to find a way into Gwen's private life at last.

Raven had better like Gwen's cooking, because he'd need a good feed after this run. Near the river, the Low Road veered downhill and around to the right, where it was narrow and much patched. Rose's brakes squealed, and she skidded.

Opposite single family dwellings to the right, four stucco double cottages stood, white with brown roof tiles, brown doors and woodwork. Gwen's far end unit displayed immaculate white lace curtains in the front room picture window. A small window flanked the door on the other side.

Tongue-lolling, Raven caught up with her bike. Rose suffered a pang, for she understood Gwen's husband hadn't left her too well off. She had to admit, though, Gwen had kept her home neat, through tending the garden, and raising her daughter alone, not to mention wringing a living from her little shop in town.

Raven dashed around to a cultivated lawn and garden behind the house. Rose caught sight of a wooded area beyond those.

Young laughter and splashing pointed the way to the river beyond.

Gwen opened the door at Rose's knock. She had dressed as for an occasion. The bright blue of her delicate wool dress emphasized her eyes, made up with a touch of mascara. She wore a ruffled, starched white apron over her dress, with her hands in the pockets. "Welcome, welcome! Where is that precious doggie?"

"He rushed down to the woods like a crazy man. Hear him barking?"

"Yes, that's his voice all right."

"I can see how he got between our houses. If he went overland to the R341 bridge, across the stream, and up the street towards Ardbear he'd stumble upon my Grandfather's house. He could easily wander back and forth once he knew the way. I wonder why he wanted to do that."

Gwen welcomed Rose with a kiss on each cheek. She studied her intently, as if seeing her for the first time. She fingered a strand of her runaway red hair. What created this singular mood?

She made Rose welcome in her small sitting room, introducing her to all her intimate treasures on shelves and tabletops and several pictures atop a small buffet. Rose noticed a clear spot in the dust where she must have removed one of them recently. Rose grinned. After all, a little dust could hardly bother a woman who enchanted clay by the handful.

Gwen pointed to two large, framed photos. "That's a nice one of my Rose and Violet," don't you think?" The large, round blue eyes could have been interchangeable in either face—the perfect Irish face which Grandfather admired.

"Yes, they both look a lot like you, Gwen. Beautiful."

"And that's Rose's father, Arthur. I don't have him as a young man, because I didn't know him then. He was widowed, like me, and childless. We met ten years after my first husband, er, after I lost him. Then it took me a while to decide if I liked him enough to make us a couple, poor man. It was none too soon when we tied the knot. That's why my daughter is so young. Anyway—" She took a deep breath and began again in a different tone. "The other photos are all in albums. For another time." She handed Rose a glass of sherry, which stood next to hers, ready on the buffet, and raised hers in a toast. "Here's to us. May we know each other better after today, and may that lead only to good."

"I'll drink to that." Their glasses clinked as they made contact.

Gwen cupped her hands upside down in her lap. As she rubbed her right thumb over the palm of her left hand, Rose's eyes fell on the gold band showing on the back of one of her fingers. A wedding ring? Again, Rose reproached herself for being so oblivious to the personal life of this dear woman who had been so good to her. A small piece fell into place in her mind's puzzle. Of course Gwen had never worn a ring to work, since her hands were always in clay.

Rose patted Gwen's arm. "I want you to do me a favor, Gwen."

Gwen's hand quivered a little.

"Yes," Rose nodded, holding those familiar eyes with hers. "I want you to tell me all about yourself. I want to know you, my friend."

Gwen answered with a nervous laugh. "Me? What would you want to know about me?"

"Everything. What it was like when you were young. Losing your little boy and two husbands. What you worry about and what you pray about. How you got over all the hard times. Because I want to learn to do that as well as you have. I want to imitate your grace and your sense of fun and your wonderful èlan."

Gwen's eyes misted over. "I can see you're already more like me than you know. We learn to cope with hard times."

"Tell me about losing your husband and son, Gwen. Don't leave anything out." Already Rose's eyes stung. "I want to know what made you who you are."

Gwen answered slowly, wetting her lips. "I couldn't believe it at first, because it was my mother who took the phone call. When she told me my family was dead, I wanted to rush back to America immediately and see for myself." She cleared her throat. "'Do yourself a favor,' my mother insisted. 'They collided with a gasoline truck. There's nothing left save the skid marks.'" Gwen shuddered. "My husband had no relatives."

The horror of that long ago moment pierced through Rose. "So, you kept living with your mother? How did that go?"

"It was all I could do. I never went back to America. I never finished university. I didn't have a trade. I was desperately depressed." Gwen paused, looking at a point outside the window, her shoulders stiff.

"I think I would have lost my senses except for the church, and I formed good friendships with other women. They made all the difference. I met the man I later married. It wasn't the same as first love, Rose. I can tell you that. But Arthur was a true and loyal friend, and I needed someone to help me feel whole again. He was a good man, and he gave me peace of mind."

Her gaze traveled to the family's portraits. "He was a good father to our daughter. He tried to be a good husband to me. God bless him. He made an honest living as a laborer, and he was home every night. He left me enough to buy this building. I live in half and rent out the other side. All those years I thought I loved him too little to miss him...but I was wrong.

"I think you're trying to tell me something, wise woman."

Gwen looked at her with mischief on her face, and tears too. Her lips turned under, though she laughed. "Is that so? Wisdom from the old?"

"Maybe you can't have what you want, but you can develop contentment with whatever you can have. Something like that?"

Gwen's lips quirked up at the corners. "Maybe so." She started to stand up.

Rose put out a hand in a signal for *stop*. "Wait. Can't I have more now that we've started? What about your first husband? Did you ever come to terms with what happened?"

Gwen emitted a long sigh. "My mother died of spite."

"What?" Rose almost choked on the unexpected words. "S—spite?"

"She feasted on it after I married my sweetheart. She didn't want me to marry an American. She didn't want me to live over there. She didn't want me to have half-breed children. And so on." Gwen paused, focused somewhere else.

Rose patted her arm. "And?"

"So she took care of the problem. She lied."

"What—what do you mean?"

"My husband—Rose's father—he did chores for one of the horse breeders in Connemara, who was very good to us, though Artie was only working class. One time this man returned from a convention abroad. Florida it was. He told Artie about one of the breeders there who had the name of my first husband. After my mother heard that, she started to turn crazy. She had hallucinations, heard voices. You know. 'Get away from me,' she used to say. 'Get away. You're supposed to be dead.'"

Rose raised her voice. "My God, my God, Gwen!" She clutched the arms of her chair. "She thought your first husband was a ghost—or alive."

"That's right. I prayed about what I heard. I went to the priest. We talked about the possibility my mother lied to me the whole time. What had she done to me, her own child? The priest offered to help me find answers. But he also counseled me about forgiveness. He insisted it would give me peace to forgive my mother. Moreover, I wasn't obliged to dredge up the past. He reminded me I had a new husband and a new child."

Rose shook her head.

"By then my mother had died, so there was no way to confront her."

The corners of Gwen's mouth turned down. She took her left hand from her pocket and picked at calluses on that palm. "Whatever my mother did to me, I did worse to myself, because I let it happen, and now I was trapped by my own doing."

Gwen told Rose that more years went by before she acted on her own behalf. She did her best to live up to her vows to Arthur. She raised her child. Then Arthur died, and she was growing old.

"I just wanted the truth. So I dug it out."

By then Gwen had learned about the internet, complete with photos and bios. She telephoned an old man in Florida, the man who had been her true love. He had burst into tears when he'd heard her voice.

Gwen's chin quivered. Her voice cracked. "He still loved me."

Rose felt a hundred horses galloping straight at her.

Gwen's hands lay in her lap. "We emailed and called and cried. He wanted to see me."

Rose started from her chair. She took hold of Gwen's hand and turned it over, revealing the back. Her brain was spinning. She could only whisper. "Where did you get that ring?"

Gwen got to her feet. Her tone pleaded more eloquently than her words. "I'm sorry, my darling. I never did put things together until today. You and I didn't talk about your grandfather, remember, just Michael, and his surname, which I've seen you sign, didn't mean anything to me." Trembling, she reached out her hands. "Now's when we find out if this story's ending is going to be a happy one."

"What? What?" Rose couldn't think. She heard barking at the back door and a familiar bass voice.

"Come now, fella. Knock it off. We'll find your women for you. There they are."

Raven rushed into the front room and slobbered over Rose and Gwen, both already unsteady on their feet. His master stood in the doorway, beaming wide enough to rip off his ears.

Gwen laughed. "For goodness sake, come in here, Sean."

The old man shifted into the light. "Well, Rose, are you going to stand there looking like an idiot? Don't you know me?"

Then her feet moved without her brain, and she dashed into his arms. All she could do was bawl. "Granddad! Granddad!" She blubbered out all sorts of things about him and Michael and Rosebud and Grandmother, little of it sounding sensible, even to her.

Still strong as aged mutton, he lifted her, as he had when she was little. "Come, my little Rose. There's all the time in the world to talk." He carried her to the couch and held her on his lap. He still smelled of horseflesh and tobacco, and she wouldn't have it any other way.

They ended up talking over each other's words and laughs and sobs all night long, always within reach of each other. Early on, she was aware of Gwen serving a glass of cold water, the best she had ever drunk. Later there were plates of beef stew with carrots and potatoes and mushy peas, along with biscuits to mop up the gravy. A massive armchair now abutted the couch, and they ate and talked right there, knee to knee.

During the evening, Rose uttered things that astounded her. "My grandmother's name was Rose. I'm named after her, and so was my daughter. How come your name is Gwen?"

"That's right, darling. That's my name—Rose Gwendo-lyn."

Rose heard the smirk in Grandfather's voice as much as she saw it on his face. "She loved me calling her name so much, that she couldn't bear to have any other man use it." The lovers smiled at each other. Gwen rubbed his hand as he spoke. "Yes, and we both remembered our promise to pass the name on. She used it with her daughter, whom I guess you know. And across the water my—our son agreed to name you Rose too."

"I couldn't find Grandmother's ring in your house, Grandfather. Where was it?"

Grandfather chuckled. "Of course I took it away to give back to my true love. And—look—she's wearing it now. You did notice that, didn't you?"

Rose's overwhelmed mind lagged. "Why?"

"It's her ring, daft one. Always has been."

"Why are you over here and not in your house?"

"This is our love nest. What else? We've been here since May playing honeymoon. Three months now. I only lived in the other house until I persuaded my sweetheart to cohabit. I didn't think I needed the family's permission."

Gwen giggled and snuggled on his arm. "I'm sorry, Rose. I should have made him call home." She lowered her eyes. "I guess we were afraid to interrupt our happiness."

"Maybe I wanted to make sure I'd made her truly mine." Grandfather Sean made his voice sheepish and playful too.

She pinched him. "Bad boy."

Rose scowled. "Really."

Gwen stretched out a hand. "We were a little afraid of what Aidan would say—after all this time."

Sean set his jaw. "It wasn't about him. We waited long enough for our lives to be our own."

In the morning, Rose felt a little murky, though ready to sort out the confusion, even if by dribs and drabs. One realization almost levitated Rose off the couch. "You are Aidan's mother, and Rose Too is my sister."

"Yes, dear." Gwen spoke in a deliberate tone, as if Rose were a bit slow on the uptake. "And therefore you and Violet are both my granddaughters. You'll get used to it." Gwen's eyes sparkled. Sean just shook his head.

Rose raised her fists next to her ears. "Oh! Now I know why I was sure I saw you before. Your eyes are just like Daddy's."

Gwen's sob was a ragged intake of air. "My boy."

Rose yawned, but she was ready to continue their catch-up marathon. In a way, she realized, she'd been waiting for this all her life.

"I've been looking for you, Grandfather. That was very bad that you let yourself get lost."

"I'm sorry, love. I didn't feel lost. What can I say? I was just a fool in love."

Gwen dug him in the ribs. "An old fool. And forgetful. He didn't even realize you were coming."

"Well, at least I finally remembered to pay my bills and put money in the bank. I suppose your dad didn't tell you that."

Had he? She recalled him informing her that grandfather was safe.

"Well, you left Pickles in the other house."

"Who?"

"The cat. Do you know he's dead?"

"Oh, that's too bad. But that's not my cat. He belongs to a widow two streets away. She kept confusing me with someone else. The cat came to me for bed and board, because we were both scared of the old hag."

"Sean!" Gwen dug him in the ribs."

"One big question, Rose." Gwen turned up her palms. "I mentioned I didn't connect you with the name Flanagan. Was that my mistake? I'm so sorry the truth passed right by me earlier."

Rose groaned, her mind racing. "I did use Michael's surname from time to time since I came to Ireland. I don't know why. I guess it caused a lot of confusion."

Gwen took both her hands. "It's okay, honey. I think I understand."

Rose shook her head. "Sometimes I've thought I was losing my mind."

Sean's arms pressed her against his big chest. His strong heartbeat made her understand things would sort themselves out, more than any discussion ever could.

She bathed in his peaceful aura, thinking how new this tranquility was in his life. The world had gone nuts long ago. Maybe now they'd help each other overcome that. She imagined Sean's strong arms hauling Michael out of his hidey-hole by the seat of his pants. She pressed her fist against her lips.

"Gwen, you're going to tell Daddy, aren't you? About you being—who you are?"

"Of course I'm dying to see him, but he's a grown up man now. He may not react as I want him to. Didn't he grow up thinking I deserted him? I'm sure he harbors resentment. Maybe hatred." Gwen's lips pressed tight, top lip over lower.

Aiden used that expression to show disappointment. "Oh—Grandmother."

Sean's voice was sheepish and a tone flat. "That's true. I may have been a little bitter, too, back in the day. Maybe I said some things I can't unsay. It's hard to tell him now. 'By the way, son. There's been a mistake.'"

Rose grew desperate. "How do you think he'll feel if you wait until you're dead?"

Gwen gave Sean a coy look. "Let's call him today. Maybe he'll forgive me if he and his wife are invited to the wedding."

Rose overheard bits of Grandfather Sean's conversation with Aidan.

He curled his shoulders over his chest and looked at the floor. "I'm sorry, my boy. I've been off the radar. I lost track of time. I never meant to disappear."

Aidan's agitated voice rumbled during Sean's Pauses.

"Yes…yes. It was all my fault…I've been a real ass. Call me what you want…I'm sorry, son. I just hope you can forgive me." His voice cracked. "You see, I met the love of my life and fell head over heels…Yes, I'm sure. I think you know who it is."

When the call was over, Rose wished she were back in Citrus County with Aidan. She wiped her eyes and put her arms around Sean instead. "You know Daddy sent me here to find you, but I also wanted to get to know Ireland and find out why you loved it so much. The truth is—I always felt bad I was half and half and not full Irish the way Daddy was—" Her voice quaked. "What I'm trying to say is…uh…I know what it's like to feel guilty when you really can't help how you feel."

Rose's grandparents looked at each other, at her, and then at each other again. Grandfather nodded at Gwen.

Gwen took Rose's hands. "Don't be shocked dear, but Aidan isn't full Irish either. I got pregnant the night before I fell for my true love here. Of course I didn't know it then. Heavens, I barely remember that fraternity party, except for some French boy and the hangover."

Grandfather offered a small nod. "Our meeting was under such intense circumstances. We had a whirlwind courtship. Trust me. She remembers that all right. We married right away. Trust me, neither of us gave a thought to Aidan's parentage until recently, as a matter of fact."

Rose's chest tightened. She turned to Gwen. "But you knew?"

"No, I didn't find out until our second courtship, when Sean told me."

Rose's thoughts raced. "But how could that be? Grandfather, how could you know, while Gwen, Daddy's own mother didn't have a clue?" Somehow, the answer really mattered to her.

"Why, it was like this, honey. Aidan and I went down to Citrus Memorial to give blood for that little boy who, uh, tangled with the alligator—remember?"

She nodded, curling her lip in distaste.

"Well, on the way out I picked up both sets of paperwork, and…I couldn't help looking at his. Our blood types didn't…um…" He waved his hands. "Anyway, he couldn't have been my son, except in all the ways that mattered to me."

Rose crossed her arms over her chest and scrunched up her face. "Gwen, how could you?"

"You're disappointed in me, aren't you? I'm sorry, darling. I wish I'd known better, but it was the sixties." She shrugged. "Fraternity keggers. Pot. Free love…"

Grandfather stepped between them. "This issue is not your business, girl, but I'll give you the true story anyway. I assumed Gwen wasn't a virgin when we met. Neither was I. We didn't hold that against each other. Period. Sex was meaningless until we found each other."

Gwen stepped up to Rose. "Anyway, the point is…Aidan is the one who's half and half."

Grandfather grinned. "Not you."

Part IV
Healing

Connemara Countryside

Chapter 16

Late August:

After Rose filled Grandfather Sean in on Michael's new modus operandi for winning her back, he waved his garden trowel at her. "You'd better go out hunting, girl. It sounds like your wild game has turned into a scared rabbit."

She flung Raven's ball toward the tree line. "Do you think I like it, Grandfather? I was accustomed to a ram charger. Now he hippity-hops around, leaving little clue pellets."

"Ha-ha!" Sean rested on his shovel. "Lord, girl, I've never seen you angry with that boy."

"No, my shining white knight worked his butt off to make me happy back in the good old days. Now he's changed the rules. More than once." Her shoulders sagged. "I don't even know this version of Michael or what to do with him when…if I find him. All I can figure is he's as confused as I am. Especially since I'm the one who ran away." She covered her face. "I did command him to leave me alone."

Gwen appeared with glasses of water. "Look, Rose, you can leave us without fear that we'll go on the lam. You'd better get on with your search."

"My woman is right, as usual." Sean wiggled his eye-brows at his one-time bride. "No telling how long your quarry will stay around."

Gwen focused on Rose. "You look peaked lately, dear. Lackluster. You need to make an end of this, one way or another."

Rose felt a shot of pain down her throat, like triple strength whiskey. "You're both right. I'm scared to lose you again, and I'm scared of one of the endings this mystery can take."

They reassured her with a family hug like the ones she'd shared with her parents. She imagined the family—all of them—assembled in her rose garden at home, applauding as Michael carried her over the threshold of their little cottage, one hand caressing her swollen belly while Puppy Joe leaped for joy.

"Am I too late?" she murmured into Sean's shirt.

He held her tighter.

Gwen kissed her cheek. "It's all right, Rose. Do leave Raven with us. He hardly knows where he belongs, poor fellow."

Rose left them at the Ardbear house, but resolved to take their advice with her. With the *fwt-fwt-fwt fwt* of her wonky front wheel, Gwen's words circled in Rose's mind. '*He hardly knows where he belongs...He hardly knows...He hardly knows.*' Maybe Michael had that half and half prob-lem these days. As for her, she rarely thought of herself that way now. She knew where her heart belonged.

The Seven Bens loomed above Clifden, more like reign-ing town elders than mountains. She imagined their censure of her failure to find Michael. Pumping one fist, she threw out her frustration at them. "Help me, then. For God's sake, you must be able to see him from there."

She paused on the 341 bridge to check out the Owenglin River. Late summer had introduced some color near Gwen's cottage on the opposite bank, where her search for her Irish roots had come to an end. She'd run out of ways to sniff out

Grandfather, but serendipity had delivered him into her hands. She needed that kind of assistance now too.

Cumulous clouds rose like fluffy chef hats above the Bens' snowy white crowns. Then the whole picture upended in the river—a reminder of how rapidly things turned upside down. The mast of a sailboat moored to the bridge pointed to the reflection of Christ Church's spire, clear and unrippled in this unbothered spot, lording it over the market square. She veered left onto Market Street, her eye on the knobby hills to the west, with their rambling stone walls and patches of spiny yellow gorse. Was that where she needed to venture?

Women called to their children from a nearby launderette. Scores of growers and artists waved and called her by name. At this hour, many of the stands stood tarped, their owners off to their lunch at the cafés and pubs. Her bike whished out its cadence. "Nevvver give up. Nevvver give up."

On Beach Road, to the west of the square, slews of vehicles nosed into the narrow spots in front of colorful storefronts, where she had shown Michael's photograph to everyone who would look. It had been a tactic to stave off the discovery that Michael did not exist.

Rose passed by the traffic circle with its obelisk at the center of the square and headed up the Church Hill Road, from where Christ Church always beckoned. She lowered her kickstand on the grass and rambled among the old grave stones, tracing the epitaphs with her fingers. "Beloved husband. Faithful wife."

Near her bike, one monument wrenched her with bittersweet pain, making her clutch at her chest. "Reunited at Last." She fell to her knees, sobbing, ripped out handfuls of grass, and flung them about.

"Help me, Michael, for God's sake. Do we have to be under the soil before we're reunited at last?" She gritted her teeth. "You're killing me. I hate you for doing so little to reclaim me, and—damn you!—I can't find you."

She stumbled to her feet and staggered into a well-upholstered bosom under a floury apron.

Rosemary tucked Rose's grassy sweater in the basket and wiped her face with her apron. "I don't know that you've ever mentioned that before, have you, dear?"

"What?"

"That you hate him." Rosemary placed a hand on Rose's cheek. "You need to tell Michael that, don't you?"

Those words caused Rose to stumble back. "I'm so tired. I don't know where to look any more, and nobody can help me."

Rosemary looked askance. "Ahem!"

Rose looked up sharply and drew in a broken breath. A surge of hope filled the silence. She seized Rosemary's arms and gave her a shake. Her voice sounded impatient and rough "What? What?"

"Well, one thing about being the rector's wife is that people don't watch you watching them. You get to see which way they go when they leave."

Rose gasped, grabbed her more tightly and gabbled. "Where? Tell me. For God's sake, tell me."

Rosemary stepped to the edge of the hill, from where she could see the northern road below, the one that led, Rose knew, to the Clifden Monument and to Sky Road, a seven mile loop that overlooked Clifden Bay. Rosemary stared into the western distance, but she had nothing more to say.

Rose sped down the hill, nearly taking a spill as she made the turn at the bottom onto the Sky Road. Her highway to heaven? Or would it bring her back to the same place at the end, always empty-handed and with empty arms?

Before long, Rose made a halt on the side of the narrow roadway, for her breath came in rough, sharp pants. The stone walls made it impossible to pull off the tarmac, so she turned to check behind her. She was utterly alone.

She sipped from the bike's attached water bottle, which, reused daily, had taken her hundreds of kilometers in her fruitless search for her holy grail. She surveyed the distance she had traveled, leaving the Bens and the town behind her, with the spires of the two churches resplendent in the noonday sun. Church of Ireland and Catholic, two different architectural and liturgical styles, watched over the town in apparent harmony. And still a broken down man and his dog could blend in with who knew what kind of shadowed places.

Climbing higher above bay and sea, she stopped often to admire the view. Vegetation grew lower here. Grass and gorse among the ever-present stones formed a border at the side of the road or a waist high wall, depending, she supposed, on the abruptness of the land's fall to the sea. At this point, the roadside on her left extended sharply downward to extensive plateaus that dropped away to the surf.

As she pedaled, she marveled at the cliffs. They made her shiver with their beauty and with the possibility of danger. Herds of Connemara ponies galloped free on the headlands. A rented pony, hardy and level-headed, had once occupied Grandfather's stable, so he'd told her. She could tell he missed the riding, and his fond tone had reminded her of her innocent years when they had ridden the family horses together, master and pupil. Until her solo ride that had killed her dog Charlie.

She cycled along the seaward side of the road. Sometimes the plateau segued into pastures and farms, the ubiquitous stone walls defining their boundaries. Clusters of prosperous-looking buildings spread out to claim their share of the never-ending, verdant meadowland. Everywhere in the vast green hue, white dots represented isolated homes, hovels, ancient ruins, or bed and breakfasts peeping from behind clumps of vegetation or hills. They reminded her of Citrus County, where everybody could afford a share of the land and access to the water, whether they lived under a Cracker style tin roof or costly tile.

In this corner of the world, all the homes wore white, and they mingled with the smaller ovine specks of wool. There were so many buildings down there, and so many sheep.

She sighed and spoke to Michael somewhere below. "You could have a sleeping bag rolled up in a shack anywhere. Tomorrow I must bring Grandfather's binoculars. I'll find you."

Positive thoughts helped Rose pump her way up and down the Sky Road for hours. Then, when hunger overtook her, she turned back toward the loop's entry. She caught a bit of grease making its way through the package Rosemary had sneaked into her basket—along with a savory scent that coaxed a gurgle from her stomach.

She looked down on the ruins of Clifden Castle amid some trees. Sheep close to the road checked her out with coy gazes, the dye marks on their backs identifying their owners. Others dotted the emerald grass all the way to the bay.

The castle was largely intact, at least on the outside. It beckoned her with shade on one end and vistas all around too good to pass up. From there a narrow, fenced path stretched into the gullies and hills to the north and east. Her instincts twittering, Rose guided her bike through a gap in the wall and overland down to the plateau, where she angled herself through an arch into an open courtyard. She let herself slide down along the far wall, thereby taking advantage of the shade while able to study the facade.

Rose tore into Rosemary's juicy packet. Mmm! She ravaged the thick-cut, full-bodied Cheddar and sausage crammed between buttered slices of brown bread. She vowed to bake this manna, when she brought Michael home. Memories spilled out of an occasion when she and Michael had broken off pieces of bread and dipped them into the seasoned oil on each other's bodies. He had licked his way all the way down her spine from her nape to the rise of her buttocks, and then he had rolled her over. How glad she was for the wisdom to make a peak pleasure out of such small moments while she could.

She leaned back to rummage through her day bag. Ah!

Her guide book. She had forgotten about that. Time to read. She felt the afternoon chill come on, though, so she cast a last look at this facade, gathered her trash with the rest of her gear, and migrated to the sunny side of the castle, leaving her bike behind. The vista over Clifden Bay, replete with white sails, filled her with wonderment. Michael would take pleasure in this spot.

The sun caressed her face while she relaxed against her newly-claimed wall. She shaded her eyes with her map and read on. The words proceeded down the pages, kicking up fleeting impressions. A ruined manor house. An heir named Hyacinth. A failed potato crop. Tenants on the lawn, begging for food.

"What a funny name for a man," she murmured, as, in her imagination, someone dressed as a purple flower faced an angry crowd. He tried to rout the mob by throwing pennies, but the peasants grew ever more desperate. "We have no potatoes," shouted Rose and Hyacinth together. "Nothing for you! Nothing." Regret not withstanding, she dozed on through her tears.

Incessant barking grew louder. Rose's eyes flew open in alarm. She scrambled to her knees. A small brown and white dog coursed down from the hills in the northeast. A few moments more and she discerned its markings. It flew into her arms, drenched her with kisses and danced around with joyful yelping. His small cocked ears, extensive ruff, and sassy expression reminded her of Puppy Joe, but this was a fully feathered adult. She tried in vain to take hold of his collar tag.

The dog's eyes pierced hers. His voice carried authority. '*Come! Come! Come with me.*' He nipped her hand with a soft mouth and pulled lightly. He lurched into her face, with a massive bark, staring, his fuzzy muzzle whiskers prickling her face. Then he hurled himself into the direction from which he had come, circled around, and returned to herd her forward.

A loud whistle came from the distance. One demanding

note. The dog flipped one ear at Rose and sped away.

Rose scrambled to her feet. Really? Was this her Puppy Joe? A mental lightning bolt sizzled through her, and she dashed after him. She had no choice.

"Puppy! Puppy Joe!" Far ahead of her, he flagged, turned, and stared at her again. Amid the heart-rending yelps and whines, she saw the man in silhouette on the rise. Surely he could hear her voice. He could see her running. He turned to face her. The frenzied little dog raced away down the hill toward Rose and then back again toward the man. Back and forth, with yelps of encouragement and frustration.

"He doesn't recognize me, Puppy!"

She remembered the signal she had used with Puppy Joe when he was small. Though not a strong whistler, her little tweet, with a pat on her thigh, always served to summon him. More important, Michael knew that signal, too.

Slipping and crawling on wet grass and mud, she struggled forward. "Fff-wheet! Fff-wheet!"

This was the moment she'd waited for, when they would come face to face. Rose's heart rose up to cut off her breath. "Look at me, Michael. Look at me!

The man leashed the dog, turned, and walked back toward the ridge and the houses.

Run!

Adrenaline impelled her. Her eyes on the houses behind the hills, she put all her strength into her goal. Her legs and arms pumped furiously. Her ankle turned against a random stone, tossing her to her knees. Rose's chest burned with desperate gasps. She crawled as far as she could. "Michael! Michael!" She stared at the dog and the retreating man until they disappeared over the ridge.

Until now, she had never thought she might lose Michael. Even now she couldn't believe it. She'd sometimes wondered how it would feel to wrap her mind around that dreadful truth. But he would never turn and walk away. As she had done to him.

She squeezed her eyes shut while panic crashed down over her. Her heart thudded with an irregular beat. She pressed her fists to her ears, gasping. Her nails pierced her palms, but she didn't feel the pain. After a while, she felt nothing at all. What had just happened—couldn't be true.

Never had Michael rejected her with such calloused blatancy.

A mental film of her life showed Michael struggling to free her from the car. Their whirlwind courtship. Michael pursuing her at the airport. His arms plucking her from the couch and dumping her on their bed with a shout. Him bursting into the shower after her and shoving her against the tile, a hand between her thighs. Holding her…rocking her when Grandfather moved to Ireland.

No, there must be some mistake. As she hobbled back to the castle, sensation abandoned her limbs, even the sprained ankle. She meandered in an unseeing zigzag, right up to a sign that warned *Beware of Bull*. She saw him, the monstrous bull, but she brushed past him. "Mmmm?" he lowed, pawing the turf with a forehoof. She didn't care.

She imagined a mental blanket tucking her feelings in tight, away from impossible notions, rendering her numb, though a few blitzing synapses announced the demise of her world.

"Hold on. Hold on." She spoke to someone who used to be her. "He always loved me, since the first night he saw me. We always slept together, since that night on the lawn. He could never wait to get his hands on me. He planted me a rose garden. He gave me a baby. This has always been my Truth."

She continued on her way, more or less toward the castle. *Talk to yourself. Don't lose your senses. Do I keep walking? I can't decide. Keep talking.*

She removed her light sweater and put it on again several times, finally letting it fall onto the grass. She looked at it as from a distance, while drizzle moistened the garment. She wrung her hands. She left it where it lay.

She veered off to her left and around the castle. She recognized a neo-gothic arch opposite the spot where she had set out in pursuit of Puppy Joe, if that was who it had been. It must be Puppy. After all, he had known her. He had reacted to her whistle and her signal. She shouted into the cloud bank "Puppy! Puppy Joe! Come back, Puppy!" She whistled until her cheek muscles cramped.

She slipped to the ground, holding on to the surface of the stone arch. Marble, like that in the Connemara quarry. No. This didn't feel like marble. Minute details were important just then. She responded to the chill on her bare arms by scratching them raw.

Something woolly pressed against her arm. "Marble." She desperately wanted to get something right, though part of her knew better. Then a substance, both stringy and wet, a hunk of grass in a wad of wool and spittle, along with two sincere-looking eyes fixed on her face.

"No! No! That's not what I expected. Get away! Get away"

The sad-faced little sheep eased off.

She wasn't crazy. She knew the creature was a sheep. But just when you had a cuddly sheep in your arms, it turned into something hideous. No sense in it, but there it was.

The mental dam that held her back from desperation leaked, little by little, until she couldn't hold back. Oceans of tears crashed against her hold on reality. She had always counted on winning Michael back, but now she knew better. There was no order left in her life. She tore at her hair. She ripped her nails against the stone wall. The love of her life had come face to face with her and had stalked away.

She had to do something, but what? It was dark now. No moon. She worked her way along the wall until she returned to the beginning. She sucked at the blood on the tips of her fingers. What if she could suck it out and stop living?

She whimpered.

She cast out the once-beloved name, like a bat in her

hair. "Michael! Michael," she shouted across the castle's demesne. She bellowed the name. She sobbed the name. A shrill scream like that of a wounded horse rent the clouds.

She covered her face with her hands and cried. "Puppy. Oh, Puppy…" She lifted her face to the sky, collecting scattered raindrops in her mouth and on her cheeks to join her tears

At last she stumbled across the courtyard where she had eaten the sandwiches. "Four walls. Warmer." She was unable to concentrate any more. Weariness got the better of her, and she hunkered down inside a ruined passageway. She made a small package out of her body as best she could and…just…disappeared into her only comfort—unconsciousness.

ℰↃℰↃ

Soft whiskers smelling of Milk Bones nuzzled at Rose's mouth. A polite inquiring muzzle dug at her crotch. A soft little body claimed a spot under her armpit.

Strong hands wrapped something woolen and snug around her and under her. It smelled of moth balls. She wrinkled her nose.

She mumbled into the warm object. "Dreaming. He wouldn't."

The man enfolded her in all four of his limbs, with his nose on her ear. She knew his smell of flower petals and grass, but she couldn't quite place the stiff hair around the lips that nibbled at her. She struggled toward awareness. Instead she reclaimed her burrow in her unconscious safe place, which she shared with this vaguely familiar other. Thunder split the sky. She heard it, but she didn't care.

A baritone voice spoke in soft tones. "I have you now. Don't worry." The rough hair rubbed against her ear. She faded again.

Much later, through slitted eyes, Rose saw the moon rise,

painting silver over the ruins. She heard the tide lap at the shore, while, farther down, it powered the waves that audibly battered the rocks. Her nostrils flared when she took in the salt air. She balled her body as the wind buffeted her. The man shivered and held her closer. She sensed all these things without discernment.

The small furry body that came with the man clung to her flank. She lowered her face to meet it, and a warm tongue lapped at her. Once, when she nearly awoke, it scrabbled against the small of her back, as if seeking purchase beneath her. She smiled in her half sleep. "Puppy..." Then she was gone again.

Her mind continued to touch on familiar things she couldn't grasp. The crook of a man-sized arm, its mate cuddling her against the scratchiness of the wool. She sneezed and rolled over. The furry lump wedged itself into the crack where her back met the stone surface. Her lips met the silken skin of a throat with its unyielding bump that, from time to time, moved up and down. She felt his strong pulse with her lips, and she warmed to the heat from his body. She reached her sore fingers up to his face. He laid his cheek against hers.

"Uh! Sharp."

"Sorry. I forgot this is new to you." He captured her hand with his and brought it to his lips. A ring on his hand brushed against her face.

The blustering wind raged against the ruined niche where they lay. She strained against the cold, and he wrapped the wool tighter around her.

He coughed, turning his head momentarily. "Don't try to move yet. You're worn out." Finally, the sounds of wind and rain ceased to batter her. "Can you stand, sweetheart? The storm is passing."

"This is a dream." She barely had strength to open her eyes.

"Come, Rosie. We're going home."

Thinking about that evening later, she realized it hadn't

been easy for him. She was a dead weight, but he managed to lift her onto his mount. He walked. She kept sliding downward.

"Whoa! Baby, this is only a pony, but I'm going to have to ride behind you to hold you on. That means we'll have to ride slowly, all right?"

They picked their way over the hills and down to the lower part of what she knew by now was Sky Road Loop, close to the bay. He held her with one arm, his ventral surface nudging against her back. The little dog yapped beside the pony, circling it and then nipping at its fetlocks. The bumping and rubbing against her made inroads into her awareness.

Her voice was dry and lumpy. "How? Why?" She turned her head partly around toward him.

He nuzzled her neck. "Shh, darling. Don't try to talk. You're in my arms. Don't worry. We have time."

The last thing she knew, he bedded her down on a low mattress with woolen blankets covering them. Puppy nested against her on the opposite side.

During the night it seemed she wept, and so did he. Then he kissed her and gathered her to his chest. They slept.

Chapter 17

September:

As the sun came up, Rose opened her eyes in a new place with familiar blue eyes peering at her.

"Michael." She didn't know whether to smile or cry. "I dreamed we found each other."

They held each other without additional words. When they separated, their eyes remained wet.

She reached up to his face to be sure he was real. "Ooow! What's this?"

He laughed and emitted a wet cough. "Camouflage. Easy to hide behind."

She delivered a mock slap. "Been smoking?"

"Naw, just can't get used to the damp. Smell me."

She did and then closed one eye.

"See? Just morning breath, but no smoked tongue."

She shared some of her breath and then tasted his mouth. "Ohh, Michael." Her arms went around his head, her lips to his lower throat. "Mmm…No hair down here. Nice."

He nuzzled her neck and grinned. "Want to see where you are?" He offered a hand to help her off the mattress, wrapped his jacket around her, and held open the door. They stepped out onto the moist grass. "Careful of your feet. Mine are always damp here. It's a reprieve riding to town by pony or bike, so I can dry them out." He paced off a short distance and then turned her around to face the house. "My home away from home."

She already knew it was small inside and shabby, but its exterior struck her as primitive. Made of the stones abundant in the landscape, with a shed attached on the end, there was but one window on this side of the structure. The rickety chimney rose between the cottage and the shed. Stones from the chimney lay where they had fallen. Several large patches on the roof were devoid of the ancient thatch, which, even elsewhere, was sparse, revealing the original turquoise color of the underlayment. The door and framings boasted a garish magenta paint.

The hovel stood at a narrow part of the bay where nearly a dozen small boats anchored. Perhaps the low tide allowed the owners to wade ashore, while high tide probably came close to the damp little house.

He grinned. "Picturesque, eh?"

"There was a horse. Where's the horse?"

Michael pulled the jacket tighter around her. "So, you remember that, do you?" His guffaw preceded another wet cough. "That ride was the answer to a lonely man's dream."

The thought of his body moving against hers as their mount plodded homeward sent a hot current through her. She looked up at him through her eyelashes. "Yes, it almost made me want to ride regularly like that, the two of us on one mount. Where is he?"

"Come see." He guided her to the other side of the building. "I put him in the shed last night since he'd been out in that strong wind and rain so long."

The memory of the rough cold caused her to shiver. She felt Michael shiver too in his shirtsleeves.

The stallion turned his head, blinking in the light. Michael guided him around with his lead. He nickered when Michael held out his hand.

"Here we are, old boy. Did you think I'd forgotten you?"

Rose held out a hand for the creature to smell. "What's his name?"

"Lucius. Don't laugh. I didn't name him."

She patted Lucius and rubbed him in all the places she remembered horses liked to be touched. "He seems to enjoy it, doesn't he?"

"Who wouldn't?" Michael replied with a leer that warmed her inside.

"Can we ride him again together?"

"Not together, I'm afraid. He's strong but really too small for two, and he's an old boy. He's a Connemara pony, not a horse."

She turned down the corners of her mouth. "Too bad. Once I really liked riding. Before I…you know."

Michael removed Lucius's halter and turned him loose in the stone enclosure. "You were a child when you had the accident. Surely, you have more confidence now. Why don't we lease a second pony for you?"

That made her frown. She'd almost forgotten how shy and fearful she'd been. Maybe she was stronger now.

Michael pulled her into his arms and tipped up her chin to look into her eyes. "Rose, I know you've had a fear of riding. I have my hangups too. I hoped we could work on them together. At last."

"Yes, fear and…lots of emotions." She toed a rock in the grass. "Anger for one, frustration, and lots of grief."

"I know it, darling, and I know I was never too good at facing my feelings, but what if I give mine to you and you give yours to me? Then we can work on them together."

Tears sprang into her eyes. This was what she had hoped he would say, what she'd wanted to do since they'd lost Rosebud, since he'd begun drinking, in fact.

"So will you, Rose?"

"I will." It sounded to her like a wedding vow. Solemn. She hoped he knew that. "And we'll tell each other the whole truth about how we feel…and about what we've done—good or bad—and the things we want to do."

He played with her hair. "Rosie, have you noticed neither of us has asked whether we want each other back?"

"I wanted to hear that for so long, and now I..."

His brows came together. "And now you don't want to
hear it?" His heart pounded against her hand, which he had
placed against his chest.

She shook her head. "No, now there's no need."

He lifted her fingers to his lips, which were still soft as
Puppy Joe's ears. He kissed her with care not to scratch her
skin, tentatively at first, and then trusting her with his need.
His tongue teased at her lips, awakening her urgency, but
she pushed back from him a little, just enough to gentle her
back away from the brink of no return.

She glowered. "The truth. I mean it, Michael. From now
on the truth. No holding back."

She heard his heart beating out his truth and saw in his
darkening eyes that he, too, was in no mood for any kind of
holding back.

He took in a deep breath, followed by a sigh and a short
silence. "All right, the truth." He grabbed her arm. "Don't
slip. We're standing a few inches from Lucius's latest crea-
tion. Ha-ha!" He responded to her stern look. "Seriously,
start with something easy to answer truthfully."

She put one hand on each of his cheeks, as she used to
do when he'd been clean-shaven, the way he'd always pre-
ferred. So he'd told her. Was that one of the games and fic-
tions he'd made up to please her?

"I asked you before. Why the face mask?"

He looked down, grinding the toe of his boot into the
grass. "Truth shouldn't be so tricky, but it is. Even mundane
things go deeper than you think."

It was hard not to touch him when she saw him wrestling
with his feelings, but she had to let him talk unmolested.

Finally, he met her eye. "This is hard to admit. When
you left, I fell into a depressive funk. I hid in bed, and I just
couldn't shave. I barely ate. I couldn't do my work." He hit

his chest hard with his fingertips. "Me! I didn't care about anything anymore, least of all shaving."

She guessed the sting of his embarrassment, which brought back her own regret. How she wanted to hold him, to lessen his discomfort. She let her nails bite into her already abused palms. Let him feel it. Let him get it out.

The words rolled out of him now. "Later I—I just liked the face mask, as you call it. It hid my shame, my grief. I was an anonymous nothing."

The tears running down into his beard were too much for her. Speechless, she flung herself around his neck. Together they let the tears flow. There were no words.

℘↻℘↻

They returned to the house, arms around each other. Thank goodness there was tea in the cupboard, and Michael had hung a kettle above the fire.

Rose wrapped her fingers around her cup. "That was wonderful. Crying." Almost like a sexual release, truth be told. She grinned at the thought. "I needed to do that with you long ago. I've wondered why we didn't."

He coughed before hunching his shoulders in a gesture of doubt. "I couldn't. I—After what I did—"

She took his hand, shaking her head in disbelief. She didn't know where to start. "No, no, no, no."

His wonderful blue eyes rounded. "Wh—what?"

"Nothing you did or do can justify hiding your feelings from me."

"Maybe I fear getting what I deserve."

She uttered a dry sob. "Michael, you were everything to me. I wanted all of you, including your anger and fear and sadness and guilt. I want to turn my feelings inside out for you too. It goes both ways."

"Well, I bet you're going to scold me about a lot of things. You should."

She wrapped her fingers in his. "No scolding, just talking. Com—mun—i—cat—ing." She couldn't help staring at his delicious lips. "And touching."

He tried out his whiskers very gently against her skin. "How's this?"

"More lips, less hair, please. There's so much hair you should name it. Truthfully, I don't want to have to be too gentle when we kiss. It's been too long."

He brushed a strand of hair away from her eyes. "Do you want to shave me...shave Bruce here?" He pulled on his beard.

She giggled at the name. "Yes, maybe. Or maybe I want to try Bruce out. Maybe he gives you a whole new personality."

He shook his head. "No, it's just me here now."

She looked around the undersized room. "I know where the toilet is, but how do you wash in here?"

"I usually bathe in the bay, but it's getting cold these days." He grimaced. "Then there's the kitchen sink. Cold and quick."

"Aww, I feel stinky."

He dove with his face into her armpit and emerged gagging. "You'd better let me wash you, pungent girl." He poured the last of the water from the kettle, along with cold tap water, into an enamel basin. "All right. Strip."

He must have seen her blush.

"What's the matter? Embarrassed?"

She nodded, unable to meet his eyes.

He yanked off his shirt, baring his chest. "Fair is fair." He eased her arms out of her shirt while she checked out his chest. She ran a finger over his trunk from his sternal notch to his navel. Her eyebrows flew closer together in dismay. "Oh, Michael. How thin you've become."

"Yes, well, at least you have maintained a good...chest."

He lathered his hands with water from the kettle and rough lye soap. No rag. Just his hands idling over her. First her face and then down her neck and around her shoulders.

Then he rinsed and dried her this far and dipped the soap in the water again. Arms, armpits, and—finally—her breasts. Around and around with extra attention to her nipples.

"Oh, Rosie, how I've longed to touch you."

She was in a pleasure trance, and then he made it worse by stripping off her jeans and soaping her feet. He nibbled on each of her toes and made his way around her knees and up her thighs. She tipped her pelvis, ready for him to remove her panties. Ohh, how she wanted that, and she wanted to touch him and memorize all of his personal terrain once more.

"Now you can do the last bit." He broke the soap into two fragments. He grabbed one with a second towel before racing outside. "I'll just take a dip, and then I'll be back to tuck you in."

Whaat? Her spiking libido crashed. "What just happened?" She scooped Puppy close and buried her face in the velvet on top of his head. She rocked with him, back and forth, just as her mind pitched this way and that. "What's the game?"

Another few minutes and Michael raced into the house, shivering. He slammed the door hard. He wore his jeans but carried his wet skivvies, which he threw into the sink. He coughed and stood there a moment, panting. He led her to the mattress, where he covered them both with rough wool blankets.

ᏨᎿᏨᎿ

They slept through most of the day, waking to share more tales of their time apart. Rose wished to find out why Michael had caused her such despair yesterday. "Why did you run away when you saw me?

"You didn't see me. I was in Galway."

But I saw Puppy, and he knew me too."

"Yes, he was with Albert, who walks him when I'm gone."

"That explains why you...that man ran like the devil."

"Yes, he's a little afraid of predatory women."

She snaked her fingers through his long hair and pulled while he chuckled. "Seriously, how did you know to come looking for me last night? Was that Albert's doing? Did he tell you a crazy woman tried to steal your dog?"

"Not really. Joe told me. Not long after dark he set up a hideous howling, and he wouldn't stop. So I walked over to Albert's to find out what had happened to him. Then I put two and two together. Joe strained to get off the leash, so I followed with Lucius. Joe took me right to you."

"You didn't want to run away from me?"

"Not me."

At some point Michael rummaged through his cupboard and appeared with an apple, a tin of sardines, and a half empty box of hard tack. Rose picked out all the fish bones. Michael laughed at her and tossed them to Puppy Joe.

She flinched when the dog licked her face. "Pyoo, Puppy. You've got icky stuff all over your mouth. Michael, you shouldn't give him such things. Now he's begging, and he stinks."

"See? Scolding." He pinched her thigh, nearly upsetting himself on his chair.

"Oops! That was close, Michael. There's hardly any furniture in here, just this rickety table with the two chairs."

"And mine has no back. And only three legs." He pantomimed losing his balance.

"Ooh, don't do that. The idea of falling makes me queasy. And that mattress on the stone floor." She shivered. "We need better furniture."

He leered at her. "We?"

She sighed. "Well, I think so. You've already got that nasty cough."

He yanked her away from the few scraps on the table and jostled her back to the mattress, leading with his pelvis. "Who needs furniture?"

She toppled onto the mattress and let him play this role,

whiskering her all over and then administering a series of belly zerberts. Their laughter took their breath away.

He raised one eyebrow at her. "You said 'we.'"

She gave him an absent-minded kiss. "Michael, I have to ask you some things."

"I should have known." His big grin told her he wasn't thinking foremost of talking.

She chewed on her lower lip as she considered how she should get to the point. "Why didn't you come for me before this if you knew where I was?"

He opened his eyes wide in mock surprise and braided a strand of her hair. "Have you forgotten you told me to get lost?"

She examined her fingertips as if counting her many actions that had defied reason. "I didn't mean it, it turns out. I just needed some time to…well, we'll have to discuss what needed—needs—to be done."

In the face of Michael's preoccupation, she decided to relax and go with his agenda.

He wound a strand of her hair around his fingers. "So I told you I would finally obey and become a hermit or some such nonsense."

She smiled. Funny. He needed to be funny. "And you kept leaving roses."

He parted off more of her hair to play with. "Well, you have to allow a man something. I couldn't force myself on you, but I damn well wasn't going to leave you to the professor either."

"How did you know about him?"

"Research kept me sane."

"Still the master of the cryptic remark I see. Mister puzzle man."

Again, a big grin. Probably thinking of another joke. He kissed her fast and broke off, as if trying to restrain himself. "Anyway, you finally made the big poster. Before that I didn't know if you wanted me back. Keep that in mind, madam." He stuck out his lower lip. "So…I tried to let you find me. It wasn't easy. You were looking for love in all the wrong places."

"So where did you spend your time while you were strewing obtuse clues about?"

"Well, I paid a lot of visits to your friends, the rector and his wife. Her baking skills kept me alive. It was warm and dry in the kitchen." He wrapped his arms around his chest and brought arms and shoulders closer to his core. "I thought she would say something to you. But she didn't."

Rose sucked on her bottom lip and looked at him askance. "You're wrong. She did. She told me when you had been at the rectory. You were a broken man, and I would have to play the white knight and go after you with more aggression."

"Hah!" he shouted. "How did that go over?"

"Well, I had little training, but that's when I finally went on the offensive and found you—er—Albert. Rosemary noted which road you took when you left the hill last time."

"So you did have a confederate. Shame on her. Good for me."

"Yes, God bless her and my other wonderful friends. Uh, we have to go home—back—Michael. They don't know where I went."

Michael looked smug. "Oh, yes they do."

"Wh—what? How could they?"

He worked a cell phone out of his pocket and dangled it in front of her face.

"Oh! Grandfather!" She yanked on his shirt. "I forgot to tell you—I found him, Michael."

He lifted his chin and sniffed. "I know."

She opened her mouth so her questions could tumble out, but he silenced her with a kiss. A long one this time, hot enough to boil the kettle forgotten on the table.

"I am the invisible man on the bicycle who lurks around town and knows everything. Don't forget that I've known your grandfather a long time. I saw him my first day in Clifden and followed him back to his...second home. I was surprised that you apparently had a relationship with his lady while ignorant of the connection."

"Hah, wait'll you hear about that."

He pressed her down on the bed. "I'm glad you finally found me."

"Except I found the wrong person. You were the one who found me. And not a moment too soon." She spread her yawn all over the room and burrowed into his chest.

"Really it was Joe, with his wonderful sniffer. If he hadn't kept carrying on, you would still be out there with that affectionate sheep." He wrapped her in the wool blanket. "Sleep now, baby."

She fell asleep thinking of her shy ovine admirer, wondering if she had scared him off people for life. Thank goodness Michael seemed all right, despite her bungling.

୧୬୧୬

When she stirred, Michael approached the bed. He'd been carving some driftwood while she'd slept. He showed her a plaque he'd finished.

"Oh, can we hang it up?"

He gouged a hole in the back of the plaque and hauled her out of bed. He pointed to an empty nail next to the door, and let her hang up his work. *Michael and Rose*.

Later, Michael brought out the remains of a hunk of cheese. "Burran Gold. Grass fed milk. Sean brought it along with your clothes while you slept." They wolfed it down as they eyed each other.

She wondered why they had not reconsummated their passion for each other. What was he thinking? Didn't he share her desire?

"Care to try for some fish to go with this?"

"I see some flour and some salt on the shelf from here, along with a can of condensed milk. I might be able to bake something that resembles bread. Does the oven work?"

"Forget it. Just the burners. And then only when the matches are dry enough."

So Rose accompanied him outside where he loaded his fishing rod with bits of leftover cheese. He stood in the bay up to his waist, searching the water for dinner. It didn't take long to nab some herring along with the raspberries growing on the wall. She looked forward to the meal. And whatever would come after that.

Finally he emerged from the water in his underpants, which stuck to his skin in places.

She ogled his details. "My, d—do you know you're all g—goose pimply?" she stammered, seeing he had caught her looking.

He looked proud. "That's what happens when you wade in for the catch."

Michael built up the fire and moved the mattress close to the hearth, banking it with cushions and blankets. They settled down, using the makeshift bed as a sofa.

Rose burrowed into the curves of Michael's warm musculature. "Brr! I just want to stay in bed. It's so cold at night."

"I agree with that, and it will grow colder. Yes, I'd better bring you back to town. You're far too delicate to stay in this ice box with me." She knew that taunting look in his eyes. Challenging her to a game. From old habit she fell into the role he had long ago written for her.

She snaked her arms around his body. "No! Michael, no!" Her voice sounded melodramatic, and it made her giggle. She spoke in a new, gruff voice. "You just try it, buster. You'll never get rid of me now."

He pressed her against the blanket embankment. The movement sparked new arousal in her, and it was easy to feel it in him. She nestled her face against his chest, stroking his man breasts with her mouth. "Seriously, Michael."

He rested his chin atop her curls. "I'm talking about the two of us, lover. It's just for a day or two if you agree. Just to dry out and warm up. Or we can stay there longer."

She combed her fingers through his beard. "Maybe, but I was thinking we'd be okay here if we arranged for some improvements. A real bedstead. A down comforter."

"I guess I could get the electricity turned on."

"Oh? I saw the wires. I assumed they were dead."

"No, I just didn't think I needed it."

"We could get an electric heater."

"I got plenty of firewood in for warmth and for the kettle. Did you see that pile outside?" He displayed his biceps.

She made her voice coy, teasing, drawing out the lust she could feel so close under his skin. "Yes, or we could just stay in bed all the time."

He swallowed a laugh down wrong, cleared his throat, and coughed. He dropped back against the mattress. "Ohh, Rosie, it feels so good to laugh. My throat's so sensitive these days, though."

"That cough creeps me out. It can't be good for you." She raised herself on an elbow to examine his face. She parted his facial hair away from his lips and bestowed a kiss, tender and firm. His delicious mouth erased all thought for a moment. "Mmmm! You are so yummy, even through all that hair, but it's like making love with your pajamas on."

Another man-sized laugh and a wracking cough brought her to a point she'd meant to raise. "Why are you living so…bare bones, anyway? You act like you're ready to grab a knapsack and walk away any time."

His eyes were serious. "That's accurate. It's not a cushy life, and yet, there's something about it here. I could stay a long time, depending…"

She lay in a shadow of quietness, the blanket clutched up to her neck. "Depending on what?"

"Well, now that we're here together, it depends entirely on you."

Her eyebrows pulled closer together. "I don't think that answers my question. You deserve a better standard of living, with or without me. You know that, don't you? Didn't this…feigned poverty bother you?"

"Well, in a way I am poor. Not working any more, you know. Spending the spring and summer here. Not earning. Bills to pay. I had to leave as much as I could in our savings account for your needs and, God forbid, for our—divorce— should it come to that. I had to accept that was what you wanted—take you seriously, you know?"

"Ohhh." A mixture of regret and self-blame throttled her, as she realized she had forced him into this life style. She lowered her head against his heartbeat.

His deep voice came to her through his chest. "Anyway, I'm rarely home. I ride around in Clifden, hoping you'll discover me. As a matter of fact, I did see you. We were both out in plain sight plenty of times. Always you passed me by. I had to assume you weren't looking."

"Not looking?" She reached for the day pack he'd retrieved from her bike. She handed him two photographs, the original, and the doctored one.

While he stared at them, she watched the blue of his eyes deepen. Finally he met her gaze, his tears brimming over.

"You did this. And it still didn't work?"

"No, and I showed them to people everywhere. It was what gave me hope."

He touched her forehead with his. "Oh, Rosie, I'm sorry."

She knelt over him, kissing his eyes, his cheekbones, the tip of his nose. She sloughed off her blouse and eased him out of his shirt. She offered her lips, tentative and brushing on his. He wound his fingers into her hair, pressing his mouth onto hers, his tongue working its way into her, insistent and needy.

He laid her down on the mattress and ground his erection against her crotch. He lifted himself on his elbows, his hands cradling her head. "Is this what you want, Rosie? Is this what you really want? Think about it, because I— can't—go back once we—"

She growled and tore at his fly. "You're killing me, Michael."

They kissed and caressed and licked at each other. He sucked her nipples and kissed her all the way to the fine hair that spurred him to go the ultimate distance. "Mmmm. Red hair. My favorite."

She gave him a sideways glance.

"My only."

She twirled her fingers in the dark trail that led to her heart's desire. Circling to delay the moment when she could only go forward, prolonging the sight of him engorged, begging her with his eyes. His pelvis bucked forward.

He pressed his mouth on hers and reclaimed her with his tongue. He broke off to gasp. "Rosie! Touch me, for God's sake."

She was in charge, fondling him, licking, taking him into her mouth. She felt him tense and grow. He breathed harder. She backed off, letting him take control.

At once he took her soft folds with his mouth, sucking and rolling his tongue over them He separated her with a finger and rubbed it around her engorged center. His thumb took over, rolling lazily around her pleasure while two fingers eased into her inner woman. She panted. The tickling heat and pleasure grew unbearable in no time, and her sex leaped toward him, pulsing with his ministrations.

Her head tipped back. She moaned. "Michael."

He gasped. "Rose. Oh, Rose. Baby."

"Michael, please. Give it to me."

He gentled his manhood into her still pulsating sex. She lifted her hips to meet him, and he entered her fully and with tenderness. They rode each other until they both cried out with shared pleasure.

He collapsed, rolled over, and pulled her onto his chest. "Oh, Rose. I guess we'll never forget."

Chapter 18

Once they leased a second pony for Rose, her body remembered how to ride. Long ago, Grandfather had praised eight-year-old Rose for her good seat. Now, as then, the way her muscles moved with those of the pony felt natural.

Every day the ponies wandered on the headlands with their riders astride. Rose tossed her hair in the shore breeze and let the late summer sun kiss her heart. She and Michael alit now and then to rest and talk while Lucius and Thisbe grazed.

"It feels right. It's as if our bodies work as one."

"Yeah, I noticed that too." He stared at her with a long, slow smile that gave her to know what he meant.

She giggled. "I meant me and the horse, not you and me. But—"

"That feels natural too, hmm?" He entwined his fingers in her flying tresses and held her still for his probing kiss.

They perched on a flat shelf of limestone overlooking the bay, while the ponies browsed through the grasses that warred for space on the bluff. He pulled her up between his bent knees, wrapped her tight in his arms, and held his lips to her ear.

She pulled his arms closer around her. "Look at those waves. They make quite a crash on the rocks. I heard the surf all night. Is that a sign of the season turning?"

"You can smell it in the air, can't you?"

"It seems cold for September. Michael, I'm soooo glad we got the new bed and the heater."

Mmm! Same here. I don't know about the winter, though. We'll want to be gone by December at least."

She snuggled inside the shelter formed by his arms and chest while the ponies feasted on the lush grass. "I think we did the right thing arranging to lodge the ponies with the breeder whenever something comes up. We can leave Puppy Joe in the house, but the shed is too small for both ponies, and it's too cold outside if we're here during, say, a winter storm. Even a fall storm."

He pursed his lips. "Mmm, I don't know. Those ponies are stronger than you think. Look at their thick coats."

"Yes, they're delicate but stocky at the same time. It's easy to tell them from a horse now that I know the difference. Thisbe is smaller than Lucius. She looks like a girl all right."

He laughed and squeezed her. "What I wanted to say was they're built to withstand the cold and damp, so don't get all worked up. Don't forget, they've got the wild ponies in their genes."

She rocked back and forth, taking him with her. "I love watching them graze side by side. They look good together."

Michael increased the momentum of their swaying until they nearly toppled over laughing. "Yes, pony matchmaker, Lucius really likes her, but there's a wary look in her eye."

She caught his drift but let it float by. "Well, I like riding her." She's gentle, and she knows what I want her to do."

"It's her Connemara temperament. They have a high I.Q."

She checked his face. Are you pulling my leg?"

"It's true. I'm telling you."

"Well, it's easy to bond with her. She's almost like a dog."

"You got it. These are wonderful animals."

"It's more than that. I feel safe with her. Thank you for helping me get over my horse hang-up." She kissed his fingers. Thinking of the things they could do to her was enough to liquefy the honey inside her, but she shook off her carnal thoughts. "Are we serious about getting a pair of Connemaras for Dad for the farm?"

He chuckled. "Did you see Sean's face when you brought it up?"

"I think he misses home now that we're here. I feel the same now and then."

Michael gripped her tightly, his cheek atop her head. "*Home*. Does that mean what I think?"

She paused for a moment to give the question weight. "All I know is when I saw you walk away from me at the airport, or thought I did, I realized in my heart where—what—home is. Being half and half—or one quarter—doesn't identify me. I belong where you are, Michael."

He sighed. "I do miss the ranch. Heck, I even miss my job."

She ran her lips over the light hairs on the back of his hand. "Mmm. Yes. I've missed the ranch for what it meant in the past, of course. There's always that. But my mind keeps wandering to what it could be in the future. If only Grandfather and Gwen could join us there. And Rose Too and Violet. That would be perfect."

"There is no perfect, sweetheart. I can't live up to it, and I sure won't demand it from you."

"I know it. I'm happy with good enough and working on the rest."

"How about sated with sexiness? Would that be even better, crazy woman?" He covered her neck with tiny pecking kisses that made her giggle until her belly cramped.

"Perfect. Michael, we're both a little nuts, and I love it."

They stared out to sea until they got cold and stiff. She wiggled in her man-shelter. "Know what? We should have brought Puppy Joe. I'm not afraid of bringing him with the horses anymore, and he would enjoy it. Plus, he would keep us warm."

"Oh, I've got enough fire in my furnace. And my hunger switch is on *ravenous*." His arched eyebrow was good for several love-starved kisses.

They extricated their cheese sandwiches from their packs and munched in silence spiced with inanities.

He had crumbs all over his beard. "Mmm! Bread and Cheese."

"And beard. Ew." She sniffed at her sandwich. "It doesn't smell yeasty."

"It's soda bread. You know that. No yeast."

"It smells like the sea."

He tweaked her nose. "That's because you have your nostrils in the air."

"Chewing is a language all its own, isn't it? There's impatient and eager, slow and sensuous—Yipe! You nibbled my ear."

"Mmm!" Michael stretched himself out atop the limestone and turned his face to the clouds. "I see a rose."

"In a cloud? I see a clown."

He pounced on her. "No, Right here."

She shrieked and tickled him back. "Here's my clown, right here."

Laughter started up his coughing. At such moments, the new lines on his face betrayed his fatigue.

He waved her away. "I'm fine. I'm fine. Sensitive throat. That's all."

"Maybe you shouldn't lie on this cold surface.

"Yeah, I agree. It's insane. But the sky is so big here."

"Your cough sounds worse. You should get it checked out. Do you have a doctor?"

"Yeah…"

"Who? Where?"

"In Galway."

"Oh, is that where you were that day when I thought I saw you?"

"Yeah." He grunted.

"Well, what did he say?"

"She. It's coming along."

"What is?"

He twisted his lips with a thumb and two fingers, as if to lock his mouth.

She rolled on top of him, unleashing more foreign sounds from his chest.

She delivered open-handed smacks to his thorax. "Better? No? Hmm. You had pneumonia, didn't you?"

"Did. Took the pills. Pretty much better."

She pulled him by both hands. "Well, funny man, your energy is impressive. Still, why take chances?"

He laughed and coughed while they mounted the ponies.

"See that flat, green stretch next to the sea? Race you down there and to the end of the strip. Show me your stamina."

She had a hard time keeping up with him. He stayed just a horse length ahead, waving his hands in the air. "Whoop! Yippee!" Witnessing his raw delight in the moment crammed her with joy. She had never raced before, and the mixture of scary and fun communicated to her mount. They pounded down the rocky hill and onto the flat land, which ended up ahead on a promontory.

He shouted a warning. "Watch the cliff!"

They both made quick turns to the right and came abreast of each other to continue in a canter along the edge of the headlands.

"Whoa!" She took a firm hold on the reins. I'm sure glad this little gal has common sense."

"Yes, she's never going to try to buck. If she does, you know to pull her head up with one rein, right?"

"Yes, I know when a horse is overly excited." *And when a man is excited.* Her man showed all the signs of exhilaration.

He dismounted and swept her off her pony, holding her close to his hardness.

The effects of his heat prickled inside her. She was ready to burst with love for him.

He turned her back to him, and they faced the waves. "See that?"

"No."

"Me neither. But somewhere out there is the You Ess of Ay, home sweet home. We need to go back soon, don't we?"

∽∾∽

The next morning they rode their bikes into town and then to a roadside beach on Mannin Bay. They waded the length of the coralline shoreline before retracing their steps to some black boulders. In the grass nearby, brown Friesian cattle grazed. One cow sniffed at their shoes.

Michael scratched her on the forehead. "Curious, girl?"

"I'll miss the animals that roam about untethered."

"Yes, in Citrus County you won't have a random sheep accost you." He seldom missed an opportunity to tease her about the love-struck sheep. She swatted his arm.

"I'm going to miss my bike, Michael. The trails in the Withlacoochee Forest are far too sandy, but we can use the bike path from Floral City to Inverness and on. What do you think?"

"Good, and I like your idea of shipping two ponies over from here. They're so hardy. They should do well in transport, especially if they're young. We need to ask the breeder about heat tolerance, though. Of course the ranch is under so many trees." She could tell his mind was back home.

He fitted a blade of beach grass between his front teeth and then teased it against her lips, tickling her until she was ready to jump inside out. "It's a good idea, us staying for the wedding. Wouldn't miss it, actually."

She rubbed her hands over her itchy mouth. "Yes, Gwen

is as nervous as a first time bride." An idea occurred to her, so she grabbed his arm. "Michael—Do you suppose they were really still married to each other all this time?"

"Hah! Maybe, and does that mean she was a bigamist with Rose Too's father?" He responded to what must have been her horrified expression. "Just saying."

"That boggles the mind. Let's hope neither of them thinks of that."

"Well, they're determined this marriage will be legal."

They set off at a lazy pace on this nearly empty section of beach, encountering a young family picnicking near a small cove. The boy hunted a gull with pebbles.

Rose sought Michael's face. "It's strange all these sections of the bay—with their unique personalities—are part of the shore, like rooms in a house."

He slung an arm around her and peered into her eyes. "Kind of like life, isn't it, Rosie. Think of the past year." He pointed in the air as though at a blueprint. "The den of despair, the salon of sadness, the anteroom of anger, the hall of hope." He ran out of breath.

"You're right, and all the bits and pieces came together to form a whole. And here we are."

"I know. It's awesome when you think about it." He took hold of her hand. The sea gulls begged for food, squawking and bending in apparent agony. "They're so desperate to get what they want."

"Humans are not the only creatures to play games."

"So you like my games after all."

Sunshine brought out the happiness in her heart. "Yes, I like playing. Of course I do. As long as we don't use it to avoid the truth."

He fingered her hair. "I know it, Sweetheart. I feel bad about that. And I know there's still plenty to talk about before we really start our normal married life."

She shot him a glance from under her lashes. "I thought we did a good job of working on that this morning. And last night."

"Thank God that's in order. I was about ready to sell my shrunken junk to someone who could use it."

Rose laughed so hard she stumbled in the sand. He let himself down on top of her, kissing his way around her belly.

"Oh, Michael. What a thing to say. Who are you these days anyway?"

He raised an eyebrow at her. "Wouldn't you like to know? I'm not merely a game-playing caballero anymore, toots. Just your randy ravisher, all directness and real emotion."

"Mmm, I like it, though we don't always have to be serious."

"Really?" He brandished a blade of sea grass in the wind. "Well, I'll always carry a small weapon with me in case you need a white knight." He put her hand where she could feel it at the ready.

∾∾∾

Another day, they rode north on Beach Road, making frequent stops to admire this rocky shore. Rose bent down to pick up a handful of stones mixed with shells. "Is this the beach the road's name refers to?"

"I think so. Your guidebook probably tells you."

"Oh," she pointed at the page. "Here's a picture of a restaurant on this road."

"I know where that café is. It's not far from my house, but this road ends after the restaurant, so you'd have to walk overland to get there from home. I've admired it from the back a thousand times."

"Let's keep going then. The sun is warm enough. Race you!" Off she went, with him close behind.

∾∾∾

Sweating from their exertion, they dismounted and walked their bikes.

"So, you beat me. It feels good that way. You've grown strong, Rosie."

"What? The white knight turns into a wimp?"

He grinned. "Yeah, hurt me some more. I can think of lots of ways you could give me a good ache." He pulled her over to him and pressed her against him.

"So I see, uh, feel, you lecher. Right now I need to drink some of my water."

"Ah! Hold it. There's the café. Let's go get some tea and scones over there." He pointed to a small A-frame. "I always wanted to try this place."

She turned serious, concentrating on his face. "It seems you've done a lot of undercover work. You're good at it, but I've also enjoyed success at sleuthing." She told him about the Shamrock thief. The admiration on his face stirred her soul.

"Hmmm, maybe we should go into business together." He pinched her bottom.

She pinched him back. "I did think of midwife training, too, since I delivered Bridey's baby."

The café stood near the cliff, where the Sky Road passed close to its peaked roof.

"Wow! It looks like a car could take the building down by over-steering just a little."

"It's an odd little place, isn't it? Do you like the portholes across the front?" He pointed. "Look at the sweep of large windows upstairs."

They ascended the three steps, entered the foyer, and continued to the upper level. They chose a table at the front window.

"I'm amazed this place is so big inside." She reached for his hands. "Michael, that reminds me...you've opened my eyes somehow to things...and people...and how different they can be from the way I supposed. It's delightful. It makes me willing to try new things."

He rubbed her hands and brought them close to his face. "What about me? Am I the way you expected?"

"Well, I haven't witnessed any angry outbursts. You've been pretty philosophical about things that frustrated you." She giggled. "Like the fire singeing the blanket on our mattress and the unexpected manure in front of the door."

They relished their scones, firm on the outside, butter tender inside. The shared pot of strong Irish tea trickled into her, restoring energy and heightening perceptions. She chattered and laughed, talking with her hands. Finally, as the second plate of scones wended its way to the contentment zone of their brains, they slowed down and held hands while they watched the ebb tide muddy the beach.

"So many kinds of beaches around here. Which is your favorite?" Holding her hands, he stared deep into her eyes, so that a fire inside her womanhood turned her too flustered to think straight.

"What? Favorite for what?" She could think of things he might have asked her, but she wouldn't like to name them in public. A hot flush crept up her neck, and she was sure everyone was watching.

"Which beach do you like the most?"

She cleared her throat. "Oh, umm…the first day we rode the ponies…the one with the coral sand."

"Oh, yes, Ballyconneely."

She giggled at his pronunciation. "That was fun. And Omey Strand was sandy, but with long grass. You hid in it. But not to scare me."

"No, it was serious business. I wanted to—"

She hushed him with a fingertip. "I know what you wanted." Another flush swept over her.

Memories tumbled out.

"Mannin Bay is sandy, too, but with big rocks along with the marram grass."

"Gwen's Rose showed me that one earlier, but it was fun climbing on them again."

"You started to stumble, and I got to catch you. That was serious and real, not just a game."

"Not as much as you thought." He could probably see her guilty expression.

"You stinker! You did it on purpose." His guffaw attracted the attention of the other diners this time. They felt for each other's hands, while their eyes consumed each other.

The tide receded.

"You know what I'd like to do? I'd like to gather those pretty little shells, the spirally little things."

"The univalves. Are you going to take them home?"

She thought about that for a moment. "No…maybe. It's something to do without needing a reason. Like talking of random trivial things the way we've been doing. Have you noticed?"

"Yes, we've jumped right into each other's worlds of bits and pieces. We just belong together. It's easy. Maybe too easy? Is that what you're saying, Rosie?"

"No I love the ease, the small details of being together. We just slide into the same mental space—physical space, too." She stopped a moment to let his grin sparkle into her heart. "But I do know we have to talk about serious things before we can…"

He moved his chair closer to the table. "What things, sweetheart?"

The lumpy throat that came before crying moved in. "Things that broke our bond, things that kept us apart."

He fondled her hand. "We already know what forces us together."

The throat lump got bigger. She hated that, when things were serious, she sounded like a Munchkin. "Yes, I know what you mean. I want you to say it. Say it in real words that show how you feel about it."

"We love being together all the time."

"And?"

He looked around at the people at other tables, his low, tender voice close to her ear. "We love fucking each other."

She gritted her teeth and emitted a low growl. "It's precious, isn't it, lover? I love that you said it. We want to keep our passion forever, don't we?"

His eyelids were red. "No term limits."

"Then we have to make sure those awful things can never happen again."

Chapτer 19

October:

Rose pulled the comforter around her. "I'm glad we stopped in Ardbear this afternoon. I wanted to see for myself whether Raven was all right. I've had him a while, you know." She giggled at the memory of the dog plastered to Gwen's side.

"Yes, Sean could hardly lure him away to go outdoors."

"Those two are so excited about their wedding. You've never attended any wedding except ours, have you, Michael?"

"Not true. I witnessed a wedding when I was a boy. Of course, the groom had a gun to his back."

"You are so funny, Michael. Much funnier without all the role playing. Hold me close, and don't snore, please. We need to talk."

He tucked the edges of the Eiderdown under her far flank. "All right, baby, but while we're acting serious— thank you for stopping with me this morning to check in with AA. I forgot you already knew where the meetings take place."

"I enjoyed talking with some of the spouses in the other room. They're great. It's good to hear they've survived some of the same things we went through and worse."

"That's what the group is for. For example, I learned to forgive myself for being a double murderer."

She snuggled into his armpit. "Seriously, Michael. I'm so glad you have that kind of help going forward, but I still have questions about the past. I know we can't deal with everything at once, but I think we have to lay some things to rest before we can, you know, be as we were before everything went wrong."

He traced her eyebrow with his finger. "Such as?"

She grabbed his hand. "Well, all right. Here it comes. You didn't drink when we got married. Then bit by bit you did. Pretty soon, over the course of months, there were times when you drank a lot. It wasn't just a beer after work."

He crept out of bed and stood over her, wringing his hands.

She put her feet on the floor. "That's when the man I married disappeared. I adored you, but you started picking away at me. Before long you were always angry or annoyed, and everything was my fault. That's what I don't understand. What did I do wrong?" She lifted her feet onto the bed again and, arms around her knees, rocked back and forth.

He held his hands on the sides of his head, pacing, "You? You think it was your fault?" He sobbed his words. "You? My precious Rose? Ahhh!" He knelt on the edge of the bed. His arms reached out and pressed her to his body. "Making you think such a thing was the worst crime I ever committed, other than—becoming a—doing what I did. Killing people." His head drooped back, and his chest heaved. He retreated to the fireplace.

His silence shocked her as much as his self-accusation, but she forced herself under control and stole over to him. "Look at me."

He shrank back as if she breathed fire.

Her tone was commanding. "Look at me!"

He showed her the torture in his eyes.

"Michael! You've accused yourself that way more than once. I no longer hold Rosebud's death against you. Believe it. It's way more complicated than that."

He shuddered at the baby's name.

She leaned over him. "I mean it. That was in the past, and we both have to come to terms with it and live with it."

Tears slid down his cheeks.

"Michael, I don't accuse you for what I've suffered either. In the end, that was my own doing. You didn't kill my devotion to you, though God knows I tried to move on from you. God help me, I haven't learned how to stop loving you." She held out her arms. "So why don't you enlighten me? Start with the reason you started drinking in the first place."

He looked straight at her and sobbed. "You don't know. You don't know."

She forced his face down to her level. "Tell me."

He trembled. "I killed my father."

ॐ

After Rose and Michael talked all night, she suspected the practice would be life-long. Though his posture mirrored her exhaustion, they rose early and saddled the ponies for the ride to the castle where they'd reunited. As their mounts grazed on the lush grass with neighboring sheep, the lovers nestled in one of the window arches and sipped hot coffee from the metal thermos they carried in their pack.

Rose's tone was urgent. "You've got to accept his death as an accident. Yes, you went there with anger in your heart, but you didn't push him off the cliff."

"That's what Doctor Meadows told me."

"My psychiatrist? You went to him too?"

"Shortly before you left. He got me right into meetings. I probably need to see him again."

"Michael, I'm just so sorry you didn't tell me about it back then. I already knew your father drank too much. And

I witnessed for myself how he treated your mother, bless her soul. All the yelling and belittling. You and I talked about that often enough." Rose called to mind the kind little woman and the Irish folksongs she liked to sing. "After he died, I thought she was better off without him. At least she had a couple of good years before the cancer claimed her. She was good to me as her daughter-in-law." She put her hand on his knee. "Even though they tried to keep his abusive behavior private, I see now that what I did witness—sensed—influenced my fear of your drinking, your anger, your frustration."

He groaned. "I can't believe we actually thought that trip to Lake Superior would be good for our family. My dad always loved northern Michigan, especially the Pictured Rocks shoreline. We had pleasant times there when I was a kid. Dad was good to my mother then, and she was happy. At least, I thought she was happy. Gosh, I thought we were all happy. Until my sister died."

Rose stroked Michael's Neck. "I wish I could have known Iris. She could have been the sister I always wanted."

"She was a nice person, just like my mom. She shouldn't have died the way she did."

"Sepsis after an injury, wasn't it?"

"Yes, she was only thirteen, the apple of my dad's eye. That was the end of our family. Booze took her place for him. Little girls—" He choked back tears. "Little girls can—can be like that for fathers, you know."

She saw his pain in his eyes. It jerked her heart, but she forced herself back on track. "So, we know what changed your father. And years later you witnessed his suicide. Terrible. What a terrible morning for you. How did you end up at that cliff?"

Michael's voice lacked emotion at first as he counted off the details—something Rose guessed he'd done many times in the past. "I found Mother that morning. Her face smashed. A gash in her scalp. Her arm hanging limp. Blood all over the floor." He shook off his list of horrors.

Rose took his hand. "That was horrible, darling. Of course you felt traumatized."

He swallowed and continued with a tight-sounding voice. "'I'm all right, Michael,' she told me. How could she be all right? How could I leave her alone? I'll never forget her voice—no feeling, controlled."

Rose scratched at the skin of her throat. "Oh, Michael!" It broke her heart to hear his pain struggling toward the surface. She forced herself not to touch him—for now, at last, he needed to speak more than he needed comfort.

"'Just watch after your father,' Mom told me." Michael's lips quivered. He swallowed hard. "I did what she wanted, Rose. I ran after him. I could hear his drunken cursing all the way to the cliff. He stumbled up to the rim and stood there tottering. I—I wished he would fall." He pinched the bridge of his nose.

"It's all right, Michael. Go on."

Waving his coffee mug, he stamped into the grass, away from her. "Dammit! It's as if I saw it occur ahead of time. I thought of my mother and how that day was going to keep happening forever. I rushed over to him. 'What are you doing, you bastard?'" Michael sobbed. "I meant to—to sound threatening. Make it a *be a man* moment."

She took his shaky coffee mug from him.

"I'll never forget it, Rosie. Can't believe what I said to him." Breathing hard, Michael clenched his fists and bellowed. "'Thinking of jumping? Why don't you do it then? Go on. Jump!'" Michael sank his face into his hands. "He turned around to face me. Then he lurched backward."

Raising his arms to the sky, Michael roared. She caught him in her arms. He bawled, and she sobbed. She couldn't help it, for she knew they'd been handed the key to their future.

After a while, she led him back to their seat in the arch. She wiped his face, and then her own.

"And you couldn't forgive yourself."

"No, I couldn't articulate what I had done, not even to you. It was unspeakable. I couldn't erase his scream from my memory. Sometimes the Guinness and the beer helped me forget. A little. In the process, I almost became my father." His voice sounded broken.

She gave him some cooled coffee to wet his throat. "But you didn't, and you won't. And you know there's always forgiveness."

✍✍✍

Leaving the horses at their cottage, they walked their bikes overland to Sky Road, with Puppy Joe behind them sniffing at sheep droppings to his heart's content. After that, the uphill road to Church Hill had Michael panting. As they climbed to Christ Church, they stopped to check out the sign board beside the path.

"Do you know, I used to check this to see if you'd left me a message or, anyway, a clue." She chuckled. "I didn't know how far you'd go in your new role. You weren't doing much to woo me. But you did let me know you were nearby—with the rosebushes and all."

He dipped his head and gave her a wily look. "Yeah, doing that made me feel you were still my girl."

She couldn't hold back a full smile. "Well, after I was done being mad at you for bobbing and weaving, it felt...safe...somehow, to know you were out there. I was grateful you'd tried to hang on to me with two hands, even if you played it shy. It felt like a kind of courtship—quirky, intriguing. I guess I knew we'd come together eventually."

He covered his cough with a chuckle. "I hate to admit it. I did think of using the church sign. You know, like at the ball park, when the score board flashes 'Marry me, Ellie Sue!' I was determined to make you search for me and find me, since you'd left me. I couldn't take that in. You—left—me! The white knight can only take so much rejection before the role grows stale, you know."

She held him back from his forward stride. "Well, even the shy damsel can play a role just so long. I was ready for a new one when you showed me what real-life distress is." She raised her open hands. "Get it? Anguish with a capital Trauma. That was no game. You became my quest. Pursuit of the bus thief was merely Detective Work One-Oh-One."

He turned his face aside.

She held his arms. "Michael. For goodness sake, didn't you realize I couldn't find you?" She shook him. "Oh!" She recoiled, sweating.

He gave her his eyes. "Yes."

His wet eyes had her in his spell, as always. He looked ashamed. Maybe she wanted it that way. She dropped his arms and stepped back.

"Why—why couldn't you have the good sense to make it easy on me?"

"I wanted you to work hard, so that—" He brushed his lips against hers.

They were so soft. She could barely catch her breath. "So why?"

"So wanting me would make you suffer. The way I did."

She knew that kind of miserable ache. It throbbed inside her now. She seized his hand, kissing his wedding ring. She led him to the door she always used to visit the church.

"Come inside, Michael. But first, give me a solemn kiss that makes me hurt like I'm turned inside out." She turned her glance to the question on his face. "There's no making out in the sanctuary, even if it is Protestant."

Half laughing, he fitted his lips on hers. Then he created a kiss that gave her his soul.

Rose and Michael entered the sanctuary from the blue door. They strolled the full length of the aisle, absorbed in the familiar allure of the windows and woodwork that had stood as silent companions in their journeys.

She slipped a hand into his. "This is the first time we…"

"I know. It seems different, doesn't it? With us together?" Michael, pitched his voice lower. "It's so quiet." They faced the organ against the side wall. Painted rose, blue, and gold, the massive pipes always made Rose sigh with the satisfaction of her senses. This time, she reached for a stuffed bear on the bench.

"Oh! Baby Rose's bear. Left from the christening."

"Winnie the Pooh."

"Shhh!" Rose trailed her fingers on Michael's lips, which seemed softer, more yielding with his facial hair in contrast. She led him toward the elevated white pulpit. "Look, Michael, the carvings are the same as the ones below the organ pipes. I just noticed that." Her eyes jerked to his face. "I'm seeing things with a new heart."

He took her hand in both of his. "Sweetheart, you see the art—the beauty—in everything." He kissed her hand. "I love that about you. And you teach me too."

They knelt. Rose folded her hands on the altar rail, and he followed suit. He studied the three tall windows before them. "No cross. Odd."

"Remember, this is a protestant church. It's not what you grew up with."

"I…hmmm. It doesn't seem to matter. I still feel very solemn in this moment."

"Yes, it reminds me of our wedding. Our marriage vows." A worm of guilt inched around in Rose's gut. "Michael, I meant the vows I spoke that day, but I broke almost all of them, as though I cheated on you."

He grasped her arms. "What?"

Her fingers reached for his chin. 'I was not the wife you needed. I concerned myself with my own hurt and my own needs. When I couldn't see where to turn, I ran as far as I could from you and your pain." She quieted his protest with a finger to his lips. "I convinced myself that fleeing was my only course." She saw the objection in his knitted brows. Her flexed hand made the sign for *stop*. She turned her eyes away. "It was a lie. I need forgiveness for that, though fear provoked me."

He took hold of her restraining hand but let her speak her mind.

"I know it was right to get distance from your addiction, since it hurt me so much, but I should not have left you. There had to have been another way."

He shook his head. They kept silent for a moment, but their bodies edged closer together. In his liberating love Rose gave herself permission to cast out the guilt that had tortured her most of all. She pressed his hand to her mouth. "Michael, when I realized that you actually gave up on me, my heart shattered." She moved their joined hands to her heart, where she could still feel the hurt. "Worst of all, I brought that misery on myself, because I let you think a lie. How could you know I hadn't stopped needing you more than life?"

He looked at her with puzzlement and pain.

She let him see her emerging tears. "Please, please forgive me." She stared at his lips, the lips that made her think carnal thoughts in a church building.

His eyes were tender. "I do."

Their wedding vows swirled in her head. She remembered the moment when he'd lifted her veil and dispensed a sizzling kiss. "Wh—what?"

"I do. I forgive you for all the things that fill you with guilt. And I forgive you for being more eloquent than I am." He grinned. "All I can say is will you forgive me too, for all the things we talked about, and for being an idiot?"

Now she was laughing. Her arms were around his neck, her cheek next to his. She took in great gulps of his wonderful manly scent and the fragrance of roses that clung to him.

"I do forgive you, and I always will. And you'll need to do the same for me, because I have the feeling I'll need it."

They held each other there on the steps. Finally he broke the silence. "This is awkward, both of us kneeling here. Would you mind standing up?"

"Okay." She reached for him.

"You first."

What was he playing at? *You first* indeed. She pushed off on the altar rail and got to her feet. Then she extended her hand, but he stayed put, solemn, his eyes fixed on her face. Finally he took hold of her hand.

All of a sudden, she understood what was coming. Her heart skipped a beat, and she gasped as he spoke.

"Rosie, will you marry me again? Will you start over with me and be my wife forever, until I'm a crumbling cadaver?"

A torrent of tears broke loose with her laugh. "Yes, yes, Michael. I will. Of course I'll marry you again." She half pulled him to his feet, and he swept her into his arms. "Just say when."

His eyes were earnest. "Now."

Eyes fixed on the chancel, they faced the altar, which, cross or no cross, reinforced the vital bond they meant to reaffirm. Then they turned to each other.

Michael's brilliant eyes dampened. "Rose, I love you for better or worse. I vowed that before, but now I know what it means. I thought I could escape painful emotions, but I lost everything that makes life real—and true—and worthwhile.

My darling, I promise to have your back and make your problems mine, even if I can't fix them, no matter how dismal things get. And I want to hear all your sadness, even if it tears out my heart. But more than that, I want to create beauty and joy and laughter for the two of us."

"Michael, I promise to make you happy if I can and share the beauty in little things. I'll never leave you or turn away from your pain again. Whatever life brings, I'm in it with you, and I love you. Never again will there be life without you in it. Because that's not life. And I will hunt you down if you try to get away."

He swept her close and held on for dear life. They sealed their promise with a kiss at once pure with awe and full of lust. "I wish we were someplace else right now," he groaned. "I know another way to seal the bargain."

She could feel the other way pressing against her.

Applause sounded from the narthex, where the rector stood with Rosemary.

"I pronounce you again and already man and wife. You're as legal as you ever were, but if you want a certificate to give you weight, I've got a lovely parchment up at the rectory. Let's hope you both know what you're doing at last."

Rosemary clasped her hands. "Come up to the rectory for some coffee and cake, and we'll discuss it."

ოოო

Later that afternoon, they pedaled a little farther, to Ardbear, where Rose had started out on her first day in Clifden. Bridget sat in the big chair in her living room, nursing Baby Rose. Claris fluttered around them, while William poured drinks.

She showed them the ring, back on her left hand. "Michael asked me to marry him. Again. So we did it."

Michael blushed. "Got married, she means. On the spot. Adam and Rosemary witnessed."

Bridget passed the baby to Michael and squealed her congratulations while covering Rose's cheeks with kisses. William seized Michael in a hearty handshake and clapped him on the back. "I never heard any more dismal news in my life." William lowered his head. Then he squared his shoulders and shook Michael's hand. "Congratulations, man. Don't let her go this time."

Sadness tightened Rose's throat for a moment as she watched Michael cooing to baby Rose. They had dealt with so many issues. All but one.

Their good news called for an immediate visit to Gwen and Sean, still ensconced with Raven in their love hut on the river bank. Rose glanced from one to the other.

"Grandfather—Grandmother."

Sean leaped up. "Bollocks, I hope it's not bad news.

Come on, dogs, go play." He let them out to ramble through the woods.

Gwen shared a wise expression. "He's trying to be discreet. We're delighted to see you. Let me turn off the stove."

Michael stood up. "Sean. Gwen. I proposed to Rosie today, and we got married again on the spur of the moment with the rector standing by. We'd like your blessing on our union."

Sean grumbled. "Aren't you forgetting something? You already have a marriage certificate, and a boatload of wedding pictures."

Michael took Rose's hand. "Yes, we wanted to make up for the unfortunate gap when we lost each other, as it were. Though, come to think of it, you two hold the record for gaps and getting lost."

Sean cracked open a new bottle of Irish whiskey, and Gwen showed her tact by producing a bottle of apple juice, which she and Michael imbibed. The women nodded to each other.

Sean offered a toast. "Here's to never getting lost again. No more gaps."

Gwen insisted they stay for dinner. The meal turned into an evening of conversation and planning, which nudged the hands of the clock to the top of the dial. Sean said he was going to bed but refused to let them brave the headlands on the way home in the dark. His was a tone of authority. "You'll stay over. And, by the way, where's your mobile, girl? I notice you never call us."

Gwen elbowed him in the ribs. "Do get Bridget to give it back to you, dear."

Sean pulled his cell phone from his pocket and tossed it to Rose. "Here—for now. You never know when you'll need it out there on the cliffs. I don't require this very much these days. I'm always just where I want to be with the person who needs to know where I am."

The wee hours found Rose and Michael tucked up on the

pull-out couch, with the dogs at the foot. Rose sighed. "I never thought I'd sleep at my grandparents' house, though it was a girlhood fantasy. I'm going to miss them, but I'm glad we're going home soon.

Michael gave a chuckle. "Why would that be, Irish Rose?"

"It's home. We have to make things right in the real world."

He rubbed his whiskers against her cheek. "You bet. Right after their wedding. As soon as we can get a flight with space for live cargo." He scratched Puppy Joe's head. "Isn't that right, boy?"

"I'm relieved you agree. We need a warm winter to get rid of your cough."

Chapter 20

The next morning was sunny and dry, so Rose and Michael took leave of the grandparents and hurried through town and overland to their cottage. There the ponies had made progress in emptying the enclosure of forage and fodder, replacing it with manure. Half an hour of shovel duty led to a mutual bath in the bay.

Michael pressed a hand to his grumbling stomach. "Whoo! Those ponies kept busy."

Rose laughed at him. "Goodness, you're loud. Here, eat this spotty banana if you're that famished, and I'll wrap some hard tack with butter and cheese to tide us over on the outing." He snitched most of the cheese while she worked. She swatted his hand away from the cutting board.

They took off across the castle demesne and into the hills. Rose detected her pony's high spirits through the saddle, and she shared them.

"Whoa, guys," Michael cautioned. "I can tell you haven't left home while we were away. Time for a good ride."

"We'll have to let them run full out."

"Yes, but not until we get onto the level headland, away from most of the stones," Michael insisted. "I don't need you to take a tumble and blame me for it. Remember when you ran headlong down the steps and into my brand new Peachy Cheeks bush? You knocked it over in its hole and filled your glorious hide with thorns? I had to tweeze them all out by hand. Boy did you howl!"

She didn't appreciate his salacious expression. "Never again," she promised. "From now on I'm to blame for my own mistakes and accidents."

He regarded her with a sly gleam in his eyes. "Speaking of which—"

"What which?"

"Accidents."

"Oh! That." She hoped he heard her coy tone. "You mean those kinds of accidents. When I burn dinner."

He pulled Lucius into a hard turn in front of Thisbe and seized her reins. The pony whinnied.

"Or the time you made me fall off the bed and bonk my head on the helmet you left lying there. Or all the times I tripped over your big feet?" She gave him a sidelong glance with a purposeful measure of the devil in it.

Michael was looking at her hard. "Think again, and don't flirt with me when I'm desperate for the truth."

The hair stood up on the back of her neck. "Oh, yes, I know, but I want to hear you say what you mean."

She saw his jaw work. The horses were now flank to flank, their riders eye to eye. "Yes, I can see you do, you strumpet. You do like me to say rather explicit things." He fingered her near arm. "Well, what do you want to hear?"

She could feel herself grinning, but maintained her mock-innocent tone. "Tell me what causes the accidents you fear."

Stirrup brushed against stirrup. He had hold of both saddle horns, and he leaned even closer. Lucius gave her the eye, as if he could explain this intensity. She shivered with the force from Michael's eyes.

"You want to hear about it, do you? Well, I want to do it. Every day. Every night. I want to make love to you in every way, gentle and rough. I love that you let me know how much you want it. That you make love to me in return. I want to lick and suck and kiss every inch of you, girl, and I want to bury myself in you and give you all I have. And when I abandon all my reserve, then sometimes—always—I—"

She panted. "Yes, you what?"

"Then I have an accident, you might say."

She giggled at his groan. "What? I'm so hurt. That's an accident?"

His voice grew rough. "No, you wanton girl. That's me wanting to fuck you more than anything. And it's me pouring myself into you desperately on purpose."

"Oh," she said, tossing her head. "Just so we have it straight, because I wouldn't want you to make love to me by accident, especially when I want it so very much."

He leapt from his horse, lifted her from the saddle, and held her in his arms like a hard-won prize. His sledgehammering heart frightened her at first, since his lungs sounded tight.

He looked around, selected a grassy spot, and deposited her tenderly onto his jacket.

"Ah, Rose…" His voice was a deep murmur. He licked her arm as far as he could get inside her sleeve. After he unfastened her bra without dislodging her blouse, his fingers played over every stretch of quivering skin within reach. "I don't want to make you cold by ripping off your clothes, sweetheart, but I do want to touch you. That's no accident. That's your wicked provocation, because you are turning me inside out with your sexiness."

The touch of his fingers made her ache inside.

He undid her jeans and slid his hands down to the hair inside her panties. From there he fingered the place that made her moan. Fire wicked up inside her.

He groaned, "Oh, baby, I want to touch all of you. Wrap my shirt around your waist. It'll make you warmer and shield your pretty bits from ovine eyes."

She thought of the cuddly sheep at the castle and giggled. "Oh, Michael, I love you to be funny, and I—" He nipped at her lips. "Ohh, I sure love you to be serious."

"Is this serious enough?" He ground his teeth. "More serious talk? Maybe some action? His slow hands crept everywhere. As they moved, he kissed and tasted. "Ahh, your skin is so soft—so supple—so sweet.

The flannel around her waist, her lower garments disappeared. No more time for thought. His clever fingers found her swollen petals and played a symphony as lust rose toward a crescendo. He circled her tingling bud, finally reaching inside the throat of her sex as his thumb kept up its rhythm on her exterior blossom. She yielded control as her desperate desire exploded into shards of pulsating pleasure.

"Oh, Michael, please—please. I can't wait."

He pounded into her with one swift, wet thrust and a trembling gasp. "I want you right now. This is no accident." He drove his passion ever deeper into her, renewing her orgasm. He shuddered and cried out her name, while he traveled with her to the ends of the world as one soul and one being.

He wrapped his limbs around her, warming her. She shivered with contentment. He pressed his forehead against hers, bringing her eye to eye with him. They clung together, trading feathery kisses that tasted of the honey they had eaten at breakfast. "Mmm, Rosie..." He growled. "Love you so much."

She murmured his name several times. "I'm glad. I'm so glad I found you, and we're making everything all right between us."

He chuckled. "It's always there, between you and me, almost ready for another workout...any minute now. Hmmm?" He buried the rest of his words in her lips with articulate kisses, more compelling than words.

She nuzzled his neck. "Yes, lover. I'm glad you were so...purposeful."

"Yes, no accidents you said." He propped himself on an elbow to search her face. "No accidents. Then we shouldn't have—"

She caressed his lips with her tongue. They tasted like

ripe Connemara gooseberries. "I don't care about that kind of accident, my love. That would be heavenly, but…"

He stroked her cheek. "But. Why is this *but* the hard part?"

"Because it is. And you know why. We're not over our first baby yet."

He stumbled over the name. "R—Rosebud. I must have cried enough to raise the water level of the Withlacoochee all by myself."

"But not with me."

He cleared his throat. "Not with you. And now I understand why we have to go through it together. I do. I paid attention to what you've told me, and I have an idea of what we must do once we get home. You'll see. It's a wonderful idea."

"You never told me if you got to hold her…you know…after."

He nodded, his voice ripe with sorrow. "She looked like her mother. I kissed the top of her head."

Her mouth turned down with emotion, and he brushed her quivering lips with a kiss, pure silk, but hinting at firmness.

"And now, if you keep lying there naked and splayed out for me, there's going to be another purposeful incident in front of God and the great outdoors." His eyes twinkled. "Unless, of course, you want to give these guys the good run they deserve."

She worked her jeans up over her legs. "Goodness, yes. There is hardly any more time to ride before we go home to America. I'm going to miss these ponies. Let's let them pull out all their stops."

☙❧❦

"Look, no stones down there to trip us up." He pointed toward the verdant cliff edge that jutted into the Atlantic."

When we get to the edge, remember it ends in a narrow peninsula and a low wall. That'll be the signal to stop—the wall looming up, so the promontory doesn't surprise you. Remember, your pony hasn't learned to deal with walls. You'll get thrown—or plunge off the cliff—if you don't stop her in time."

"Don't worry about me. I take care of myself now." She studied him through lowered lashes. Just know I'm thinking of a reward for the victor in our race." She smirked. "Whichever of us that would be."

"See you at the wall then. Go!"

She stretched her arms upward before taking the reins. No mere win today. She wanted to stay well ahead of him so he could admire her classical seat while he ogled her bottom. She rode straight in the saddle, as her grandfather had taught her, head lifted, eyes straight ahead, reins loose.

Rose started with an easy walk, letting her hips move with the sway of the horse. She chirped to the young mare, who lifted one foot at a time in a calm walk, sharing her confident energy with her rider. They segued into a trot, and the diagonal one-two beat of opposite hooves matched the thump of Rose's two ventricles, making her one with her mount.

One two one two. Rose squeezed her fingers lightly in the reins as communication with her pony, letting her know by the even contact of her seat bones to trot straight ahead. From time to time, light pressure from one buttock alerted her to step to one side around boulders. Rose's thighs lay alongside the mare, open and relaxed. She imagined she felt the mare smiling.

"It's just like driving a car, Thisbe. Instead of feet, my butt and thighs apply the gas, and my hands on your reins are the steering wheel. I'm gonna miss you so much if I have to leave you behind."

Michael maintained his position a few seconds behind her. So he intended to let her win by a nose, did he? Nuts to that. Time for her to get serious. That sexy man needed to play a little bit of the white knight after all. Let him chase her.

They neared the areas where the grass grew thicker and stones were rare. It was safe to go faster now. She would lead Michael a merry chase. Thoughts of their love fest kicked up her adrenaline.

"Come get me, then!" she called to him. The pressure of her thighs told the mare to canter. "Good girl! Back-Back-Front—and sail!" She loved how this pony moved like a rocking horse in the canter. No bouncing. "Good girl, good girl!" She scooped her bottom along the saddle to match the lunges of the pony.

Rose had reached the strip of smooth, emerald turf. Michael lagged behind her still, though there was no way she would forfeit the race by turning to look back at him. "Time to give it your all now, Thisbe. Make him want us."

Rose assumed the two point crouch, standing in the stirrups, her bottom barely above the saddle and her upper torso parallel to the pony's back. The animal sprang ahead, and the ocean wind blasted against Rose's face as they hammered down the home stretch.

Far behind, Michael shouted. "Rose! Rose! Stop!"

What now? Trying to get ahead of her after all? Fat chance! Her thighs gripped tighter. His voice grew louder, closer, and with it the sound of frenzied hoof beats closing in. He drew alongside of her as she neared the stone wall, causing her thighs to release their grip on the pony. The fright in his eyes took her aback as he leaned over to grab her reins.

This intervention pulled her pony's head up and to the left, while Michael struggled to stop his own mount. Rose and her pony screamed. The mare's forehooves clawed at the air, bucking Rose to the grass.

Clutching at both sets of reins, Michael pitched down onto the wall. Head first.

Rose heard her own scream as if at a distance. "Michael! No! No!"

She limped over to Michael and crumpled to the ground, where his blood ran over the limestone.

"Come on now, Michael, sweetheart. You're all right. I know it."

But his eyes were flat. She located the merest pulse in his throat. She shouted his name and shook his shoulders. There was no response.

She wanted to lay her head on his chest, where she might listen to his feeble heartbeat and cry and force him with her will to come around.

"No! No! No! You're going to wake up. We can't end this way. Hear me? I'm going to get you out of this." She must somehow hoist him up and across the pony's back. But first she had to stabilize his spine. "What am I going to do?" Finally she thought of Grandfather's cell phone, an unfamiliar lump in her pocket.

After her nine-nine-nine call, there was nothing more to do, except keep him close to her and alive.

Somehow. She covered his face and hands with kisses and keened his name. She scolded and pleaded and prayed. Then, afraid to lose track of his heartbeat, she laid her head on his chest and crooned the songs they used to sing together. "...Alive, alive-O! Alive, alive-O!"

Until she heard the siren.

Men spoke in urgent voices, but her eyes were all for Michael. Her hair blowing wildly and her bereft cries made her a destination for the rescuers, she knew. "Here, over here," she murmured through aching vocal cords, at the same time wanting to stave off the moment when she must let them take him.

Their voices were staccato points of sound in the wind. Clad for a seaside emergency, with rain macs, black rubber wellies, and rain caps, they made her think of bizarre sea mammals in a horror movie. The impulse to scream was already growing into a hard knot in her throat.

"There she is."

"Bollocks, look at the blood under his head."

"Good luck to us pryin' her offa hem."

"Madam, what's his name? Tell my chum here while I get his vitals, will ya please?" The tech grunted, searching for a pulse. "Fok! There's not much to work with here. Look at the bloody great hole in his head. Gimme a dressin' will ya, Terrence? Jaysus, man. Give me plenty of gauze, will ya?"

Rose sobbed over the blather between the men. On hands and knees, she cowered close to Michael, as close as she could get, hands in contact with some part of his precious body all the time.

"All right, mum. His heart is beating, but—as you can see—he's out of it, fer sure. Don't know if that's a sign of something really bad. Concussion at the very least. I guess ya agree we've got to take him in. Ya can see that, can ya? I'll call dispatch, but I'm sure we'll go straight to Galway. You the missus then?"

"Yes, I—" Her tongue rolled over the word. "He's my husband."

Chapter 21

It was tough for Rose to focus on the technician's words. "Well, he's alive, but ya should follow as soon as ya can arrange for the ponies. Do ya know someone nearby who can do for them?"

"I—I never thought we'd need to do that. I could take them to the place where we leased them, but I can't leave Michael—" Her aching throat pinched off her words with a spasm, leaving her with nothing but tears.

"Hey, look there, missus." The fellow with the carrot-colored hair pointed up the rise to Sky Road. "That your da and ma comin' there, those old things?"

She reached up a hand to clutch at Sean. "Oh, Grandfather, Michael thought I was falling, and he reached for me, and now—now I might lose him."

Over Gwen's shoulder she witnessed the miserable look the tech shot at her grandparents. The one who cradled Michael's neck in a rigid collar took charge. "No need to work yerself up more than necessary, mum. I've seen far worse. Of course we want to protect his neck and his brain, and we want him to come back to his senses, don't we, mum? That's right. That's why we have him in charge now, and we're going to get him in the vehicle." He turned to Gwen. "Know the way to Galway hospital, madam? You'll want to bring her after."

"Yes," Gwen said. "But she's going with her man, and I'll accompany her. If you're driving, I'm next to you. Look at the state she's in, for pity's sake."

Grandfather enclosed Rose in a bear hug. He didn't hide the tears in his eyes. "I'll take the ponies, girl. I know the breeder, you remember? And I'll fetch your little laddie home with me too. Don't have a care."

"Puppy Joe." Rose's voice was flat. She'd stopped thinking. She only had eyes for the still form the techs loaded into the van. Whether they liked it or not, her body moved of its own accord into the van next to Michael, her hands always in touch with him.

⟨⟩⟨⟩

The stretcher transferred into the emergency room of University Hospital. People made space for Rose, as if they all understood her need to breathe the same air as the un-conscious man. She laid her head on Michael's chest when she could. She found a feathery heartbeat. Shallow breath-ing. She must let him experience her hands on him. Over and over she murmured, "Not again."

No one paid attention to her remarks. The crew worked around her. No one tried to shove her away. Machines went about their business, and everyone conveyed without words what she never wanted to hear. Michael was dying.

Presently, a familiar arm crept around her waist and stole her away to the waiting room. Even outside the trauma room, the clanking of instruments and urgent voices of those toiling to save his life stabbed at her heart. Rose would have given anything to hear Michael's voice among theirs. Surely at any moment his hearty laugh would ring out. She held her breath and then gulped for air.

"Come sit with me," said Gwen, who reached for her clenched hands.

"Grandmother, I—I'm lost."

Soon the neurology resident appeared to give them an

update. His eyes looked tired, but he found the strength to smile, and his voice was unhurried and kind. "Mrs. O'Leary, right?"

Why had she insisted on remaining a Flanagan? What did it matter now? Her crazy ideas could have made poor Rosebud a hyphen, and now she didn't even have Michael's name to hang on to.

She offered her hand. "I'm Rose, Michael's wife."

"I'm Doctor O'Shea. I'm here to help his brain heal."

Fretful-looking eyes answered her unspoken questions. She uttered a shattered sob.

"I'm sorry if that sounded ominous. I do expect neurological functions to return as he recovers. Of course, with a concussion, one never knows. His X-rays reveal cranial fractures at his occipital lobe." He placed his hand on the back of his head. "Here."

She tried to follow him, though bewilderment and dizziness had the upper hand now. "He landed on his back—" She mimicked the gesture. "—hit his head."

He nodded. "That's right. Of course, we still want to make further scans. Right now we can only confirm the anatomical damage. We need an MRI to assess functional damage."

She groaned. "Now. Do it now."

"I'm sorry to say we don't have anybody in the MRI department until Monday. This is Friday night."

"What? No. Do something, please. You have to help him." Her mind whirled, casting up worst case scenarios. Anxiety tightened her chest. Her hands went to her temples. "My fault. It's my fault."

He kept talking. "Most of all, we have to watch for bleeding in the brain. That's always the major concern when the patient loses consciousness."

If only she could focus. "Still bleeding? How?"

He patted her arm. "A concussion in itself is pretty simple, but there can be complications, especially with bleeding and swelling in the brain."

The magic word slapped her alert. "Complications? What complications?"

"There are a number of them—headache, confusion, amnesia, ringing in the ears...um...slurred speech, difficulty with concentration, personality changes, depression." He waved his hand, as if to dismiss the list. "Even blindness, though that can be temporary or partial. Or not. That's possible with damage to the occipital lobe." The doctor's rapid swallowing attested to his discomfort. He fumbled in his coat pocket for a pamphlet, which he handed to Gwen. "Don't worry yet."

Yet? She looked at him, unbelieving.

He placed a hand on her arm. "We'll know more when he wakes up."

What wonderful words—*wakes up*. She leaned forward, stifling her misplaced laughter. "When will that be?"

"Michael might come to by tomorrow, but it could be a day or a week." He looked at her intently. "That's what you're here for. If you're up for it."

Did this nice young man say what she thought he said? Michael could soon be awake? She would look at his beautiful eyes, hear his laughing voice, hold him close, and take in whatever scents clung to him now. She would enjoy them all, even rubbing alcohol and disinfectant, as long as they cohered to the living man.

"Talk to him all the time, and touch him a lot."

She blushed. This was something she could do, for as long as it took. Pinching. Tickling. Singing. Dragging a feather against his skin. Oh, she would make this her finest hour.

Sean came to drive Gwen home. He parted with optimistic words. "Don't worry, Rose girl. The boy will be all right. I once had a concussion when I fell on my head, and look how good my gray matter is." *Dear Grandfather. Bless him for trying to lighten the mood.* He knocked on his skull. "I've got precious little to spare up here, though."

Into the wee hours, Rose chattered to Michael. She

traced love messages into his palms. She whistled. She even read the pamphlet on concussion and brain damage aloud. "You don't want all that. So snap out of it soon, lover." She lay down on the edge of the bed and tickled his cheek.

Periodically, staff checked Michael's vitals and examined his IV. Early in the morning, a grim-faced white coat stethoscoped his chest several times.

ꙮꙮꙮ

Another day passed, and Michael slumbered on. Staff came and went off shift. Increasingly often, they checked his chest. Always, Rose touched him, held his hand, rubbed his limbs. His skin was very warm to the touch and his rough breathing alarmed her.

After two more chest X-rays, the pulmonary specialist pulled up a chair and sat backward on it. "Well—"

She cut him off, her tone urgent. "He's not awake yet. What's wrong?"

His lowered eyebrows made him look somber. "I'm not concerned about that."

She stared, unbelieving.

"Your husband has pneumonia, and lying down all the time has worsened his chest."

"Yes, he's had a cough. He was treated earlier this summer."

"Well, had we seen him since then, it might not have gone so far."

Her shoulders slumped. Now she could blame herself for this.

The doctor gave her a shoulder pat. "It's a good thing he showed up here now. Antibiotics—that's the thing he needs."

"I read about a woman who died of sepsis at this hospital. Are you sure he'll be all right?" She rummaged in a pile of literature she had picked up and handed him the pamphlet.

He chewed on a hangnail. "Yes, I know about that case, but we have new guidelines on infection these days, and our staff has been very careful with your husband. Try not to worry."

What a useless thing to say.

Someone showed up to remove Michael and his IV pole for another X-ray. Rose walked alongside him, his hand in hers.

"Try not to worry," a volunteer lectured.

The nurse hung a new bag of liquid…and another…and another. She made a clucking sound. "He's very resistant, your man. This new medicine should do it, though."

Rose wanted to shake her. "What if it doesn't?"

"Well, there's always something, isn't there now? He's a long way from being on a respirator. Try not to worry."

Tears stung Rose's eyes. She paced back and forth in front of the bed, rubbing her arms. "You listen to me now, Michael." She made an effort to back off her strident tone, but her nerves stretched taut. "Michael. This is enough. You have to do better. Accept the antibiotics and breathe."

She threw herself onto his bed face down and listened to his chest. His lungs were wet and raspy, yet strong heart sounds flooded her with hope.

"Michael, you listen to me now." She grasped his shoulders. "You have a strong heart. So breathe. I know you hear me, darling." Her voice turned wheedling. "Come on, you always let me have my way." She slung a leg over his and placed a palm on his chest. Nuzzling her face into his neck, she struggled to maintain a soft albeit tear-strained voice.

"Michael, my love. When I couldn't live with you, I left, though you begged me to stay. When I told you I was through, you followed me, lurking in the shadows while I worked out what I needed. I'll repeat what I need. I want you to stay close to me, lover, and build the life we planned. What do you need, Michael? I know it's really up to you."

Her voice came strangled now. "What if the last few weeks—months—were all we get?"

Tears interrupted her train of thought, flowing freely. Rose rubbed her face, her mind struggling to flee this reality. Still, as best she could, she held Michael tight until he gasped several times. A jolt of adrenaline shot her off the bed. She cranked the upper part up, raising his head and chest. He gasped once more, and then his breath sounds came easier. She moistened his washcloth in the sink and sponged his face, arms, and chest, following the cloth with kisses. Before long, his forehead was cooler.

"Thank you for this, baby," she said. "It's enough, now that I know you're trying."

Hour after hour, she traced the wet rag over his upper body, then downward, over his long legs all the way to his elegant bare feet. She nipped over his limbs with fluttering kisses and trailed her longing over him.

The nurse nodded. "Keep touching him. Sensation is our ally right now."

"Oh, Michael. I want you so." Slowly Rose walked her fingers down his torso, around his navel, and over the trail of hair leading to the thicker growth and the erect sentinel below. Her hand took possession, contented in the heat sent from him to her. "Thank you, Michael. Yes, I know what you want. We're not done yet, are we?"

How lovely to hear him sigh.

જીન્જી

Darkness took over the hospital room. Rose rested in the armchair and slaked her needy throat with tap water, enjoying a rare respite from talking. Tonight she had finished reading the Clifden telephone listings aloud. That had tested her staying power, but she couldn't face the Galway phonebook, not yet. Gwen had promised to bring her a new novel.

Meanwhile, she intended to take out the Bible from the drawer and read the whole thing backward, starting from Revelations.

That should shake Michael up.

In the dark, she heard him swallow hard. He grabbed a ragged breath. She took in the micro sound of flesh sliding over sheet. Then a deep-pitched groan. Every sound was a gift.

After a deep yawn from the bed, the smell of his breath wafted over to her, and she smiled, thinking of how she had brushed his teeth this afternoon and maintained her regimen of bathing all of him with soap and water morning, noon, and night. Vigorously. She wasn't sure what all the rubbing had accomplished on his behalf, but it had dosed her with an elixir of contentment in the aching heat between them.

"Dark," he murmured.

She pressed the call button on his bed rail.

"Someone there?"

Oh, he can't see me in the dark. She scooted closer to the side of the bed. "It's Rose, Michael."

"Rosie." His voice shook with emotion. "I prayed you would come." He winced when he fingered his bandaged head, where he had struck the stone.

"What's wrong, Michael?"

"My head. Hurts. My skull fits too tight."

"It's all right. The nurse is coming. Do you remember what happened?"

"Assassination attempt?"

"No, silly. You fell off your horse. You've had a concussion. You're under treatment for pneumonia too."

"So glad."

"Why, Michael?"

"Brought you to me." He drifted. "Searched—long time. Now you're here."

By the time the nurse arrived in Michael's room he was under again.

"He seems a little incoherent," Rose said.

"He'll be in and out. Try not to—"

Rose interrupted her. "I know."

The rest of the night progressed as predicted. Near dawn,

Michael rustled about in agitation. Irritable, and then some. Hadn't the doctor predicted that? Even some change in personality? She wanted him to be himself, the love of her life, just as he had been. That was all she needed, and everything else would work out in time.

Now they had time. She hugged herself.

He continued to grumble incoherently, poor darling. No wonder he was crabby, with all he'd been through. She looked forward to putting a smile in his heart and on his handsome face.

"Why is it so damn dark in here?" he growled. "Am I shut up in a stall?"

"Take it easy, darling. I know just what you need." She moved to the window and opened the blinds. Then she sprawled in the chair.

"It feels like it's been night a long time," he said. "Why the hell don't you open the curtains? I want to see you."

Her flesh grew cold.

Michael wasn't looking at her.

Chapter 22

The day Michael found out he was blind was a trip into hell for Rose. She would rather take his affliction on herself and allow Michael to see. She wished to rail against fate, scream out her anger and loss any way she could. His pain was hers. She turned to the window and shook her fists at the sky. She made herself hoarse, for she fled every so often to the park, where she could scream her pain undeterred. Tears swelled her eyes. What a sight she must be. Did it matter? Michael couldn't see her—might not see her ever again.

The ophthalmologist struggled to get his attention. "Michael! Michael." He tapped him on the shoulder. Michael shuddered and turned in the direction of the voice.

"It's Doctor Lynch, Michael. I'd like to examine your vision. Is that all right?"

Michael cleared his throat. Rose had never heard his sardonic tone before. "My vision. You're too late, I'm afraid. You can do anything you want, and I won't know it as long as you don't touch me."

Dr. Lynch focused his lamp on Michael's face. Michael's pupils narrowed in response to the intensity of the brightness.

"How long has it been since you were able to see any light?"

He shrugged. "How long have I been here?"

The doctor squeaked his stool to the side. Michael turned his head in that direction. The doctor fluttered his hand on the other side of his patient's head. "Now look at my hand." Nothing.

Doctor Lynch tapped Michael's nose with his pencil. "Look at my pencil. Michael, look at my pencil." Michael looked right in front of his nose. "Keep looking." Michael kept looking in the same place, but the pencil was now three feet away. "All right, now look for the squeaky mouse." He depressed a rubber duck." Keep looking." Michael looked at the location of the sound, though the toy kept moving in front of him. "Take the mouse in your hand, Michael." He snatched at the air to his left. The doctor put the object into his hand. "What do you think of this mouse, Michael?"

Michael rubbed it between his fingers. "Some mouse."

Michael's pain dragged Rose into a dark place.

Dr. Lynch looked at Michael's face. "What do you hear, Michael?"

"I hear Rose crying."

"Do you know why she's crying?"

"She tends to feel bad when I'm in trouble. She's afraid my eyes don't work."

"Uh-huh. Michael, there's nothing wrong with your eyes or your optical nerve. It's your brain."

Rose could see the big question mark on Michael's forehead. "What? Is that good?"

Dr. Lynch shrugged. "Could be. Michael, you don't have ocular blindness at all. Your eyes are perfect, lying in wait for your occipital lobe to accept their signal. You have cortical blindness, because your brain got hurt."

Rose leaped up and rushed to Michael's side. "How do you know?"

The doctor explained how Michael's eyes responded to brightness, although he did not see it. His pupils opened and closed in response to the amount of ambient light in the room.

He turned to Rose. "You noticed how his eyes don't track—move toward a moving object? His head moved, but not his eyes. He heard it or felt the movement. But he didn't see it."

Rose trembled like a skittish horse. "If his eyes are all right, and this—" She pointed to Michael's eyes. "—if it's all due to the brain injury, does that mean he can heal?" She was holding on to the doctor's arm now, laughing and talking fast. She knew her voice was too loud, but—God! Michael was going to be all right.

"I'm sitting right here, Rose." Michael turned his face toward her. "I can hear you."

The doctor told them that, yes, it was possible Michael would recover at least partial sight—eventually. "Usually the ability to detect light is the first to recover, then seeing motion, and maybe seeing objects. Or not."

Rose could not speak. She placed her arms around Michael's neck. The doctor cleared his throat. "There is also relearning therapy, retraining the brain. Recovery of sight can take a long time—or happen fairly soon."

Rose glanced up brightly.

"Remember, though, the impairment may be permanent."

⁋⁊⁋

Michael left the hospital with a white cane and a manual on braille. Rose slipped her arm under his as they waited for the taxi.

"You don't have to hold me up, you know. I'm not ready for you to cart me to the knacker's yard to be made into glue."

She released an outsized breath. Gosh, he'd been grouchy lately. "No way. You're a randy young stallion yet, mister."

"Blind or no, I can't understand why I can't go home to my own goddamned hovel."

"You remember we discussed that with the doctor. You're not ready to walk among all those rocks. Besides, I don't want any more falls for either of us." She squeezed his arm. "Look on the bright side. Your lungs are clear. You're still weak, but you're going to survive. If your head keeps getting better, we can keep our reservations to home sweet Florida. Enough details to tide you over?"

He threw his hands up and groaned. "You ask a lot of an uncoordinated, blind amnesiac."

She poked him in the ribs. "Try not to give me any more cranky sass, darling. Tomorrow's the wedding, and we're going to celebrate all day."

"Who's getting married? It's not you and me, is it?"

"My grandmother and my grandfather. You know that, don't you?"

He shrugged off the question. "Apparently I don't remember everything I should."

Rose shook her head, speaking quickly. "No, but you will, darling. You will. And if you don't know that we're already married, you're going to be surprised when we get to our bedroom at the Ardbear house and I crawl into bed with you. I've already pushed the twin beds together upstairs." She grinned at him in delight, until she realized he couldn't see her face. That dealt a blow to her mental compass.

He turned her to face him full on and focused his sightless gaze by centering on her breath. "I do know who you are, Rosie."

Her insides clenched for him. Here in the sights and sounds of the outside world again, her senses sky-rocketed, and her sex filled with honey at his mere proximity.

"Not being able to see you is the cruelest blow. You know that, don't you? Your blue eyes always defined the world for me." His voice cracked. "I'm a deaf man at a symphony, but blindness doesn't mean I don't know you. I can smell you, for example." He pressed his nose to the top of her head. "And touching you feels the same as ever." He ran his free hand down her arm. I'm just pissed not to be able to look at you." He broke into a smile. "I remember you being rather good looking."

He was trying to keep the mood light, wasn't he? Hmm...She would follow his lead. "Since your memory is so sketchy, I'll just agree. I'm beautiful. I'm Venus."

He laughed. "Let's not go overboard." Turning serious, he reached for her. "What if I chase you? Do you think you could let me catch you sometimes?"

ⲉⲟⲉⲟ

"We're never sure if Gwen and Grandfather will show up to sleep here, so I wanted to claim the guestroom. It's nice, isn't it?"

"Yeah, I like the color."

Rose directed a dirty look at him. She threw open the dormer window and turned down the bed. She placed a glass of water on the bedside table and settled Puppy Joe on a floor cushion. While she stripped off her underwear, she watched Michael undress. It was odd to know he couldn't see her, after he had once been such an enthusiastic spectator. He didn't know, either, that she was raking over him with her eyes, and that was even more unsettling, because, without the subtle visual cues between them, she felt like a seedy voyeur.

Before the accident, their mutual disrobing had constituted an amorous ritual, whether frenzied or tender, which had contributed to the ardor of their coupling. Always, undressing had made their bodies ripe and their passion undeniable. Her peaked nipples, his long, hard manhood, their heaving chests had been visual cause and effect that opened the floodgates to mind-rattling carnal delights. No more. After he skimmed his pants off on his side of the bed, he rolled under the down comforter.

She extinguished the lamp and lay down facing him, reserving a little space in the middle. Precious seconds elapsed. Was he even aware of her nakedness? The moonless night hid his reaction, but, obviously, her silent, smug smile was lost on him. With equal footing in the dark, should she make the first move?

"So, how's the memory doing? Um...do you remember much about our lives together? About me?"

He propped himself up on one hand. "I know we lived together. We were married, and we were very happy, and lying together like this meant everything."

"Mmmm." She laid a hand where he could reach it. However, his body's tension indicated his mood had darkened. "When you left me, I deserved it. I remember that. It broke my heart. I knew there was no chance of getting over you, even when you told me to back off. So I came to Clifden and wooed you from afar while I lingered nearby, contenting myself with odd glimpses of you." His laugh was short and dry. "Finally, you let me know you wanted to find me, so I tried to make it easier. I remember repainting the door jamb and window frames a rose color. I hung around the church more. I brought more rose bushes, and I was more careless delivering them. More than once your dog barked. Raven. You should have caught me then."

She reached out and touched his hand. "What else?"

"Then you did find me—and I found you. I took you home, and we were happy all over again. Is that enough to remember for now?"

"What about during the last day? Can you remember that?" She wanted so much for him to recall their rampant love-making. She wanted him to remember it almost as much as she wanted to repeat it. And what about the reprise of their wedding?

He fidgeted. "It's the last bit I'm not sure about. They say that's normal."

"That's your accident. It was horrifying and better forgotten. But you've lost some things we said and—did together at the end. Those things were beyond compare."

"And you think I'll remember some day?"

She scooted closer to him. "I'm going to remind you."

Abruptly, Michael clutched the back of his head and emitted a wretched moan.

She reached for him, her mind racing to find a means of relieving his pain.

He pounded his head with his fists. "Oww! I wish I could cut off my damn head." He uttered a shriek like a lament from hell.

She hurried to the door. "I'll get your pills from the bathroom."

He fumbled for his cane beside the bed. "I'll get it. I'm not a goddamn cripple on top of everything. Don't treat me like a fuckin' gimp, God fuck it, woman!" The stick slashed out at the foot of the bed.

Rose shrank back, horrified. She followed a few steps behind him as, stumbling, he reached the bathroom cabinet and swallowed down his medication without water. He pressed a hand to his chest. "Ohh…that burns. Damn it!" He drooped over the sink, shoulders shaking.

She loathed herself for eavesdropping on this personal moment. She longed to reach out to him, yet she was reluctant to humiliate him, for suddenly she grasped the limits of a blind man's right to privacy. At any moment, someone could observe him unwanted, and she didn't want to be that person.

He turned and leaned against the sink, his expression blank. He rubbed his face with a quiet groan. Then he peered intently into the darkness. "You're standing right there, aren't you, Rosie?"

She stepped toward him, her heart breaking.

He crossed his arms in front of his torso, where she wanted to lay her head for comfort. The corners of his mouth turned down. "I don't want you to treat me like a freak."

"That's not what I'm after either, lover." She walked into his arms and brushed her lips against his, intending to help him know her by touch alone. "I wanted you to take me back to bed so, when you're ready, I can treat you like a man. That includes giving you privacy. It also includes weeping or cursing or feeling low—whatever you need to do. I hope you're not ashamed to do it with me."

He grunted, swallowing hard.

She spoke in soothing tones. "That was one of the things we agreed on."

His cane tapped its way back to the bedroom. Her arm lay on his shoulder as she shadowed him.

"It's easing up. You're good for me, and leading you makes me feel like an adult. And a man, yes."

Rose's teeth chattered. "It's cold in here." She closed the window and directed his hand to her arm. "Feel my goose bumps. Shall we put on our pajamas?"

He sat on the edge of the bed and extended his arm for her. "Hell, no, woman. There's one more thing I remember about our past. The raging lust I always felt for you. It's a fantastic memory, and it's a heat I still feel." He pulled her down on the bed on top of him. "I'll lie on the crack."

"What? Which crack?"

"The crack between the beds. Didn't you realize? I notice everything now. Next, I'll take up oil painting by braille."

She stifled his rambling with her lips and made love to him every way she knew how.

Chapter 23

The bridal couple had arranged to pick up Rose and Michael in a limousine. They stood at the curb, swinging their locked hands while they waited. He rested his forehead on hers. This mannerism gave the impression of looking into her eyes. She appreciated this nod to their past, though it provided a pang of loss.

He rubbed his cheek against hers. "You were a Florida panther last night, my love. I think you've found a fondness for playing that role." Thank God, he still used his sexy eyebrow lift to melt her insides.

"Maybe I just needed to play the white knight for a change."

He kissed her hair. "I needed my woman. We were stuck in that hospital way too long."

"I know, Michael. The truth is, I was afraid you wouldn't want me anymore, with all you went through. That would kill me." She struggled to hide the break in her voice.

He turned an expression of incredulity on her. Indignation sounded in his suddenly strident voice. "I'm blind, baby. My cock didn't fall off."

She raised a finger to her lips. "Shh! Shh! Shh!" She giggled. "You made that abundantly clear. And I have to warn you when you might be overheard. They're pulling up to the curb."

Gwen and Sean looked radiant. Her upturned face had never appeared so beautiful to Rose. Her eyes danced, and she spoke in a voice as bubbly as a central Florida stream bed. Sean offered compliments to all the ladies. Rose could almost visualize the pair when they were young and newly in love.

Bridey and baby Rose were in the car already. "I'm about to turn inside out. I heard from Evan. You will never guess what happened. He finally got courage to tell me he's shacking up with a woman doctor he met over there."

Michael looked as if he wanted to tear the car apart. "What an asshole!"

Rose made comforting noises in Bridey's direction and rolled her eyes at Michael, though he couldn't see her. Come to think of it, he probably knew she would do that. How splendid to know each other's faces so intimately.

Bridey patted the air in their direction. "Don't be sorry. I suspected it when the Marines didn't acknowledge his disappearance. He was there all the time—missing only to me." She tutted, while Rose did her best to put an arm around her and the bonneted infant. Bridey's eyes were downcast. She shook her head slowly and choked out her words. "Not a single message, all this time." Her free hand rubbed absently at the baby's bunting. "I would never have believed it. He's not the man I married." Her lip quivered, and the baby snuggled closer to her bosom.

Rose ran furtive eyes over Michael His handsome, kind face, his welcoming arms and broad shoulders. She couldn't say it here, but she was overcome with relief that, despite all loss, he remained himself.

Bridey clung to Baby Rose, covering her cheek with kisses, and produced a croaking whisper. "How dare he let me worry?"

Rose's brow creased in concern. The troubles they had lived through together flitted through her mind. She swallowed hard. "What about the baby, Bridey? Will he want joint custody? Is he even coming back?"

"Oh, that's the worst part." Bridey turned hurt eyes on Rose, continuing in a new, sardonic tone, "His dolly won't let him take an interest in the baby. Can you believe that?" Her laugh was half sob.

Michael looked as if he'd just bit into a sour kumquat. He fumbled with his words. "How c—can the asshole let—let go of his baby girl? What—what kind of a bastard would do that?" Then a new thought seemed to cross his face. He scrubbed his hands over his eyes and directed his sightless gaze out the window.

Rose caught hold of his hand, and he directed his look of regret her way.

Bridey rushed her words. "We're going to move in with Dad and Claris in Galway for a while. Dad is crazy about little Rose, so maybe we'll go home with them when his sabbatical is up. Heck, I'm an American, after all." She cooed to the infant. "I guess you are too, sweetie poo."

Baby Rose giggled.

Rose hid an unexpected smirk. "*Heck?* Looks as though you've cleaned up your mouth, while Michael has embraced his id."

Gwen turned to Michael. "That's just part of your post-trauma rigmarole, isn't it, Michael? We have faith you'll get over that. You're not going to keep swearing in front of your grandmother-in-law, are you?"

"No, ma'am. I'll try to hold it until we leave town. I'm going to become a profane street fighter back in Citrus County, though."

Sean looked as if he had just bitten his tongue.

⟡⟡⟡

The car left them at the bottom of Church Hill, where they met Gwen's daughter Rose and little Violet in her white organza dress.

Violet looked ready to leap on Rose. She spouted like a

disorganized geyser. "Guess what? Grandmother says it's all right. I may sit with you, Rose. We're both...er...grand-daughters. Isn't that brilliant? Ma is just a daughter. She has to...uh...walk in front of Grandmother, so her mom can keep an eye on her, but you and I can take care of each other." Her little face clouded over. "I'm sorry you're going to America, Rose. I hope you won't forget me."

"Of course I won't, dear. And when Grandma and Grandpa come to America, I hope you and your mama will come too. You're an honorary American, I suppose, and I'm only a quarter Irish myself, so you'll fit right into our mixed up family." Rose directed a grin at Sean, who looked at her with a lemon mouth.

He walked ahead with Violet, explaining it all to her. "Yes, and you'll meet my—our—son, your uncle, who's half and half himself."

Michael grinned and linked arms with Rose. "That's a losing battle." They proceeded up the hill behind the rest of the party. By and by, they stopped to sample the air and the noises of birds migrating.

"Ahh. I remember this hill. I rode up on my bike. Sometimes I walked it uphill if I had a rose bush on the back." He squeezed her arm with a smile that told her more about his pursuit of her than his words had done. "Yes, I remember all that."

"Tell me what you see—in your mind's eye—what you remember."

"Then you have to let me use my cane, and I'll guide you." He lifted his face, sniffing at the fall air. "See? Right about here is the notice board. Am I right? The church steeple is in view ahead. Now the path is bearing a little to the right."

Rose's mouth formed a circle of amazement at the accuracy of his memory vision. This frequently traveled path had meant something to him, and that touched her heart, giving her a glimpse of his feelings back then, when he'd pursued his covert quest.

"And now we're almost at the baptistry at the end of the narthex. We can go in here, but I always went in through the blue door. Which are the others using today? Ah, probably went in already, right?"

Rose saw he'd figured this out by directing one ear forward in a way that let him verify the absence of chatter ahead.

Several steps farther, Michael paused with his hand on the blue door. "This door leads to the apse and the chancel." He flashed her the telltale smile of sudden insight.

"We went in here together, not too long ago." Which was most important, really—recovering his memories or his sight? Rose was glad she didn't have to choose for Michael. This was his personal journey. All she could do was stand by him and pretend she didn't mourn the loss of those things they could no longer share. Especially the mutual recall of passion shared during his last sighted days.

Since the accident, she hadn't mentioned their loss of Rosebud, from whom the past year had issued. It would break her heart if he didn't remember her. He waited at the blue door. "Mourning for what we can't have together, Rosie?"

She caressed his face, ready to deny it. Then she changed her mind. "Truth, my love?"

He nodded. "Truth. Always."

Her voice hitched. "Yes, your vision loss wasn't just your loss. It was—it is mine too."

He held her head in both hands and whispered, "Oh, Rose."

She whispered back. "But we have this, and it's new and exciting and it's sexy as hell."

He cupped her bottom and brought her close to his hardness. "Feel that?"

How could she not? Her womanly center turned moist. He turned his sly grin on her then. "Kiss me quick, Rose. No making out in church."

Did he remember her saying that here before? He kissed her, one hand on the door.

൭ൟൟ

They found their way to the front pew, where little Violet tugged on Michael's hand. "You made it. Rose has to sit next to me, since we're granddaughters." She squeezed between them, looking smug at her maneuver.

"Where's your mama?" Rose delivered a hearty hug, but Violet kept peeking at Michael.

Violet waved a vague hand. "Oh, she's somewhere in the back. She's the matron of honor. When they're ready they'll come to the front or whatever you call this part here. It's a funny church, isn't it, with the big bath for babies in the round part there?"

Rose laughed, lifting her eyes to Michael's face from habit. Her heart skipped a beat when she realized his eyes centered on her right ear, and she swore a gleam revealed his amusement. She cleared her throat slightly before she responded to Violet. "You're talking about the font back there in the baptistry."

"Well, I thought it was strange when Bridey's baby got christified. We could see her fine in the bap-tis-ty, but other people in the pews here wouldn't have seen her at all."

Michael grinned at her. "I never thought of that, chatterbug. You're pretty smart, aren't you?"

She slipped her hand into Michael's. "Yes, I am." She sucked on the inside of her cheek and kicked her legs in a way that suggested she wanted to say something impertinent.

Rose scooted closer to Violet. "Do you want to say more to Michael? It's okay to ask him questions."

Violet looked from Rose to Michael and back again. "Is he looking at me?"

"He's trying, dear."

She tugged at Michael's sleeve. "Are you going to get new eyes? Because I like the ones you have very much."

Rose kept a straight face, as did Michael. His tender manner with this child tugged at her heart. Michael spoke close to Violet's ear, shaking his head.

Violet put on a solemn face. "Well, isn't it sad not to be able to see? The way you look without your face hair, you must want to admire yourself in the mirror all the time."

Michael stifled a chortle. "Someday my brain might learn to see for me a little bit."

Violet's eyes went to the back of Michael's head, perhaps searching for extra eyes there. How astonishing she was, this little girl. They would miss her. His arm around Violet, Michael squeezed Rose's arm, letting her know his thoughts held another little girl, lost more than a year ago.

While the organ played Bach's "Now Thank We All Our God," the rector started the procession, ending up in front of the altar rail, where he waited for the groom. Sean passed the handful of guests and stopped next to Michael. You haven't forgotten, have you, Michael? You're my best man." He slipped his arm through Michael's and continued with him into position at the front. Finally, Rose Too and Gwen took their places at the altar, and the service commenced.

Looking at Michael, Rose thought back to the day when they had knelt at this rail together while they spoke their spontaneous vows. Tears rolled down her cheeks.

Violet tugged on her sleeve. "Rose, why are you crying?"

Rose hugged her and whispered back. "It's so beautiful. Let's listen to what they say, darling, for these are words to remember forever, and we must help them do that."

In a tone of reverence, Adam intoned, "Dearly beloved, we are gathered together here in the sight of God, and in the face of this congregation, to join together this man and this woman in holy matrimony."

Rose felt touched, for the liturgy reminded her of society's importance in sustaining a marriage. She had left her community when she'd fled from Michael, but they'd found this new group of people who cared about them and helped them come back together.

Violet poked her, watching her face. "...that children might be brought up in the fear and nurture of the Lord..." Rose squeezed Violet's hand. Yes, her grandparents, though past child-bearing, had acted like loving parents to many of them here.

Now Gwen and Sean spoke their vows, promising each other love and comfort no matter the vagaries of life. They spoke of honoring each other, forsaking all others, living together as long as they lived.

Rose Too stepped forward and sang in a lyrical soprano.

> "Be thou my vision, O Lord of my heart;
> Naught be all else to me, save that thou art;
> Thou my best thought, by day or by night;
> Waking or sleeping, thy presence my light."

Rose wanted to cry. When she saw the tears on Michael's face first, she couldn't hold back. Regret flowed out of her bruised soul and hope muscled its way in.

After the service, Michael rejoined her in the pew, his expression mischievous. "Here I am, a witness who can't see. I can tell you, though, that Sean was crying up there. And now, while we wait for the photographs, Violet is having a grand craic sprinting between the pews." He nuzzled her face with his bare cheek. "I'm really relieved I didn't disgrace myself. I even handed the ring to the right person."

She clung to his hand. "You did very well, darling, though for a moment I thought you were going to collapse."

"Yes, I remembered something, and it made me a little dizzy. I remembered you and me kneeling at this rail. It was painted white, wasn't it? And I asked you to marry me again. And you agreed. And we spoke wonderful, meaningful vows to each other that we made up right on the spot. I recall everything I felt about you then, much of it rather disgraceful. I feel the same way now. And I want to take you someplace private." His customary lustful expression was all over his face, even if he could not see her.

She giggled. "You said the same thing then."

Chapter 24

November:

Rose and Michael agreed he should gain some independence before their return to Citrus County. Hence, their prolonged stay at Grandfather's house, where she devised therapeutic challenges for him. Today he was having a hard day. Rose saw it in his flaring nostrils and the reddening of his handsome face. He planted his legs wide and thrust out his chest to gulp some air.

"Go ahead, Michael. Be true to our deal and say it—how much it hurts you to be curtailed as you put it. I want you to tell me, even if I suspect it anyway."

A vein pulsed in his neck. "Damn it, woman! Can't you just say something to make me feel better?"

"What? And enable you to keep your crap stored inside? Again?" Her posture mirrored his, while she thrust her forefinger at him again and again. "Own it, buster." Her muscles quivered as she struggled to make him release his anger.

"Fuck it, Rose!" He powered his fist in midair and connected with the wall. He cradled his hand with its partner. "Ahhh! Holy fuck!"

Rose hurried to his side and seized his reddened hand. "That was much better, dear. Got any more?"

He ground his teeth in frustration. "I've got plenty, but I've only got one more fist."

She applied an ice pack around his hand. "Well, why don't you tell me why you're upset at the moment?"

"You've got to be kidding." His laughter had an edge. "I'm fuckin' pissed at everything right now. Don't I have a right?"

"Why, Michael? Why?" She knew, all right. She snorted. She'd have to be a simpleton not to know.

He shouted his aggravation. "I can't cross the street by myself. I can't give my dog the evil eye when he's stolen a rancid bone. I can't tell black from white." He stood still, panting. "I'm not allowed to ride my bike. I can't get any damn exercise. I'm so damn frustrated. I can't even leer at the woman I want to fuck, and I'm so damn pissed I could explode." He slammed the cupboard door, shattering a glass. His voice dwindled to a near whisper. "I can't even be sure to pick up all the glass."

She waited.

"Shit, Rosie!" he growled. "I feel so damn sorry for myself." He kicked the shoe molding. "That's for my father. I've been mad as hell at him. Now I'm annoyed that I can't hate him anymore." He punched the air with his good fist. "Damn it!"

Her chest heaved in tune to his anger. "Good enough for today, Conan. Now can I tell you what's troubling me? Then you can help me with that."

The glower forsook his face, tenderness in its stead. "What is it? Tell me, sweetheart."

"It's not so bad. It's just...sometimes I'm scared, Michael. "Her eyes powered up at him, and he seemed to know it, for he caressed her face with his very close.

"Please, Rosie, tell me." He did not move to kiss her. Rather, he listened with a newborn intensity. She could almost see him prick up his ears.

"It's hard to say."

"Give it to me, love."

She nodded, trusting him enough to let him see inside with his special vision. "What if I never get over Rosebud? What if I can't get pregnant again? What if I do, and it ends...I lose..." She shook her head. She couldn't say it.

His face was still very close to hers. "You used the wrong word, my love. It's *we*, not *I*."

She laid her head against his chest, and he closed his arms around her. The strong beating of his heart told her he, too, knew these qualms.

"Trust me. As I told you, I do have a plan, and it will help us with Rosebud. We'll find closure together, and we'll be able to keep her close. This is something I can handle, Rose. Please let me."

She nodded her head against his chest. Her small voice found a direct line into his heart. "Okay."

"As far as the future goes...Will we have children? Will I still be blind? Will I be fit to take care of a child if I am? Time will tell, but every page in the story has us hand in hand from here out."

They swayed to their mutual rhythm.

All the way upstairs, his hands rode on the small of her back and the curve of her bottom in front of him. She knew what that did to him, so she took her time climbing—and letting down her hair. Locked inside the dormer bedroom, she turned to face him, nearly upsetting his balance. Instead of waiting for him to recover from his surprise, she jerked his shirt over his head and arms, tweaked his nipple roughly, and pitched the garment at the door.

She would let him guess at the fire in her eyes. "Still got a good head of steam? A little rage? Self-pity? Good." She dawdled, working her shift over her head. Close, certain he knew what she was up to. She kicked her clothing to the floor and over his instep, grinning all the way. She weaseled her thumbs inside his sweat pants and skimmed them down in one motion, unleashing his erection. She tugged on it forcibly and rubbed it against her triangle of curls.

"Give your anger to me, Michael. Make it rough."

During their last month in their adopted city, they devised ways to exercise together. They started by walking the streets and beaches of Clifden hand in hand. When Michael's long legs outpaced Rose's, she modified Puppy Joe's retractable leash.

"You've heard of a man purse, haven't you, Michael? Well, this is a man leash."

He acted a bit grumpy about it, until he realized that, with one end around his waist and Rose holding the leash on her bicycle, he could run flat out. In return, she let him tie her up sometimes. They rented a tandem bike. He liked pedaling, he declared, especially pumping close behind her rounded bottom while she steered. One way and another, they were able to ride to all the places that had meant so much to them before.

They visited the pony farm to say goodbye to Lucius and Thisbe. Using helmets, they were able to ride a little bit, not too fast, with the horses attached with a rope, either side by side or single file. Soon, Lucius learned he must always stay close to Thisbe, so no rope was needed.

Michael turned his face toward Rose by his side. "I have a confession to make."

She grinned at his newly lightened tone. "Uh-oh."

"I don't know how much more anger I can extrude. My spleen feels practically empty."

"What happened?" She expected a goofy story. He'd been that much more his old self.

"No, nothing. It's these strong, capable ponies and their gentle ways. I really think ponies like this will keep me riding, and, now more than ever, I want to bring some home. With the railed racing track we have on the horse ranch, I can ride full out without you leading me."

Rose jerked her head back and widened her eyes. She didn't know what to say, so she just kept smiling.

Michael sent her a full, sparkling beam of delight. She hoped many would follow, especially now that he'd improved his eye contact. Even though he didn't see, his attention to this social refinement confirmed his desire to please her. Since it was his occipital brain that preluded his vision, his eyes still displayed the emotions that originated elsewhere. She adored the flashes of anger, the glint of a chuckle, and the smolder of passion that let her in on the inner Michael.

He chuckled. "I just feel so...liberated. I'm no longer so trapped in the darkness."

Tears sprang into Rose's eyes. At last!

Rose and Michael did take the ponies out one last time, for they had always intended to pay a visit to their hovel at the bay. Signs of late autumn were near. Even the cushiony pink thrift flowers had nearly disappeared from the headlands. They arrived early one morning, with the idea of bundling up bedding and leftover belongings before releasing the building to the rental agency. Michael pried open the long unused door.

"I forgot to carry you over the threshold after our wedding, Rosie." He braced himself against the doorframe. "Well, come at me." He opened his arms, and she rushed him. She leaped. He lifted. Then they stumbled inside shrieking and fell onto the bed.

"Bah! It's musty." She rued the neglect of a nice new bed. "What a shame."

"We got our use out of it, didn't we, darling?" She could swear his eyes twinkled at her.

They shivered in the cold room. He gave her a sweet kiss for old time's sake and a deep one for the future. "I'll be glad to return to our cozy bed on Aidan's farm."

She wiped dust from the window and peered out toward the cliffs. "I have an idea. Let's ride Lucius and Thisbe in the direction of the site where you had your accident. We'll dump all our leftover issues there, and—that will be the end of them. Do you think you can do it?"

The next thing she knew, the guide rope was back on the ponies. She kissed him lightly. "We have plenty of good light this morning."

"Good. I want you to tell me what you see. Maybe I'll see it in my brain too."

"That's what I'm hoping." She smiled to herself. Today they wore the same garments as on their last ride over the headlands. Because she knew by now that he enjoyed it so much, she put her foot in the stirrup and let him take hold of her bottom to hoist her onto Thisbe's sturdy back. Michael tested his way over to Lucius. She enjoyed these new roles, because she knew they made the testosterone thrill within him, making him feel strong. And, darn it! Watching the movements of his well-toned leg muscles and ass created a delicious tingling inside her.

She'd been foolish to harbor a sense of loss when he failed to remember their love-making on the cliffs that last day. After all, they'd had so many other notable moments of passion and would have more.

Off they went, parallel to the North Sky Road. "I can feel how the land is rising, Rose. I can remember how green the grass is here. Are there still sheep near the castle? Remember the miserable night we spent there?"

"It wasn't miserable for me, Michael. You held me tight the whole time."

"Yes, but you had sheep breath. Ha-ha!"

"Stinker. You were feeling no pain when you rode behind me."

"You're right. I do remember that."

As they neared the boulders, Rose had trouble keeping the ponies nose to tail. Time to make a stop.

"Hard tack and cheese."

"What?"

"We had hard tack and cheese—and lots of butter."

Rose worried the trip would take too long. Maybe it would wear Michael out.

"I had on that blue jacket, didn't I, Rose? Whatever happened to that?

"I had to throw it away. It was soaked with blood."

"I really liked that jacket. I wrapped it around you."

"Slow down, Michael. We'd better keep the rope on. We can't afford another accident." Her stomached clenched.

"We talked about accidents then. I remember your face—so coy, so teasing."

His words set off a tingling in Rose's groin. "What did you say?"

"We talked about accidents. You baited me. 'I want to hear you say it. Tell me what causes your accidents.' You pretended not to understand. You were panting. You wanted me to talk dirty—tell you more about my rampant desire for you."

Rose's brain was cottage cheese.

"'Just so we have it straight, because I wouldn't want you to make love to me by accident...'"

Rose finished the sentence. "Especially when I want it so very much."

"Then I lifted you out of the saddle and laid you on my jacket. I wrapped my flannel shirt around you."

Fire wicked up inside her, as it had then. "What happened next?"

He was out of his saddle in a flash, finding her and lifting her up. "My darling, my love. Let me show you."

It was later than Rose had feared when they returned to town. They were both exhausted.

೮⁄つ೮⁄つ

December:

On their last day in Clifden, their close circle gathered in Grandfather's home in Ardbear. Rose brought platters of scones to the table. On the sofa sat Violet with her mother's arm around her. Bridget's baby girl lay on a cushion in Violet's lap, her innocent blue eyes fixed on her face. She held onto Violet's finger and cooed and blew bubbles. Violet laughed and made round eyes. Baby Rose imitated the sound. "Ah-ha-ah-ha-ah!" She blew in and out when she laughed.

Violet talked to her in baby-speak. "You are a perfect little baby. I am so glad Rose brought us together. Someday you will be in my wedding, and we will look as beautiful as Grandmother did in her wedding dress. Won't we? We will hold flowers, but I will have more than you, because I am the bride. Yes I am. Until then, I'm going to teach you everything I know, including how to use the toilet." Baby Rose seemed to agree. Then a frown of concentration clouded her face. "Bridey, look what the baby did." Bridget bore her away, and Violet followed.

Rose murmured into Gwen's shoulder. "The small teaching the smaller."

"Yes. They're both lucky. Children need children, almost as much as they need adults."

Rose hugged her. "You're such a wise grandmother, and such a good friend. Violet is fortunate to have you."

"I'm the lucky one. I hope you understand why I can't move back to America without Rose and Violet. Will you help Aiden understand too? See…I have a chance with Violet."

A taste of bitter bile reminded Rose that she and Aiden would never mean to Gwen what Rose and Violet did.

Gwen fetched a medium-sized package from the sideboard and handed it to Rose. "I already shipped one to Aiden. I made this one for you. I hope you can fit this into your hand luggage."

It was an oil painting. In the middle sat Gwen and Sean in each other's arms, partially turned toward each other. The top row depicted Rose Too next to Aiden, peering down at their parents.

At the bottom sat Rose with little Violet in her lap, her

hair bow askew. Rose beamed at someone unseen in the foreground.

Gwen kissed Rose on the forehead. "We'll visit when we can. I promise. In the meantime, remember—you have a family."

Part V
Homecoming

Citrus County, Florida

Chapter 25

Watching the pair in line at Emigration and Customs brought home to Rose that Michael and his dog had grown up together. Moreover, Joe's heart belonged to his master. Though still an impulsive young animal accustomed to running full out across the headlands, he had qualified as a service dog. As such, he guided Michael through the airport and lay at his feet for the flight to Orlando.

Still, there would always be a bond between her and her Puppy Joe. She valued memories of comfort he had afforded her during her grief, but she knew that his joy came from his master. She was proud of their accomplishments.

While the white knight still resided in Michael's spirit, he admitted, he would never again emerge with his former abandon. On the other hand, Rose reveled in Michael's deep joy in all he had gained.

In charge of bringing Michael home, Rose knew she too had grown, especially into her new role as his protector and guide, though this required tact, patience, and consummate skill—attributes she would never have given herself credit for. Her success made her feel proud and lent additional layers to her role as his devoted lover and soul mate.

Would Michael ever recover his vision—or some of it? Regardless, she read his joyfulness in the brilliance of his smile and the enthusiasm in which he snatched her into his arms.

As for her, she'd found and fought for her heart's desire.

She glanced past him at the cliffs of Connemara below the plane, still green in early winter. He curled his arm around her, pressing her head onto his chest, where his manly scents and voice and indefinable heat assailed her with tenderness. She heard his deep voice rushing directly to her ear from within him.

"Rose, I'm so glad you saved me." He brushed her lips with his, and her center of pleasure stirred for him. He deepened the kiss that went on and on.

She sighed and snuggled into his chest. "Same here."

A crusty voice spoke from across the aisle. "Excuse me. I hope you two aren't going to monopolize the lavatory for sex. I'm sitting near it for a reason, and, if my bowels blow, things will get unpleasant for all of us." The speaker looked like a sad-eyed sheep.

છળછ

When Aidan and Maria picked up the exhausted travelers at MCO, Rose's impulse was to run into her parents' arms. Instead, she steered Michael toward them with the pressure of her hand on his arm. Holding onto him still, she leaned forward into her father's embrace. Her mother took possession of Michael. "Welcome home, son."

During the drive to Citrus County, Aidan left the turnpike for the dark back roads. The foursome chatted about Sean and Gwen—and Maria's hopes to bring them home to the ranch.

Rose thought Aidan acted subdued. His wrinkles went deeper.

"Daddy, you haven't gotten out a word. "You must have a lot of mixed feelings about your mother. You're going to love Gwen, I promise."

Aiden rubbed his lips.

"She is so sweet, Dad, and Grandfather is flooded with love." She leaned forward in her seatbelt to squeeze his shoulder. "Now you understand your mother didn't abandon you. Can you get your head around it?"

"Not yet, but she's been writing to me."

Maria turned around to look at her daughter. "And we talked on the phone. She's very nice."

"You're so much like her, Dad. Even before I knew she was my grandmother, she reminded me of you."

Michael cleared his throat. "Do you have any memories of your mother, Aiden?"

"Well, I remember her holding me. I was...mmm ...three. I still hear her singing to me, and I recall what it was like—her carrying me around while she talked to me constantly." He swallowed several times. "Different phrases run through my mind. 'Here's the new foal, Aidan. No, he doesn't drink chocolate milk from his mama.' Things like that. Who knows? Maybe more will come back in time."

"That's how it was when Michael started regaining his memories, wasn't it, sweetheart?" Rose squeezed Michael's hand, and he reciprocated. New shorthand to replace the secret glances they used to send back and forth.

Aidan's voice sounded shaky. "I spent my life missing my mom. All this time she missed me too. She says she wants to come see me—us—soon. She talks like she thinks of me as her little boy."

Maria placed a hand on the back of Aidan's neck. "In a way you are, dear. You both have to recapture parts of your relationship that were cut short. It'll be hard to adjust."

Rose wished Michael could see what she saw—her parents' tactile communication, so like theirs. She rubbed his arm.

She gave Aidan another shoulder pat over his back rest. "It's going to be a process, Dad. It's going to be that way for all of us."

"Yes, I'm pretty sure Gwen—Mother—and I will be all right with each other in the long run."

"How about Grandfather? Are you angry with him for not telling you who it was he went to Ireland to see?"

"Not really."

Maria squeezed his shoulder. "Admit it, dear. You were really hurt. You felt he was wrong to let you suffer longer than you had to."

Michael cleared his throat. "Yes, but maybe he wanted to save you pain in case things didn't work out."

"And maybe he didn't want me messing with his business. He always thought I did that, and I guess he was right. Especially when he got older. I didn't treat him like his own man."

Michael growled into her Rose's ear. "Ho-ho, wait until he sees the bridegroom act like a man."

For a while, all remained quiet until Maria changed the subject. "Have you been quilting or drawing, Rose?"

"I did a little drawing, and I crocheted dozens of Irish roses for a friend's church bazaar. I gave Violet some lessons. I thought of sending Bridget the pony quilt for Baby Rose, but I'm not quite ready to let it go."

Maria sent her an eye hug. "Recently I entered three quilts in the annual show in Atlanta. I won first and second place. And, Rose, I brought your landscape quilt for display only. I hope you don't mind. You did say you wanted to show it."

"Oh, I didn't have the binding on it, though."

"You won't believe what people offered for it as it was. Of course I wouldn't sell it. But I did take hundreds of orders for framed photographs of it. The orders are waiting if you want to proceed."

Rose felt belly punched and elated at the same time. "Well..."

Maria nodded. "Yes, it's true. And a magazine wants to feature your work, both fabric art and drawing. And there was a massive request for a website and a virtual show.

Somebody from the Central Florida art department called too. I think you can make a living with your art from now on."

Rose covered her face and sobbed, while Michael cuddled her. "I knew you were going to cry, and I didn't need to see you for that."

"Oh, Michael."

He nibbled her ear and whispered. "Right now I can taste your tears and hear your heartbeat and smell the sweet fragrance of your hair and your own peculiar sweatiness. And pretty soon I want to test out my tactile senses on you, my dear stinky girl."

∞∞∞

Rose and Michael climbed the steps to their porch. He held her in his arms as they waved goodbye to Aidan and Maria. Puppy Joe ran around in circles, yipping.

"I hear him ripping up the grass. His vocabulary has really developed, hasn't it?"

"Yes, that behavior there means passionate delight, and I agree with him. The peeing says 'All this is mine.'"

"Yes, it's good to be home. How does the garden look? I don't smell anything in bloom."

"Um…the roses need dead-heading." She saw with one glance that some of the bushes were done for, but, in light of Michael's recent concussion, a blow like that was more than she wanted to deliver.

Michael brought his fist down on the porch rail. "No, Rose, don't do that!" He glared at her—nearly at her. His irritation took her aback. She stepped forward to touch him. His voice was stony. "Don't you get it yet? I can't stand it if you lie to me. I'm blind, not senseless. You think I can't detect the absence of fragrances I should smell? You think I can't hear the crackle of the brown leaves as Joe brushes by them?"

She lowered her head. "I—"

He splayed his fingers in her hair. "I can dig out dead roots. I can shovel manure. I can prune by feeling for the junctures of the shoots from the stem. I know what colors every rose should bloom. I recall the soft feeling of rose petals. Damn it, I remember what red and pink and yellow look like. I know you hate puke green." He leaned back on the support post, breathing hard. "Let me be a whole person, for God's sake, as much as I can."

"I'm sorry, Michael. I wanted to protect you." She walked into his arms. "It was an impulse."

"Like my impulse to protect you. I know. Can't help it." He rubbed his face on the top of her head. "Neither of us likes being half and half, Rose."

"I'll try not to do it again." Her voice was small.

He descended the steps. "Okay…Well, I'll go get the chain saw now and cut up some firewood."

Her stomach lurched. She produced a sound that started squeaky and ended in a low croak. She rushed over to the path, where he stood doubled over in laughter. She flailed away at him, and he grabbed her arms.

"You! You! That was awful!" she scolded.

"Oh, trying to restrain me from using the chainsaw?" He pulled her against him. "Well, thank you, Madam White Knight."

❧❧❧

Someone had been there to turn on the overhead light and fan in their living room. Rose reacted to the surprise above their mantelpiece.

"Oh! Oh, my God!"

His arm around her let him follow the direction in which her body had turned. "What is it? Are you going to remind me that I can't cut any more wood for the fireplace?"

"Grope your way to the mantel, smartypants, and you'll find out for yourself."

His fingers tested the surfaces of wood and glass. "It's something framed. It's very big. Knowing your mom, it's probably a textile, but, large as it is, it's small for a quilt."

"Yes." she stepped up behind him. "It's not full-sized, a very sharp photograph of a quilt."

"Is it the quilt you showed me before you left, the panorama with you and me and all our family for generations?" His hand held her neck, and, when she nodded, he felt her assent. "Then I love it, and—even better—I remember it. When you brought it over, you spread it out on our bed. Our bed that had been empty of you for too long."

"Mmm..." She wrapped her arms around his waist, forcing her breasts against his back.

"There it all was, the grandchildren and old people, the lovers in the bushes, the school, and the homes. A whole community. When I brought the tea in, I found you with your head on my pillow, your hand on the world you'd created in that quilt." He turned to face her and ran his fingers over her features, practicing the lines and planes he rememorized every day. Then he palmed her bottom and clutched her pelvis close to his body. Now she was the one reading his emotions by braille. "I remember how much I wanted to get under that quilt with you."

Their kiss lingered, sweet and tender. "Let's get ready for bed, Rosie. Our bed."

"You claimed I'm stinky."

He kissed her nose. "To the shower, woman."

Puppy Joe herded them to the bathroom, where the water was warm, the soap slippery, and their bodies receptive to touch.

Chapter 26

Four years later:

It was the cool evening of a hot summer day. The porch door slammed behind Rose when she brought out a large pitcher of iced tea and a small one of lemonade, placing them on a table near four white-painted rocking chairs. She paused to revel in the sights and fragrances coming from the rose garden.

She called to him inside. "The roses are perfect, Michael. Never better. You know I wouldn't lie to you."

"Told you! Varieties planted for their aroma can be gorgeous too. Look at that *Sugar Moon* next to the porch. It smells like heaven."

She sniffed at the bush. "Ah, the white one. Mmm. Intense. Citrus and rose together."

"How about the raspberry in that red next to it, huh?"

She envisioned him smirking. "I like the deep rose scent in this pink *Falling in Love*." Its name reminded her of every day with him.

Puppy Joe scratched at the screen door. When she let him out, he ran around and around the rose and flower beds arranged inside the expanded front yard. They needed the picket fence now as a supplement to the hedge that hid the cottage from the road. It had been Michael's idea to include the centenarian oak tree, the picnic table, and a paved walk inside the enclosure too. He had done all the gardening, paving, and fencing himself. Aiden had painted most of the fence, because he'd insisted Michael sucked—his word for *missed a few spots.*

Rose's heart swelled when she thought about all her husband had accomplished here in a few short years.

Tongue lolling, Joe plopped down in front of the large, rose-colored stone under the tree and fell asleep.

Michael descended the porch steps. "Rose?"

"He's still doing it, sweetheart. After all this time."

Arm in arm, they strolled to the spot where the dog lay. He wagged his tail at them, but they could not induce him to move. Michael petted him. "Let him be. He knows where he's needed."

"It's a beautiful stone, Michael, such an unusual color. I still love it."

"Rose granite."

Her voice turned tender. "I like the way you worded it. 'Rosebud Flanagan O'Malley. Our daughter." Tears came to her eyes, even after all this time, and Michael wiped his eyes too.

He bent over to touch the stone. "We love you, Rosebud."

Time stilled with their embrace.

"Yoo-ooo! Hello there! Aidan and Maria edged through the gate, bearing a picnic basket and a large rubber ball.

Aidan shouted. "Here comes the man! Three years old today."

A sturdy little fellow barreled into the garden and rushed over to Michael and Rose. He hugged Michael on the leg and squeezed Rose around her belly, kissing it. "Hello, Daddy! Hello, Mommy! I had a lot of fun at the big house. Did you miss me?"

Rose scooped him up in her arms and smoothed back his curly dark locks. "I always miss you, Mike, when we're not together."

"I missed you too, Mommy, but I'll be your little boy forever, like you always say."

She peered into his solemn blue eyes. "That's right. Even when you're a grown man, you'll be my boy."

Mike sat down on the stone under the tree to pet Joe. "He sure likes to sit by this stone. Come on, boy. Let's see if we can get a soda." He ran to the porch with the sheltie at his heels.

Aidan shifted his grip on the small white rocker. Maria handed Rose the quilt with the ponies. "Here's his banky."

Rose put an arm around each of her parents and led them toward the porch.

Michael hoisted his son over his shoulder and carried him giggling through the door. "You, my man, may have lemonade—and a good tickling."

The End

About the Author

Judith Kammeraad grew up a good girl under the triple onus of preacher-teacher-author's kid. A fecund imagination counted as a survival tool, and making up stories proved almost involuntary. Books were her best friends, and Dad showed her that words were the best fun ever. Mom voted for ladylike behavior and cookies. Fate led her to marry her high school sweetheart, who brought out her naughty side at last. The Kammeraads settled down in Michigan and raised two daughters as creative as their mom, who encouraged them to embrace their inner quirkiness. Kammeraad devoted herself to a teaching career and created her stories and poems on the side.

These days the Kammeraads and their talented sheltie live in Florida near their six grandchildren, who inspire her to write stories about children and spicy novels that break hearts and warm the spirit. And keep her laughing and crying all day. Meet Judith on Face Book, on Amazon Central, and on judithkammeraad.com where you can join her newsletter.